ALSO BY JEAN THOMPSON

NOVELS

She Poured Out Her Heart
The Humanity Project
The Year We Left Home
City Boy
Wide Blue Yonder
The Woman Driver
My Wisdom

STORIES

The Witch and Other Tales Re-Told
Do Not Deny Me
Throw Like a Girl
Who Do You Love
Little Face and Other Stories
The Gasoline Wars

A CLOUD
in the SHAPE
of a GIRL

A NOVEL

Jean THOMPSON

SIMON & SCHUSTER

NEW YORK   LONDON   TORONTO   SYDNEY   NEW DELHI

Simon & Schuster
1230 Avenue of the Americas
New York, NY 10020

Copyright © 2018 by Jean Thompson

First Simon & Schuster hardcover edition October 2018

SIMON & SCHUSTER and colophon are registered trademarks of Simon & Schuster, Inc.

For information about special discounts for bulk purchases, please contact Simon & Schuster Special Sales at 1-866-506-1949 or business@simonandschuster.com.

The Simon & Schuster Speakers Bureau can bring authors to your live event. For more information or to book an event, contact the Simon & Schuster Speakers Bureau at 1-866-248-3049 or visit our website at www.simonspeakers.com.

Interior design by Carly Loman

Manufactured in the United States of America

1   3   5   7   9   10   8   6   4   2

Library of Congress Cataloging-in-Publication Data

Names: Thompson, Jean, 1950- author.
Title: A cloud in the shape of a girl : a novel / Jean Thompson.
Description: New York : Simon & Schuster, 2018.
Identifiers: LCCN 2018000350| ISBN 9781501194368 (hardback) | ISBN 9781501194375 (trade paper)
Subjects: LCSH: Domestic fiction. | BISAC: FICTION / Literary. | FICTION / Contemporary Women.
Classification: LCC PS3570.H625 C58 2018 | DDC 813/.54—dc23
LC record available at https://lccn.loc.gov/2018000350

ISBN 978-1-5011-9436-8
ISBN 978-1-5011-9438-2 (ebook)

In memory of my parents
And of their parents
And of all those gone before

A CLOUD
in the SHAPE
of a GIRL

part one

LILACS

*To thy happy children
of the future
Those of the past
send greetings*

Inscription, *Alma Mater* sculpture
by Lorado Taft, 1929

I.

It was the end of lilac season, that brief, heady time. The long mid-western winter retreated, the sky was a blue vault unrolling for-ever, and the lilacs came on. The best were the old-fashioned lilacs that could reach seven feet tall or more, leggy, ambitious growers. There were newer varieties now, compact and smaller-scaled, ad-vertised as better suited to yards with limited space. But they dis-appointed, because their fragrance was so much less. They didn't make you want to bury your face in them or bring home staggering armloads of branches.

By mid-May, the lilacs would fade and dry into brown pods. Then would come spirea, pink-sprigged or with branches like white fountains. Then iris, all colors, rust and purple and pale blue and white, and gold with orange tongues. Then peonies and early roses. But the lilacs were both humble and extravagant, the true wild heart of spring.

The old lady who was dying had always loved lilacs, and her daughter clipped some of the woody stems from the backyard bushes and set them in a vase near her bed. She thought that the scent might still reach her. The old lady no longer spoke or opened her eyes, nor did she stir or call out. She had been like this for some days. The end could not be very far off, but it seemed to be taking a long time.

A hospital bed had been set up in the first-floor sunroom. The hospice nurse visited, and there were home care assistants who worked rotating shifts. The daughter spent time sitting with her mother, sometimes speaking or reading aloud, sometimes silent. She fielded calls from friends and other family members, she went through her list of things that had to be done. She had moved back into her mother's house during this final illness, and so there was also her own house to run, a twenty-minute drive across town.

She made trips back and forth, bringing stacks of mail and bills with her. She left Post-it note reminders for her husband. At her mother's house she slept upstairs, in the same room she'd had as a child, although she had been forced to buy new sheets for the bed. The old ones were sour with age and no amount of laundering and bleaching could get rid of the smell.

The house had been declining along with its owner for some time now. It would need shoring up and attention before it could be put on the market. Once the old lady died, there would be no need in the family for a big, expensive-to-maintain house. It would be sold, although this had not been discussed with the old lady beforehand, in order to spare her feelings and avoid the impression that the family was making coldhearted plans. Which they were, in fact, but these were necessary.

If you lived in a place long enough, as the old lady had, you grew used to it and saw nothing wrong. But the basement seeped water when it rained and the foundation bricks showed cracks. The daughter had called in a service to evict the raccoons from the attic, then someone else to seal up the place under the eaves where they got in. The plumbing was balky, the wiring needed an upgrade. The air in every room was stale with disuse and regret. The furniture had sat so long in one place that it had worn the carpeting thin. The heavy curtains held dust in their folds. Small black beetles lived in the kitchen shelves.

When her husband had died almost ten years ago, the old lady's son and daughter had tried to get their mother to move to the excellent senior living facility in town. But this was the house where she had been a bride, a wife, and now a widow, and she had no wish to leave it. It had been a grand house and it was still solid and imposing, a dark brick built in the Foursquare style with a hipped roof and a front porch supported by stone pillars. The neighborhood had many such big old houses and was still considered desirable, with its shade trees and quiet brick side streets and its nearness to the campus. The town had grown outward over the years, like the rings in a tree trunk, from postwar bungalows to ranch houses to the daughter's newer district with its mishmash of architectures: citified farmhouses, Colonials, contemporaries. Nowadays the most prosperous people built out on the edges of town, the farthest ring, where they could have attached three-car garages, media rooms, open-plan living spaces, and his-and-her bathrooms.

Once the lilacs by her mother's bed had wilted, the daughter removed them, threw them out, washed and dried the vase, and set it in the pantry cupboard that held any number of other vases. She and her brother had made some effort at clearing things out when their father died, but there was a limit as to what their mother would allow, and now there would be that project to contend with as well. The closets, basement, and attic were full of old and worn-out items. Most things would be discarded or donated but first you had to sort through it all and depress yourself with the thought of how much of a life came down to useless possessions, how much there was of vanishing.

Although it was true that there was also the archive.

Both of her parents, her father in particular, had been prominent people at the university. Her father had been on the faculty of the law school for more than forty years. Much of her parents' lives had centered around the familiar routines of a college town, its circumscribed news, its issues, its ceremonies. The parents had been boosters, donors, and later, benefactors. They had been a reliable presence at fund-raising campaigns, fixtures at alumni luncheons and receptions. They attended sports events, choral concerts, theatricals, lectures, welcome sessions for foreign students, homecomings, convocations. Her father had served on all the notable campus committees and in the faculty senate. He had received many awards and honors, all duly noted in his obituary.

After his death, a scholarship at the School of Law was named for him. And the university library archived his publications, his personal papers, and the plaques and framed proclamations, the distinctions that had charted and crowned his career. Archivists had sorted through it all, arranging and cataloging. Her father would have liked the idea of having his own well-ordered and climate-controlled space, preserved for all time.

There might be other items that could go to the archives; the daughter would keep an eye out for them and set them aside. Her mother had held on to a share of memorabilia, scrapbooks, and such. Her father was older than her mother and his memories of the university went back to the Great Depression when he was a student here. The monthly room and board at his fraternity house was eight dollars, and there were times he and the others struggled to come up with even that much. A loaf of bread cost ten cents, a bus ride a nickel. To hear her father tell it, it was a time of hardship cheerfully borne, when he and other students still managed to have their share of thrifty fun with dances, serenades, and hayrides. There were ice cream socials and organ concerts at the music building. They gathered to listen to the radio, they made fudge and popped popcorn. There were no cars on campus, no smoking allowed. (After some passage of time, this was again the case, although the language used now was "smoke-free campus.") Certainly no alcohol, although this last was always announced with what seemed like an audible apostrophe: except for those times when . . . Women students had to be home by ten thirty at night, eleven on weekends, a view that carried over to the raising of his own daughter, and which had caused a certain amount of friction.

But that too had been such a long time ago.

His wife might not have her own archive, but she did have her own story. She was dreaming bits and pieces of it even now, lying in the hospital bed. Her story was not yet over because there were these final pieces to finish.

She had grown up and gone to college back east. She came from educated people who expected daughters as well as sons to better themselves and to make their way in the world.

She had met her husband when she arrived at the university to take an instructor position in the history department, her first teaching job. These were the war years, and as men were in short supply, the department was obliged to make do with whoever was available. She settled into her rented room and the routine of classes and grading papers and loneliness.

The war hung over everything, the excitement and dread of what happened in those unimaginable places half a world away, where bombs fell and armies marched and there were so many dead that they too were a kind of army. The war was a constant, solemn reminder of the many things larger and more important than any one person, certainly more important than yourself and your own silly problems.

The history department had her teaching a patchwork of courses: Medieval, and Intro to American, and one called the

7

Golden Age of Exploration. She was on shaky ground with everything but the American, and kept waiting for her students to find her out and denounce her as a fraud. She was only a couple of years older than they were, and conscious of her lack of authority and credentials. But the students (mostly women, a few men either unable to enlist or waiting to be conscripted) were too distracted by the hysteria and romance of wartime to pay her much mind. They sat politely enough in class and turned in their blue exam booklets filled with haphazardly written answers.

It was her job to hold them accountable and to insist on standards of knowledge and scholarship, but it was difficult to be very severe with them. History was something that had already happened, and life, their lives, were in the anxious now. Most of the girls had boyfriends in the service, or at least wrote letters to someone away at war. The boyfriends wrote letters back from the places they were not allowed to identify. The girls followed the war in newsreels and radio broadcasts and looked at names on maps and pieced together a good notion of where the boyfriends were. There was an urgency to it all. Some of these romances ended badly, tragically. It was inevitable.

The whole country was at war. The war effort involved not just the obvious, the weapons and implements of war, the planes and bombs and tanks and trucks, but the manufacture of canvas for tents and for the webbing that was used for holding canteens, wood pulp for paper, fine optometry lenses for binoculars and scopes, leather for shoes, feed for animals, copper for electrical switches, great quantities of wire, of cable, of cement. All manner of commodities and substances were needed, scrap metal, rubber, aluminum, tin foil, cooking grease, all of it elevated and consecrated by the solemn necessity of war. Everyone was to do their part. People trained themselves to recognize the shapes of enemy aircraft overhead. They saved up to buy war bonds. The boyfriends came home on leave wearing their uniforms. The girls left school to marry them and wait out the war at one or another army or naval base. Who would care, at such a time, about the Golden Age of Exploration?

And yet history shifted underneath your feet, she knew that. The present was a dizzy perch that every so often began to spin and slide. If you built a plane you were also bringing into being the sheets of flame that sprang up in the bomber's path, the ruined town, the ghosts that blew through it like rags of smoke, and then the town rebuilt and its memories put into museums. You held on to your life with both hands, you told yourself to pay attention to this moment, the here and now. But one minute passed into the next, and then the next, and at some point you looked back and everything was over and people called it history.

Anyway, at that moment in the here and now (which had in fact long since passed), she needed to slip into the shared bathroom and wash out her underwear in the sink with the bar of yellow soap that was provided. Then carry the bundle, wrapped in a dripping towel, back to her room, where she would hang it over the radiator to stiffen and dry. There were times you wished that history would just go ahead and swallow you down.

Her daughter too was thinking about history, in the sense of things lost, as she stood at the back door of her parents' house looking out at the garden.

Her mother's death would be hard, but it was almost harder going on about the business of normal living, more or less normal, until it happened. When her father died it had not been unexpected, exactly—he was by then a very old man—and it had gone quickly. A collapse at home, a trip to the hospital, his death the following day. Everyone should be so fortunate.

In her mother's case there had been a series of setbacks, declines, crises, decisions to be made about interventions and treatments. The choices presented to you only gave you the illusion that anything made much of a difference. Was it a terrible thing to wish that it could all be over?

Like everything else here, the garden had been neglected. Once her parents had reached a certain age, the daughter had made a project of coming over to help with it. But just as she had uselessly nagged and prodded them about keeping the house up, her efforts with the garden had never been enough. Now she was going to have to hire someone, a landscaper or a maintenance company, to come and weed and cut things back and restore order.

The original beds and borders were choked with honeysuckle bushes and all manner of stalky and creeping weeds. In the daughter's growing-up years there had been a grape arbor, long collapsed, its timbers now leaning against the fence, a few vines still bound to them.

You could lie on the grass beneath the arbor and look up at the grape clusters and the blue sky between the sifting leaves and feel as if summer would never end. She and her brother had been greedy and impatient for the grapes to ripen and had always picked some of them too soon, when they were thin and sour. When the fruit turned heavy and purple-red, they had raced the birds and wasps to get to it. The grapes were sun-warmed and slightly bruised and she had stained her chin with the sticky juice. She had never tasted any grapes that were as good since.

She had her own garden at her own house, of course, and she tended it and took pride in what she'd brought into being. But it never seemed as wild and splendid as the garden she'd grown up with.

She supposed she could get someone to prop the arbor back up and build new supports, if she decided it was worth it. The wild roses still bloomed. The lilies and the columbine had disappeared. A hydrangea had found a place it liked and had overgrown the ferns. Two huge weeping cedars stood at the far end of the lot, their shade black and dense. They would have to come down or at least be trimmed. Any grass that remained had turned thin and untidy.

Where to begin? The lilacs needed pruning and this was the time to do it, right after they had finished blooming. She didn't stop to change into better clothes for yard work so as not to lose the impulse, but fetched the big clippers from the garden shed and went at it. It felt good to be outside, doing something vigorous and physical. She couldn't reach the highest branches so she trimmed carefully lower down and was satisfied with the neatness of the job. Encouraged, she kept going, cutting back the nuisance growth, the trees of heaven and honeysuckle bushes that had taken root everywhere. They would have to be entirely dug up, but it was a start.

The day was warm but it wasn't yet humid the way it got later in summer, when the air was so thick and gray it was a misery to even look outside. She found a square-bladed spade and turned over the dirt in the place where she remembered her mother planting annuals.

More than an hour later, she'd cleared enough of the garden to feel she'd reclaimed some part of it. She might get some flats of marigolds or verbena to make the yard look less forlorn. Less like the neighborhood haunted house.

The daughter was no longer young herself. A year or two past fifty. Her own children now grown. When your parents died, you lost your childhood, or at least the best witnesses to it. More and more she had difficulty not just remembering herself as a child— that girl with the dark bangs cut straight across her forehead, standing crookedly in all the pictures—but believing that she had been such a child, had not always been a fully formed adult, with opinions and a credit rating and a hundred distracted thoughts.

Along with the loss of the parents was the loss of the parents' history, as it was told to you, as you understood it through their living memories, until nothing was left except the curious odds and ends in the house, like the songbook in the piano bench. "Ragtime Cowboy Joe," "Song of India," "Annie Laurie," "Old Black Joe," "Danny Boy," and her father's favorite, "The Sweetheart of Sigma Chi," which he used to play with lush arpeggios, swaying a little as he sat before the keys.

She swept the walkways and put the garden tools away and went back inside. It was time for the home care aide to leave and there was a space of time before the next one arrived. Assuming that she in fact arrived. Sometimes there were lapses. Once this new aide was here, she could make a trip back to her own house. Her husband, Gabe, had not been entirely understanding about her extended absence, the disruption of essentials such as meals and clean laundry.

The aide who was leaving went through the checklist of what had been done and would need to be done and wished her a good evening. The daughter settled into a chair with a magazine. There was nothing else to do but wait and then wait some more. She kept expecting grief to seize her and make her weep, or some other normal reaction, but so far there was only exhaustion. The hospice service had a grief counselor who was available to family members after a death. Maybe by then she'd be more suitably bereaved.

A small fan blew across the foot of the bed, ruffling the sheets. It was the only noise in the quiet, quiet room. The sheets were tented with a kind of frame so that the nurse and the home care assistants could easily check her mother's feet and toenails for discoloration. Discoloration was one of the signs that might mean the end was at hand.

It was strange to witness her mother's silence. Her mother had always been one to keep a conversation going. She had a quick mind and a gift for easy speech. Her father had always joked that his wife was the one who should have been the lawyer, she could wear anyone's arguments down with sheer persistence. Her mother had been silent only when she was unhappy or angry. So that now the silence made her daughter anxious, as if something must be set right. But what?

She said aloud, "You were a good mother. I hope we made you happy." And then, because that seemed self-centered, self-important, she said, "I hope you were happy."

Her words dropped into the small mechanical purr of the fan. She was embarrassed to have spoken. Usually she talked about normal, everyday things, like what her children were doing, or she read the less depressing newspaper headlines aloud.

The home care aide was half an hour late, but at least she came. The daughter spent some time going over what was needed. She said she would be back later this evening, after she had fixed dinner for her husband. The aide appeared to simultaneously listen and ignore her. This was the daughter's least favorite aide, a slow-moving woman with a belligerent air, as if anything you said to her was an occasion for offense. There was always a logical, unimpeachable reason the aide gave as to why her chores were not completed, and the daughter suspected she prowled the house snooping into things when left alone. And, although she had to be imagining it, there was something smug and knowing in the woman's attitude, as if to say, Afraid of a little death? I see it all the time. You don't know the first thing.

Yes, she was imagining, or projecting, all that. The woman was simply disagreeable. But she was better than nothing, and if you called the agency to complain, that was probably what you would get instead: nothing. Anyway, there would be an end to everything soon enough.

The daughter, in a hurry as always these days, drove to her own house. It was a beautiful mild evening, with the trees just now coming into full leaf and the new grass looking cool and shadowy. She took a deep breath to steady herself and fill herself with calm and make way for the tasks that would come next.

She was tired of managing, coping, arranging, bearing up well. Maybe that was what real grief did, prostrated you, rendered you incapable of being so idiotically useful.

Just as she reached the intersection of one of the downtown streets, she happened to look to one side and see a man locking the front door of an auto parts shop, closing up for the day. A tall man, thin, with iron-gray hair. She only saw him from behind for a moment, she had not seen him for more than twenty-five years, but she had no doubt who it was.

She drove on without stopping. It was the damndest thing. That someone might turn up after all this time, perhaps had been in the same place all along without you ever running into them, ever looking up at the exact right moment. And with that one glance she had the extraordinary sense that she knew all about the life he had lived in those years, how he had changed and how he had not. The damndest thing, she kept saying to herself, turning it round and round in her thoughts. There was no one else she would tell about it.

Because she had a past too, much as it might be hard for people to believe.

II. LAURA

The lilacs were in bloom and she thought it would be nice to cut some and put them at her mother's bedside.

The daughter's name was Laura Wise Arnold. Arnold being her married name. (And daughter still for a little while longer.) Before her marriage she had been Laura Catherine Wise and she missed the particular chime of those pretty syllables. Maybe she should go back to it. Not a legal change, just for everyday use, like writing letters. People called themselves any old thing these days. Look at Lady Gaga or Caitlyn Jenner.

Or look no further than her own daughter, who had been christened Patricia Grace and called Patti. For a time in her teenage years she announced that she wished to be known as Vera. Vera, she was happy to tell anyone who expressed an interest (and many of those who did not), meant truth. As if her parents had conspired to name her after a lie.

Eventually her daughter had dropped both Patti and Vera and settled on Grace, which was still hard for her mother to get her mind around, as well as her mouth, but at least it was some part of her name that she wasn't throwing away.

So she might if she wished begin calling herself Laura Wise again. Her husband wouldn't like it and would see it as some kind of hostile act. And even if he had been the kind of man who was supportive and sympathetic, the kind who tripped all over himself understanding feminism and women's issues—and her husband was so not that kind of man—other people would wonder what you were up to. They would wonder if you were making some pitiful effort to promote your unremarkable, insignificant self. Because what were older women meant to do with themselves, besides prop up everybody else's lives and drink too much wine at book club meetings? No one, Laura was convinced, was as invisible and as easily dismissed as the tribe of women like herself, with short gray hair and glasses.

Perhaps she ought to leave her name alone and concentrate on her hair.

She was in the habit of analyzing herself and her impulses, or, if analysis sounded too grand, in the habit of second-guessing herself. Now she wondered what wanting to change her name might mean. Some restlessness or discontent surfacing unbidden? Simple caprice?

Or more than that. Her mother was now very ill, and while there had been any number of false alarms in the past, this looked like the inevitable end. A parent's death was a milestone. It put you in a strange territory of fear, dread, ache, bewilderment. It made you greedy to get back to your own life, and then you felt guilty because of your selfishness.

Maybe she wanted to be a child again, Laura Catherine, a child who still had a mother.

She would be spending another night at her mother's house, as had been her habit these last two weeks. Right now she was at her own house, waiting, with lessening patience, for Gabe to get home. The hospice nurse was scheduled to visit and Laura needed to talk with her. But first she wanted to tell Gabe what had to be done with the food in the refrigerator meant for his dinner. (Her son was not home either, but he was always out late and fed himself, as far as Laura could tell, from foods that came in Styrofoam containers.) Her husband was not accustomed to making an effort in the kitchen. It was easiest to prepare things for him. Or not easiest, but one of those trade-offs and calculations you made when nothing could be done entirely well.

Finally her husband's car pulled into the driveway. Laura's own car was parked on the street so she wouldn't get boxed in by his. She met him at the back door, impatient to be on her way. "Hi, there's barbecued pork, corn bread, and salad. Put the pork in a 350-degree oven for fifteen minutes and the corn bread for five. Don't use the microwave, you'll just dry everything out."

Her husband pushed past her. If he was in one of his moods, she was just as happy to be leaving. He set down his keys and took a highball glass from the cupboard, filled it with ice from the refrigerator door, and fixed his usual bourbon with a splash of water. Just to be saying something, Laura told him, "There's extra barbecue sauce, it's in a square plastic container."

He drank, set the glass down again. "Why thanks for asking. In fact, my day sucked."

"I'm sorry. What happened?"

"Sales figures came out."

"Bad?"

"Let's just say, toilet territory." He took another drink. Then picked up the bourbon bottle and poured out a small portion more, what he called floating it on top.

"Well," Laura said, calculating how much longer the hospice nurse would be at her mother's house, how much longer she could stand here without missing her entirely, "they can't think it's your fault. You told them they were pushing the pricing limits."

"Has to be somebody's fault. Might as well be mine."

"Don't let it be. Push back." Gabe worked for a computer software developer as an analyst and marketer. He had begun in computer science, then made the switch to business. It was a decision that he now regretted. Laura tried her best to coax or console or suggest positive courses of action whenever it came up, which was often. But over time it had come to seem like Adam and Eve eating the forbidden fruit, a kind of original sin that could never be erased or remedied.

Gabe didn't answer. By now her helpful suggestions were only made so that he would have something to ignore. And she didn't have time to be ignored tonight. She went to him and kissed him lightly. "Oven at three-fifty," she reminded him. "Why don't you call me later?"

He allowed himself to be kissed, his expression ironic and knowing. He was growing round-shouldered, developing a bit of a stoop. One of those slight men who seemed to be curling up into themselves with age. Every time she noticed such things, she felt her critical eye turning toward herself. It wasn't as if her own declining looks didn't distress her. "Bye," he said.

"Call me?"

"Sure."

Laura left by the back door, started her car, and drove off. It would have been nice if he had asked her how her mother was doing.

At least the hospice nurse was still there. Laura found both her and the home health aide in the kitchen, drinking coffee. Which was not really a transgression, but annoyed her just the same. She would have liked to feel that someone else was on her side and backing her up, not turning into one more problem she'd have to manage. "How's my mother?" she asked, and the hospice nurse said that she was about the same, and that she was just getting ready to go back in. "No, please, finish your coffee," Laura said, not wanting any more explanations or scmiapologies, and went down the hall to the sunroom.

Everything about what the hospice nurse called "the dying process" had been explained to Laura. It was all entirely natural, but understandably distressing for those not used to it. The fitful consciousness, swimming up from the surface of that state between sleep and death for brief intervals. The skin losing warmth and color. From time to time her mother opened her mouth in a way that, the nurse explained, did not indicate either a desire to speak or pain. The aides had coaxed sips of juice or broth into her, but she was losing the ability to swallow, part of the body's breaking down. Everything possible was being done for her comfort.

Nothing could be done about dying itself.

"Hi Mom," Laura said, sitting down and pressing her mother's hand lightly with her own. She was aware of the nurse and the aide coming up behind her. They must have decided that the coffee was not such a good idea right now. The nurse had her paperwork to fill out and the aide made herself busy with tidying the room, and for a time the three of them were quiet as the late-afternoon sunlight lengthened and the east-facing sunroom grew shadowed.

Her mother's eyelids fluttered and her eyes rolled back and forth behind the lids. The aide saw Laura move her chair closer, attending to this. "It doesn't mean nothing," the aide said. "A reflex. A muscle thing. Like when they start picking at the bedcovers."

Laura said nothing. Who were "they"? It was no way to talk. The aide had only been here one other time and Laura already disliked her. She never seemed in a hurry to do anything.

"Everybody thinks they're going to sit up and give a big speech and it just never happens."

"Well, every patient is different," the nurse said after a moment.

Laura wasn't expecting any big final speech. But she wanted to believe that her mother was still here, in some way.

Laura had questions for the nurse about when it might be necessary to switch to the twenty-four-hour care, and the nurse said she did not think it was required at present, and that things might go on like this—that is, her mother would not die—for some unforeseen amount of time. She said again that every patient was different, as if this was a consolation. The nurse went through the availability and limitations of services as prescribed by the insurer. Laura knew all these by now. She had become fluent in the language of policies, exclusions, providers, and so forth. It was a part of her exhausting new knowledge.

The nurse suggested some respiratory therapy, comfort care, and Laura agreed that this might be helpful, and they talked about how soon this might begin. Laura liked the nurse, who was cheerful without seeming too brusque or matter-of-fact. She checked the patient's vital signs one more time, then made ready to go.

Laura walked her to the front door, then, not wanting to go back into the sickroom while the unpleasant aide was there, took a pair of shears out to the garden and cut some of the lilacs. She gathered a reckless amount of them because what other use was there for them?

She found a vase in the pantry and arranged them, smashing the ends of the woody stems as her mother had taught her, so they would better soak up water. She carried them into the sickroom and cleared a space on the bedside table.

The aide said, "What are those for?"

"So she can smell them," Laura said, not caring to explain herself even that much.

The aide didn't answer, but her dismissive expression plainly said, Whatever.

Laura went back to the kitchen and was surprised when the aide followed a minute later.

"Did you want her to get a sponge bath tonight?"

"No, that can wait until morning."

"What do you call those flowers?"

"Lilacs."

"They do smell pretty."

"Yes, they do." She had begun making herself a cheese sandwich but now she stopped, waiting for the woman to leave.

"She seems like a real nice lady. Your mom."

"Thank you." Although how the aide might come to such a judgment about someone who neither moved nor spoke was unclear.

"Some of them turn nasty at the end. Won't let you help them. Cuss at you. Of course they can't help it. Their minds are gone. Be glad she's not in that kind of state. Is your dad still alive?"

"No, he passed away."

"I figured. So you been through this once already. That helps."

Laura didn't answer. How was that supposed to help anything? She felt the aide was hoping she'd share some confidence, or maybe break down sobbing, something that would make an interesting story she could relate later. She resumed making her sandwich. She was too hungry to keep waiting.

"Wish somebody gave me flowers. Well, I can dream. Ha."

The woman's name, Laura remembered, was Angela. She had short, slick hair dyed a profound black, and a way of squinting at you, almost leering, that might have just been nearsightedness. Laura said, "I'm going upstairs to get some sleep. Please come tell me when you're leaving if I'm not down already."

She waited while the woman, Angela, lingered in the doorway, seeming not to want to leave. "Did you need anything?" Laura asked her.

"Just, not to worry too much about your mom. She's not going to have a bad time. She's found a door and she's working hard to unlock it."

She, Laura, was her mother's only daughter. Just as Laura herself had one daughter, the fluidly named Vera-Patricia-Grace. One daughter made for a certain claustrophobia, a push-pull of closeness and distance. Laura liked the idea of the Old Testament matriarchs who gathered their daughters to them for purposes of counsel or consolation. A whole tribe of daughters.

Instead, she and her mother had been their own small tribe. They occupied the female territory of the household, its daily maintenance and needs. Evelyn, her mother, was not enthusiastic about domestic matters. From time to time she announced that anyone who didn't like whatever fish sticks or hamburger patties she served up could fix their own dinner. But she taught Laura how to scramble eggs and to be careful pouring out hot grease, how to pair socks together and roll them into a ball, and how to iron so that she could take over the chore herself. Evelyn bought Laura's clothes and scrutinized Laura's image in mirrors, not unkindly but with a certain objectivity. Laura came to understand that she was neither pretty nor homely, but a serviceable in-between.

They didn't look alike. Not really. People would see them together and say things like, "She favors you around the forehead, just a little." Laura was dark-haired and compact, while her mother was leggy and had fair, freckled good looks. It was said that Laura took after her father, and she supposed she did, although it wasn't any striking resemblance. She went through a phase when she wondered if she was a changeling, or adopted, which was romantic and satisfying, until some undeniable family trait, like her allergies, collapsed the whole notion.

They were mother and daughter, even if uncertainly bonded. It was not as if they had any memorable, heart-to-heart talks. (At least, trying now to recall any, Laura came up empty.) Her mother was too detached, too often absorbed in things beyond her family to make occasions out of talking. But there was an ongoing conversation between them, bits and pieces at a time, when information was conveyed or implied. Such as, Laura should not think that being a girl who got good grades would be enough for people to take her seriously. Or the more modest reach of sexual appetite in females as opposed to that of ravening, insatiable males. Her parents were, after all, old-school about many things. Laura and her brother had been born to them later in life than was usual.

Or the time when she and her mother had been watching television, some show where a pretty actress fretted about keeping her boyfriend. (It was a girl program. Her father and brother were elsewhere.) There was a series of made-up obstacles, a happy ending, a wedding. The theme music jingled. Laura was relieved at the happy ending. She was still young enough to feel anxious as to whether the shows would provide them. There was also something that stirred and teased her about romance, even a make-believe romance, as if some unreliable promise had been made to her.

"Ah," her mother said, nodding at the screen, where the happy couple were getting ready to exchange vows. "Two perfectly good young lives, ruined."

"Ha ha," Laura said, wanting it to be a joke.

"They'll be fine until they start having children."

"What?"

"Nothing."

"Can I have some more Oreos?"

Her mother said, "No, you've had about enough for tonight." She shut the television off and the picture faded to a point of light and winked out. She said, "I never planned on getting married.

Even back when everybody felt sorry for you if you didn't and called you an old maid. I was going to go on and get my doctorate and be a real professor."

"But then you met Dad, right?"

"That's right," her mother said. "Saved by the bell. Now it's time for you to get ready for bed."

Why had her mother said such a thing? Perhaps she had been drinking wine, as she liked to do in the evening. Or she'd felt injured, resentful at something Laura's father had done, or failed to do. Laura was aware that her parents were not always as harmoniously aligned as they appeared to others, when they hosted get-togethers or official university functions, and Laura and her brother sneaked sips of liquor and marveled at the unfathomable boredom of adult events.

Her father was used to running things: classrooms, meetings, departments, committees, and to having people pay attention when he spoke. His life had been a steady progression of goals achieved and victorious struggles. He seemed to grow more and more solidly righteous as he grew older, more and more certain in his pronouncements. Laura was still a child during the Vietnam War, when the streets turned angry, when protests and peace signs broke over the country, and the campus, in a cresting wave, when her parents sent her out of the room during certain portions of the television news. When stoned kids played stoned music and talked about the system, and feeding your head, and the doors of perception. How alarmed people were, and how outraged, at so much ridiculous, dangerous, gleefully obscene behavior! Some of it was just fashion, the hair and beads and hippie finery, but it signaled something much worse to people like Laura's father, perhaps Communists egging the whole enterprise on for purposes of creating moral rot. He was quoted in the campus newspaper, in his capacity as head of the student honor court, as urging swift and certain discipline for antiwar demonstrators and other transgressors: "We seem to have become so broad-minded that our brains are falling out."

At home their father threatened his young children with punishment if they committed certain terrible but unspecified offenses. "If I ever catch you doing drugs, I will personally call the police and have you arrested."

"Oh you will not," their mother said. "Why are you trying to scare them?"

"I'm keeping them from ruining their lives."

"Children, don't take illegal drugs. They're bad for your father."

"I suppose you'll think it's funny when they end up in jail, or in a mental institution."

More than forty years later, taking her own son to his first stint in rehab, Laura would look back on this memory with grim amusement.

"Pity's sake, Andrew, they're nine and seven. Where do you think they're going to get their hands on drugs?"

"They are actually dirty. It's not just a figure of speech."

"Who's dirty? The students?" Their mother now both exasperated and mocking. "I don't imagine you get close enough to them to tell. This is such a silly fit you're having. You don't like to have a bunch of pip-squeak students standing up to you. That's what you're really so upset about."

Her father muttered something and left the room. Laura understood that her mother had won the argument, worn him down with her words. The argument between them continued, in one form or another, throughout their marriage. Her father issued opinions and pronouncements, and her mother undercut them. She did not always win, or ever win completely, since her father was still so unshakably himself, so armored with his importance in the world and the deference it paid him. But her mother sniped and shrugged and rolled her eyes often enough to unsettle him.

There was an imbalance between them. Her mother chafed against it. Had she always been so discontented? To which of them, her mother or her father, did Laura owe allegiance and sympathy? Her father might be more remote, difficult to entirely understand, but he was at least always the same. Her mother might go from happy, or at least her unremarkable everyday self, to sarcastic and resentful.

Why had they married? Why had they stayed married? Even people of their parents' generation divorced, it wasn't unheard of. When they were both older, Laura and her brother maintained the attitude that both of their parents were crazy, in their own ways. But that was glibness, and was only a way of not thinking about them.

Most marriages had their share of bad spells, or of just bumping along. Laura knew that now. Knew that most people stayed married in spite of the unhappy parts. They hung on and waited for things to get better, or they walled themselves off from each other, or built their enmity for each other into a solid and enduring structure.

Laura had never asked her mother for marriage advice. Maybe this was the deathbed speech she was waiting for. Her mother would rise up, clutch at her failing, fading heart, and deliver herself of some undoubted truth. And what would that be? *I thought I loved him but I was wrong.* Or, *You do the best you can. Then you run out of patience.* Or nothing at all. Words forgotten, wisdom canceled out.

If you lived in a small-to-medium city, like this one, for some number of years, or almost all your life, as Laura had, there were circles of people you knew, from the different layers of your life, different strata, like an archaeological dig. Fallen-away friends from middle school, old rivals, old sweethearts. Your brother's old friends, rivals, sweethearts, etc. People you'd forgotten all about, until they appeared at your door, selling lawn care services or running for city council.

Of course the circles might overlap. Someone you knew from high school worked with the wife of your kids' former soccer coach. Your waitress at lunch was the daughter of your parents' lawyer. It was not unusual for Laura to make a trip to the grocery, or the library, and encounter one or two or more acquaintances. She liked having this network of known, interlocking people, this seemingly inexhaustible supply of connections. Even if you left town for a long time, when you came back there would still be some old neighbor, or your doctor's receptionist, to bump into at Walgreens and share some agreeable conversation. People remembered you, asked after your family, told you who to call if you needed a plumber or an HVAC guy. It was a comfort, feeling that you knew a place and that it knew you.

But Laura was aware that there were other circles of people she did not know and did not care to know: the impoverished, the criminal, the casually dangerous young men cruising the bad neighborhoods in cars that throbbed and shook with music. Nor did she know the men in Hi-Viz shirts who worked on road crews, or the women you saw buying cigarettes and oversize plastic cups of soda at gas stations first thing in the morning, or the kids who drove in from the little towns organized around grain elevators and railroad tracks so they could party in the bars, or the Mexicans bicycling to work at the paper bag factory, or the half-grown girls at the mall with their looking-for-trouble clothes and makeup. She could not say she knew any of them. There was no occasion to do so.

Laura's town, the one she'd always considered hers, contained the university, of course, its grandly shabby old buildings and the newer, more utilitarian structures of hulking brick, its lawns and statuary, athletic fields, frat houses, its rowdy district of bars and student apartment buildings. There were monuments, inscriptions, dedications that bore witness to the traditions of the place and those who had left their mark. The town had grown up around and away from this campus center, so that civic life was no longer entirely shaped by it. Although most people still had passionate opinions about the sports teams.

Some things about the university itself had also changed since her parents' era, architecture and most everything else. One college summer Laura had a job moving old files from the dean's office. She and her fellow workers spent a lot of their time plucking out the handwritten records of problem students who had been called in for stern conferences, among them young women who had been discovered in compromising situations and then had to divulge the details to the maiden ladies who served as their deans. Laura still remembered the best one: "Says she could not have had intercourse with girdle on." They had all roared with glee.

Just beyond the university were districts of modest wooden houses with couches set out on the front porches, gravel driveways, shade trees in need of trimming. Students lived there, or older homeowners who'd had the students crowd in around them, or young families who had chosen the slightly eccentric over newer, pricier real estate.

Nowadays more and more of these houses were being knocked down and replaced with large and profitable apartment buildings. But when she was a kid, Laura used to ride her bicycle through blocks and blocks of such streets, which adjoined her parents' grander neighborhood. She could not have said, then or now, why the little houses sided with old-fashioned green or white shingles, their blowsy yards planted with daylilies and phlox, their uneven porch steps spoke to her so strongly of mystery and possibility. It was as if someone might come out of such a house, or she herself enter one, and everything about her life would change forever.

When did you reach the point when you began counting up losses, rather than looking forward to adventures?

The downtown that people were always trying to revive, although so much business had moved out to the mall. Around the refurbished courthouse, a number of hopeful, short-lived shops and restaurants tried to take root. If you knew where to look, a second-story window still held an electric sign indicating the meeting room for the Knights of Pythias.

And past downtown, depending on the direction, were either districts of small houses that were not intended as anything other than inexpensive shelter, or else grand neighborhoods where the streets curved and circled and were called Something or Other Trace, or Way, or Court. And past these—or perhaps right up against their back lot line—were the farm fields of monotonous beans and corn, the few hedgerows that had not been turned into acreage. Here and there a stream running beneath a road through a concrete culvert. At the east edge of the county, a small, meandering river with its belt of woods, where people built getaway cabins. Habitat for fish, beaver, fox, deer, raccoons, coyotes, possums, hawks, wild turkeys.

Politics: Laura's father voted Republican, her mother Democratic. The town divided up pretty much the same way, older business interests versus different varieties of center-left. Both sides found plenty of things in the local news coverage to infuriate them.

Weather you could complain about most of the time. Winters that made people say, "If hell was cold, it would be like this." Sleet in spring, summers that didn't let up, rain at harvest. And in between these, many days of ordinary beauty.

This was the place where Laura had been born and where she still lived, and she knew it too well to see anything remarkable in it.

In March, before the air had any hint of spring in it, Laura and her friend Becca went out for happy hour so that Becca could find a new boyfriend. They were work pals from their jobs at the university's alumni association. Becca wasn't a townie. She'd moved here from Chicago because she had wanted to put some distance between herself and her ex-husband, who she referred to as Popeye. Anyway, after the divorce she couldn't afford the Chicago cost of living. She missed the city and her life there, or parts of her life, the parts that had involved money. She was trying to make the best of things in this new place. She was trying to have a good attitude.

She and Laura were the same age, although Becca made more of an effort with hair and makeup, so that she looked, if not younger, at least less resigned. She had a pretty mouth, a round little chin, and short, curly hair that she tinted different shades of honey or butterscotch. Every couple of weeks she talked Laura into one of these after-work excursions. She liked to say that she was through with men, but that seemed to mean men she had already met.

Laura didn't mind being the wingman to Becca's bomber pilot. It had its amusing moments, as when the men who approached them or offered to buy them drinks were people Laura recognized, people she knew a thing or two about, maybe knew they had someone waiting for them at home.

As did Laura. She nursed her one glass of wine through Becca's two, then said, "I have to get back."

"Aw."

"Michael's home with a cold, and if I'm not there, he and his father will kill each other."

It was just something you said. You didn't really mean it.

"Aw," Becca said again. "They can't be that bad."

"You have no idea."

"How's it going lately?"

"OK. It's like one of those signs they put up in factories: NO ACCIDENTS IN EIGHTY DAYS."

"You're amazing. An amazing mom. I hope somebody tells you that once in a while. I couldn't cope the way you do." Becca didn't have kids, either from Popeye or the husband before him. It just hadn't happened, she said, but she also volunteered that they hadn't tried very hard, whatever that meant.

"Coping means I get out of bed in the morning."

"Call home and tell them we're going out for dinner and they can fix their own."

"Sorry. I just can't."

"They'll be the sorry ones when you get tired of doing things for them and they have to take care of themselves."

Laura thought that was probably true. These days her family spun in a centrifuge while she tried to pull them back into the center. Michael, at twenty-one, was in college, or this time around junior college, trying to get through the basic courses. It was a start, or rather, a restart. A kind of probation, with all of them acting as if things were better (they were) and would stay better (perhaps). Michael was living at home, paying rent—one of the ground rules—and working the only kinds of jobs he could find. Convenience store clerk, waiter. His schedule kept him out late and made for the irritating sight of him eating breakfast cereal at noon in front of the television. He liked music, he wanted to do something with music. It was not the sort of career path that inspired confidence in his parents, but they had learned to pick their battles. Whenever Michael was home, smothered, amplified bass chords shook the house like the soundtrack of doom.

He was cheerful, creative, kindhearted, smart. A mischevious kid, sure, but in a lovable way, unlike his sister's prickly brooding. And for an escalating period of eighteen months, he had ingested

Adderall and Vicodin and cocaine and whatever else he could get his hands on—a polydrug user, it was called in the language of addiction—all of it washed down with alcohol. He had stolen checks from his mother's purse, wrecked his own car and one of his parents', lied about being high, lied about being sober, passed out on the front lawn in January, thrown up blood, needed IV fluids, B$_{12}$ shots, legal representation.

They hadn't seen any of it coming. How could you? There had been some of what was considered normal adolescent screwup trouble, then episodes of careless, sullen, evasive behavior. Then the all-out catastrophes, the confrontations, the promises made and immediately tossed aside. Who was he, or who had he always been, so practiced at lying, at anger, at horrible talk? Laura's nerves were still shredded from all the emergencies and panics, and the effort of forgiving her son again and again. One night they woke to the noise of cupboard doors slamming over and over and found him barefoot and shirtless in the kitchen, his nose running and his hair standing up in wild, stiff patches from days of lying in his own sweat.

"Michael? What in the world?"

"I can't sleep." His upper lip was raw and crusted with snot. His crazy hair looked like it belonged on something dead.

She and Gabe glanced at each other. He had never been this bad before. Laura said, "Honey? How about we take you to see a doctor." She was light-headed with fear. She had been sound asleep and the overbright kitchen had the quality of a dream or a nightmare.

"I don't need a . . ." He trailed off, rubbing at his nose. His pants sagged from his skinny hips and his bare chest was too naked, starved looking.

Gabe said, "Come on, Michael. Let's go get you fixed up." He reached out to take hold of his arm and Michael spun around and threw him off.

"Let me go!"

"Come on. Get some clothes on."

"Fuck you."

"That kind of talk isn't going to fly, Michael." Laura could see Gabe losing patience. Once he got angry, things never went well. He seethed and wound himself up and wouldn't back down.

"Yeah, OK, screw you. How's that. Both of you. You and your shitty, shitty, totally bogus . . ." He doubled over, in some kind of pain. Laura started toward him but Gabe blocked her way.

"Apologize to your mother."

"It's all right, Gabe. He doesn't know what he's saying."

"Oh I think he does." Her husband nodded, agreeing with himself. "How much are we supposed to put up with?"

"He's sick, you can see that."

"He wants to be sick. Michael, I'm waiting for you to apologize."

Michael straightened himself, took a step closer. He smelled sharp, unpleasant, spoiled. "Make me."

"I'll make you sorry if you don't."

"All right," Laura said. "This isn't helping anything." She wanted to move away from her son but made herself stay still, as she would with a dog she didn't know. She could see Gabe stiffen also. "Watch yourself," he said warningly, but she couldn't tell if he meant her or Michael.

"Both of you," Michael said, "died of boredom years ago, but you forgot to drop dead."

They had called the police, and then an ambulance, and Michael had ended up in hospital detox for the first time, but not the last.

Later he told them he was sorry. He'd told them he didn't mean any of it. But he'd still said it.

They were all trying to climb out of it now, the whole saga of active addiction, with its crises and crises revisited. Laura thought that at least they'd gotten through the worst parts. She had her son back, her funny, affectionate son, and for that she was grateful, even if there were still moments that were shadowed with bad memories, times Michael retreated into silence and brooding. If addiction was a disease, as everyone said, no one had yet found a miracle cure.

It had been made clear to Michael that there were now real limits, and consequences for any backsliding. "Detach with love," all the counselors drummed into you. So many counselors, so many versions of the same advice, only fitfully useful. Gabe wanted to give Michael a deadline to find his own place. He'd run out of patience with what he called coddling. He was still deeply angry at everything Michael had put them through. Laura didn't want to yank the rug out from under him. They compromised, agreeing that as long as Michael was making some progress in school and going to therapy and going to meetings, they wouldn't force the issue. Then they got to argue about what that meant, progress.

You had to allow young men their freedom, and the space to make mistakes, while molding them into responsible, productive, caring adults. Laura knew all the parenting mantras, thank you very much. But you also had to intervene, as they had, to keep your child from falling (or jumping) off serious cliffs. She was still hopeful that Michael would eventually grow into a more settled life. First he had to survive the catalog of disasters she imagined for him (car crash, overdose, AIDS, homeless addict). "Come on, Mom," he told her, exasperated at yet another episode of her fretting and cautions. "Don't tell me you never had any fun. I mean before Dad came along and all fun stopped."

"Don't. I also worked toward a degree and got a job."

"And then you lived happily ever after. Sorry. I don't mean to sound snotty. But quit worrying. I know you won't, but try."

"Don't start calling substance abuse 'fun,' Michael. Really."

"I was joking, come on! Sorry! But Jesus, Mom, don't you ever want more than being overworked, and really pissed off about it?"

"I am not either of those things. All right, some days I'm overworked."

"Nobody said you have to give things up for us."

Oh but they did. The whole world did. It was beat into you so many different ways. In spite of a million women's magazine articles about good career moves, and claiming your own interests and hobbies, and your right to your own sphere. Just try and get away with putting yourself first. Maybe younger women no longer felt such pressures. Maybe they were now free to be selfish. It was something she might ask her own daughter, if they ever accidentally blundered into a real conversation. She said, "Everybody gives up something." It came out sounding forlorn and melodramatic, which she had not foreseen.

"Well don't. Quit it."

As if anything was that easy. But at least he cared about her and understood her this much. In ways that her husband seemed incapable of doing. An unhappy thought. She said, "I just want you to be happy." One of those weak, fallback remarks you could drag out when you didn't have any good answers.

"I am happy. Yay. Joy. I want you to be happy too."

"I'm happy as long as you keep working your program. Your dad is too."

"Let's not bring him into it."

"We both want the best for you."

He looked so much like his father. Same sandy hair and sharp, clever features. Why couldn't they get along better? Had the two of them always hated each other? Why couldn't people ever do what you wanted them to? Michael said, "This is about money, isn't it. He thinks I should make more money."

35

No, it was about sobriety, and taking responsibility for your own actions, and making good decisions, and all the other lectures that were such a big drag. Laura felt an unwilling sympathy for her son. No one enjoyed being the object of so much hectoring good advice. She wanted to understand his recklessness, even as it terrified her. In order to love him again she had to love the part of him that was foolish, dangerous, willful. Love that he was impatient with practicalities and long-range projections and niggling doubts, love that he had blown off the stupid vocational tests that came back saying he was suited to be a medical assistant or culinary worker, love that he had no use for what was safe when he might have a chance at something magical and passionate. Drugs had been the wrong way to go about it. He would need to give up on the romance of self-destruction and of excess. And who were you, once you did that?

She could do it. She could bend and stretch herself into that shape and so understand him, after a fashion. But it had taken a toll on her.

"Don't screw up," she told Michael, and from then on he'd turned it into a joke and said he wouldn't as long as she didn't either.

About her daughter, the intelligent, ironic Grace, Laura's worries had less to do with how she would function in the world. Grace would manage just fine, once she outgrew living like a student and decided to be a grown-up. She was levelheaded, she had cooly removed herself from the rest of the family when her brother's troubles had blown up in everyone's faces. But there was a deep current of dissatisfaction in her that Laura recognized and wished she did not.

Becca was talking about Popeye and his various unpleasant habits. "Acres of porn. He totally polluted the computer. All the different varieties of disgusting stuff. They have them organized so you can shop for them, like on Amazon. You have no idea."

"I do have an idea, and I'd rather not dwell on it."

"Not to tell tales out of school, but there were requests I was not going to go along with."

Laura raised a hand, meaning, Enough. She dug in her purse for her wallet so she could pay her share of the bar tab. "Are you staying or going?" she asked Becca.

"Going. There's nobody here." The bar was crowded with sociable groups of people enjoying themselves. Becca meant nobody who had caught her eye.

"Do you want to get married again?" Laura asked. "I mean, I guess I thought you didn't. But I shouldn't assume."

"Sure. Why wouldn't I? If I find the right person. That's been my problem up until now. Settling for less-qualified applicants." Becca opened her purse and took out a lipstick and slicked it over her mouth without looking in a mirror.

"I think I've outgrown being married. No, it's not anything tragic. More like, can't we renegotiate the terms?"

"Whoa."

"People wear out," Laura said vaguely. "That's all I mean."

They counted their money out and looked around for their server. Laura sighed, and Becca said, "There it is."

"There what is?"

"Your I-have-to-go-home face."

"I'm not making a face."

"You need a vacation."

"I don't think Gabe can get away."

"You and me, then. Alumni association tours of the Holy Land."

Laura giggled. "Lucy and Ethel in the Holy Land."

"We could dress up like nuns. Trip over a bunch of holy relics."

"Get arrested for sacrilege. It's all so tempting. But it wouldn't go over big at home."

"What if something happened to you, God forbid. They wouldn't last a week."

In fact they would last almost a year.

Laura began to say that nothing was going to happen to her when her phone chimed, a text coming in. She picked it up, studied it, and then looked up with a different kind of face.

"It's my mother," she said.

III. EVELYN

There was not much of a garden in their new house, the house of their new marriage, and Evelyn wanted to plant some lilacs in the yard.

Hydrangeas too, and peonies, columbines, lilies. A grape arbor and roses. She had sketched it all out, and begged plants from people who already had their own gardens, so as to keep the costs down. Her husband was not openhanded with money and she wanted to avoid any fuss. They had already spent quite a lot on furnishings, and the mortgage itself, and he still felt aggrieved by that. He made good money and it wasn't that they couldn't afford things. She wished he was more generous, but there was no point. Everything was settled now, and she was married.

Evelyn wanted to get some of the smaller plants into the ground by herself, without waiting for the Negro man who came through the neighborhood with a wheelbarrow full of tools, looking for yard jobs. Andrew was at work and couldn't object, as he otherwise might. It was March and still chilly. She dressed in trousers and an old pair of boots and a short wool plaid jacket that belonged to Andrew, and tied a scarf underneath her chin, babushka style. She worked a spade into the earth alongside the fence, testing to see how much effort it would take. She thought she could manage. She was four months pregnant. She had been married for two.

The columbine went in first, as they were a spring plant and needed a head start. Then some of the early lilies, because she knew where she wanted them. By then her back hurt and she was sweating beneath her heavy clothes. The rest would have to wait.

She took off her boots at the back door so as not to track anything in, and hung Andrew's jacket in its place in the coat closet, and moved through the downstairs rooms as if she was in a museum, not wanting to disturb anything. She wasn't yet used to the house and all the things the house contained. Draperies and lamps and rugs, dinner plates, silverware, bed linens, pictures in frames. All that and much more. It was hers now, that is, hers to tend and polish and scour, and she had no idea of how to go about it.

And a baby on top of everything. She couldn't stand to think about it.

Most of the furnishings had been bought new, since there was so much space to fill. Evelyn had nothing to contribute beyond a couple of bookcases and her set of teacups. Andrew brought a set of chairs, his heavy walnut desk, and a chifferobe from the bachelor house he'd lived in. As formidable and challenging as this house seemed to Evelyn, at least she did not have to move into Andrew's. His rooms were airless, wallpapered in shockingly ugly patterns, salmon pink or spinach green. The boards around the kitchen sink sagged with rot. There were no doors to the rooms, only curtains strung across the openings. He'd eaten most of his meals at his desk in the study, spilling crumbs as he read over his law books.

Evelyn had only seen the inside of it once, which was quite

enough. He'd hurried her in and out, since it was not proper for her to be there before they were married.

He had not minded, or had not noticed, the shabbiness. But this new house was to be different. Evelyn understood that it was meant as a gift to her, the foundation of their new life. With the house and the marriage and now a child, he was establishing himself, a settled man, a family man who would go out into the world from there. And she would have her place alongside him. It was all coming together in ways no one could have foreseen.

She changed clothes and lay down to rest, not meaning to fall asleep. But here was Andrew sitting on the side of the bed, patting her shoulder. "Wake up, Little Mother."

Evelyn disliked it when he called her that. But rather than say so, she yawned and sat up.

"What time is it?"

"Four. I left work a little early." He was smiling in a way she had come to learn meant that she was supposed to do something, but what? So often it felt as if she had blundered into the middle of a play or a game already in progress, which no one had explained to her.

"I should see about dinner," she said, and this was the right thing to say, or one of them, because Andrew said it was still early yet, which meant that in fact it was time for her to go downstairs and hope there was something in the icebox that could be made into a meal.

But first she went down the hall to the bathroom, closed the door, and sat there on the toilet for a long while.

Dinner turned out all right, or mostly all right: chicken salad from the leftover bird, peas and carrots, biscuits. The biscuits were scorched on the bottom and the chicken salad was drippy from the jar of pimentos she hadn't thought to drain. She was still a new enough bride that there could be jokes about such things,

41

although they were wearing thin. Evelyn had to remind him that she'd never claimed she could cook.

"That's right. It's not as if I married you under false pretenses."

"What?"

"It's not like you told me you were a blue-ribbon cook."

That was all he'd meant. "No," Evelyn said. "I wouldn't say that to anyone."

In fact she'd never taken much interest in food, and had only ever eaten enough to get by. These last four years she'd boiled eggs or soup on the hot plate in her room, made meals out of saltines and sardines, or eaten at lunch counters. She couldn't say she was making much headway yet. She could manage things like pork chops and boiled potatoes, and she made a hamburger casserole with noodles and mushroom soup that usually turned out all right. But she despaired of the fancy creations you saw in the magazines, the pretty layered sandwiches frosted with cream cheese, the ham stuffed and sliced so as to make a pinwheel, the perfect, glossy deviled eggs garnished with paprika and snips of parsley. You could get all the sugar you wanted now, and Andrew had let it be known that he favored meringue pies. Meringue! Where did you even start?

And now for the first time in her life she was hungry, really hungry. She was past all the throwing-up mornings and now she ate whatever she could quickly get her hands on, mostly sandwiches made of store-bought bread and store-bought jelly. She was going to have to do better.

Now, watching Andrew scrape the blackened biscuit with a table knife without complaint, she said, "I'm sorry. I haven't figured out how to keep the oven from getting so hot."

"Well, that oven's pretty old. Tricky."

He was being kind. She should have been more careful. He was older than she was. He said he'd never expected to marry.

He'd had to work so hard to get where he was, taking time off from school to earn money, and then from law school when the war broke out. He'd come back from the army, finished law school, clerked, studied for the bar, passed, practiced law at one of the offices across from the courthouse, then only last year had joined the university's law faculty as an adjunct. He had a chance to do more teaching if he wished. He loved the university. It was a natural for him. Meanwhile, there was his law practice to keep up. There was no end to the work.

He had thrown everything into his career. There had been no time for girlfriends, courtship. Anyway, he was not the kind of man who had an easy time with women. He didn't have the knack for small, agreeable talk and flirting. He was tall and he carried himself with an air of apology for his height. His ears stuck out and undermined the dignity of his features. He had resigned himself to doing without a wife. And here she had come along. He had cast his lot with her, and she with him. He was not yet disappointed in her. She would try harder.

Evelyn said, "I was thinking, I should get some kind of a cookbook. Study up on it."

"Really?" She could tell he was pleased. "I expect there are some good ones out there. I could ask Louise." Louise was his secretary at the law office, a severe woman who wore old-fashioned hairnets and lace collars. She and Evelyn had only met on one occasion. Louise had looked her over, come to some conclusion, and closed her mouth in a line.

"Oh no, please don't. That would be embarrassing. I'll ask someone at church." They were members of the Presbyterian congregation downtown, or rather, Andrew was and she now attended with him. She had never given much thought to religion. But it wasn't such a hard thing to do, going to church. "I'm sure if I just asked around . . ."

"Yes, that's a good idea. Plenty of the ladies there are good cooks. I expect they could point you in the right direction."

"I'll ask next Sunday." She wondered if she might persuade one or two of them to bring over their chicken divan or cherry pie once in a while. "I'm sorry I never learned that much about cooking. It wasn't anything I paid attention to, growing up."

"Well, you thought you'd be busy with your studies," Andrew said, and this was true, although it was perhaps uncomfortable to have it set out like that and said out loud, how her life had changed. They both smiled briefly, then returned to eating their watery chicken salad. They did not know each other very well yet.

They had met last fall when Evelyn attended a concert at the music building. A girlfriend had talked her into it. It was a classical program, nothing she would have gone to on her own. She would rather have gone somewhere with a dance band and, well, someone to dance with. The music building had limestone facings and a grand lobby, and the main recital hall was supposed to have near-perfect acoustics. It was a respectful temple of music, designed to encourage your solemn appreciation. Not that you were likely to hear any music of the toe-tapping sort there.

Evelyn's friend said, "I know it's not your kind of thing, but it's free. Please? I don't want to go by myself, I'd feel funny."

So Evelyn accompanied her, and listened with half an ear to the concert—was it Brahms?

She had not paid attention. The violins sawed up and down. A clarinet and piano chased the notes around. It was all very accomplished, she supposed, with its intense musicians and angry-looking conductor, but it did not transport her as it did other people. At least it was a break from the constant pressures of her marginal job.

The GIs had come back from the war, using their government payments to enroll. The men were being hired, or rehired, for teaching positions and the women were being crowded out. She should not have expected otherwise. She had not been taken seriously; she was a part of the war effort, like a scrap-metal drive. Her three courses a semester went down to two, and they had yet to promise her anything at all for the spring. She decided to work toward a doctorate and persuaded one of the faculty to be her dissertation director. "I don't understand why you want to get the PhD," he told her. "You're not at all bad looking."

She liked keeping company with men and she had a steady boyfriend for a time, a young mathematician who took her to the movies and talked about the intricacies and beauty of the proofs he was working on. When he got a position at a college in New York state, she half expected him to ask her to marry him, and was relieved when he did not. What did that mean?

She was twenty-three, twenty-four, twenty-five, twenty-six. She had always assumed she'd get married; it was what people did. But it kept not happening. She kept going along as she always had, teaching her classes, correcting their papers, and now, spending time in the library taking notes on index cards. Her dissertation would be on the deliberations of the Second Continental Congress, the one that issued the call for independence. The library was known for its size and its excellence, and contained some of the primary sources she needed. She took to research naturally. Her notes were meticulous. The structure and sequence of her ideas and arguments were both logical and fluid. She felt she might distinguish herself, given time. There was a part of her that was deeply contented with such work, and only with such work. It absorbed her but it also lightened her, freed her from herself. She could not have entirely explained it to someone else.

She could support herself, just barely. The doctorate would make a difference, if she could hang on long enough to pull herself over the line. She wished she had a boyfriend who was just for fun, and could be summoned when you needed cheering up, or sex. Since that was not likely, she guessed the world would simply leave her alone.

The concert came to its thundering and triumphant conclusion. The conductor bowed. The musicians stood and bowed. Evelyn and her friend gathered their coats and gloves and handbags and moved toward the exit. "Well that was . . ." Evelyn began, not yet knowing how she might end her sentence. That was impressive. That was noisy. " . . . a very nice evening," she finished lamely.

"Don't look now," her friend said, "but there's a man watching you."

"What?"

"I said don't look."

So of course she looked. A tall man in a bulky, uncomfortable-looking overcoat dropped his gaze, his face reddening. Evelyn's friend giggled. "You have an admirer."

"Who is he?" Evelyn asked, but her friend didn't know. He was now paying elaborate attention to the hat in his hands, examining it critically, as if it belonged to someone else.

Evelyn started toward him. "What are you doing?" her friend whispered.

"If he's going to stare at me, he can talk to me."

As she approached the man, he gave his hat another beseeching glance, then raised his eyes to her, trapped. "Hello," Evelyn said. "Did you like the concert?"

"Very enjoyable," he managed, looking so stricken that she felt a little bad about cornering him. How old was he? Older. Neither good-looking nor ugly. One of those men you saw doing serious things, running offices or standing behind elected officials in newspaper photographs.

"I don't know that much about music, so I have to ask other people's opinions, to find out if I like something," Evelyn offered.

"Oh, I know less about music than anyone alive. But some-times you have to make an effort."

"Broaden the mind," Evelyn said. "That sort of thing."

He nodded. He didn't realize she was teasing him. He said, "The chamber pieces are lovely, but I believe you'd have to know the symphonies to really appreciate him as a composer."

Evelyn couldn't think of anything to say to that which wouldn't have been glib or foolish. It had been a silly, smart-alecky impulse, confronting him. She looked back at her waiting friend, who was rolling her eyes at her: *Come on.* "Well, very nice talking with you. Enjoy the rest of your evening."

Without waiting for him to speak, she turned and crossed the lobby to rejoin her friend. "What did you do?" the friend asked. "Were you trying to get picked up?"

"No! I asked him how he liked the concert."

"I bet he could really show you a good time."

"Shut up."

"You're such a fast little number."

"I mean it, shut up."

Then he was standing in front of them, his hat still in his hand, holding out a card and saying, "Would you allow me to introduce myself? And might I have your permission to call on you?"

Call on you! How funny, how antique! As if she still lived under her parents' roof, and expected to be serenaded on a ukelele! It was so hard to keep a straight face! Hadn't they all lived through enough of war and shivering fear and destruction to take the shiny edge off things? Hadn't they all wised up? A man didn't call on you, he took you out for drinks. You either clicked or you didn't. Who was he, some kind of joker?

But of course she said that yes, he could, and of course he did.

He escorted her to football games, a lecture by a distinguished judge, a supper at the Presbyterian church. That kind of thing.

Nothing rowdy, and certainly nothing extravagant. Evelyn was amused by his serious good manners. She could do with a break from the library now and then. Her girlfriend teased her that Andrew was a great catch, an ambitious lawyer on the way up. Evelyn supposed that this was true, if you were in the business of catching men, which she was not. From time to time he spoke about his law practice and the principles of impartiality, evidence, and precedent that governed all legal matters. She liked that he was someone who considered things like principles. Most people, herself included, didn't give them much thought.

She couldn't tell if he was courting her, or if he only needed someone to squire around and to present to any of his colleagues whom they might encounter. Aside from that first evening when she'd caught him staring at her, there wasn't much she could recognize as sexual pursuit. She was reminded of a pair of white geese she'd seen once in a park, waddling around together in what was either a chase or a promenade, nothing in their goosey expressions giving any clue as to which it might be. Surely the geese themselves knew what was what. About Andrew, she could only guess.

Evelyn didn't mind going to the football games with him. He was patient about explaining the plays and the positions to her. The team was not having a good year. People went to the games out of loyalty, school spirit, it was called. Andrew had been a student here and he knew the words to all the school songs and sang them unself-consciously in his tuneless baritone.

Evelyn's attention wandered from the game, which did not seem to be going very well, to her surroundings. The grand stadium was dedicated to the student dead of the last great war. Their names were carved on the lonely stone pillars you walked through on the way in. It felt irreverent to her to be a part of the excited crowd in their looming presence, but maybe that was as it should be, and the honored dead enjoyed the fun. All around her, people were hooting, cheering, or groaning as the plays unfolded. It was November and chilly, with a steely afternoon sky. People had wrapped themselves in plaid blankets and mufflers. They wore earmuffs and mittens and drank from thermoses of coffee or hot chocolate.

She had tried to dress warmly, in a sweater and flannel skirt and her wool coat, but her feet were cold and her nose kept running. She counted down the minutes left on the game clock, willing it to advance. She was determined not to shiver or complain, because then Andrew would be likely to remove his own coat and drape it around her, the kind of chivalrous, irritating thing he was prone to do.

The home team lost, no surprise, and the disappointed crowd filed out of the stadium. As always, Andrew saw people they had to stop and talk to. This or that old schoolmate or someone he knew from his law practice. How at ease he was with them all. They talked about the game, about court cases or other old friends, a smooth surface of talk with its own familiar rhythms and rituals. What an amiable, reassuring presence Andrew was. A goose among goose-men. People liked him, they would trust him to do what needed to be done. She saw how a man might be successful in business, how Andrew might be successful in his element, even if he was often stiff and awkward with her.

Finally they emerged and set off down the sidewalk. It was a number of blocks to Evelyn's rooming house, and the cold made them hurry. The setting sun had fallen below the cloud cover and sent out a red flare that lit them briefly before it was shut off like the lid of a box closing. "It gets dark so early now," Evelyn said, just to break a silence.

"Yes, well, November," Andrew said, by way of agreement. One more topic going nowhere. Evelyn tucked her chin into her scarf for warmth and watched the lights come on in the houses along the street. He had not invited her to dinner—she was annoyed that he had not done so—and she was hoping she had enough of last night's hamburger soup to get by. Really, he could have taken her to Steak 'n Shake, like a normal date. She was getting tired of him.

"They ran out of gas in the second half," Andrew said, harkening back to the football game. "I expected more from them."

"At least they kept it close for a while," Evelyn said, just to be agreeable. She was fine with them losing, perfectly lighthearted about it, while Andrew appeared to be brooding. When he didn't respond, she said, "Honestly, it's not the same as losing a war."

"No, it isn't," he said after a moment. "I was in Frankfurt after the bombing stopped. Not at all the same thing."

"Well," Evelyn said after a moment. "What were you doing there?" She was accustomed by now to men telling their war stories.

"I was in the quartermaster corps. Support and supply. I was fortunate, it was toward the end of things."

"So you were in Germany," she said helpfully.

"Yes, for a few weeks. France too. After Normandy."

"Oh, of course." It could be such an effort, dragging his dead weight through a conversation. "And Frankfurt? Wasn't it . . ."

"One of the last air raids used eight hundred bombers. Each of them dropped thousands of pounds of incendiary and high-explosive ordnance. When we say 'bomb,' what we really mean is 'burn.' When a fire gets big enough, it draws in more and more air, like a chimney. You get a fire tornado. The city was leveled."

Evelyn tried to envision a fire tornado springing up in the middle of the dreary cold. She couldn't do it. The war had numbed people with each new unimaginable thing. "What about the people?"

"People burn too," he said shortly.

"That's horrible."

"It was an industrial center. A legitimate target. Don't think for a moment they wouldn't have done the same to us."

They walked on for a time without speaking. She felt that she had been rebuked. A silly girl who had been shielded from harsh realities and therefore should not offer her foolish opinions. Andrew said, "I'm sorry. I shouldn't dwell on it."

"How could you not," Evelyn said.

"All that's behind us now. Anyway, as I said, I was one of the lucky ones."

"Yes," she agreed, but she felt cold, dismal, and somehow implicated.

Here was her block, and the big white house where she lived. It had been built forty years ago as the town residence of a prosperous farmer, then divided into individual and inconvenient living quarters. One of which Evelyn now inhabited. On the sidewalk at the bottom of the porch steps, she turned to Andrew, anxious to get inside.

But he started up the porch steps so as to see her properly home. At the front door she opened her mouth to begin her thank-yous, but he cleared his throat with such thoroughness that she stopped, alarmed.

"I very much enjoy," he began, then stopped and turned his head away to cough. "Excuse me."

She waited for him to set himself to rights and begin over. "I have very much enjoyed your company these last few weeks."

"Yes, it's been such fun." Not entirely an untruth. There had been some intermittent fun. A premonition, a warning. All she had to do was say good night, open the front door, and pop herself inside. But she was neither that quick nor that rude.

"I know that this must seem hasty, or premature," Andrew went on, as Evelyn, helpless to stop him, stood rooted. "But would you consider . . . would you do me the honor . . ."

She gaped at him. He tried again. " . . . do me the honor of entering into an engagement . . ."

"No, please," she blurted. "I mean, why?"

This threw him off his stride. "I suppose . . . we're both at a point in life, that is, I am more so than you. Being older, I mean. I mean, you're not old in the least. Not wanting to miss out on things, you know. Miss out on things in life. Before it's too late."

He did not seem aware that it was customary, when proposing marriage, to say admiring and ardent things to advance your suit. Really, he was ridiculous! Evelyn said, "I suppose there are those reasons. But as you say, it's somewhat hasty." She thought she could talk her way out of it if she just kept going. Why did she feel she had to come up with reasons? It was preposterous.

He seized on this. "Then perhaps you would keep it in mind. As a serious possibility."

"Yes," she said, seeing an escape route. "I would be happy to keep it in mind."

Andrew inclined his head toward her. She braced herself, knowing that she was about to be kissed. Just then the door behind them opened and they had to step apart. One of Evelyn's fellow lodgers came out and hurried down the stairs without speaking to them. "Thanks for the lovely evening," Evelyn said, stepping inside and shutting the door behind her.

She accepted his proposal a few weeks later and they were married on New Year's Day in the pastor's study of the Presbyterian church.

Andrew was surprised and delighted that she got pregnant right away. Then, at the end of March, she miscarried. It was one of those things, the doctor said. Not uncommon with a first pregnancy. He'd see her back here with a healthy baby or two, and very soon.

But their children were not born for years and years, after they had come to believe it would never happen.

Had Andrew known? Had he suspected? They never spoke of it. They went about their lives. They did those things that needed to be done. Time passed and passed. It built up like layers of glass. You could see straight through it, but every so often there was a shimmer, a distortion, something that threw you off.

Where was her baby daughter, her Laura? The woman kept talking and patting her hand. She was gray and tired looking. "It's me, Mom." Of course it was. It was so irritating when they thought she did not know things. Laura was old because everybody was old. Andrew was whatever it was that came after old. Dead.

Why was she driving? She didn't know how to drive.

He said, Take your time. You got it. Now you're cooking with gas.

You could see the storm rolling in for miles and miles across the big open flatland. From west to east, a great dark mass of cloud that opened its throat and shook the air and sent down red and yellow forks of lightning.

One of the courses she was teaching that fall was a survey, World Civilization I. The textbook made mention of Babylonians and Sumerians. In faraway places such as India and China, people were busy doing things that might be considered civilization, if one lived in those parts. Civilization had really come about in ancient Greece, with its philosophers and playwrights. The Romans had made it more efficient. During the Dark Ages, it was a wandering orphan. The Renaissance revived it, the Enlightenment argued about it. Kings and queens tugged it back and forth. Finally, on the eve of the founding of the Republic, it was ready to be perfected. That was where the next course, World Civilization II, began.

Her students were now distracted by fun and hijinks rather than war. They giggled and jostled in the classroom's wooden chairs, so that a constant scraping sound accompanied Evelyn's lectures. She raised her voice and carried on. The course was part of a basic studies curriculum and most of them were required to take it. Evelyn began to develop a dangerous contempt for her students. She gave pop quizzes and called on the sleepiest and most distracted of them to answer questions. She was getting a reputation as one of the mean instructors.

Most of the GIs went into practical fields of study, like business or engineering. The few who did take her classes stood out as older and more studious. They kept to themselves and didn't say much in class, aside from asking when a paper was due, or some other requirement. They were in a hurry to make up for lost time.

The man who stayed after class in World Civ I was a veteran, Evelyn was certain. She noticed him as she was packing up her books and notes. He sat near the back, one foot tap tap tapping, and wrote in a spiral notebook. He kept his head down and Evelyn didn't speak to him. But after the fourth or fifth time of this, she said, "Are you writing a letter?"

He did look up then. "No ma'am. I don't take real good notes the first time around. So I run through them again while I still have them fresh in my head."

"That's very conscientious of you."

"Well ma'am, that's the only way I can get through it. I'm not much of a school type."

He smiled. He had fair, reddish hair, sandy eyebrows, and sun-burned, unemphatic features. His voice had country in it.

"I'll leave you to it then. See you Wednesday."

The seating chart told her that his name was Russell Hatch. "Call me Rusty," he told her on another day after class. "Real original, right?"

She was careful to keep their conversations brief and impersonal. She'd had previous experiences when she'd become friendly with students, even fond of them, and then had to give them bad grades. And Rusty's first written assignment was bad. Objectively, even terrible. Whatever he had been trying to say about the Greek city-states was lost in a pileup of sentence fragments and odd assertions. ("The army in Sparta was a very important part of military life.")

She didn't put a grade on his paper but handed it back with a note: Please see me. After class he approached her desk. "Not so good, huh?"

"You don't seem familiar with basic composition. Are you aware of that?"

"I guess so." He shrugged. He didn't seem especially troubled by her criticism.

"You're going to have to improve in order to pass the course."

"OK," he said mildly. "I do a lot better with multiple choice."

"Do you have a few minutes? Let me show you what I mean about your paper."

He hitched a chair next to her desk and Evelyn did her best to go through his writing and explain the problems. She drew diagrams and put arrows in the margins. Rusty followed along, nodding his head and seeming to agree. He didn't seem able to stay entirely still, and kept shifting around in his seat. When she was finished he thanked her. "I guess I'm not much of a writer type either."

"You could get a tutor. I can help you find one."

"I do appreciate that, but tell you the truth, I'm kind of doing this at my own pace."

Evelyn put his paper, now bleeding red ink, to one side. "Do you care about getting a passing grade?"

He looked embarrassed. "College was sort of my mom's idea. She said, as long as they were handing out money. I told her it wasn't my best move, but, well, mothers."

"You were in the service."

"Navy. Stateside. Just dumb luck we didn't ship out. San Diego. We had ourselves a time there. You ever been to California? You should go see it if you can, it's a beaut. I really like your class. You do a great job, you make it all interesting."

"Thank you." You took your compliments where you found them.

"No, I mean it. I'm supposed to be taking an English class but I quit going, it wasn't nearly as good as yours. Honest? I don't think I even knew there was an ancient Greece. Just the modern one."

She guessed she could stop worrying about having to give him a dismal grade. She asked him where he was from and he named a small town more than a hundred miles away. His family farmed, corn and beans and a few beef cattle. He'd go home and help out once he'd put in enough school time to convince his mom it wasn't working out. It wasn't a bad life, farming. The government was going to help with that too, with the new price supports. He was taking an ag course on soils, well, he was not exactly enrolled in it but he sat in the back and listened and that was just great. He was buying the textbooks so he could follow along. You could pick up a lot of things if you kept your ears open. "Man, I love the university. I think the smartest people in the country work here. I should have just stayed home and signed up for some ag extension courses but, you know . . ."

"Mothers," Evelyn finished for him.

"She looks at me and sees a college man. Nobody else does."

Listening to him, Evelyn thought how at ease he was with the world, how confident that it would give him what he wanted. He was the history that was yet to happen. He talked about his idea for a side business. Farm implements, tractors, and such. He'd taken plenty of machines apart and put them back together. He had a knack for it. He figured there was good money in it, the markets were going to be wide open now. Watch how big it got.

The war had made him. There were people she would never meet, that no one would. They had been trampled under, erased. But for those who were young enough and lucky enough, there would be opportunities. Windfalls.

"How about you?" he was saying. "You seem real young to be a professor." And she had to explain that she wasn't a professor, only an instructor. "That's just as well," he said. "I don't think I'd have the nerve to ask a real professor to come out for a drive with me. Especially one as pretty as you."

How long had it been since a man flirted outrageously with her? You took that where you found it also.

Rusty had a GMC half-ton pickup, a farm truck, battered maroon, with bits of straw and other loamy debris in the corners of the homemade bed. Evelyn walked downtown to meet him since he was still her student, no matter how temporary or unserious, and she didn't want to court trouble. He was younger than she was, twenty-two. She knew how it looked.

He pulled up at the curb and got out to help her into the passenger seat. "Not exactly limousine service," he said cheerfully. Evelyn settled herself in the cracked leather of the seat. He had made some effort at cleaning. A section of the dashboard had been wiped free of dust, and the ashtray emptied, although the smell of cigarettes hung on like a fog. "No radio," he said. "You'll have to talk to me."

He drove them out of town heading north on a two-lane. She

could never get used to the flatness here. The horizon went on forever, with nothing to stop it. Here and there a tree line. The farm fields were laid out like a grid, cultivated right up to the edge of the road. She loved plants and flowers but this kind of growth had more to do with industry than nature. It was October and still warm. Rusty pointed out the things a farmer would know. The good or bad condition of corn waiting for harvest. The drainage problem with a particular acreage.

The truck didn't have much speed, but it went fast enough to kick up a breeze. She tried to listen to him, nodding along, but the noise of the truck drowned him out. She was so ignorant of so much. In the new world that had already begun, there would be no room for anyone like herself, anyone who looked to the past for answers, or who did not eagerly embrace change.

The railroad tracks ran parallel to the highway. Little towns, some no more than a street or two deep, appeared at intervals. There was a depot, a water tower, a café or a tavern. In the larger ones, a bank branch, a church. One or two big houses, with shade trees and pillared front porches, then a string of smaller and frankly poorer ones, the town trailing off into sheds and grass lanes, an abandoned barn, a graveyard set inside a rail fence. On the side of a brick building now serving as a garage, a painted advertisement for a livery stable, faded but still visible.

They stopped at one of these towns and sat at a lunch counter and ordered pie and coffee. No one knew them here. Rusty got on with the waitress like they were old friends. He understood small-town small talk, which might begin with the weather and progress into accounts of children and grandchildren, national politics, and local scandals. He left a dollar tip by his plate and they went back out into the fading afternoon.

"You get along with everyone, don't you?" Evelyn asked as they started out again, this time heading south and home.

"Maybe not everybody. Ask my lieutenant. He thought I was a, well, a horse's patoot."

"Everybody you want to, then."

"You know who I get along best with? Pretty women." He leaned over the gearshift and kissed her.

They took three such drives, and each time afterward they went to his rooms. Evelyn was not inexperienced, thanks to the mathematician. They were awkward with each other at first but that didn't last. She said, "It's probably against all sorts of rules. Teachers and students."

He had been dozing, his arm around her, and now he roused himself. "I'm only an accidental student. Besides, people are people." He would be leaving school soon to help his family with the harvest. There was no point in saying much more about that part of things.

What point, indeed, in saying more about anything? But she couldn't help herself today, when the perfect strangeness of her situation overwhelmed her. She said, "Do you ever miss the war?"

"What? What brought that on?"

"I don't know." But she did know. "I don't mean, I miss people fighting and dying. I miss the way it was for us here. Everything was for a good cause. A purpose. Even teaching my classes was important, because it meant somebody else could serve. Now they don't need me. It's not their fault."

She could tell he was considering his options. Sympathize or try to talk her out of it. "Well, don't they still need you? Here you are teaching. Here I am, your ace number one student." He reached down to give one nipple a friendly tweak.

Evelyn allowed his hand to stay there, exploring, teasing, then going lower to tickle and spread her, and then they were both breathing hard again, and trying not to make the kind of noise that would carry beyond the thin walls.

Then it was time for her to leave. Rusty went out into the hall-way first to make sure no one was there, and they went quickly down the hallway and out to the street. "Would you do something for me?" Evelyn asked.

"Sure," he said after a beat. After considering what kind of in-convenient something she might have in mind.

"Teach me how to drive."

"Yeah?" He was relieved. "Of course. If that's what you want. How come?"

"I don't want to be . . ." She might have said "left behind," but she didn't want him to think she was talking about him, complain-ing about his leaving. " . . . unprepared. Now that so many things are going to be different."

"Why sure. Lots of girls—women—drive nowadays. My chance to play teach, huh?"

The next time they went out driving, which turned out to be the last time, he stopped the truck at a crossroads with nothing and no one else in sight. "Your turn," he said. He put her behind the wheel and showed her the starter, accelerator, and brake. How to work the clutch when she shifted gears. "Feel that little whine at the top of the gear? That means you shift. There you go." She was a natural, he said.

No she wasn't. She was terrified to feel the engine rev or falter every time she hesitated or made some inexpert move. The size and weight of the truck made it feel like a large and wayward ani-mal with a mind of its own. "Take your time," he said. "You got it! Now you're cooking with gas."

It took her a while to get a feel for it. She stalled out twice and had to restart the engine. Nobody would have called her a natural. Still, Evelyn managed to wrestle the truck into reluctant compli-ance. Rusty joked about giving her a grade.

Evelyn had managed almost four miles when he said, "Looks like we got a little weather moving in."

It was far enough away that it seemed like a curiosity. A dark patch you could cover with a thumbnail, off to the west. The darkness glinted. "Oh, lightning." Everything was so flat, it was like viewing a giant map, a battlefield map, perhaps, where generals had planted flags and moved toylike troops from one place to another.

Rusty said, "You want me to take over now?"

"No, I'm all right. Really."

"Then you might want to go a little faster."

At first it seemed they might outrun it. But the storm was in a hurry, as if it had a mind to catch them. They watched it take up more and more of the sky. Lightning froze a moment's view of the dark lowering underside of clouds. Soon it was close enough for them to hear thunder.

"Oh my God," Evelyn said, not in panic but with a kind of awe. Wind was shredding the dry cornstalks and blowing the long, papery leaves across the windshield. The sky ahead darkened. The steering wheel shook and her hands along with it.

"Don't stop now. You stop, we could get hit from behind." He told her how to work the headlights. They rolled the windows up and the inside of the truck turned stuffy. "Slow down a little. You don't want to overdrive your lights."

The storm was straight ahead. Sheets of lightning turned the fields white. Rain hit the windshield in hard bursts. Rusty leaned over to turn the wipers on. Were they still on the road? It was hard to tell. Rain streamed over them. The wipers couldn't hold it back. She hit the gas by mistake and the truck jumped. "Sorry," Evelyn said, or tried to say, but the thunder spoke an awful word.

And then it was over. The rain slackened and turned to mist. They looked at each other, both talking at once.

"I never—"

"—that was some—"

Evelyn said, "I think I would like you to drive now, if you wouldn't mind."

"You are something else. Courage under fire!"

"I think I was too scared to stop." It was going to take a little time for her to catch her breath and decide how to feel about it. Terrified? Exhilarated? Probably both. The sky behind them was purple, lit by sunlight. Water shone in the ditches along the road. The storm moved east, still complaining to itself. She pulled the truck over into a muddy lane and when they got out to trade places, her legs sagged and she leaned against the hood.

"Hey." He went to help her and she turned and they kissed for a long time and he said they should probably get a move on. Head on back to town. But first he gave her backside a squeeze, and then let his hands do other things. Right out there in the open, in front of God or anybody else who came along, but no one did.

By the time Evelyn suspected she was pregnant, he had gone back home to be a farmer again. Day after day, she trod a circle of worry and panic and blurry disbelief. They had been careful. They had not been careful enough. She had to do something. Or she could do nothing at all and her life would become unrecognizable. She would lose what was left of her teaching job and they would remove her from the doctoral program. They could do that. How would she live, how would she raise a child? Her parents had their own problems of declining health and declining fortunes and anyway she could not present her shameful self to them when they had made such a proud point of boasting of her.

There were ways in which you would not have a baby, but she knew nothing about these, nor even whom she might ask.

Or she could leave and find somewhere that would take her in, some grim Catholic or Lutheran institution where the girls were the object of a lot of disgusted prayers, and they took your baby and gave it to people who would be better for it than you would be.

She would have to get married. Wouldn't she? She didn't trust her own thinking. There was a hole in her brain and she kept shoving possibilities into it, then watching them erupt like geysers. Married to Rusty? Would he have her? Wouldn't his mother weigh in and tip the balance? And say they did marry. She would be a farmer's wife and she would be no good at it, no good at all, useless and feeble when it came to wrangling calves or canning vegetables, complaining about dirt and flies and bad-tasting well water. She would be just as big a mistake for him as he would be for her. An educated girl, she knew, was not always a welcome thing.

Andrew invited her to a reception at the home of one of the law school faculty. Evelyn understood that this was an important occasion for him, one where he hoped to present himself as a logical, inevitable choice for a greater presence at the school. And she would be a part of that presentation.

She had a good dress that he had not seen (because he had not taken her anywhere that required it), a full-skirted blue taffeta with a waterfall bow at the back of the waist. She fixed her hair with care and did what she could with rouge and powder. She'd been feeling sick and wretched most mornings. Now she hoped to look blooming and pretty. Although Andrew's offer of marriage was still on the table, so to speak, it was important that he repeat it, and that everything should be his idea.

She was too desperate to feel guilty for trying to deceive him. Andrew both was and was not stupid. He believed it was reasonable to propose marriage to a woman he had not known very long, or very well; he believed it was reasonable that she might accept him. But if they did marry and if she had a baby too soon, a healthy, full-term, red-haired baby who would grow up to take an uncanny interest in tractors—she didn't know what he would do. Unleash the power of the law on her, cast her out.

She would have the baby in secret, put it in a basket, and leave it at the farmhouse's front door.

Waiting for Andrew to come get her, she felt her stomach churn and heave and had to run into the bathroom and drape a towel around her as she retched.

"Don't you look nice," Andrew said when he arrived. Evelyn murmured a thank-you. She had a roll of Stik-O-Pep Life Savers in her handbag and she kept one under her tongue to settle her stomach. Andrew steered her outside. "It's only a few blocks," he said. "I thought it would be all right to walk."

He had a car but he was stingy about using it. And so they set off through the early darkness. The weather had turned frosty and the sidewalk had patches of thin glaze that she had to pick her way around carefully. Her shoes were low-cut shell pumps and no good for walking. Why were they walking? She knew where the host lived; it was a neighborhood clear on the other side of campus. And at the end of the evening, she would be expected to walk back. What was the matter with him? Why wouldn't he spend enough on gas to take her out in decent fashion? Had he even looked at her shoes? Of course not. He didn't think about such things. They would have to be pointed out to him. Again and again.

Her ankles were cold; they were making her steps clumsy. Andrew had to slacken his pace to keep from bounding away from her. He often walked for exercise and was a believer in the curative powers of fresh air. It was another of his principles, maintaining good health. Wasn't that admirable? Yes, but it was also infuriating, as were the entirety of his thought-through notions, his reasons for distrusting soft-cooked eggs and voting for Hoover, some number of which she had already heard and some unknown number of which she had not, at least not yet. This would be her life with him, or some portion of it: the receiving of opinions.

But you could not entirely dismiss such a man, or entirely resent him, or even make fun of him. He was too upright, too serious and substantial. When he said a thing, he meant it. If he had any dark or conflicted thoughts, any bad wartime memories, he would put them in their place and move on. If she married him, he would always be himself, a pillar of certainty. She might rage against him and argue, but he would not be moved. And that would be exasperating but also a relief, to have someone so close at hand, who could be so reliably contradicted, scorned, denied, and who would always, always be there to accept more.

Her face felt frozen. The cold had turned her feet into hooves, scraping along on the uneven sidewalk. They had reached the low brick wall that surrounded the library. Evelyn sat down on it. "What's the matter?" Andrew asked.

"I want you to go get your car."

"What?"

"I can't walk any farther, this is stupid. I'm not dressed for it. I'll look like a hobo by the time we get there."

"But we're most of the way to the house."

"No we aren't."

Andrew swung around to the empty street and sidewalk, as if wanting someone to witness how unreasonable she was being. "It would take me a lot longer to go get the car than to finish walking."

"I'll wait."

"I can't just leave you sitting here on the street."

"Yes you can."

"Let's at least walk a little farther so we can talk about this."

"Unless you go get the car," Evelyn said, "I'm not going to marry you."

He stood there for a moment, his mouth opening, then closing, reconsidering whatever it was he had meant to say. Then he turned and walked off in the direction from which they'd come. As she watched, he began running.

You didn't lose a baby. It wasn't something you misplaced. The baby simply didn't take hold. It was a failure of the body, a false start. She lay in bed for days afterward. From time to time she wept, but for the most part she stayed wrapped in a cottony numb fog. The church ladies sent casseroles. The doctor's office sent a nurse. Andrew sat with her in the evenings and went up and down stairs to fetch things he thought she might want or need. He was allowed to be there, consoling and anxious, like a dog shoving its nose into your hand. After all, he was her husband.

It had been explained to him that she was in mourning, it might take her time to come to terms with it and move on. And she was in mourning, not for any baby but for her only, her irreplaceable, her precious life, which she had mortgaged out of fear and now could not get back. Andrew would be her life, or at least he would take up most of the space in it. They were now each other's life, even more so than before. A sealed contract, no longer subject to invalidation due to fraud.

She would make an effort. He would make an effort. There would be arguments over who was making the greater effort. The children helped, when they finally came. She had not been unfortunate. She had enjoyed many advantages and comforts. Over time, her discontents became familiar and lost some of their sharp edge. What were you allowed to expect from life anyway? Not much. Nothing, when you came right down to it.

That did not keep you from wanting all of it.

But it was not so entirely strange, in the drifting, fitful process of dying, with so much that was misleading or uncertain, like a dream you might still wake from, that she would go back to the time when all possibilities were hers. Driving into the storm, all amazement, the rain hitting the glass like a volley of diamonds.

IV. LAURA

Syringa vulgaris was the Latin name for lilacs, the old-fashioned ones her mother had planted. *Vulgaris,* unfortunate word. Laura had looked it up after she found her mother's handwritten notes. Evelyn had sketched out a plan for the yard on an oversized scroll of paper. Everything else was indicated with its common name, columbine or hydrangea or lily, but the lilacs had been given their proper designation and labeled according to variety: Madame Lemoine, Belle de Nancy, Charles Joly. Her mother's handwriting was small and precise, unmistakable. She'd drawn tiny sketches of all the plants as well. Graceful branching stems, puffy bushes. She'd put in a crosshatched border, as if it was a needlework sampler. It was all quite lovely, a miniature landscape. One more thing Laura felt she ought to understand about her mother but did not.

Dust balls might roll across the floors like tumbleweeds and the refrigerator might be home to many cheerless, half-empty jars of pickles and jam. But her mother's yard was always kept in trim shape, at least until her mother aged. Once, when the house had been in its usual state of mild uproar—Laura and her brother bickering, their father stamping around like an old bull elephant, indignant about something no one else cared about—they had all looked around and registered her absence. "Mom? Mom?"

They found her out back, sitting in the child-size chair under the grape arbor. "If you are all going to stay out here," she said, "then I will go back in the house."

The garden plan was in a brown accordion file inside an old suitcase inside a closet inside a first-floor room that had once been a play space for Laura and her brother. There were a number of such files, filled with potentially important papers, although that had not yet proved to be the case. The closet also held some old toys meant as keepsakes: A cloth doll with one side of her face stained orange. Some of her brother's fleet of miniature vehicles. Old board games and jigsaw puzzles, their cardboard boxes gone soft with wear. What was anyone meant to do with them now? Why keep a thing in the first place, what kind of power were you hoping it had?

It was mid-June, a month since her mother's death. Laura had taken more time off work to go through the house. ("No fair," Becca said. "I miss you, there's nobody here to help me make fun of my dates.") There was pressure to get the place cleaned and sorted out, painted and patched and put on the market before the weather turned cold and people got out of the house-buying mood. The realtor had been through and had made suggestions. Some things, aesthetic things, could be deferred or done on the cheap, but the house had to be able to pass inspection. Workmen were already tackling the wiring. A number of unsatisfactory bids had come in for foundation and roof repairs.

Mark was the executor of the estate and he would have to approve any expenditures. He had been here for the funeral but now he was back in Pennsylvania, being a lawyer like their father. (Or not like, since he mostly represented workers in lawsuits against employers.) There were many back-and-forth phone calls about what ought to be done and how much it should cost. There would be more conferences necessary once the house was, with any luck at all, sold off and all the legalities satisfied. Laura was beginning to appreciate ancient Egyptian funeral practices. Build a new house for the dead, lay them within it alongside their possessions, seal it up, and go on about your business.

She heard a car pull up in the driveway, and then the front door opening. "Mom?"

"In here."

Footsteps coming down the hallway. Even before she reached Laura, Grace was saying, "You shouldn't leave the door unlocked. Anybody could walk right in on you."

"Go lock it, then."

"I already did."

Grace stood in the doorway, disapproving. "You should just get a dumpster."

"I don't suppose you'd want any of this." Laura nodded at the heap of old playthings and metal cookie tins and cockeyed lamps that she'd herded into a pile needing further consideration.

"No one would. I brought us some lunch. Vegetarian vegetable soup and some beet and farro salad. You can't keep eating cold cuts. They're a bullet aimed at your heart. I'm going to go heat the soup, I'll call you."

"All right," Laura said, although her agreement hardly seemed necessary, and Grace was already gone. She was used to her daughter bullying her about one or another thing. She didn't mind so much. At least it was a way they could talk.

She heard Grace making exasperated noises in the kitchen. Cupboard doors slammed and pots rattled. Then Grace called her and Laura got up from the floor, stiff-legged, and went to wash her surprisingly filthy hands.

Grace had set the kitchen table with soup bowls, plates, and the paper carton of salad. There was a stack of brown, recycled paper napkins and two bottles of whatever it was that Grace thought she should be drinking, probably some tonic made of green tea, ginseng, and celery. Grace worked at the healthy grocery in town that sold these things. "This looks nice," Laura said, because Grace had made an effort, even if the meal was somewhat severe, and you wanted to encourage Grace in making an effort. "Thank you."

"This kitchen should be towed out to sea and burned."

"We're going to pull the appliances and repaint."

Grace looked around the room, her expression cool and un-amused. She had streaky blonde hair she wore pulled up in a knot, and thin, restless features. She hadn't turned out looking like any-one else in the family. You're tall like your grandmother, Laura al-ways said. "What are you going to do about this floor?"

The floor was red and gray checkerboard tile, not quite old enough or clean enough to be considered vintage and desirable. "We'll see how it goes," Laura said.

"I bet you had some mighty fine meals in this room."

"Well, Grandma wasn't very interested in cooking," Laura said, ignoring the sarcasm. Laura had been the one in her family who put her nose in the cookbook from an early age, figuring out what went into meat loaf and spaghetti sauce and layer cakes. Good plain cooking that people actually ate. You shouldn't be surprised that each generation headed off in a different direction from the one before. Evelyn had no use for cooking; Laura baked her own bread. Grace cooked, but she always seemed to be trying to prove something with food.

The vegetable soup was tasty, even if Laura thought it could have used less . . . texture, perhaps. Fewer beans and chunks of imperfectly peeled carrots. She didn't get very far with the salad. The soda tasted like iced tea that had undergone some kind of religious conversion. Grace finished her own portion and got up to help herself to the rest of the soup on the stove. She never gained weight no matter what she ate, even growing up on Laura's short ribs and mashed potatoes and desserts. There were times that her thinness seemed like a willed, an obstinate thing, although Laura knew that was silly.

Grace had volunteered to spend the afternoon helping, and once they had finished eating, she asked where she should start. "How about right here," Laura said. "Scrub the cabinets out and put down shelf paper. Try and make it look like a place people could imagine cooking a meal."

"Their last meal, maybe," Grace said, then, "Sorry." There had, in fact, been a couple of last meals prepared here, and rather too recently for jokes.

Laura let it slide, which was her default mode with Grace. She pointed out the cleaning supplies, scrub brush, bucket, rubber gloves and left Grace standing at the sink, contemplating the unsatisfactory cupboards.

Laura went into the dining room, where the table held stacks of dishes, cookware, silver, and serving pieces. She'd already set aside anything that she or anyone else might want—anyone else being Grace and Mark, neither of them enthusiastic—and the rest was going to be boxed up for donation or an estate sale. There were some jadeite pieces that would be of interest to people who collected such things, and a pair of clawlike salad forks that would not be. She filled one box for the Goodwill and started in on another. She heard Grace in the kitchen, scrubbing away, bumping into things, swearing under her breath.

I have lived my life sandwiched between two angry women.

She had not put it to herself in quite this way before. Yes, both her mother and her daughter had their angry, impatient moments, but that wasn't the entirety of them, it wasn't fair to reduce them to that. But she recognized the truth of it. Her mother had been happiest when she was away from them, teaching her part-timers classes or doing work for the League of Women Voters or some other project. She'd done what was required of her at home. She had joined Laura's father and supported him in his many social and civic enterprises. Sometimes with better cheer than others, and determined to carry it off with style. Sometimes begrudging it all, holding back, saying sarcastic things, making everyone unhappy.

There weren't as many opportunities for women when her mother was growing up. That was certainly true, though once you started blaming other people for your unhappiness, as Evelyn had (mainly Laura's father), it curdled something in you.

And what about Grace, who had grown up with wide-open opportunities, who could be a doctor or an astronaut or any other goal she set herself? So far, it seemed, she wanted to be a part-time yoga instructor and a grocery clerk, with a series of drippy boy-friends. She was twenty-five years old. Weren't you meant to have decided some things by then?

It was hard not to have opinions about all this. It was also not allowed for Laura to express these opinions, but they tended to leak out anyway.

A final, energetic burst of door slamming and water running in the kitchen sink, and Grace came in, looking grim and triumphant. "Done. Well, I didn't put down shelf paper yet. You need to spray for bugs first."

Laura waved this away. Bugs could be put off for another day, once they'd finished clearing everything else and didn't have to inhale poison. Grace said, "What do you want me to do next?"

"How about you take all the pictures and mirrors down from the walls and bubble-wrap the ones we're keeping."

"Which ones are those?"

"You can help me decide."

Grace thought this would be an interesting chore, at least more interesting than kitchen cleaning. She said she'd bring everything downstairs so they could look them over. Laura heard her industrious feet on the steps, sounds of scraping and hauling. She was glad that her daughter was the one taking down the pictures, the photographs, the framed maps and mirrors. She didn't want to see the walls made bare. It was one more too-sad thing.

Grace arranged everything gallery style, propped up against the living room walls. There were a lot of mirrors, one in a twig frame, others in gilt or painted wood. Family photographs that would have to be kept, dutifully, even if no one looked at them again for another fifty years. Here were the grandmothers of grandmothers in black, antique clothes and hats, Evelyn in a graduation cap and gown. (High school? College?) Evelyn and Andrew dressed up to do battle at some university reception. Laura and her brother eating birthday cake and probably kicking each other underneath the table. Baby pictures of Grace, of Michael, of Mark's kids. Laura had put a number of these around her mother's sickbed, although that was probably more for her own comfort than Evelyn's.

"What's this?" Grace asked, lifting a framed picture from the pile. It was a print of the idealized, highly colored sort, popular eighty years or more ago. A storm at sea, with a three-masted schooner tossed by violent waves. On a cliff in the background, a lighthouse sent out a narrow yellow beam.

"Your grandfather had that in his study. I always liked looking at it. You could tell yourself that the ship was going to make it to shore, with the lighthouse showing the way."

"Or they only came close and shipwrecked on the rocks with all hands lost."

"Honestly, Grace." As usual, her daughter enjoyed being a smart-ass. And as usual, Laura felt she had to respond with disapproval. A pattern that had been going on since Grace's teenage years, at least.

Grace rummaged around in the frames and came up with another. "And this?"

It was a reproduction of Picasso's *Guernica,* with its stylized, shocking violence: dying horse, dismembered soldier, broken sword, mother grieving her dead child. "Grandma's," Laura said.

They regarded the picture for a time. Laura said, "She was a different kind of person. Your grandmother. I never felt we had that much in common."

"Different, how so?" Grace asked. Laura could tell, from her casual tone, that she was paying attention.

"She was always restless. Always wishing she was somewhere else." She had wanted to be alone. But Laura didn't say that; it would have been too hurtful to admit it even to herself. "She would have liked to be more independent. And she never liked living in the Midwest. She thought it was provincial. She would have liked to go back east, where things were more civilized. Her opinion."

"She really did a lot, though. Her and Granddad. They were like, famous around here. All the fund-raising and speeches and newspaper articles. They went on all those alumni association trips. They went to Greece. They went to India!"

"She had a full life," Laura said, but that was the kind of rubbishy thing you said about people, and anyway there was a difference between full and long.

"She could get pretty snippy at Granddad."

"They always managed to work things out," Laura said shortly. She did not wish to get into a discussion of whether or not her parents had been mismated, any more than she wished to discuss the dynamics of her own marriage, or why Grace couldn't seem to pair up with anyone who had much lifetime earning potential.

They didn't make a lot of headway with the pictures. There was no reason to keep most of them. The too-pretty landscape paintings, the many renderings of university landmarks. They would need to be thrown away, but Laura could not yet bring herself to do it, and so they were set aside to wait for her to harden her heart.

Grace said she had to get back to work. "How's Dad and Michael?"

"You know, you're welcome to come over and see for yourself."

"I will, OK?"

"Come for dinner." Her daughter gave her a pained look. "You can bring your own food if you want."

"Yeah. So is Michael home for dinner a lot?"

"If you say you're coming, I'll make sure he is. We'll make a plan."

"Maybe it's better if I try to run into him downtown, when he's working."

"Better than coming to see us?"

"Come on, Mom. It's miserable being in the same room with him and Dad. They can't go five minutes without screaming at each other."

"We're all trying to get along better."

"Those guys aren't."

Laura said, "You don't know that if you haven't been around at all. Besides, your father would like to see you."

"He knows where I live. I'm sorry, Mom. I want to see you guys, I do. I'll call Dad, I promise. But I don't want you to knock yourself out cooking some big meal and then have it turn into a drunken brawl."

"Michael isn't drinking."

"I didn't mean Michael."

"That's about enough of that."

Grace closed her mouth then and gave her mother the benefit of her most irritating expression, a look of cool, detached pity. *Fine. Clearly, you possess superior insight and strength of character and would never allow yourself to be inconvenienced and unappreciated, certainly not by your own family.*

They let it rest after that. Laura thanked Grace for coming over to help, and Grace said that she'd have more time this weekend if her mother wanted her to come back, and they half hugged good-bye.

Well, she had helped. That was something. Neither Michael nor Gabe had, not really.

But why not come for dinner? Why argue about it? Just when you thought you already knew all the ways your children could be hurtful.

Surely they weren't as bad as all that, her family, not as bad as Grace seemed to think. Everybody had their difficulties. Everybody managed as best they could. Grace was just being her usual hardheaded self.

She finished filling the last kitchenware box, checked to make sure all the lights were off and the house secure. She was going to have to get used to the fact that the house would change hands and other people would live here. The process had already begun. People who had known her parents had sent realtors around to make discreet inquiries. Laura was helping it all come about. She ought to be over any soppy, boo-hoo feelings by now, but she wasn't.

When she got home and opened the back door, a murky wave of sound greeted her. Michael was in residence. Laura climbed the stairs and knocked on his closed door. No response. Knocked louder. "Honey?"

He opened the door without turning the music down. Laura had to pantomime: Too loud!

Michael retreated back into his room, adjusted the volume

down but not off, and presented himself again at the door, which he held closed behind him. His parents had access to his room and the ability to make regular searches of it, that was part of the postrehab deal. In practice, it was a lot harder to barge in on him.

"Hello," Laura said in a meaning-to-be-ironic voice. "Just checking in."

"Yeah, hi." Michael not having one of his better days. She could tell. Requests for information would be taken under consideration. His face had a blurred, muzzy look to it. Old alarms seized her, the fear that he was using again, the conditioned response that you couldn't shake yourself loose from. But no.

"Were you asleep?" He nodded. Often enough he fell asleep to the racket of his music. "Sorry. Are you working tonight? Will you want some dinner?" No point, she knew, in trying to coax anything nonfactual out of him.

"Yeah, I have to go in to Rocco's. I'll get something to eat there." Rocco's was the restaurant where he worked as a server and was, by all accounts, charming and attentive to his customers. Perhaps they should consider having him work for tips at home.

"All right. I saw your sister today."

"Yeah?"

Three yeahs in a row. "She says hello." She had not, literally, but she might have, if urged to do so.

"Uh-huh." Michael yawned. "I need to catch a little more sleep before I go in. Can you get me up in an hour?"

Laura said she would. "Michael? Turn the music off."

He opened his mouth to argue, maybe, but Laura kept her eyebrows raised, her half-stern, half-mocking, you're-being-ridiculous face, and after a moment Michael ducked his head and smiled and once he closed his door the music went blessedly silent.

Back in the kitchen she thought about sitting down, thought the better of it, and started in on supper. Pork cutlets pounded thin, dredged in fine crumbs, pan-fried and served with lemon. A simple pasta with cheese and garlic. Salad. Reasonably healthy stuff. She'd make enough for Michael too, no matter what he said. It was a mom thing.

You could measure your life out in meals. Too depressing.

Gabe got home while she was cutting up tomatoes and celery for the salad. "Chop chop," he said, clapping his hands together. There were some jokes you were so tired of, they didn't even register anymore.

Gabe fixed his drink and went in to watch the news until it was time to eat. Laura cooked up a portion of the meat and pasta and put them on a plate for Michael, along with some salad. It was time for him to wake up for work. She put the plate on a tray, added silverware and a napkin and a can of Coke.

Gabe raised his head as she carried the tray on her way upstairs. "What's that?"

"It's for Michael."

"He's home?"

"Yes, but he's going in to work."

Gabe said something she couldn't hear. Laura knocked on Michael's door. Knocked again until she heard him answer. "I'm coming in," Laura said, and balanced the tray to work the door-knob. Michael was sitting on the edge of the bed, awake but not very. Laura set the tray down on the clearest available surface, his desk. "Here. In case you decide you're hungry."

"Oh, sure. Thanks." He rubbed his eyes and his T-shirt rode up, showing his meager stomach. He was still way too thin. "Yeah, thanks, Mom. Looks good."

When Laura went downstairs, Gabe said, "What was that about?"

"I took him some dinner."

"Why can't he come downstairs and eat?"

"He has to get ready for work."

"What's so complicated about putting on a white shirt and black pants? He doesn't need his food delivered to him."

"It's not a big deal," Laura said, heading into the kitchen. She knew Michael wouldn't sit down to eat with them. There was no point in going into it.

She and Gabe ate at the kitchen table. Gabe worked through his food as if he had some grievance against it. Should she ask him how was his day, what was wrong, or any other kind of useless wifely noise? He could talk if he wanted to. She said, "I saw Grace today. She came and helped me at Mom's house."

"That's good."

"She said to say hello."

They heard Michael bumping around overhead, then his feet on the stairs, descending. He had to ride his bike in to work—his driver's license was long gone—and he came through the kitchen in a rush. "Bye Mom. Dad. See you later."

Gabe said, "Bring those dishes down from your room."

Michael paused and tilted his head, as if he might not have heard. "Your mother took the time to bring you your dinner, you can take the time to bring the dishes back to the kitchen."

Laura kept silent, but she nodded to Michael: Just do it. Hoping he'd go along without it turning into a stupid fight about nothing. Gabe looked peevish, ready to start in. Just do it. Please, no power struggle. And of course Michael ought to take care of the dishes, and Gabe was not wrong to say so, although he could have done so less unpleasantly, and here they were again, she, Laura, the enabler, and he, Gabe, the unsympathetic hard-ass, everything that had come out in the counseling sessions, everything they'd said they understood now, as if that ever changed anything.

Michael shrugged, headed back upstairs, came down with the tray of dishes. He rinsed them and set them in the sink. "It was all real tasty, Mom, thanks." Then, in his best waiter's manner, he presented himself at his father's chair. "Freshen your drink for you?"

"No thank you."

"Bye guys." And then he was gone out the back door, his bike tires crunching on the gravel of the driveway.

"What's with his hair?" Gabe asked.

"It's a kid thing. It's how they're all wearing it." The sides of Michael's head were shaved close, and the top was a fluff of curls.

"It looks half-witted."

Laura didn't disagree. She was just glad when there was something as trivial as hair to worry about. Gabe got up to fix himself another drink. He said, "Who's going to hire him for a real job, looking like that? I wouldn't. He'd get laughed out of the office."

"He's still in school."

Gabe made a particular kind of face, meaning, school was an excuse for their son to not do much of anything else with himself, anything adult and well paying. He'd said it all before. She'd heard it all before. He said, "How's the house coming?"

It wasn't entirely a change of subject. Selling the house would mean money for them, though how much depended on things that had not yet happened. Michael's treatment in rehab, Michael's legal fees, Michael's work-in-progress counseling had put them deep in the hole. Insurance only paid so much. "It's getting there," Laura said.

"What's the big holdup? It's been a month."

"That's not a long time." She meant, not a long time for your mother to be dead. He could try harder to understand these things. He could try a lot harder.

"What's your brother waiting on? Doesn't he want to get the estate settled?"

"Of course he does." It was her family, not his. She hated when he was like this, greedy and angry, his lower lip pushed out like a baby's. A crabbed and aging baby with his scalp showing through the thin spots in his hair. There was no talking to him. "It's going to take as long as it takes. Call Mark yourself if you think he's dragging his feet."

Gabe started in about the particulars of the roofing companies and other contractors who had been consulted, or who should not have been consulted, and how they were gumming up the works, and what should have been done instead. Laura let him run on without further comment. She'd long ago made her own peace with his drinking. Let him run on, let him exercise his grievances and fall asleep in front of the television and come to bed in the small hours and wake up in the morning convinced that everything was stacked against him. Meanwhile, Laura got up to start the dishes. She could have asked Gabe to do them, there had been times she'd made a point of it and turned it into an argument, but really, it was just easier to do them herself. As it was easier to let some things go. You got used to them. You could get used to almost anything.

After a bad spell, a bad evening, he felt guilty and tried to make it up to her. Then things would be fine between them for a while. They would be fond and easy with each other, a reminder of their best times.

They both made an effort these days. He only drank at home, in the evenings. He allowed himself two or maybe three drinks, and if he didn't pour them especially light, Laura made no mention of it. This was the bargain they had come to over the years, although there had been no such thing as a discussion of terms. He could drink, and she would allow it, at least as long as he did not become mean or stupid or soggy. And she would not use a certain tone of voice.

She thought they still loved each other, sure. But it was a worn-down kind of love by now, like an old silver spoon polished thin.

Back in their first married years, the drinking had almost been the end of them. Laura had seen Gabe drink a lot before, of course. She drank herself, all of their friends did, at bars and parties. They were all young and no one had yet got themselves into bad trouble over it. They made jokes about hangovers, they made liquor runs at parties when they ran out of supplies. They were in their twenties, single or coupled up, and none of the married ones had children yet. Gabe was still in grad school, earning a teaching assistant's salary. Laura worked at the city's development office, helping to coax commerce and industry into relocating. They and all their friends had jobs like that, good enough for now. No one was looking very far ahead, because the present was so effortless, and so much fun.

One night they had gathered at someone's house, late in the evening, after drinks and dinner and then more drinks. A few people had gone home already. Some of those remaining were watching a horror movie in the den, others a basketball game in the kitchen. Laura was on a couch in the horror-movie room. She was falling asleep, she would have liked to go home, but there was still a lot of rowdy noise coming from the kitchen, where Gabe and his buddies were carrying on. The movie was one of the killer-in-a-mask ones. They had all seen it before and had their favorite death scenes. Laura tried to keep up but really, it was just a lot of annoying screaming.

She was asleep. And then she wasn't, because the noise of the movie had grown so much louder. She opened her eyes to see Gabe and another man, the man whose house it was, pushing and swinging at each other, clumsy, red-faced, clinching and breaking apart, breathing hard, neither of them doing a good job of keeping their feet underneath them. "Hey," somebody else said, but they were all too confused to do anything, and anyway it didn't last long. Gabe fell over the coffee table and the other man landed on top of him and there was a noise of things breaking, things broken: wood, metal, glass.

Gabe tried to kick his way free. "Get offa me. Fuckin' . . . asshole!" The other man was bigger and heavier. Gabe rolled from side to side, trying to get some purchase to right himself. Their clothes were disarrayed from grappling with each other and their eyes were streaming and when they finally disengaged, both of them were making huh-huh sounds, very unwarrior-like. They didn't seem to have hurt each other, at least, nobody was bleeding. They got to their feet, swayed, feinted. Finally other people got between them.

Not Laura. She was still on the couch with her feet tucked underneath her. One of those times when your life takes a turn and you're too stupefied to catch up to it.

"Get outta here, fuckhead."

"Oh yah, don't worry, fuckhead, I'm going."

"The Battle of the Fuckheads," said someone else conversationally. It wasn't as if any of them were sober.

They took a few swings at each other, wild ones that didn't have any chance of connecting. That part of things was over. Gabe said, "Pussy," one last stupid insult, then, to Laura, "You coming?"

She felt the others watching her. She got up, looking for her shoes, her purse. Gabe was already on his way out the door and she had to hurry to follow. Once they were outside she said, "What was . . ."

Again he didn't wait for her, but set off down the street to the car. "Do you want me to drive?"

He ignored her, opened the driver's door, got in, and revved the engine. Laura barely got herself inside before he took off, punching the accelerator and getting as much noise as possible out of the tires. He took off down the street, the car well over the center line. "Stop that," Laura said. "Do you want to lose your license?"

That at least made him slow down, and when they came to a red light, he stopped for it. "Tell me what happened back there."

"He kept getting in my face. About Iran-Contra."

"What?"

"He said the Contras weren't terrorists. You believe that shit?"

"You got into a fistfight over Iran-Contra?"

"Ah, he's . . . a dick." The light changed but Gabe only sat there. His chin drooped to his chest.

"Gabe!"

He shook his head to rouse himself, accelerated, and ran the car hard into the curb.

They got home eventually and fell into bed. The next day they both came down with the flu, the actual flu, not the drinking variety, though the drinking surely hadn't helped. It was a while before they could think about anything except bodily misery. The fight was something that had happened in the receding past before they got sick, a bad time before the more recent bad time. It was almost a week later that Laura said, "Are you going to talk to Ian?" Ian being the host and combatant of that evening.

"Talk about what?"

"About what happened." They were eating grilled cheese sandwiches in the kitchen, the first real food they'd managed in a while.

Gabe finished his sandwich and started in on a bag of potato chips. "There's nothing to say."

"Come on. You guys have to make it up."

"No we don't."

"It was a dumb fight, you were both drinking. Everybody's cooled down now. Just talk to him."

"Not going to happen." He had the chip bag propped up and was reading the list of ingredients and promotional copy. The flu had hollowed him out. He looked even thinner than usual, the knobs of his backbone visible through his shirt.

"Well . . ." She didn't yet imagine it was anything more than pride and stubbornness and his needing her to coax him out of it. "What's going to happen when we go out with those guys again, or see them at the bars? Don't you think that's going to be awkward?"

"Yeah, I won't be anywhere they are, so that's gonna make it a lot less awkward."

"You don't mean that," Laura said. Although she was beginning to sense the shape of some other obstacle, like a rock surfacing in seawater. Maybe he did mean it. "Those are our friends."

"Your friends, maybe. I'm not having anything to do with them."

"Because of Iran-Contra," she stated, hoping that if she said it out loud, he'd hear how ridiculous it was.

"What? Sure. It was a last-straw kind of thing."

"You're being childish." He was still engrossed in the bag of chips. "What is the matter with you? You're in some totally stupid fight and you're too stuck up to apologize so you're turning it into this huge grudge."

Gabe finished eating and wadded up his napkin. "You know what I finally figured out? None of those people are especially bright. They're OK if you want to watch *SportsCenter* in a bar and throw peanut shells at the screen. That's all they're good for. Adios. We can do better."

"I don't understand you," she said, because she really didn't, and perhaps she didn't want to understand this part of him. "That's not fair to them. Or to me. What am I supposed to do, tell everybody I know they're not smart enough for us? I didn't get into any fights."

"Do whatever you want," Gabe said, getting up from the table. The bread and cheese were still out on the counter. He put a slice of each together, then doubled them over into an unappealing sandwich and ate it standing up.

Laura went into the bedroom and lay down. She was still not yet entirely well. She still had headaches and weak spells. She saw how it was going to be, how everyone would keep their distance now, how she would be a part of Gabe's feud because she was a part of Gabe.

It was different for him, he hadn't grown up here. He'd come to the university from one of the prosperous Chicago suburbs. Everyone here was a chapter in his life, not the whole of it, even she, Laura, was a chapter, a portion. But Laura had known some of these now-discarded friends for longer than she had her husband. Knew their brothers and sisters, knew what they'd looked like in the seventh grade and who had been the first to get their driver's license. It wasn't as if she wouldn't see them anymore. They would just turn away and go on without her.

Gabe came into the room then and lay down next to her on the bed, fitting his front to her back. "How are you feeling?"

"Tired."

"Yeah, that flu kicked our butts."

They were quiet for a while. Laura wanted to go to sleep and wake up and leave all the wrong, stupid, and complicated parts of what had happened behind. Gabe said, "It's OK. It's OK if it's just you and me."

But it wasn't, and it wouldn't be. There would always be other people, you couldn't shut yourself in or shut them out. Gabe was the smartest person she'd ever known. He knew so much about things like computers, chemistry, electronics, hard, complicated, brainy things. She thought that his being so smart was what made him stubborn. She said, "Let's let a little time go by. Give everybody a chance to calm down."

"I'm perfectly calm. Do I seem not calm to you?" Laura felt him shift his weight and roll away from her. Now he would be sulky and she would have to talk him out of it. But she didn't mind that part because after all, everyone said you had to work at a marriage, it wasn't all sunshine and rainbows, and wasn't this what they meant? He had chosen her, out of everyone else in the entire world, and she had chosen him. Now it was time to make all the words mean something. There was a thrilling, adult quality to it all.

They had been so very young.

Laura was part of a volunteer group that did fund-raising and work projects for the public library. She liked that it was a responsible, public-interest, good-citizen thing to do, and she also liked the library itself, which she'd been visiting since she was a child. The library was one of the Carnegie buildings, with a temple-like front entrance up a flight of limestone steps. Inside, the lobby had high, vaulted ceilings. People spoke in hushed, echoing voices that always seemed to Laura like the cool and orderly sound of all that collected and transmitted knowledge.

One of the other volunteers was a woman named Jeanine, who was the girlfriend of Ian, the man Gabe had wrestled with. The group had a meeting scheduled a few days after she'd had her unsatisfactory talk with Gabe. She'd see Jeanine there; maybe there would be a chance to set things right.

She got to the meeting early, hoping to have a chance to talk, but Jeanine got there late. She found a seat at the big table at the far end from Laura and didn't look over at her, but then, there was the meeting itself to pay attention to. Jeanine wasn't a friend, exactly; she was too cool and self-contained, one of those head-turning girls who are always conscious of their own value. Laura was only another hopeful girl trying to get someone to notice her. She had not had a notably successful adolescence. But she and Jeanine had known each other since high school, knew everyone each other knew. Jeanine and Ian were the ones who had the parties, the ones who kept the ball rolling. Laura didn't want to stay on their bad side.

The meeting was over. Jeanine was out of her chair and through the door before Laura could get to her. Laura caught up with her in the parking lot. "Jeanine! Wait up."

Jeanine stopped and opened her handbag to find her keys. She had a small leather bag on a chain, the kind that was expensive for no good reason. "Hey, can I talk to you?" Laura said once she'd reached her.

"I have to be somewhere," Jeanine said, managing to sound both bored and impatient. She had short, dyed black hair that she wore in bangs across her forehead, like a 1920s movie star. And Laura should have stopped right there, backpedaled, said sure, some other time. But she was in a rush to get things settled, and to demonstrate her own blamelessness.

"It'll just take a sec. I'm sorry about the other night, I don't know what Gabe was thinking."

"Maybe you should ask him."

"I guess he wasn't really thinking, you know, it was one of those crazy times when everybody's drinking too much—"

"He said that Ian had the political smarts of a third-grader. And that third-graders were actually smarter."

"Oh, well, that's . . ."

"He said a lot more. All of it nasty."

"I don't know what to tell you. I'm sorry."

"In Ian's own house. Then he throws a punch while Ian's back is turned. Which is so classy."

"I guess . . . Gabe has a problem."

"You know who else has a problem? You do, if you go along with his bullshit." Laura started to say that she didn't, she didn't go along with it at all, but Jeanine was still running hot. "Why are you following around after him, apologizing? Why isn't he apologizing? Huh?"

"I'm hoping he will. Apologize. Men, you know." A sisterly appeal. They all knew what was wrong with men, didn't they? If

Gabe had won the fight, or at least landed some good punches he could brag about, Laura was pretty sure he'd be magnanimous and willing to forget the whole thing.

Jeanine wasn't buying any of it. She said, "I really do have to go now. I'm meeting my mom, we have some shopping to do."

"Sure, say hi to her. Maybe you can talk to Ian . . ."

"And say what? You're sorry your husband's a big jerk? We should feel bad for you? I don't. You were always so impressed by the smart guys. So-called smart. It should have been by your picture in the yearbook, 'Most Likely to Marry an Asshole.'"

"That's not fair, Jeanine."

"So he acts like a prick and we're supposed to give him a pass because, what, he's such a superior being? Him and his computer talk. I never heard anything so boring. There's something really wrong with you."

Laura turned and fled. She reached her own car and it was as if she had never driven before, had to think through the pedals and the steering.

She couldn't remember a time when she'd been attacked in such a way. It left what felt like a bruise on her heart, something that would darken and stay sore for a long time. She thought Jeanine was probably right about her. Other people were always right about her, saw her mistakes and flaws more clearly than she did herself.

But right about Gabe? No. They didn't know him as she did, the caring part of him, the goofy, funny part, the times he made her laugh like crazy over nothing at all. He was an outsider, he didn't bother to hide his intelligence, he had his prickly, sarcastic moments, and they resented all that.

She cried a little, which was another stupid thing. What had she done that was so awful, besides try and smooth things over? Was she really such a terrible person?

She couldn't tell Gabe about any of it. He'd just start in again about everything that was wrong with everybody else.

Three days later she got a call from one of the librarians. This was not a usual thing. "Hi Shelly, what's up?" Trying to sound brisk and cheerful, although Shelly was neither of these things herself. Shelly wasn't one of the nice librarians, who smiled and helped little kids find books. She was more the kind who told them to go blow their nose and then wash their hands.

"Laura, I'm sure you know why I'm calling."

"Not really." No clue.

"It's about the magazines. The ones that rotate out of the displays."

"Yes," Laura said, switching her tone to one of mild impatience, although she knew now what was happening, and why. She felt the cold touch of disaster.

"Those magazines are meant for prisons and the county nursing home. It has been reported that you're taking them for your personal use."

It has been reported. By which mean-mouthed, black-dyed bitch? Laura said, "I didn't think . . ."

She'd scooped up a few of the ones without covers, with wadded-up or torn pages. A few of them, a few times. Jeanine had seen her and had stored it up to humiliate her at this later date.

She said, "They were damaged. No one would want them." She would have been embarrassed to give them away as charity.

"Laura, that's for the librarians to determine. If you still have any of the magazines, I'm going to have to ask you to return them. And in the future, do not remove any library property."

"I'm sorry. I already threw them out." Thank God Gabe wasn't home to overhear this.

"Because any further such incidents—"

Laura hung up the phone. She didn't go back to the library again for years. Years and years.

It was the start of one of the most unhappy times of her life. Their routine, hers and Gabe's, went on pretty much as before, except that they either went out alone or stayed home. Gabe kept a lid on his drinking. There were days, whole weeks, when he did not drink at all. This was to demonstrate how little its hold was on him. He would do this from time to time over the coming years, and it was successful, except for those times when it was not.

They were pleasant and mannerly with each other. Laura supposed that as far as Gabe was concerned, everything was working out well. They had separated themselves from the people he did not wish to see and they were fine, weren't they? He'd been right about that. He would keep on being right about things and they would keep on being fine.

Laura was bewildered by the turn her life had taken. She missed her friends, or the people who she had thought were her friends. Maybe they had always felt a secret contempt for her. If she caught a glimpse of any of them in a grocery store parking lot or picking up the dry cleaning, she hurried to turn her face away and retreat. She lived in dread of people finding out about the humiliating episode with the library, small-scale and farcical as it was—that she had been accused of stealing something, even a worthless something, that the library staff had seen fit to intervene! For all she knew, it was now a topic of general conversation and people were having a good laugh over it. For all she knew, no one and none of them had ever wished her well.

She told Gabe she didn't have time for the library group anymore, she'd burned out on it. She didn't want to tell him the whole story and have him say it was no big deal and she should rise above it, get over it. Advice he probably wouldn't have taken himself. But even if he was right, there would have been no comfort in it.

One night she said she thought they should get some counseling. "Counseling?" He was genuinely surprised. "Why do you think we need to do that?"

She had rehearsed this part. "To help us identify our issues. Our goals. So we can communicate. Communicate better, I mean."

"Sweetie, what's this about?" He was working at the computer. It was difficult to find a time when he was not at the computer, or watching television. But now he turned it off and swung his chair around to face her. "Are you mad about something? Unhappy?"

"No." She was going to have to find some way of saying yes. "But I think it would make some things easier if we talked them out with a third party."

"Huh." He frowned, as if considering it. He didn't want to do it and was looking for reasons. "I have to tell you, a third party is the last thing I want to have snooping around in our business. I don't trust most of them anyway, I mean, what, they have a certificate or something? What does that mean?"

"They have training. Experience. People go to them all the time, they can help."

"Help." It was a trick he had, repeating something so that it turned into irony and was undercut.

"Never mind," Laura said. "Forget I brought it up."

"No, hey, I expect they help some people. The really bad-off ones. Believe me, if we were anything like my parents, I'd be dragging us in to a counselor. A lawyer too."

Gabe's parents had been famously unhappy and combative before they divorced. Afterward too, he said. Laura wouldn't know. She'd only met them once, at the wedding. Each of them had attended with a new companion and had made a number of amusing, vicious remarks about the other.

"I mean," he went on, "I know I spend too much time working, I know you resent it. But I'm busting my ass for you. For us. You know that, right?"

She nodded. She wasn't sure if she knew it or not.

"I'll try not to be so wrapped up in it. I'll schedule some breaks. That's what you want, right? Me to pay more attention to you?"

"You make me sound like a dog that wants somebody to throw the ball."

"You're still mad about that thing with Ian, aren't you? You think it was all my fault."

"I don't know whose fault it was."

"I tried to fit into your old gang. I tried for your sake."

"They aren't my gang, Gabe, I don't have a gang. And there are some people we met together."

He raised a hand, both to concede the point and to wave it away. "You know what would be great sometime? If you were on my side. Totally. Like married people are supposed to be."

"Of course I'm on your side, you're being ridiculous."

"Yeah, well, it doesn't feel that way."

"Ridiculous," she said again, but Gabe had gone silent. He turned the computer on and waited for the screen to brighten. She could keep talking if she wished. She could have pointed out that this was exactly the kind of issue that a counselor could help you sort out. But there was no way she could make herself heard.

Now she felt guilty, as he had no doubt intended. Because he wasn't entirely wrong. She'd coaxed him into friendships with the people she knew, spent time explaining them and telling him stories. She thought he'd wanted to know things about her, as Laura wanted to know everything about him, everything she'd missed before they met. She'd wanted Gabe to like the people she liked and get along with them, why wouldn't she? She'd thought he did, but now there was this drawing back, and it seemed she had gone about everything wrong.

She was lonely without them. She was lonely in her marriage. What if that never changed? What if your life sneaked up behind you, tapped you on the shoulder, and said, Guess what, I'm already here.

Laura took the car in for an oil change to a new garage, a franchise that had sent out coupons. She sat in the waiting room as other customers came and went. A television mounted up high in a corner was tuned to a soap opera, nothing she ever watched, and it was restful to watch the pretend people getting so worked up about their pretend problems. Different mechanics came in to discuss air filters and synthetic oil with car owners and to ring up the charges. When her name was called, Laura presented her credit card and signed the receipt. The man at the register said, "You don't remember me, do you?"

He had blond hair curling around his ears and over his collar, the way guys who worked in garages wore it long. Wide-set blue eyes and a high-bridged nose and wide, curving mouth. His shirt was embroidered with his name, Bob. Laura said, "I'm sorry, I guess I don't."

"I went to school with Mark."

"Oh, sure." She still couldn't place him. Everybody had known Mark. He'd played football and run track and spread himself around. "Bob . . ."

"Bob Malloy."

Laura nodded, running through her mental files. Bob, Bob, there had been any number of them.

"I ran cross-country," he said, and maybe she did remember him. A tall, skinny kid with legs like a heron's, though she couldn't recall one thing about him or one thing he might have said. But it was enough to claim acquaintanceship.

"So what's old Mark up to these days?"

"Law school. He's at University of Pennsylvania."

"Well, he always was a smart guy," Bob Malloy said, stapling her receipts together and handing them to her. Laura didn't ask him what he was up to these days, since it was all around them. He indicated Laura's hand with its freight of rings. "You got married."

"Yes, almost two years now."

"Any kids?"

"Not yet." Another customer came in behind her and needed his attention, and besides, Laura was done with announcing the headlines of her life, the way you did on such occasions. "I'll tell Mark I saw you."

"Yeah. Law school." He made an owlish face of mock amazement. "Tell him I bet I can still dust him in the eight K."

Laura said that she would. A few weeks later, when the car developed a shimmy at high speeds, she took it back to the same garage. Gabe was too tied up at school and it was easier for her to run such errands.

"The dreaded shimmy," Bob Malloy said. "Leave it here, we'll take a look at it. You need a ride to work?"

He drove an old Pontiac with patches of Bondo along the hood and one fender. Laura guessed you wouldn't trust a mechanic who drove a new car. You wanted the guy who could keep a wreck going for a long time. He asked her what her job was and she told him and she could see him chewing it over, trying to figure out exactly what it was she did. "What line of work is your husband in? If you don't mind my asking."

"He's getting his master's degree in computer science. He's doing a little work for a software company."

"Now, there's something I couldn't know less about," Bob Malloy said cheerfully. "Computers. If you can't fix it with a wrench, I'm out of my depth."

Laura might have told him that Gabe wasn't the best at wrench work—really, he didn't do household repairs—but that would have seemed disloyal.

He said he'd call her once they knew what the problem was, and Laura said she hoped it wasn't anything expensive, and he said it might be a tire problem, or front-end alignment, or well, those were the easiest things. It felt funny, comical, to be getting out of such an old, beat-up car and she wondered whether anybody she knew was watching, and wondering who Bob was.

He called to tell her the car needed an alignment, and he walked her through what that meant, and how much it would cost. Gabe wouldn't be happy about spending the money. Laura said she'd have to talk to her husband and maybe bring the car in some other time, and he said he could run the car over to her and she could drop him off back at the garage, all right?

By the time Laura took the car back in for alignment they chatted away like old pals, which she guessed they were in some sense. Laura said she'd wait for the car, it was just as easy as going back and forth. She settled into the waiting room with a cup of garage coffee and a word puzzle. Through the big window into the shop she saw Bob Malloy and two other mechanics working in the bays. Bursts of shrieking, pneumatic noise came from the power tools. People came and went. They had starter problems, dead batteries, worn timing belts. For every problem, there was a fix. It was all so businesslike and logical and reassuring. If it hadn't been costing her money, and if there weren't whole lists of things she ought to be doing at work and at home, she would have been happy to spend her time there.

When the car was finished, Laura paid, and Bob brought it around to the front and held the door open for her. She thanked him and said it was nice to see him again and catch up, and he said, "You really don't remember, do you."

"Remember . . . I guess not."

"The party Mark had where we all ended up in the basement."

"He had a few parties. They were always . . . Oh my God!"

She stared at him, stricken, and he grinned back. "Oh my God," Laura said again. Their parents had been absent, off on a trip? Mark and his friends had gotten famously drunk, and Laura had helped herself to the flavored vodka, was it strawberry? Cherry? Some kind of red. And helped herself again, and after a while you lost track, lost any sense of how one thing might have led to another. People were in the basement and the lights were off and Laura was off in a corner with some boy, whoever it was that had pulled her down onto his lap, and they weren't having sex, not exactly, but they were having some teenage approximation of it, involving hands, mostly, and clothing shoved aside. At some point they had fallen asleep or passed out, and she woke up alone in the predawn dark and made it to the bathroom, where she got sick and fell asleep again on the floor.

Laura sat down on the edge of the car's front seat. Her body was overcome by roaring heat, as if she had stepped into a furnace. "I don't believe it."

"I guess you don't have to."

"Did anybody else . . ."

"I didn't tell anyone. And it's not like there's pictures or—"

She held up her hand to stop him. "I'm trying to think this is funny. Why didn't you say something? Back then, I mean. Come up to me in the hall and . . . I don't know, made dirty jokes?"

"I guess it was kind of awkward. And after all, you were this hot older woman—"

"I was not hot."

"—hot older woman, and I was this skinny little knucklehead.

Anyway . . ." He seemed to have embarrassed himself at this point. He shrugged and looked away.

"We didn't really do anything," Laura said severely.

"Nope."

"And even if we had . . ."

"We were just kids."

She found it difficult to look at him now, or rather, she found it difficult not to look at him. He was still thin to the point of skinny, but work had put some muscle on him, and the open collar of his shirt showed the workings of his throat and collarbone. Fair-haired, blue-eyed looks, pleasant, servicable, good-humored good looks. Again, hot humiliation overcame her. There were things she thought she remembered.

Abruptly she said, "I have to get home." Swung her legs around, shut the door, put the car in gear, and drove off.

When Gabe asked if the car was all right now, if they'd fixed whatever it was, she said it seemed that they had.

The next week she went back to the garage. She didn't go inside, but pulled up outside and waited for him to notice and come out to her. She kept the car running and he leaned against the door, bending down to talk to her. Laura said, "I want to know why you told me. Why you said something, after all this time."

"I guess it was like, now or never." He shrugged. Not wanting to meet her eye.

"Never would have been just fine."

"Sorry. I wasn't trying to embarrass you. But here you showed up after all this time, and it was, funny, I don't mean, hilarious, but kind of amazing, really, to think of all those years ago and then see how life turned out for you. Turned out for me too."

"I don't want to be finished yet with the turning-out part," Laura said.

She might have tried to blame Gabe for what happened after

that, might have summoned up times he was indifferent or inatten-
tive. Or it would have been easier to justify if he had committed
some new offense of anger or cruelty. But he had not. What she
did over the next month with Bob Malloy she did for her own self
and her own reasons, namely, she had too much unhappiness to
keep to herself.

They spent parts of evenings, parts of weekends, at Bob's
rented house twenty miles outside of town. No one was going to
see them there, north of the bridge over the interstate, on a turnoff
down the road from the red and yellow Big Mart and a Citgo station, past endless flat fields of corn and soybeans, here and there
a farmstead built up new next to the old collapsed barn. Cows in
a pasture, a pair of horses in someone's muddy back lot. The di-
rections involved unnamed roads like 1050E, and tenth-of-a-mile
increments. No one followed her. No one ever knew. Not Gabe,
Laura was certain. There were any number of things he was not in
the habit of noticing.

The first time she went to see Bob Malloy, he drove them out
even farther into the country, to a little cemetery, a pioneer cemetery, he said, a dozen or more graves surrounded by a rail fence.
They walked among the old, softening stones, trying to read them.
There were dates from the 1850s, 1860s, 1870s. Bob said there was
a county historical society that did research and handled the up-
keep.

BRUMLEY, Laura read, and RIEFSTECK, and one that said only
DAUGHTER, which she found disquieting. There was a single oak tree
in one corner and they sat in its shade and drank the two beers that
Bob had brought from home. It was September and hot. Locusts
shrilled around them. The cemetery was on a little rise and they
could see the grid of roads in the near and far distance, here and
there a car kicking up dust. The sky was blue and piled high with
clouds. They had not yet made love and she wasn't yet sure it was

going to happen. It seemed like something you already should have decided, but she didn't think she had.

"Nice day," Bob said, and Laura said that it was, glad to have something that easy to say. She was too full of confusion and heat and nerves to come up with any real conversation. They were close enough to touch, although they did not do so.

"See that cloud? Looks sort of like an alligator, don't you think?"

"If you say so."

"Come on, you have to use your imagination. That one there? It's a . . . race car. Sure it is. Those are wheels. Your turn."

She shook her head. "I can't."

She looked away to try and keep herself from any stupid crying. She said, "I can't see the sense of anything anymore. It's all just a big mess."

He put one hand under her chin to raise it up. "You see that cloud way up there, the one with the sun lighting up the edges? You know what that looks like to me? A pretty, pretty girl."

Bob's house was a two-story white frame, with some green-painted cinder blocks shoring up the foundation. There was a cement cover over the old cistern, a detached garage, and a couple of sheds that had outlived their usefulness. His landlord, a farmer, was his nearest neighbor, a quarter mile away. "Why do you live in the middle of nowhere, what's that about?" Laura asked him a week later.

"It's cheap."

"Gas back and forth to town must cost you. And the driving must take forever."

"Ah, I fly that left-lane airplane. Anyway, it's peaceful out here. Quiet." They were in the upstairs bedroom. The window next to them was open and the curtains belled in and out with the breeze. The landlord was harvesting corn in the field across the road and there was the steady, droning noise of his tractor, which was not exactly peace and quiet but was pleasant to hear.

"Besides," he went on, "I'm a hick. Born and bred. My folks didn't move into town until me and my brother started junior high."

Laura said she hadn't known that. Just as she hadn't known much of anything else about him. The room was warm and she felt drowsy, her skin damp and hot. They had been going at each other like the teenagers they once had been. She put her head against his chest and felt his voice reverberate, like an organ playing chords. He said that his grandparents had farmed. And went broke doing it, like a lot of other people. They'd sold out to one of the big operators. He didn't remember much about the place. A smell of hogs and cows. A barn. A ride on a tractor.

Laura roused herself. "You could have been a farmer."

"Maybe."

"Or you could have gone on to college. You're an intelligent person. Sure you are."

He raised one hand and rubbed the fingers together, the universal sign for lack of money.

"OK. But you could have—"

"I'm a pretty good mechanic," he said. "And I'm not likely to turn into anything else."

She was quiet then. She knew what he was saying. He wasn't going to be part of her world, nor was she going to be part of his. There was only this little space of now, however long that lasted. This moment and this one and this one. To keep from feeling melancholy, she drew herself closer to him and his arms went around her.

Some time later he said, "So what is it that you could have been?"

"What?"

"Since you don't seem too real sold on your present situation." Laura didn't answer. "If you don't mind my saying so."

"I don't mind. But, I don't want to talk about my husband."

"Sure."

"OK. In my family, we went to college. I mean, you knew my folks. No way we weren't going. I majored in speech com."

"What's that, exactly?"

"The study of communication. One of those majors that doesn't get any respect. I use my communication skills to write memos and press releases. It's a job, I don't expect that much from it."

Although she might have expected more from herself. She wasn't ambitious like Evelyn, never aimed herself at any remarkable, prestigious career. What had she thought would become of her? She said, "I guess I didn't think I'd still be living in the same place I grew up. I went to Europe for a couple of weeks after I graduated, and Gabe and I went to San Francisco for our honeymoon. But I never took any big road trips. I didn't move to Chicago or New York City like some of the kids I went to school with. I don't know why not. I guess I'm not the brave and bold type."

"This isn't such a bad place to live. Come on."

"But I always thought I'd have some great . . . adventure, some totally unexpected, transforming thing happen, like in the movies, I know, silly . . ."

"Well what do you think this is?" he asked, and Laura felt their two hearts beating next to each other, keeping pace.

She told him about Gabe and Ian's fight, and the horrible things Jeanine had said, and her humiliation at the library. "Jeanine Waller? That Jeanine?"

Laura said it was, and he started laughing, long and hard, while she waited, a little offended, for him to tell her what was so funny. "Good old Jeanine," he said, shaking his head, out of breath from laughing.

"Yes, she's a hoot."

"You know, her family's kind of sketchy. Her dad's roofing company got charged with fraud, you remember that? The neighbors used to call the sheriff when him and Jeanine's mom got drunk and started throwing things. No wonder she gives you a hard time, her sketchy self is jealous."

She was silent, trying to puzzle this out. It seemed she might have gotten things wrong, or at least there were other ways to look at her past besides through the lens of her own adolescent misery. Other layers to her hometown, people who lived different, more complicated lives. She'd always known that, but she hadn't paid enough attention. Bob said, "Want to hear a story?"

Laura wasn't sure if she did or not, but he didn't wait for her to say. "I had a girlfriend for a while who lived in the same house as Jeanine. Candy Tucker. You know her? Old Dandy Candy—"

"Never mind that, what about Jeanine?"

"It was a party-time house. Everybody's first place after graduation. Jeanine's boyfriend lived there too, from time to time. One or another boyfriend. I forget who. And some other characters. So one day Candy and I are up in her room and we've just finished, well, you know, just fallen back on the sheets, and the door opens and in walks Jeanine. She sits right down on the bed with us and asks if she can join in."

Laura gaped at him. "What happened?" It was so purely awful. She didn't want to know, but she had to.

He put his hands behind his head, pretending tiredness. "Some other time, maybe I'll tell you."

Laura punched him in the arm.

"Nothing happened. It was gross, you know? Listen at doors much, Jeanine? Ever think about knocking, Jeanine? Jesus H. Christ. Come right on in and make yourself at home."

He sounded angry, disgusted. As if he'd been the victim of a violation. You didn't expect it, not when you'd been told that men regarded sex the same way they did pizza. Sex was sex, pizza was pizza, both good things and it didn't much matter whom with or what kind. One more thing she seemed to have gotten wrong. "So you didn't . . ."

"She didn't take it real well. If you ever want to get up in her face, tell her Bob Malloy said hello."

"You turned her down." Jeanine, with her pretty, sulky face, her green eyes, and her breasts that the boys all visited in their dirty dreams.

"Girls like her, they think they can get anything they want. Well, not my fine white ass."

"But I did," Laura said. Happy now. She couldn't stop giggling.

"That's right. You sure did."

Laura let her laughter trail away. "Why do you think Jeanine did that?"

"Ah." Shrugging. "Cheap thrills."

"That's not me." She raised up on one elbow. "Look at me. That's not me. I needed this. I needed somebody to talk to."

"Somebody to talk to naked."

Laura hid her face again, and she felt him stroking her hair. "I know, girl. I know."

She and Gabe had decided to delay starting a family until their jobs and their savings were a little further along, but it was the very next month that Laura determined she was pregnant.

By then she and Bob Malloy had parted company, a clean break, both agreeing that was best. She had no wish to seek him out and tell him all the embarrassing reasons (having to do with contraception, having to do with, well, what one did in bed) that she was 99 percent certain the baby was his. There was worry, and guilty shock, and what if there were problems with blood type or inherited diseases, the same kind of thing you mocked when it came up on the soap operas. But it was so much easier to go ahead and have a baby than not to have it. And as time went on, and it seemed likely she would get away with everything, it began to feel like a happy accident. Because who knew when, or if, Gabe would decide they were sufficiently financially secure, sufficiently well-established, for a baby? It was something that might steer their marriage onto a better, less lonesome path. And Laura discovered that perhaps what she had imagined and expected and wanted of herself all along was to have a child.

part two

SACRIFICE

Ours was the privilege of sacrifice . . .
Our willing selves the offering
The price demanded to make fierce the cleansing fire.

Richard Dennys
1884–1916

I. GRACE

Grace was awake but she was pretending she was still asleep. The night before they'd had, if not quite an argument, an impatient, sharp-edged discussion. Or not even a discussion, because that implied two people exchanging views, rather than one of them staring at a computer streaming episodes of *Fear the Walking Dead*. This nondiscussion had been about the future, which Grace believed they should give some thought to, and which Ray believed would take care of itself. And maybe it would, but you might want to give it a nudge, and you might want to determine if your needs and goals were sufficiently aligned to make a mutual future possible and desirable, and that required words. Talking. She was tired of being made to feel she was some needy hyperemotional desperate controlling etc. etc. female for wishing to have such a conversation.

So this morning she kept her face turned to the wall and tried not to be too artistic or complicated with her breathing, which was always a dead giveaway. Ray ran the shower and dressed, being quiet about it, then he drank his protein shake and rinsed the glass. He probably didn't want to deal with her this morning, all right, but it would have been nice if he'd kissed her or touched her or woken her up to say any stupid little thing that wouldn't mean anything in itself except that everything was fine between them, the two of them were fine.

There was the click of wheels as he walked his bicycle down the hallway, then the door opening and closing quietly.

They were not fine. Perhaps they had never been.

Grace got out of bed, did her sun salutation, and made coffee the way she liked it, strong, with milk and sugar, her secret vice. The water heater was still thumping, so she waited to take her shower. They were trying not to run the air conditioner any more than was absolutely necessary, and the apartment was stuffy. Heat lurked in the corners, ready to regroup and attack. The place needed cleaning. It always needed cleaning, it was too small for the two of them and everything they had jammed into it. You were supposed to be so goo-goo in love that you didn't notice such things. Or they weren't supposed to matter. Or you got past them. None of these applied or were helpful.

There was a banner hanging on one wall, something she'd had for years. It read: WILD WOMEN DON'T HAVE THE BLUES. It was from an old blues song with lyrics about getting full of good liquor and putting your man out if he didn't act right. If you let things keep going along and going along, and brooding about your own low-grade unhappiness, it was just another amusing item to put on a wall.

She worked until six and then she taught classes at the yoga center, so she didn't get home until almost nine. Ray had not called or texted her all day, nor had she tried to reach him. When she walked in, Ray was sitting in front of the television with his laptop open. He was playing World of Warcraft and watching *SportsCenter*. Incredible. When had men decided to stop growing up?

Ray didn't move his gaze from his screen when Grace came in, stowed her bags in the bedroom, and went to the refrigerator for water. Was he ignoring her? Or just engrossed in his game? Did it matter?

She drank her water and walked behind the couch so that she could see the small figures on his computer screen and his fingers busy on the keyboard. "I think one of us should move out."

There was the sound of an on-screen explosion and a burst of vivid colors, some episode of simulated violence coming to an end. Ray turned around to look at her, blinking, trying to refocus his eyes. "Did you say something?"

Ray was the one who moved out, two weeks later. He was disbelieving at first, and then angry. He said great, if that was the way she wanted it. Grace was calm as he emptied out the closet and stuffed his clothes into black plastic garbage bags and made trips up and down the stairs and out to the car and back again. He'd had to borrow a car, as Grace would not let him use hers, even to move. No more free rides. Money was one more thing piled on the heap of reasons.

She watched him wrestle with the plastic crates that held his books and his many varieties of sports equipment: bats, rackets, mitts, balls. She guessed she was meant to feel sorry for him or guilty or regretful and she did, a little. They had breakup sex and Grace thought that even then it might not be too late if he would only try harder, or promise to try harder. Or say or do anything at all, anything besides sitting in a puddle of his own entitled feelings. She was tired of trying to claim his attention. Boys began by ignoring their mothers, then they moved on to ignoring the other women in their lives.

Although she had promised herself never to do so, she had

ended up with a man who was just like her father, at least in all the ways that counted.

Grace's friends all said, "Wow, I thought you guys were doing so great," and Grace said it was just one of those things. They had a lot of the same friends and it was better not to tell tales or give people too much gossip fuel. She went out for drinks and dinner with two girlfriends, an occasion that was meant to cheer her up as needed, and to welcome her back to the world of exciting singlehood.

One of the friends said, "There's so much pressure on relationships these days because they're so optional. Just about anything they provide, women can do on their own. Like the economic motive. We can support ourselves."

"You can have kids and raise them by yourself. Well, with a donor."

"How about sex?"

"There's an app for that."

"I mean good sex."

"No guarantees. Not anywhere."

"What if you're lonesome? If you just want to love somebody?"

"Get a dog."

This struck them as funny, in a potentially lewd sort of way, and they began to giggle and snort into their drinks.

Grace had not thought she needed any cheering up, but in the middle of all the giggling, melancholy crept up on her, like ink dropped into water. Talk it up all you liked, nobody really wanted to spend the rest of their life alone.

But for now she had her pride to consider, and she was a Wild Woman, not some fragile bruised flower, and so when some guys in the bar started talking and joking around with them, Grace made barking noises behind her hand and sent them all into laughing fits.

The next time her mother called her, Grace let the conversation go on for a while, mostly her mother talking about the problems with Grandma's house—the roofers had discovered an unexpected layer of rot—and complaining that she was tired these days, more tired than she ought to be.

"You could do some meditation," Grace told her. "And cut back on sugar and caffeine. They jack you up and then they wear off and you end up feeling worse." As if her mother ever listened, or changed anything about her lifestyle to deal with stress. "Let Dad and Michael clean up after themselves for a change, or cook a meal for themselves. Go on strike."

Her mother laughed, or rather, made a small, explosive noise meant to signify amusement. "Oh yes, I'd like to see how that goes over. Your father and your brother, planning a menu."

"Well, why not? They aren't handicapped. Just spoiled."

"Honestly, honey, it's easier if I do things myself. It saves on wear and tear."

Grace kept silent. She had shared her opinion on this topic a number of times already. Her mother chose to martyr herself to some domestic-goddess routine that everybody else in the world had wised up to long ago. "Well anyway," her mother went on, "I'd better get back to it. Love you, honey. Say hi to Ray."

"Ray and I broke up."

"Were you going to tell me?"

"I just did."

"Oh dear." Her mother was trying to avoid saying the wrong thing, whatever that might be. Or voice too much false sympathy. She had never been a big Ray fan. "How are you?"

"I'm good. It was for the best. We had irreconcilable differences," Grace said, trying to talk without really saying anything, or at least anything that could be used against her later. "It's just one of those things."

"If you're sure . . ." her mother began, another effort at tactful consolation. "I mean, if you think it's the right decision for you."

"I do." No equivocation. She couldn't stand her mother feeling sorry for her.

"I know that if you just hang in there, you're going to find a new boyfriend—"

"Partner, Mom. Nobody says 'boyfriend' anymore."

"They don't? All right, sorry, partner, anyway, somebody new who can make you happy," her mother finished, and Grace let that pass, because it was one of those reassuring mom things to say, like, you would certainly outgrow your bad complexion and once you were older your feet wouldn't seem so big.

"Okay, well, thanks," Grace said, in a hurry now to get off the phone.

"I'll tell your father you said hello."

"Sure."

"Love you."

"Love you too," Grace said. It depressed her to think that another part of her mother's martyrdom was worrying about her children much more than the children worried about her.

There were other things, other worries that her mother did not bring up on this occasion, although they hung over all their conversations. How Grace, despite having been given every advantage, every enrichment and opportunity, having been encouraged, supported, counseled, despite having been provided an excellent four-year liberal arts education and the resources to pursue further study if she chose, was still living an unserious, financially precarious existence that failed to live up to her potential. And she was doing so just to be difficult. Just like when she'd tried out different names. She was never going to live that one down, was she. It had been one of those teenage things, like the time she dyed her hair pink. Now she was stuck with her parents' notion of her as a willful and rebellious girl whose complaints did not have to be taken seriously.

Her parents didn't get it. Life was different now. The future, her future and that of everyone else her age, had blown up in slow motion. She lived the way she did because greed had sucked the juice out of the world and it was no longer possible to get one of those humble but promising jobs that led, with hard work and perseverance, to something that might be considered a career. Instead you competed with ambitious, underpaid people on the Indian subcontinent for the sucky customer service jobs, or you might choose to go the tech route and work as a coding slave, or sign noncompete and binding arbitration agreements with some major corporation that still required human bodies to do their dirty work for them.

Yes, you could go to medical school, or business school, you could aim to be a big deal of one sort or another. You could try to be rich. She had not done so, or at least, she had not done so yet. All options remained open. She thought she might like to travel and see more of the world, teach English in Japan, perhaps, or volunteer with a world poverty organization. She thought she might like to open a restaurant, or even a coffee shop, a place that would promote healthy foods and products. These personal choices were all you had left in a world that seemed so intent on steamrolling you and chugging along to its own destruction. How depressing was it to try and plan a life in such times? Look at climate change, for God's sake.

And in spite of everything you could say about the unfairness of it all, the ongoing, escalating, flaming catastrophe of the world around you, there was no dismissing the lurking fear that perhaps you simply did not measure up, and it was your fault you could not afford your own vehicle, or health insurance, or real estate, and you would spend the rest of your life at the bottom of the heap, frantically promoting yourself and your ventures on social media just as everybody else was promoting themselves, and complaining about it all.

Or, as her father had said, and kept saying: "What did you expect, being an English major? That's like walking around with 'Unemployable' tattooed on your forehead."

Thanks. Thanks ever so much. She really really really did need to get out of this town. But she didn't, she hadn't. She suspected herself of cowardice and irresolution, for all her big talk. She was a townie through and through, and she had the townie's comfortable familiarity and comfortable contempt, both at ease with and chafing against the place. Every block seemed to hold some of her history, her own personal bronze plaques: here she'd broken off a portion of a front tooth jumping from someone's porch steps, here had lived the boy she'd had a crush on in sixth grade. The one in seventh, the one in eighth. And so on. Here had been parties, babysitting jobs, encounters with members of law enforcement while in possession of contraband. Here was the university, her alma mater, whether she wanted it to be or not, clasping her to its oversized bosom.

When she was in high school, the university campus had been a playground for her and her friends, a place for them to hang out and try to get away with the same things the college kids did, sneaking into bars and parties, horsing around. There were summer nights when the school grounds had been a kind of giant hide-and-seek field, where they met up and ran away and met up again, climbing through unlocked windows, running down empty, echoing hallways, writing rude things on blackboards. Kids' stuff. Grace had been up in the bell tower as well as down in the steam tunnels. She'd ridden a horse in the stock pavilion and climbed down into an empty and disused swimming pool. She and her friends drank beer on the playing field of the stadium, with its statue of the legendary football player from almost a hundred years ago, which was just about the last occasion when the school had a decent team.

By the time she started college herself, as a freshman, she had trouble taking any of it very seriously. She lived in one of the dorms—she'd insisted on that—but she spent her free time much as she had before, with those of her friends who had not gone away to school. It was all fun and very absorbing, this new, emancipated life, and it wasn't until she got the worst grades of her life at the end of her first semester that she had to stop and rethink things.

Did she even want to be in school? Did she belong there in the first place? There was a series of unpleasant conversations with her parents. She made a new effort with her courses, even the required science and math ones she had no real liking for. She petitioned to have some of her worst grades dropped from her transcript. She declared herself an English major with a minor in ecology, which was not exactly a clear path to a career, but she did well enough in such courses. She was supposed to be intelligent, at least that was what everyone told her, in encouraging, bullying ways. But what if she was not, what if she was just getting by? There was so much knowledge in the world, an infinite vaulting structure, like a temple, and she hardly seemed able to pry off a little piece of it.

Meanwhile, many of the people she met at school, people who came from all manner of different places, were often curious and disbelieving that Grace actually lived here in town. For them, the town only existed as a subset of the university, since you had to put the school somewhere.

She got through the four years mostly because she realized that her classmates were not necessarily more brilliant than she was. She graduated and worked in one or another disappointing job, that is, disappointing to her parents, and it seemed that this would be the pattern and shape of her life, at least for now. Then the now of everything changed.

*   *   *

First, her brother took a magic carpet ride on drugs and crash-landed. Grace knew he had his wild and crazy moments and sometimes he went overboard, trashed himself having one or another kind of good time. But that surely wasn't the same as their father's life of sad, stupid drinking. Michael knew better than that, he and Grace both did. Although in hindsight Grace realized they had assumed a fallacy: that problem drinking or problem anything else was the exclusive territory of their father. And since neither of them was or ever could be him, they had no such problems of their own.

But it took quite a while and many mistakes for Grace to unravel and sort out her own thinking. In the meantime, nothing Michael did seemed that different from what other guys his age did. They all experimented, they all had boozy nights and strung-out mornings and bragged about how wasted they got. It was sort of obnoxious, but, as Grace liked to remind him, he was still in his obnoxious phase. "Yeah, what phase are you in?" he said, pretending to slug her in the arm. "Overeducated?"

Her hilarious, aggravating, pain-in-the-ass brother. The Kid. The Brat. He'd started out as a chubby, worshipful baby. As he got a little older, he discovered that the surefire way to get attention was to be annoying. He teased and mocked her and made up silly songs. If her friends came over to play, he lurked outside the door, elaborately spying. "Mom!" Grace would complain. "Michael's bothering us!" And her mother would disappoint her by failing to dispense justice and telling them both to behave or else nobody would be allowed to play.

Both her parents would have denied that they showed any favoritism, that they treated their children differently in terms of preference or behavior. Yet it seemed that Michael's future, the promise of his future, was different from her own. Of more consequence; while Grace was only expected to find something to do with herself. Nowhere was this stated. Her mother would have made horrified denials. Michael shrugged off anything that suggested a hopeful and accomplished destiny. It seemed to annoy him. Grace kept any grievance to herself. It was undocumentable.

But for all that, she and her brother were allies, coconspirators. They agreed on the impossibility of their parents, the wild unsuitability of their union, the awfulness of their lives, and how the first time the two of them met they should have turned and run in the other direction, except that would have left Grace and her brother unborn, which wasn't really what you wanted. Still, what had possessed them? One more cautionary tale, one more mistake they themselves would never make.

Michael's troubles started when he was in his first year of college. He was a good but careless student, the kind who put off reading the textbook until the night before the exam, and then got the best score in the class. Grace had already graduated and gained a toehold on an adult life. Unlike his sister, Michael had chosen to live at home rather than on campus. Grace thought that had to do with their mother waiting on him all the time, her baby boy. It wasn't anything Grace held against him. It was just the way things were, and anyway, Grace wasn't someone who wanted to be babied herself.

She saw Michael more seldom now that she was out on her own. She was busy with work and with her yoga, and with trying out one or another idea of herself, and fighting off the feeling that nothing much had changed since she was in high school. She had a boyfriend, not Ray but the one before Ray, who was good enough company for now, and that too was the same as high school.

Some nights they went out to their favorite bar. Grace had

pretty much stopped drinking, as a part of her developing preoc-
cupation with all things healthy, though she didn't mind keeping
company with people who did. One Saturday night with a crowd
just beginning to pack the place, football on the television and a
rowdy country song on the jukebox, they came in for cheeseburg-
ers, or rather, cheeseburger for the boyfriend, veggie burger for
Grace. They sat at the bar, eating. And here was her brother, swimming through the packed bodies to wave a hand in her face. "Hey,
meathead." He had a vodka and tonic in the other hand.

"Meathead? Since when is that my name?" Grace pushed her
plate toward Michael, who was already helping himself to her
fries. "Please, have some. Brian, this is my brother, Michael."

Brian had been watching the football game. He said hello,
waited a moment to see if his further attention was required, decided it wasn't, and turned back to the television.

"How did you get a drink here?" Grace asked him. "You're way
underaged." Michael rolled his eyes. He might have been trying
to look smug, or mock-innocent, or something else, but the effect
was distorted by his bulging mouth full of french fries. "What, you
have a fake ID?"

He ducked his head, chewing. "Gyut," he managed, meaning,
"Quiet."

"Seriously? You better not get caught."

"Gont." He finally swallowed. "I won't."

"Right, because nobody ever does." She guessed it was his
business if he wanted to risk a fine or some other expensive shit
storm just to get into a bar. "So how are your classes?"

"Boring. I have to take all basic requirements. 'Bum jeer, mon
sewer.' That's conversational French."

"Is it now. How's things at home?"

"Ah, I'm never there. Some guys I know have a practice space,
we're getting a band going."

"What happened to the last band?"

"Keyboard player sucked." Her brother was scanning the room, looking for someone he wasn't finding. He wore a grubby T-shirt that said "I Can't Adult Today." He'd done something with his hair that Grace couldn't quite figure out, until she realized he'd pulled some of it into a knob at the back of his neck. It was as if he was wearing a costume. He felt her staring. "What?"

"Nothing."

Michael pulled out his phone and checked the screen. "Gotta go." He maneuvered himself to come into Brian's field of vision. "Later, man."

Brian raised a hand in acknowledgment, and they watched Michael work his way through the crowd and out the door. Brian said, "That's your brother, huh."

Grace waited while he found his beer on the bar and drank from it. "All right, maybe I shouldn't say this—"

"Say what."

"—but I saw him a few nights ago, I'm pretty sure it was him, leaned up against a car in a cop stop."

Grace felt something within her go dead quiet. "Where?"

He mentioned an intersection. Grace knew it, a stretch of busy crosstown street, but after dark a no-man's-land of closed businesses and the kind of glaring, anticrime lighting that always seemed to encourage crime. "It was late, after eleven. I went out for groceries," he explained, but Grace waved this away.

"What kind of car was it?"

"Old Toyota. Green, I think."

It was Michael's car. "What was going on?"

"Not much. Couple of cops talking to him. They didn't have him cuffed or anything."

"All right," Grace said. The noise and racket of the bar rose up around her. She didn't know what to think about Michael, if there was anything to think at all. They didn't get into each other's shit, didn't interfere. She wasn't that kind of crummy big sister. She would let things ride.

But the next time her mother called, Grace waited for her to finish going on about the usual, her father had a cold, her uncle Mark called and talked about maybe coming out for a visit. Once her mother's stream of talk ran down, Grace asked how her brother was.

"Michael? He's fine. Why?"

"I hardly ever see him these days."

"You hardly ever see any of us," her mother pointed out.

Noted. Thanks. "I was just asking."

"He's not around that much either, he's always off at school or practicing. He has a new band, did you know? It has some silly name. The Idiots. No, The Useful Idiots. I have no idea. It's been very expensive, they have to buy amps and microphones and who knows what else."

They talked for a while longer, and Grace promised to stop by the house sometime soon.

Should any of them have known or guessed? Perhaps. But it was secret behavior and people took pains to hide it, at least until there was no more hiding possible. Her mother did say at one point that she didn't care for a couple of the boys that Michael was spending time with, although she disapproved of most young people aside from her own children, and sometimes them as well. There was a refrain of complaints about money, about Michael needing money. Grace's father said Michael was going to have to get a real job soon, not just screw around with this music thing, which was money down a rat hole, but that also was one of his usual complaints.

In September, Michael got a DUI. "I thought you knew," Grace's mother said to her in another phone call. "I thought he would have told you. It's the biggest mess. At least nobody got hurt. This had better be a wake-up call."

It took a while for Grace to get the story out of her, or at least some version of it. Michael had been out late as usual, musicians being late-night people, everyone understood that. Musicians were also the type to encourage the creative process with different kinds of self-indulgence, everyone understood that as well, or at least his mother was inclined to understand and excuse certain excesses. The cop who stopped Michael said he was weaving back and forth between lanes. He had failed a field sobriety test.

"Anything else?" Grace asked.

"What do you mean?"

"Nothing, never mind." Her mother was so, so thick. "How's he doing?"

"Embarrassed. He's pretending it's no big deal. Your father had to have a talk with him."

"I bet that was one for the books."

"What? You know, we're having a crisis here, a serious situation, and it's been very, very hard on all of us, and we're trying to handle it the best we can, and if you can't bring yourself to be helpful, maybe you could at least keep from making snotty observations."

"All right, I'm sorry." Grace was a little surprised at her mother's vehemence, but then, it had to be tough for her, worrying about Michael and how much the lawyer was going to cost and everything else. "How about I call him?"

"Yes, that would be nice. Call him and try to be . . . encouraging."

Grace said that she would. And she did call, and got his voice mail, and called again but still couldn't get through. Both times she left messages that she kept on the light side, saying she was trying to reach Uber and was this the right number, or call if he wanted to borrow her cross-country skis. Neither of which was all that funny, but she was trying not to sound like their parents, like it was the end of the world. Michael didn't call her back.

Well, he didn't have to. He probably had his hands full dealing with their parents and the residual damage from the DUI. She assumed she'd hear anything she needed to hear, and went on about the business of her own life.

Then, a couple of weeks later, there was a phone message from her mother sounding abrupt and rattled: "Grace? If Michael calls and asks you for money, do not give him any. Just don't."

Grace called her back. "What's this about money, what's going on?"

"I can't stay on the phone."

"Mom? What's going on there?"

Her mother was whispering now. "He'll use it to buy drugs. Tell him you don't have any money."

"I don't. What drugs? What happened?"

"I have to go, he's coming downstairs."

"What—" Grace began, but her mother had hung up.

Grace tried to call her father, both on his cell phone and at work, and both times got his voice mail. She was at work herself, manning the cash register at a store at the mall that sold athletic shoes, and it took her some time to persuade them she had to leave. She tried calling the house again and no one answered.

She kept calling as she drove. Still no answer. She swore, uselessly. She reached their street and slowed to a stop at the curb in front of the house. Her mother was sitting on the front porch steps. It was October and cold, but she wore only a sweater, her usual sweatpants, and slippers.

"Mom? What's the matter, what's going on?"

Her mother regarded her with a peculiar stony look. "I guess everybody thinks I'm stupid."

"What are you talking about, come on. What did Michael do?"

"He stole money from my purse. It's not the first time. I guess I was stupid, at the beginning."

"Is he all right?"

"Not really. I don't mean he's bleeding or anything. Yes, I suppose he's what you'd call all right."

Her mother had wads of tissue scattered around her on the stairs, although her eyes behind her glasses were dry, and if she had been crying, she had stopped some time ago. Looking down on her, Grace could see the part in her mother's gray hair, the scalp showing through the thin places. Grace looked away again. The front yard was covered in red and orange leaves. Someone, her mother probably, had begun raking them into piles and loading them into yard waste bags.

Her mother was absorbed in picking at the sleeve of her sweater. "Go talk to him if you want to. I'm done talking for now."

"Come on in, Mom, it's cold out here."

"It feels all right to me."

Grace left her there, crossed the porch, and let herself in the front door. They almost never went in that way. It was another thing that felt wrong. The front rooms were quiet and empty. She didn't know what she'd expected. Overturned furniture, maybe. "Michael?"

He was in the den, sitting in the middle of the couch. His feet were flat on the floor. His arms were at his sides and he appeared to be doing nothing at all. "Hey," Grace said. "What's up?"

"She called you, huh?"

"Yup."

"Such a stupid stunt."

"She's worried about you."

Michael shrugged. He looked sweaty. His skin was unfresh, like the skin under a bandage. Grace said, "She told me you took money out of her purse. Did you?" He made an impatient face. "Talk about a stupid stunt."

"I told her I'd pay her back. I will too."

"What's going on with you? You don't look so good."

"Fuck you very much."

"Nice. I'm trying to get up to speed here."

"Don't bother."

"Come on, Michael."

"Come on what, what do you want? Everybody needs to leave me the hell alone. All of a sudden I'm this great object of curiosity for people who don't have anything better to do, and they can back off. That means you."

Grace was alarmed by him but she wasn't afraid of him. "What are you doing, coke? Tweak? You a big tweaker now? A druggie kingpin? I wouldn't care what you were polluting yourself with if you had it under control, but it sure doesn't look that way."

He tried to stare her down but gave up and let his head fall back against the couch. "I can't stand her. I can't stand her worrying about me."

"Then don't do crap that makes her worry."

"Everything makes her worry, it's sick! Everything I do!"

"So move out, Michael. Get your own place. That's what grown-ups do." Her brother muttered something. "What's that? You don't have any money because you spend it all on partying? Wow, that is a problem."

The front door opened and shut and their mother walked through the kitchen to stand in the doorway. "He hates me," she said to Grace. "What did I do to make him hate me?"

"Mom, he doesn't hate you, come on."

"Then why is he doing this to me?"

"Doing what?" Michael said. "Doing what to you? It's not

about you. Nothing is. Why are you supposed to be so important, huh? Where'd you get that idea?"

Their mother started crying. She slid down the wall behind her until she was sitting cross-legged on the floor. "Oh, way to go," Michael said. "I still don't feel sorry for you. You stick your nose into everything and then you act all hurt when the door slams on it."

"I've wasted my life on you children."

"Looks like," Michael agreed.

"He doesn't mean it, Mom," Grace said.

"Sure I do."

"Stop it, both of you," Grace ordered uselessly. There was a feel of performance about what she was seeing, as if the two of them had needed her as an audience, a witness to their unhappiness.

"I have to get back to work, I can't stay here and referee."

Her mother had found another wad of tissues and was applying them to her nose. "He needs to admit he has a problem. Nothing's going to get better until he does."

"She's the one with the problem."

"Adios," Grace told them. She went through the kitchen and out the side door to the driveway. She couldn't have stayed inside for another minute.

She drove back to work through the pretty, leafy streets where she'd grown up, the houses decorated with pumpkins and seasonal wreaths, or maybe flying the team flag for another doomed football season, or one of those gift-shoppy banners depicting autumn leaves. The same mass-produced, expected stuff you saw every year, and she thought for the hundredth hundredth time that she had to move to Alaska or Costa Rica or anywhere that people didn't take so much pride in commercially available self-expression.

She felt bad for walking away from her mother and Michael, but not bad enough to go back. She had no doubt that her brother was screwing up, and would keep doing so for a while. He was probably making a mess of school too. That would be enough to make her parents lose it. They'd lay down the law, stop providing free room and board, and everyone would go on from there. Michael would have to do some growing up. It looked as if he was determined to do it the hard way.

It was simple self-preservation not to get involved in her family's messier dramas. It was like trying to save a drowning person and getting dragged under yourself. It was what you had to do. There was no way to feel good about it.

Her father called her a week later. "Oh, hi Dad." She steeled herself for one or another variety of unpleasant conversation. "What's up?"

"Ah, your brother can't get his head on straight."

Grace waited for him to elaborate. "He wants to be a drug addict. It's part of being a creative type, you know?" Her father had a low regard for anyone who chose to pursue the arts. How many people ever managed to make a living from it? One in ten thousand.

Grace had heard this view expressed many times. Sometimes it was one in a hundred thousand, or a million. "What's happening, is Michael all right?"

"No he's not all right. He's a drug addict."

"What does that mean, exactly."

"He takes whatever it is he takes and stays out all night and comes home and is disrespectful. Your mother wants us all to go to counseling," her father said abruptly. The real purpose of his call.

"What kind of counseling, what for?"

"Family counseling." Her father didn't like the taste of the words, Grace could tell.

"Well, I don't know about that." It was the last thing she wanted to do. "Michael's the one who needs counseling. I don't see where any of us can help."

"That's what I told your mother, but you know how she gets." Her father sounded relieved. He hadn't wanted to sit in an office sharing his feelings any more than Grace did. She was glad he wasn't going to go along with it, but she didn't like this invitation to consider everything, somehow, as being her mother's fault. For being oversensitive and unreasonable and failing to instill desirable character traits in her children.

"I'm sure she just wants to help," Grace said, offering up this weak tea of a defense. Was there anything about her family that didn't make her feel bad? "So what's going on with Michael, is he getting some help?"

"He hasn't been around for a while. He's staying with some girl. Just as well. Your mother doesn't see it that way."

Her mother would want Michael home. "Is he going to get help, you know, a program or something?"

"He says he will. Believe it when I see it." Her father shifted gears. "All right, I'll tell your mother you don't want to do any family counseling."

"Not right now."

"You're a smart girl," her father said, making Grace feel he was approving of her for all the wrong reasons. For being coldhearted and reluctant to take on any more of her family's unhappiness and discontents. For being grudging and wary around them and not wanting anything to do with Michael's new, self-inflicted catastrophe. She disliked her father's anger and impatience as she disliked these things in herself. But neither did she wish to be her mother, who carried her complaints around in a basket and kept collecting more of them and was so endlessly willing to be hurt.

Michael had come back home after a spell, she heard that from her mother, and after that she didn't hear much of anything for a time. Then her mother called to say they were taking Michael to an in-patient treatment program in Chicago and if it wasn't too much trouble, would Grace come over a couple of times to take in the mail and water the plants?

Grace recognized the spitefulness in this, and the intent to make her feel guilty, but she wasn't immune from either anger or guilt. She asked her mother if the program was one of the religion-based ones where you prayed to have your druggie sins lifted from you? Or did they use a more cognitive approach?

"They use the very expensive approach."

After a moment Grace said, "Well, it's probably good to have professionals, people who know what they're doing—"

"We had to call the police. We thought he was going to hurt himself. Hurt us. He spent two nights in the hospital. Yes, I am happy to turn things over to the professionals. I don't understand him anymore. I don't understand why he's doing this to us."

"Mom, addicts don't do things on purpose. And they don't think about anybody but themselves."

Michael's problems were bringing out the worst in everybody: her mother's grievances, her father's anger, her own cowardice. "Try and, ah, detach," she added. She knew that was something you were supposed to say.

"I always wanted a family. I still do. But sometimes I wish you were all different people."

She hung up then, leaving Grace to put the phone down quick, as if it burned.

Michael stayed in the rehab program for three weeks. He was said to be making progress. He came back home. He was all re-habbed, he said. Or maybe he was a retread, like a tire. "Really, I'm great, I'm just making dumb jokes, I mean you gotta laugh, right?"

Grace met him for coffee. It felt awkward and stagey, like a date of some kind, like an inspection of his new, tuned-up self. She asked him how the place was, you know, the program, as her parents called it, as if it were something other than an expensive semijail, and Michael said, "It's tough. They have to be tough, they know all the bullshit you try to sell. They're big on slogans. There's a lot of cheerleading. One day at a time! Let go and let God! Gratitude is an Attitude!"

"Yeah, they need some new writers." Grace let a beat pass. "So, are you clean and sober now?"

"Oh, totally, I mean, I'm still an addict. It's a disease, and the only cure is if you keep working your steps. You know, examine your motives and make amends and all."

"Amends?"

"That's when you apologize to everybody for being a giant pain in the ass. So. I'm sorry for all the times when I was a giant pain in the ass."

"All right, well, it's all good. I'm glad you've got the lingo down." He kept beaming at her in a way she found unsettling. "You're looking sharp too."

"Thanks. Got tired of the just-puked look."

Michael did look better than he had in a while. He'd shaved his scruff of beard and either that or gaining weight made his face fuller, less gaunt. He wore a cotton shirt with a collar, and jeans that had been laundered in some not-too-distant past. Even his hair seemed a lighter shade of blond, wispy and floating around his forehead, not dark and slick as before. All positive things, but wasn't there the faintest hint of a Communist reeducation camp? To suppress this unworthy thought she said, "It's a new start for you."

"Yeah." He nodded. "I want to get back to my music. I want to see if I can do it straight. That was part of the problem. Being the crazy artist who romanticized self-destruction."

"You sound like Dad," Grace said, to tease him.

"Well, maybe he's not all wrong."

This was unexpected enough to turn Grace quiet. She looked out the window to the parking lot beyond. Michael had picked this place, a franchise coffee shop in a strip mall, because it was away from the usual hangouts where he might run into people he knew. That is, the bad friends who might drag him back into the old lifestyle. How long could you keep avoiding everybody you knew? "This town," she said, following her thought. "Nobody ever leaves, do they?"

"Well, you haven't."

"Yeah, not yet." She wasn't anxious to discuss this. "I have to get ahead of my bills, save a little more. I'm not going to move someplace and then have to sleep in my car."

"But you still want to move, right? What, to California or somewhere?"

"Somewhere." She should probably shut up about California. She'd been talking about it since she was thirteen, and she'd still never made it there.

"There's this thing in AA called 'the geographic cure.' When people think all they have to do to solve their problems is go somewhere else."

"Huh." Grace wasn't sure she liked this new, evangelizing version of her brother. "Except I don't have AA-type problems."

"Why is it you want to leave anyway? What's so bad about living here?"

"How about, it's a big world and I want to see some more of it. So you're a lifestyle guru now. Wow, Mom and Dad really got their money's worth."

"You don't have to be so defensive. I'm just trying to get some insight here."

"It's not some big mystery. I don't want to be stuck here. I don't want Mom and Dad constantly in my business."

Michael said, "You're always mad at them. I don't know why."

"Because they pass judgment."

"Ah." He nodded. " 'It's so annoying that my children aren't perfect.' I believe I've heard that before."

"All right." Grace waved a hand, dismissing him. "Fine. Moving on."

"I guess you think it's weird to talk about stuff like this, you know, all the bad feelings and unhealthy expectations, but that's what they had me do the whole while I was there, and you get to where you want to figure it all out, why we do the things we do and get into these destructive behavior patterns."

"Whatever floats your boat," Grace said. She thought that Michael had taken too many bites of the rehab cheeseburger, and he was going to go on this way for a time until he settled down.

"I'm happy now. I want everybody else to be happy too."

"I am happy," Grace said. "I'm fine."

"I'm not bulletproof. I'm scared shitless I'm going to slip up and start using again."

"You better not." She was alarmed at this. "I will personally beat your ass if you do."

"Yeah, if only threats worked. Did they tell Grandma?"

"What do you think?"

They were quiet then, watching the parking lot and the ordinary traffic, people coming and going with packages, errands, dry cleaning on hangers, coffee cups, people with their own problems.

They got through Thanksgiving, a meal fussed over by their mother and prayed over by Michael, who volunteered to give a blessing. This was not their custom. Michael gave thanks for his sobriety and recited the Serenity Prayer, while the rest of them examined the tablecloth in shared embarrassment. They were not a family who was accustomed to overt declarations of gratitude. Grace contributed a stuffed acorn squash and a dairy-free pumpkin pie. Their father set the table without wineglasses. He wrestled with the carving of the turkey. Their mother worried about whether the breast meat was too dry. "It's all great, Mom," Michael said, and Grace and their father chimed in, yes, great, thank you.

By Christmas the shine had worn off the rehab thing and there weren't any more dinner-table blessings. Their mother insisted on the usual elaborate cookie project she undertook every year, rolling and frosting and decorating dozens of cookies with colored sugar and tiny sugar pearls. There were also Santa cookies with gumdrop hats and beards made of shredded coconut, and chocolate pinwheels topped with crushed peppermint, lemon squares, pecan bars, molasses crisps. As if all manner of distress might be warded off with enough cookies. Michael missed one of the family dinners, and was absent when the rest of them decorated the Christmas tree. He was trying to get his band started up again, it was explained. It was proving to be very time-consuming.

In January there was a new crisis, or a series of crises, involving more damage to automobiles, more misappropriated funds, hospital stays, lies about lies, and Michael's parents put him in the backseat of their remaining car and drove him north for what proved to be his last stay in rehab.

II. GRACE

Grace and her grandmother were not fond of each other, exactly; neither of them did fond. But they maintained a wary mutual respect, based on what they had in common: a lack of sentiment and an impatience for weakness. When Grace (Patti, back then) had been a small child she had taken a fall down Evelyn's back steps and broken her arm. Evelyn made a splint out of towels and a kitchen cutting board and drove her to the emergency room, telling her that if she cried, the doctor would have to give her a shot. She didn't cry all the way through X-rays and having the arm put in a cast. When Laura showed up at the hospital, full of fluttering maternal concern, Evelyn said, "Now don't go getting her all upset. It's just a little break and if it doesn't heal well she can always learn to use her left hand."

While her parents were away writing more checks for Michael's second round of rehab, and sitting in counseling sessions designed to elicit painful truths, Grace was tasked with checking up on her grandmother. She phoned and asked Evelyn if she could bring her some scones from the health food store's bakery.

"The kind they don't put sugar in?" her grandmother asked, not sounding all that excited.

"They use natural sweeteners and whole wheat flour."

"I don't see why they bother."

"Come on, Grandma. People eat them all the time."

"You know what I have a taste for? Some plain glazed dough-nuts. Why don't you hunt up some doughnuts for me."

Grace bought a package of supermarket doughnuts and headed over. It was clear, cold January, with a steady wind going about its impersonal business of making everyone miserable. Grace rang the doorbell and waited on the big front porch, hugging her-self against the cold. No one and nothing moved on the street. A crust of old snow turned everything untidy. There was nothing for the eye to take comfort in, nothing to make you feel that tomor-row might be better than today. She thought she was probably depressed. Well, this was the season for it. And she was worried about Michael, without feeling there was anything she could do about him, no way he'd allow her to help him. Even when he was a little kid with a skinned knee or a finger slammed in a car door, he'd howl and rage on his own, resisting consolation. He'd always had that side to him, volatile, unreasonable, bewildering. For the first time, she considered that there might not be any happy end-ing to his story.

Evelyn was a long time getting to the door. Grace's mother car-ried a key to the house with her for fear of all the things you saw on television commercials, old people lying helpless in bathtubs or at the foot of the stairs. But Evelyn didn't like being barged in on, as she called it, and even if she did fall and hurt herself, it was easy to imagine her dismissing it as just a little hip fracture.

Eventually Evelyn appeared and unlocked the door and swung it open. "Don't let that cold in," she ordered. Grace held out the doughnuts. "Now, those look good. I've had a taste for doughnuts lately, I don't know why." She was wearing one of her usual at-home outfits. Pull-on pants made out of shiny, heavy-duty acrylic, a cotton turtleneck, and a cardigan sweater with its pockets full of tissues.

"Sugar is addictive," Grace said. "They've done studies." Then she wished she had not said "addictive." Evelyn was not supposed to know about Michael's problems, at least not while they were active and ongoing. She had been told that Grace's parents were having a fun extended weekend, shopping and sightseeing in Chicago. "Do you want some coffee with these? How about I make coffee."

"Don't make it too weak," Evelyn said. She shared her granddaughter's taste in this.

They sat at a table in the sunroom, the doughnuts cut into quarters. "Go ahead, have some," Evelyn said, and Grace cut an even smaller piece for herself. It was so sweet it made her tongue curdle. She flooded her mouth with coffee.

Evelyn took her time eating. Everything she did nowadays was slow. How old was Evelyn? Somewhere north of eighty. In the old pictures in the albums, the pictures hung on the walls, she was a woman with a pretty if angular face, her hair pinned up in the fashionable rolls and bunches of the time, facing the camera with a what-do-you-want expression.

There was no hint of this younger self now. It was as if the winds outside had blown her into tatters, like clothes left too long on a line. Her skin was crosshatched with wrinkles and her mouth was marked by deep hinges. Her hair was fine and white and disordered. Grace felt hopeless when she thought about getting older, like she was running out of time already, without yet having launched her life. Age was a catastrophe that overcame people. Maybe it was something you got used to. How else would you keep on living?

But Evelyn still had a clear mind and a sharp tongue and no longer cared what anyone thought about her. She ate what she wanted of the doughnuts and set her coffee cup down in its saucer without any unsteadiness in her hands. "What is it I'm not supposed to know?"

"Pardon?"

"Your mother pretending she had to go shoe shopping at Nordstrom's in the middle of winter. You'd better tell me."

"She didn't want to worry you."

"Too late for that."

"Michael got into trouble with drugs. They had to call the police a couple of times. He's not in school anymore. They're up in Chicago, the suburbs, I guess, putting him in a treatment place so he can get some help."

Grace stopped there. She watched Evelyn for some reaction, but her grandmother only said, "What kind of drugs, what does that mean?"

"Different ones. Painkiller pills. Cocaine, I think."

"And what do those do for you?"

"Ah, they do different things." It was an odd conversation to be having with your grandmother. "Different kinds of getting you high." She hoped she wasn't going to have to try and explain "high."

"You take this stuff too?"

She did and she didn't. "Some. Not a lot."

Evelyn tightened her mouth and looked Grace up and down. "At least you have some sense. You don't make yourself sick with it."

Grace didn't answer. At this point it seemed like the less said, the better. "She's spoiled that boy," Evelyn said. "No wonder he thinks he can get away with anything."

"No, Grandma, you can't make it Mom's fault. Michael did it to himself."

"Can they get his head put back on straight? This place? What kind of treatment? Never mind. I don't need to know." Evelyn pulled a tissue from the pocket of her sweater and worked at her nose with it.

Grace kept quiet. She figured she was already in some kind of trouble, or would be, for blabbing. It was so easy to be in trouble in her family. All you really had to do was speak up.

Evelyn raised her head and regarded the brilliant, painful winter sunlight that lit the glass in almost liquid streaks. "This room gives me such a chill lately."

"Really?" The entire house was overheated. The thermostat was set to Bake. You could have grown orchids in the sunroom. "It feels warm enough to me."

"The windows aren't glazed right. Even when the sun's out, the radiators can't keep up."

"You need a new furnace, Grandma."

"The old one works fine. It's the windows that let the drafts in."

"Then get somebody out to work on the windows. Not in the middle of winter. Later, when they can take the glass out and replace it."

"Maybe I'll do that," Evelyn said, but she wouldn't. She wasn't somebody who spent money on a house. Grace's mother was always trying to get her to repair or replace one thing or another: The balky water heater that made noises like it was tumbling rocks. The yellowing kitchen sink and the bathroom tile that resembled that in a 1940s public washroom. The sunroom was furnished with white wicker armchairs and love seats and floral cushions so old that it seemed spiteful to keep using them. Everywhere you looked, something needed more or less urgent attention.

It wasn't that Evelyn couldn't afford to do such projects. It was Grace's understanding that she was modestly wealthy, although she couldn't have said what that meant in terms of dollars, or where the money was meant to go once Evelyn passed away. Money was like certain forms of misbehavior, not considered suitable for conversation.

Although there was the time that Grace's mother said the problem was that Evelyn was afraid of outliving her money. Like a lot of other old people. "And if they start spending it, it's like admitting they're going to die. That's one problem I guess your father and I won't have. Since there's no money to begin with."

Grace wasn't sure how she was meant to respond to this information. Everybody she knew worried about money and she didn't think her family was any worse off than most. But her parents always made it sound as if an injustice had been committed against them.

"Grace," Evelyn said out loud, startling her from her thoughts. "You through changing names for a while?"

"I thought we were done talking about this." Her grandmother had not been enthusiastic about her decision.

"Still trying to get used to it. You one of those who won't change your name when you get married?"

"I haven't thought about getting married." That is, she had, but she and Ray agreed that marriage was an intrusive legal construction.

"We didn't have a choice. You got married, you were Mrs. So-and-So. It was the way things were. I'd have liked to hear what your grandfather would have said if I'd told him I wanted to stay a Miss or a Miz or whatever. He was not a forward-thinking man. You probably don't remember that much about him."

"Not a lot." He'd been so old. Like one of those dried-up spider bodies you came across in the corner of a window frame, ready to crumble at a touch.

"He fought in the war. He was in France and in Germany. He saw terrible things."

Anytime someone attempted to summon the past, the past she

had not been a part of, Grace was impatient, not wanting to pay it any attention, since it had nothing to do with her. But there was also the thing she shied away from, her fright at how the world swallowed up everything you were and everything you knew and then you too became a boring story to somebody else.

"Yes," she said now. "I saw the pictures of him in uniform."

She waited, but Evelyn was done talking. Sometimes there were these silences, as if she might be carrying on a conversation by herself and no longer had need of you.

Grace gathered up the plates and coffee cups and took them into the kitchen to wash up. Evelyn was ready for her to leave, she could tell, so that she could fall asleep in front of her afternoon television programs. "All right, do you need any other groceries? Anything from the drugstore?"

"Everybody thinks I can't use a telephone if I have to. You call and they bring anything you want, right to the door."

"I can go to the store for you too, it's no problem."

"Don't knock yourself out."

"Come on, Grandma."

"No, I mean, don't fuss like your mother. She's always telling me I need one or another thing and then making a production out of it."

Grace got her coat and put it on in the entryway. "She likes to be useful."

"She likes to fret and worry and wear herself out for everybody else and then you're meant to feel bad for her."

"I guess."

"But that's not you, is it. You're not the suffering type."

Grace tried not to look as if she had an opinion one way or the other. Once Evelyn got on your case, she stayed on it.

"But that's all right. You should do whatever you want. God knows women hardly ever get to do that. They don't even try."

"All right, Grandma." By now Grace was anxious to be gone. "I promise, I'll do whatever I want. I'll call you tomorrow."

But what was it she wanted to do, and how to live? And why did everybody seem to think it was easy? As if all she had to do was exert her will on the world, and declare herself one thing or another, an artist, or an inventor, and that would come to pass.

All she could think of, driving home through the winter-bare streets, the everyday ugliness of traffic and billboards and power lines, was that she wanted to open her eyes in the morning and see something different.

Grace's mother said, "I'm worried about your father."

It was nothing new to get such a call from her mother. Sometimes she was worried about Michael. Sometimes it was Evelyn. Grace assumed that at other times, different family members got calls announcing that her mother was worried about Grace. "What's the matter, Mom?"

"He's so furious at your brother. Addiction is a disease. You can ask people to take responsibility, but you can't blame them for it."

"So is being a drunk a disease," Grace said, but her mother ignored this.

"Your father starts in on him, then of course Michael feels he's being attacked, because he is, and he retaliates. It's horrible. Your father needs to make more of an effort. He's supposed to be the parent. The adult."

"Well they're both . . ." Whatever they were. Totally sick. "They both have problems, Mom. It's probably inherited. Genetic." She hesitated, charged ahead. "I worry sometimes about me. I try not to drink or, get carried away with anything. So I won't be like them. Another famous screwed-up Arnold."

"Oh honey, I don't worry about you one bit," her mother said, which was just like her, to dismiss any of Grace's little problems. You'd think you'd be used to it by now, but you weren't and you never would be. So much for trying to tell her mother something actually important and personal. "But I wish you would come to the counseling sessions with us."

Fat chance. "How are those going?"

"They're very productive. Everyone has to sit and listen to everybody else."

"That would be nice." And different.

"The counselor would like you to attend. She says she gets an incomplete picture if all family members aren't there."

Grace thought the counselor could get a pretty good picture from the fact of her absence. "Pass."

"I could really use some moral support from you. Somebody has to calm Michael and your father down when they get carried away."

Grace contemplated the exciting prospect of piling on in the family arguments, while a counselor took notes and kept score. "No, why does that have to be your job, or mine, or anybody else's? You treat them like little boys, no wonder they keep having stupid, juvenile fights. What are you supposed to get out of counseling anyway, isn't any of this for you?"

"Oh, P—, Grace. Maybe one of these days you'll have somebody who's so precious to you, you won't worry so much about yourself. Now I have to take Grandma to her doctor's appointment. Unless that's something you decide you want to help with."

Evelyn's funeral was more than a year later. She had been stubborn about her dying, and right up to the end she'd taken her time. Everyone said that Grace's mother had done a wonderful job of caring for her. Had kept her out of a nursing home and out of the hospital so she could die at home. That was supposed to be important to people, even though by the end, Evelyn had been beyond knowing where she was, except, perhaps, that she was still tethered to the world.

The family had attended the Presbyterian service and the graveside ceremony and had now gathered for lunch at a steakhouse. Grace ordered salad and a bowl of vegetable soup. It wasn't a day to make waves. Her uncle Mark and aunt Brenda and her two silent teenage cousins, Dylan and Tracy, had come in from Massachusetts. They were her only other relatives, her father being an only child, and she wished they were more engaging. She liked Mark; he was a lawyer, but a nice one, and he was good at keeping up steady, cheerful conversation. Brenda was thin and sniffy and was always pulling Mark aside to talk to him privately about something that was not as it should be. The cousins might eventually grow up to be interesting, but right now they kept their faces in their phones and displayed all the personality of a couple of cabbages.

Also at the luncheon were a few of Evelyn's longtime neighbors and a few university people who had felt obliged to attend for her grandfather's sake. Also two old, very old friends of Evelyn and her husband, the Radishes. That was not their actual name, but Grace and her brother had not been able to pronounce "Radisson" when they were younger, and so the Radishes they remained, although not to their faces. John Radish had begun as a junior member of her grandfather's law firm, almost sixty years ago. They were people who went to a lot of funerals. They ate quietly and lifted their water glasses and coffee cups with care, and through most of the day's events they had seemed not entirely present, as if preoccupied with mournful, mortal thoughts.

Her mother had checked out. So Grace thought, watching her sitting at one end of the long table, her chin propped up with one hand. There were hard white lines around her mouth. At the grave site she'd cried a little, quietly, while the rest of the family had stayed self-consciously dry-eyed. Now she'd reached the end of her obligations and the end of her rope and she was only waiting for the day to be over so she could go to sleep. And if the day was not yet over, she would get a head start on sleeping right where she sat.

Mark sat next to her mother and said what looked like encouraging things, although her mother did not seem to be paying him much attention. Losing Evelyn had been harder on her mother than on Mark; Grace knew this without entirely thinking through why. And Mark, who was a nice man, who probably felt some guilt for living out of town, for not being more of a help, was trying to make it up to her. Now that Evelyn's dark hair and Mark's red-blond had turned gray, they looked so much alike. Hansel and Gretel, grown old.

Her father and Michael were down at the other end of the table with a cousin between them. They both wore unaccustomed suits and ties, and both of them had managed to squirm half out of their collars and rumple their jackets. They were looking off into opposite corners of the room, two different versions of the same morose, sandy-haired man, reluctantly present in the here and now.

In fact, Grace realized, she was probably the only person at the table who was not somehow paired off.

As if everyone else might be about to notice the same thing, and think how pitiful she was, Grace turned to John Radish on her right. "You must have known my grandparents back when they were practically newlyweds."

He took his time swallowing his food. He raised his napkin to his mouth and then returned it, still folded, to its place alongside his plate. "Arthur's older than me."

"Well, yes, he was."

"That's why I'm still kicking around and he's not."

"Oh, hush, John, what's the matter with you," his wife said.

Her name was Alice and she had skin as white and translucent as milk glass. "Nobody wants to hear something like that."

John didn't answer. The restaurant window looked out onto a small pond with a fountain. He stared out at the rise and fall of the water's spray as the wind tossed it. Alice went on. "You'll have to excuse him. He has the tiniest little bit of fuzzy brain going on."

Grace murmured that she was sorry to hear it. "Oh he's still a big sweetie," Alice said cheerfully. "Anyway, it's too late to get rid of him now. Oh poor Evelyn. I'm sorry to say we didn't keep up as well as we might these last years. I sent her a card when I heard she was failing. I don't know if it got through to her."

"I'm sure it got there and my mom read it to her."

"That's not what I meant," Alice said.

Grace was distracted by her father and brother, who were having some terse conversation over the head of the preoccupied female cousin. She hadn't had a real chance to talk to Michael lately, what with all the worry and exhaustion of Evelyn's dying. He always said he was fine, things were fine. And maybe they were, though that depended on what you were willing to call fine.

"When she lost that baby. Now God knows that's a terrible thing."

"What?" Alice was still talking, but Grace hadn't been listening. She tried to catch Michael's eye. He was standing now, jamming his hands into his pockets and saying something to their father that their father did not wish to hear. "What baby?"

"Their first. So sad. She went east to see her family and sent word to Arthur that she wasn't coming back. Nobody was supposed to know. But of course we all did."

Michael had turned his back and was headed for the exit. Grace said, "Would you excuse me?" Or began to say it, when John gripped her arm above the elbow, hard enough so that it was difficult for her to dislodge.

"Arthur took care of the trees."

She managed to get her arm free. "Thank you. I wasn't aware of that." She looked at Alice, who only shook her head, as if to say, No accounting for him. Michael was out of sight by now. Her father was still at the table. He said something to a waiter. Grace guessed he was ordering another drink. "But she did come back. Obviously."

"Yes, I don't know what Arthur told her or had to promise her. She was a pistol, Evelyn was. Times were different then. People stayed married."

John Radish said, "They planted trees around the parade ground. One for each soldier. Arthur was in charge."

"John, this is Arthur and Evelyn's granddaughter. She doesn't want to hear about any silly trees."

"You go look it up. Or you could ask Arthur."

"Now, John, you know very well that Arthur's beyond asking. Anyway, it's Evelyn we're supposed to be remembering today."

Grace's father appeared behind her chair. "So this is where the party's really happening."

"Hi Dad." Grace felt herself shrinking away from him, a familiar, involuntary recoiling. She hated everything about his drinking, especially his smiling, insouciant confidence that his drinking made no difference. "Where did Michael go?"

"Who knows. Off to play music. A reggae version of 'Goodbye Cruel World' . . . John, Alice. You get everything you need? Enough to eat?" He leaned over them, an attentive host.

Alice said, "It was all very good. Of course we've slowed down some, we don't eat the way we used to." A small section of her breast of chicken entrée looked as if it had been surgically removed.

"How about you, John? What are you drinking? It's on me."

"He's not drinking anything, Dad."

"Well that's because nobody asked him what he wanted. What say, John? You a beer man?"

"Ha ha," John said. "Now you're talking."

The waiter came by then and replaced her father's empty beer glass with a full one. "Thanks. Bring another for this gentleman, why don't you." The chair next to Grace was vacant and he sat. He said, "This has all been very hard on your mom."

"Yeah." She waited to see if he had more to say, but he only nodded and looked up and down the length of the table at the rest of the guests, the old acquaintances and university people who were finishing up their desserts and coffee. Her mother had planned the whole menu. She hadn't wanted anyone else to help.

Her father lifted his beer glass. "Here's to your grandmother. Wherever she is, I hope she's happier now."

"Dad." Grace couldn't tell if anyone had heard him. It didn't seem they had. "Cool it, OK?"

"What? Simple truth. She was one of those women with a persecution complex. The whole world is out to get them."

You could make the case that the whole world actually was, in certain ways, and especially for women of Evelyn's generation. But this wasn't the time or place for a drunk argument. "Come on, Dad. Mom doesn't need to hear that."

"She'd agree with me, a hundred percent."

"Fine. Let's talk about it some other time."

Her father gave Grace an unfriendly look, but subsided. The waiter set a beer glass down in front of John Radish, who tried to pick it up without spilling it. He settled for leaning over it and slurping it direct from the glass.

"Where's Rich?"

"Ray. He couldn't get off work."

"Doesn't he work in a bike shop?"

"So?"

"Just how vital to the national interest is his presence at work?"

"That's really snotty. Like other people's jobs aren't important."

In fact Ray hadn't wanted to come with her to the funeral and they'd had a huge fight about it.

"Snotty, I like that." A trick her father had of saying something offensive, and then being the one who took offense. Grace hitched her chair away from him. She purely hated him.

Grace's mother got up from her chair and made her way around a corner to the restrooms. Grace's uncle Mark got up too and came over to where Grace and her father were sitting. "Gabe. Gracie. How's everybody holding up?"

Grace murmured that she was fine. Maybe you were meant to be overcome with grief, but she wasn't. Evelyn had been so old and so sick. It had been time. Her father said, "Where's Laura? We need to wrap this up."

"She'll be right back. She is what they call plumb tuckered out."

"Aren't we all," her father said, making a droll face. "I mean, not just with Evelyn. We've had our hands full at home. Maybe you heard."

"Ah," Mark said, nodding in a noncommittal way that Grace thought of as lawyerly. "Has to be hard on everybody."

"You ask yourself where you went wrong. Feed them, provide for them, wipe their noses, tie their shoes, buy them whatever they want. Then they turn around and sink their teeth in your leg. I don't mean you, Gracie. You're a good girl."

"Thank you," Grace said. Her phone chimed. She dug it out of her purse. It was a text from Michael:

IS THE ASSHOLE STILL THERE?

She texted back:

YES.

Mark said, "Hey, he'll straighten himself out. Wait and see. He's a smart kid."

"It's not a kind of smart that's doing him much good."

Her uncle allowed himself a glance at Grace, and Grace moved her shoulders ever so slightly. Meaning, Those two. What were you supposed to do?

"This rehab business. Boy, do they ever have a scam going."

Shut up shut up shut up shut up.

Mark said, "Come on, Gabe. It's a process, not a quick fix."

"I'd like to own some stock in that process. That's all I'm saying."

Mark's wife, Brenda, was trying to get his attention. "Excuse me," Mark said, navigating around the other guests to where Brenda sat at the far end of the table. Grace watched him bend over the back of Brenda's chair, listening to whatever it was that Brenda wanted. They were flying back to Massachusetts this afternoon and there would be one or another thing that had to be packed or purchased. They would be anxious to be on their way. Everybody was. Where was her mother?

"What a screwed-up situation."

She turned toward her father. "What?"

"Is your brother coming back here?"

"I don't think so."

Her father rubbed at his eyes and yawned. "We need to clear the air. Me and him."

"What do you mean, exactly?"

"All his problems are my fault. For being a bad parent."

His eyes were bloodshot from the rubbing. Their expression was belligerent and challenging. Grace said, "I don't know what he means by that."

Her father seemed suspicious of this answer. Then he waved a hand, dismissing it. "Nobody knows how hard having kids is until it's their turn. It changes everything."

Wasn't it supposed to? Should she apologize for her own existence? Or just keep up her usual silent, mutinous, and yes, snotty
commentary.

"I'd like to see them try. See your brother try. Earn a good living so you can keep the whole outfit chugging along. Let's start
with that. People take it for granted. Times I lost sleep, times I
thought I was going to get fired. And I still could, you know? Stiff
upper lip. Soldier on. He thinks that part's not important." Again
the challenging look.

"Of course it's important," Grace said. She hated having to be
simple-minded and patient with him, agree the way you might
agree with a baby, just to keep him from getting stupidly mad,
often enough about something else entirely. "You do work hard,
everybody knows that." This happened to be true, but saying it as
a way to placate him felt craven.

John Radish spilled his beer glass into his lap then, and Grace
jumped up to keep from getting wet herself. "I'm going to go find
Mom, all right?"

She didn't wait for an answer. She got up and crossed the room
and went into the small vestibule with the restrooms. The ladies'
was empty except for a woman at the sink, absorbed in tweez-
ing her eyebrows. Grace went back out and scanned the restaurant. John Radish was being tended to by a couple of waiters with
napkins. He allowed himself to be moved this way and that, like
a horse being shod. Still not seeing her mother, Grace walked
through the front door of the restaurant and a little ways into the
parking lot.

She found her sitting on the hood of a car, not her own, watching the fountain rise and fall back into its shallow pool. "Mom?"

Her mother turned her head toward Grace in an unhurried
movement. "Are you all right?" Grace asked.

"Of course I am. How are you?"

"I'm fine. Did you . . ." She meant to ask, Did you want to be alone, then decided it was better if she was not left alone. The car her mother was sitting on was a Lexus in some power shade of dark charcoal. It was not the kind of car often used for sitting, and it might have an owner with strong feelings about people doing so. Screw it. Grace sat down on it also. The hood made a foreboding sound of metal giving way beneath her, then springing back. The afternoon was warm and the fountain teased with its promise of coolness.

Her mother said, "I don't believe in heaven. Not the goopy one they talk about in Sunday school, and not some homemade version with psychedelic angels. When you're dead, you're dead."

"I haven't thought much about it," Grace said, which was true. It hadn't been any kind of urgent question. "I guess we'll all find out." Then she wished she hadn't said it. It sounded flippant.

Her mother didn't seem to have registered Grace's remark. "Remembering is all you can do for anybody."

"I won't forget Grandma," Grace said. She meant it as consolation, though again, her mother wasn't paying any particular attention. She was watching the fountain's column of spray and seemed content to keep watching it. Back inside, people would be heading out, wanting to say their good-byes and last condolences. Mark would have to handle it.

They sat for a time longer. Her mother roused herself, looked away from the water, and sighed. She hadn't worn black, none of the family had, except for Grace's black skirt, and that was only because she had a lot of black clothes. Her mother wore one of her good summer dresses, a blue-green paisley that Grace thought, unkindly, made her look as if she was wearing a shower curtain.

"What was your father doing when you came out?"

Grace considered how she might best respond. "Nothing. He was still at the table."

"I should probably go back in and help out," her mother said, although she made no move to do so.

"Michael left. Him and Dad kicked up some kind of fuss between them."

Her mother sighed but didn't respond. Same old same old.

"Why is it always so hard for them to get along."

Grace hadn't meant it as a question, or at least she hadn't expected an answer, but her mother had one ready. "Well, fathers expect sons to go on and represent them in the world. Validate them. My father was so pleased when Mark went to law school."

"Oh, so, standard patriarchal dynastic crap," Grace said, forgetting that she was making an effort to be supportive and understanding. "I guess Michael's not enough of a success for Dad. They're too different."

"No, honey, I always thought they were too much the same."

Grace saw a man and woman coming around the corner from the restaurant's entrance. Based on nothing but intuition, and their well-tailored good looks, she knew they were the owners of the Lexus. She slid down from the hood and held out her hand to her mother. "Come on, let's go find Dad and Uncle Mark and Aunt Brenda."

Her mother got down also, wobbling a little. On the way back they passed the Lexus couple, who looked at them uncertainly. Grace avoided their eyes. She heard the electronic chirp as the Lexus unlocked its doors. Just as they reached the restaurant, her mother laughed, a breezy half laugh. "Care to say what's so funny?" Grace asked her.

"Not funny, exactly. Your grandmother never thought I was smart enough, or ambitious enough to suit her. Because those were things she prided herself on. But don't you worry, dear. It's just fine if you don't turn out one bit like me."

*   *   *

155

Grace was scheduled to work later that afternoon. She could have asked for the whole day off, but it had seemed prudent to have somewhere else to be if the day dragged on. As it was, people didn't linger after lunch. Her aunt and uncle and cousins were going straight to the airport, and her parents were visibly ready for naps. Michael wasn't answering her texts. Grace left the restaurant, drove to work, changed into her green apron, and clocked in early.

In the restroom she washed her hands and faced the unfriendly mirror. She certainly looked like she'd just been to a funeral, or perhaps as if she were getting ready for her own. Her skin was as pallid and puffy as bread dough. She'd left her hair down and it was so lank and defeated, it might have belonged to a drowned woman. Now she pulled it back with a rubber band and pinned it up. She didn't fuss much with her looks, on general principle, but there were times she could have gone for some really, really expensive makeup.

She would have liked to find Michael and, well, he couldn't have a drink, not these days, but they could sit down over whatever the clean-and-sober equivalent was, coffee, probably, and kick around the whole exhausting day and end up feeling better about it all. Raise a mug to their grandmother, who had been nobody's fool, even if she wasn't like other people's cuddly grandmas.

They could have talked about whatever bludgeoning Michael had received from their father, and the rest of the bumps and bruises. It was family life as they knew it, and there was even a sort of familiar comfort to it. Because at other times she stood outside their circle. Had chosen to remove herself from it, perhaps. But she was also unclaimed, somehow, extraneous. A daughter, an afterthought, left to her own devices. They made her lonely.

It was some relief to get to work, to take her place behind a register and ring up heirloom tomatoes and squares of plastic-wrapped corn bread and jars of immune-boosting supplements. Her work friends asked how the funeral was and Grace said it had all been fine, thanks. The store and the people who worked and shopped there made up a world of its own where people cared about fair trade and the treatment of animals and the genetic manipulation of crops and the loss of honeybee populations and everything else that was made to seem quaint, an amusing affectation, by people who ate fast food and spent their weekends at shopping malls. Grace's coworkers were rasta white boys, aspiring ecoterrorists, crafters of natural fibers. Dispossessed oddballs, the kind of unprosperous young adults who were making up their lives as they went along. She fit right in.

For the next two hours she worked the register, or took breaks to help stock shelves. Back at the register, she looked up to see Ray in her line, holding a container of soup and shifting his weight impatiently. She both did and did not want to see him. Things had reached that point between them.

"Hey," he said once he reached the front of the line. "So how was it?"

Grace weighed out his soup. "Three sixty-eight." He paid and she counted out his change. "Did you need a bag?"

"I just got off work. This was the soonest I could get here."

She put the soup in a brown paper bag and folded the bag's top. "Did you want your receipt?"

"Come on, can we talk?"

There were people in line behind him, waiting. "I'm working," Grace said.

"Well how was it?"

"It was a funeral. How do you think it was?"

Ray made an impatient face. She was being difficult. Why was she always so difficult? The customer behind him was unloading a shopping basket and lining up groceries on the belt. "I'm sorry, OK? I really couldn't get off."

"Thank you for shopping at Nature's Market."

He stalked off, soup in hand. Grace watched him push through the glass doors and outside, his shoulders tense, long legs in a hurry to get gone. Why was she always watching him leave? She was tired of feeling bad about him.

She turned to the man next in line. "Sorry for the wait."

"No problem."

She'd seen him before. Black, or more probably mixed. Coffee with cream skin, curly hair. Cute. He kept his eyes down so as to maintain some pretense of not having overheard her and Ray. She rang up his sandwich and the rest of his ordinary groceries—really, you got so you didn't even notice what people bought—then she forgot to offer him a bag and a receipt and the rest of the routine. "Sorry," she said again.

"It's OK." He smiled. Grace smiled too, another kind of apology, told herself to get with the program, and moved on to the next person in line.

She worked until nine, when the store closed, and when she checked her phone she saw that Michael had texted her back:

HEY COME OUT TO THE WAGON WHEEL WE
ARE PLAYING

and she texted back

SURE.

First she called her parents and got the answering machine. "Hi," she said. "Just checking in." She had wanted to say something encouraging about the funeral, wanted to glide over any of the weirdness at lunch and offer what comfort she could. "It was a good way to say good-bye to Grandma." She hung up, feeling dumb, that she'd made a dumb sort of effort, but at least she'd tried.

The Wagon Wheel was a downtown bar that started out country western and now booked all comers, especially for weeknights. It was a relief to have somewhere to go besides home. For all she knew, Ray was boycotting the apartment too. Dueling tantrums.

When she got to the bar it was early and Michael's band hadn't set up yet. She didn't see him, although she recognized some of his friends. Most of them she'd known all her life, had watched them grow up from bratty little kids to whatever the older version of brat was. Any effort Michael had made to avoid them had been abandoned. He was either going to use or not use, he said, and it wasn't anybody else's job to keep him out of trouble.

"Have you seen my brother?" she asked one of them, a tall kid named Benny. He wore one of those yarn caps with earflaps, knit by Bolivian villagers. Honestly, she was all for self-expression and individuality, but it made him look simple-minded.

"Yeah, I think he's bringing stuff in from the van. Are you staying for the show? Cool."

Grace went back to the restrooms and followed a passage beyond them to what she guessed was an exit. Pushing the heavy door open, she found herself in the sudden dark of an alley. At the far end, a streetlight. Nearby, a group of dark figures next to a van. She couldn't make them out. "Michael?"

One of the figures detached itself. "Gracie?"

"What are you doing?"

"Getting ready to get ready to play."

She smelled pot. She thought she recognized one or two of the others. She still thought of them as high school kids, though they had to be older than that now. "Great." She turned and went back inside, shutting the door behind her and walking away fast.

Michael opened the door and followed her. "Wait up."

She stopped. "It's only weed," he said.

"I'm not your probation officer."

"Don't get upset."

"If Mom and Dad—"

"How about just for once, it's not about them. Because it's not, OK?"

"I didn't say that," Grace said, but her brother was only getting started.

"They've been so deep in my shit all this time, you have no idea, all the stupid meetings and stupid conversations and everybody sharing their feelings, well fuck, excuse me, I have a few I don't care to share. Mom blubbers and Dad gets mad. That's something new? That's supposed to help?"

"All right, take it easy."

"Look, I don't want to go back to using and being wiped out and sick. This isn't the same."

"All right," Grace said again. It didn't much matter what she thought about it, or whether she believed him or not. She knew that much about addiction by now.

"Music's the one thing that's mine."

She guessed that getting a headful of pot was part of music for him, either as some brain-opening creative process, or else it was just what you did if you were a guy in a band. "I'm not going to tell them," she said.

"Well I know that." Michael was relaxing now, as if he really had not known.

"But make an effort to be extra nice to Mom. She's really worn-out and sad about Grandma."

"I'm always nice to her. OK, you're right. Extra nice."

"What went on with you and Dad?"

"What do you think? I'm not perfect enough. I have a rotten attitude. He was in a bad mood and it must be my fault. You going to stay and hear us?"

"Sure."

"Great! You don't think, I mean, is it disrespectful? Playing a show the same day as Grandma's funeral? We already had it booked, nobody knew."

"I think she'd probably get a kick out of it."

He brightened, looking once more like his best, most light-hearted self, the kid who could charm and entertain at will, the little brother who had gloried in finding creative ways to aggravate her, the one who had gotten away with everything, or almost everything except of course using, and for God's sake she hoped he wasn't going down that road again. "I'll make sure you get a really good seat. The crowd's gonna be huge tonight."

Huge was a stretch, but the bar began to fill up with the kids Grace recognized as being part of Michael's set. His longtime friends, plus those college students who went in for scruffy fashion and offbeat music, plus people Grace's age and older who might have come just to drink or play darts, but who didn't mind a little background noise. Michael and his band were busy with the equipment and the sound checks. This went on for a while, long enough for Grace to wonder what Ray was doing, if he'd gone home or if he was doing the same thing she was, ostentatiously not going home. Oh screw it, she was allowed to have a life that didn't involve him, revolve around him or against him. She drank a glass of wine and then another, and by the time the band drifted onstage and played a few tuning chords, she was determined to have some sort of a good time.

The house lights went down and the stage lit up with blue and red. The first song hit with a wallop, an exploding riff from Michael's guitar on lead, and the bass backing him. A sax player added some high notes. The keyboard doubled the melody and the drummer crashed the party with his own beat, and somehow it all came together. The crowd whooped and cheered. The lights blinked and changed color, blue blue and red red, crisscrossing in beams of lurid crimson violet. Michael and the rest of the band bent over their instruments, leaning into the music. No vocals, only the amplified sting of guitars and the driving rhythm, on and on, then a show-off solo from the sax, a final eruption of something that by now was less music than pure noise. Michael swung his guitar around, dipped, and strutted. It had been a long time since she'd seen him in any kind of performance, and those had been more casual, garage or basement shows. This show was like a brand-new and hungry animal.

The sound hammered on for a time, then stopped, leaving a shocked emptiness in the ears.

"All right!" somebody yelled from the audience, and Michael stepped to the front of the stage.

"Thank you! Thank you very much! We are The Useful Idiots. And if you don't believe us, just stick around." Whatever that meant, the room laughed along, ready for more. "We're so very very very glad to be here tonight. We're going for a ride. You wanna come along?"

They did. More cheering. Michael played a couple of chords, bright and loud. Teasing the crowd, not yet ready to play. "You know what's great? This is a town where people come out to hear music. People support us, you support us, we want to thank you. For telling us that what we do is . . ."

More chords. He walked along the stage. "Because there's times it sure seems like nobody's listening. You know what I mean? Them deep dark, stinkin' . . . And the hell of it is . . ."

The crowd uncertain now what he was up to, if he'd lost his train of thought. Michael played a scattered line of melody. Behind him the stage was dark and quiet, the rest of the band waiting too. "The hell of it is, we got the best thing in the world going on right here, right this minute! Live music! The power of a hundred hundred superheroes!"

Right then the band swung into the next song, something low-down and bluesy, played with cool energy and polish. The crowd went nuts. He'd pushed them up to some brink and then yanked them back, and they were grateful. The music was in charge now, and what was it about music, or music and drinking alcohol, that pulled you out of yourself and into some place of pure feeling. Michael was front and center, and if the band had any stage presence it came from him, with his swagger and theatrics. His voice was hoarse and sweet, singing about the lonesome sad bad times, the no-good women and the no-good nights, and Grace guessed if anybody knew about that, he did. If music was the only thing that was his, then it was a damn fine thing. She felt loose and light and glad, at the same time it was like being dragged under the surface of a deep river when you really, really wanted to drown. Drunk? A little. It felt good. Someone sat down at her table. The cute guy from the checkout line.

She laughed. He laughed. The song ended. He leaned toward her. "Where's the boyfriend?" Grace lifted her hands and made a fluttering gesture, intended to mean who knows, who cares. The blues song was still going strong. "Dance?" he asked. She had to think about it. Other people were dancing in the narrow space that was the open floor. She guessed it was all right, even if she couldn't remember the last time she'd danced in a bar.

He offered his hand. She liked that. They found a spot to one side of the stage. "Cedric," he said.

"What?"

"My name. Cedric."

"Oh. Grace. Hi."

"Yeah, it was on your name tag."

"Oh. Sure," she said articulately. Had he followed her from the store to the club? Or maybe this was just a random encounter. With some random guy. Well why not and who cared, random fun in a random world. "That's my brother," she said, pointing. "We went to my grandmother's funeral today."

She didn't think he'd heard her. That was just as well. She was so out of it, she was babbling. He was a graceful dancer and she tried to copy the easy way he moved his hips, though she felt like the Great White Klutz, like she was wearing wooden clogs. He didn't seem to mind and after a while, neither did she.

She had to turn half around to see Michael from here. He wasn't looking her way. He'd put his guitar down and had both hands around the microphone, singing in the voice that was his and yet not his, recognizable to her but also made strange and strong. They must have been playing a song they'd written themselves, she didn't know it. Cedric—was that his real name? She didn't know anybody named Cedric—put both hands around her waist and drew her in closer, so that if she had forgotten about sex, she was now reminded. It was one more strange, random happening.

Where did you go when you died? Anywhere? Maybe you turned back into atoms. Sparks like colored fireflies, like the bits of light scattering overhead, chasing the music. Why was she thinking such a thing at such a time, with the boy's warm mouth up against her ear, with small rippling explosions passing through her skin? His hands were warm and stealthy. She let them go where they wanted to go. And all the while the flecks of light flew and circled, preventing her from paying full attention to him, as if her grandmother was zooming around in her head, saying, Here I am, yoo-hoo!

What a wonderful invention, the body. This lovely cage of skin, with its tides of breath sifting in and out. And it moved here and there as you wished it to. (Even if dancing bewildered it.) It was an entire garden of sensations, the ordinary ones, and then you turned up the dial. This boy, Cedric, was doing his best to make a case for sensation, in ways that she couldn't ignore. But she was also not a part of it. She was outside of it, looking on. Because you couldn't forget that it didn't last.

I might have told you so, her grandmother said. But nobody listens to an old lady.

Like that wasn't weird. Grace laughed, ha ha, to show she knew how wacked-out it was, having spooky little conversations with her dead granny. She was only pretending to have conversations. Because it had already been such a long, difficult day, and now night, because she was balancing on the edge of some new and bigger sadness. She would have liked to explain this to someone but the music was too loud. This boy trying to convince her of something, who was he?

In a moment, it all turned strange. She stopped moving. The boy leaned toward her, smiling, meaning it to be a question? It was too loud for talking. She shook her head. The lights had gone blue. "I'm sorry," she said, but he wouldn't be able to hear her.

She left him there. She got through the crowd, moving sideways, and reached the front door. The music was still going on, as wild and rowdy as ever. She'd have to apologize to Michael for not staying longer. But she'd heard him through and through.

She drove home and let herself into the quiet apartment. The light was on over the stove. The bedroom door was open and the room beyond it was dark. It took her eyes time to adjust. Ray was lying in bed, not asleep, with his arms stretched out above his head. She went to him and lay down with him and his arms closed around her. This dear and familiar comfort, in spite of everything, and for a little while longer, at least.

III. GRACE AND LAURA

Whenever Grace taught a yoga class for the park district, she could expect three or four of her regular ladies to enroll. She was fond of them, and they of her, but privately Grace would have been just as glad to see the last of them. They took class after class without ever getting much of anything right, they chattered away while Grace tried to explain things, and they bossed the new students around under the guise of encouraging them. Peggy, Helen, Rita, Flo: they were all senior citizens with enthusiasm for self-improvement activities, and they all assumed that Grace needed their opinions, commentary, and cautionary advice about her personal affairs.

Grace did what she could to keep them gently at arm's length, but they were oblivious. Why didn't she have a boyfriend? They knew some nice boys she could meet. She was such an independent modern girl; they worried about that. Tonight Flo, who was somewhere north of seventy, and who favored hot-pink headbands and T-shirts, had told Grace that she shouldn't wait too long to have babies. "I know you're just as fit as a fiddle, but Mother Nature has a few tricks up her sleeve. My daughter had her first when she was thirty-six, and her little private parts have never been the same."

"That's something to think about." Grace made a point of nodding gravely. She knew Flo's daughter, who ran a carpet-cleaning franchise. Fortunately, there were other options in town for carpet cleaning, operated by people who kept their private parts private. As for having babies, if that was something that kept not happening, she guessed she was all right with that. Mother Nature could go jump in a lake.

The class met from six thirty to seven thirty. The students finished up their corpse poses and namastes and helped her roll up mats and stow blocks. Grace waited until they'd all gone, then used a push broom to sweep the studio floor. It was a welcome moment of quiet that helped her center herself, get back a little of the tranquillity that was always lost when she wound up directing traffic in Yoga for Life. She said good night to the park district guy who worked the front desk and walked out into the fine October evening, a welcome edge of chill in the air.

And this was the very last moment she would be untroubled by dread, the last before all the sorrow in the world was let loose. She followed the sidewalk out to the parking lot and her little car. The park district classes went on for another hour and there were still people coming and going. Lights were on at the outdoor basketball court and three boys were shooting hoops, the ball making a pleasant smacking sound on the pavement. Her muscles were light and loose from the class. The hot shower she'd take when she got home would feel good. She got into the car and started it, then dug her phone out of her bag to turn it on and check it. There was a text from her brother:

MOM IN HOSPITAL.

She tried to call Michael back and got his voice mail. Then she rang the landline at the house and got her mother's recorded voice. Her father never answered his phone but she tried it anyway. She texted Michael:

WHAT HAPPENED?

Nothing came back from him. She wanted to get out of the damned parking lot, go to where she needed to be, but where was that? There were two hospitals in town. Grace kept the engine running while she looked up the numbers. Her fingers were clumsy and she was dialing wrong. She called one hospital and then the other, swearing at the voice mail, struggling to make herself understood by the eventual human being who came on the line. Was her mother a patient there? No and no. "Did you want to check the emergency room?" one of the operators asked.

At the emergency room, a clerk took Grace's mother's name and typed it into a computer. Yes, she was here, but no one was available to speak with Grace at present, if she would just take a seat. She tried Michael's phone again. She was going to kill him for not answering. A nurse in blue scrubs came out and called Grace's name and she followed the nurse back through a hallway lined with metal carts and wheelchairs. There was a nurse's station, and someone talking loudly behind a curtain in Spanish. An old man with a bandage of gauze and tape over one eye glared out at Grace, daring her to stare. For all she knew she was in the wrong hospital.

But here, finally, was her father coming at her down the hall, though he was not looking at her and nearly went right past her.

"Dad?"

He stopped short and visibly recalibrated to account for her. "Gracie."

"What happened, was there an accident? Where's Mom?"

"Upstairs. They're admitting her. Did you see your brother? I don't know where he went."

"Dad, tell me what happened."

Her father rubbed at his nose with the back of his hand, an ugly gesture she'd never seen him make before. "She was feeling sick. She couldn't breathe. They did a heart procedure. They had to drain fluid from around her heart."

"She had a heart attack?"

He shook his head. "No, it was just this fluid. It's from something else, I have to talk to the doctor."

"How is she? Who's the doctor?" Everything about her father seemed vague and slow, as if he was moving underwater. "Dad!"

"The doctor's Chinese. Chin or something. He's upstairs, we should go find him."

She kept waiting for him to say her mother was all right and he kept not saying it. "Where upstairs, show me."

They took an elevator up two floors. Grace checked her phone again, hoping Michael had answered; nothing. "This is it," her father said when the elevator doors opened, but he didn't move to get off, and Grace had to tell him to come with her.

At this nurse's station she asked for her mother and her mother's doctor. She was told that her mother was being brought up from X-ray—X-ray for what? Why?—and that Dr. Chang would be with them as soon as he reviewed the results, and would they like to wait in the family lounge?

The hospital was the older of the two in town, and the lounge was furnished with chairs upholstered in cracked green vinyl, like the seats in an old taxi. The walls had been painted a bright, flat brown, a mistake. They had entered some zone of hospital procedures and protocol, where all you could do was wait for someone to remember you were there. The only other people in the room were a black family, a middle-aged woman and a young couple and their sleeping baby. They looked like they had been sitting there a long time, waiting purposefully, as if they were being paid by the hour.

Grace's father, restless now, tapped his foot. She wanted to smack him to make him stop. Instead she asked him what had happened, how her mother had ended up in the hospital.

"She started feeling bad a couple of days ago, she said she was tired, but you know, she's tired a lot." He frowned, trying to adjust the ordinariness of everything to what had happened. "And then tonight she didn't want dinner because she thought she was coming down with something, and then she said she couldn't breathe, it was hard to breathe. So we all drove over here." He stopped and looked around the room. "It wouldn't hurt them to clean this place up a little."

"What happened when you got here, what did they say?"

"Well, there was this heart thing. It's been very confusing."

Grace gave up on him. He wasn't even drunk, just overwhelmed. The door opened and a doctor, an Asian man, came in, followed by Michael. Grace and her father stood.

"How's Mom?"

"This is my sister," Michael said. "This is Dr. Chang."

Dr. Chang was serious, tired looking, gray haired. His English was flavored with strong vowels and a hitch in his consonants that made some words come out in forced barks. Grace watched Michael's face as the doctor spoke. She saw the bad news before she heard it. Mrs. Arnold was comfortable, she was resting, they could see her soon. She was getting the best of care. Michael looked away. "But what's wrong with her?" Grace asked, couldn't keep herself from asking.

Dr. Chang was deliberate, patient. Not allowing himself to be thrown off script. The heart procedure, the draining of fluid, had been necessary to give her immediate relief, to ease her breathing. But it had happened because of an underlying condition, and that was what they had to diagnose now.

Their father asked what underlying condition was that, what was he talking about, and Dr. Chang said there were indications—at this point that was all he was prepared to say—of growths in the lung.

"You mean lung cancer? She doesn't smoke. She never has."

Their father was insistent on this point. He did not say "bullshit," but he clearly wanted to. Dr. Chang said it was preliminary. Nothing was certain yet. But say this was the case. There were patients who developed pathologies in the lung due to exposure to chemicals, perhaps. Or for unknown reasons. And if that proved to be the diagnosis, there would be a treatment plan. Medical interventions. Supportive care.

This was all the time it took, to go from a well person to a cancer patient.

Their father said he wanted a second opinion. The doctor said that as of now, there was no first opinion. Very very early for that. Of course they could arrange for Mrs. Arnold to be treated anywhere they chose. If she stayed here, there would be a team approach, they could certainly consult with others on the medical staff.

They were no longer listening.

Grace asked what room her mother was in and Michael said he knew where it was. Dr. Chang said that Dr. Park would be the one to see them in the morning, Dr. Park could tell them how things would proceed in the morning. He was very sorry about the delay.

Dr. Chang excused himself and left them there. Michael said, "Come on. It's down this way."

They followed him. The halls were bright but quiet. Doors to patient rooms stood half-open. It was hard to tell if anyone was inside, and whether they were sleeping or awake, dreaming or dying. Michael said, "She was asleep a little while ago. I think they gave her something."

Here was her mother's name written in marker on a whiteboard on a door. They hesitated, then Grace took a step forward to peer inside. It was dark except for a small light over the bed nearest the door, her mother's. The bed next to the window was stripped and empty. Her mother slept on her back with her mouth open and crumpled looking. She wore a blue flowered hospital gown and a plastic bracelet around her wrist. Without her glasses her eyes were the eyes of an old lady, veins standing out on the eyelids. This room was the first of the things they would have to get used to seeing.

Grace backed out again. "I can stay with her," she told her father and Michael. "Somebody should stay."

"Do they let you do that?" her father asked.

Michael started to say something, then tucked his chin and kept silent.

They decided that Grace's father would keep watch while Grace drove home and showered and made ready to spend the night at the hospital. She would drop Michael off at the house on the way. "How could she have lung cancer," Michael said, as Grace drove. "That's screwed up."

"Maybe she doesn't, maybe it's something else."

"Like what, the flu? He already knows it's cancer, he's just giving us time to get used to the idea."

"Well," Grace said after a moment. "I'm not used to it yet."

They didn't say any more to each other. There was something almost like shame in the enormity of their fears.

She left Michael at the house, drove home, showered, tried to think of things she would need to do: call work, call the yoga center where she taught classes tomorrow night, call her friends, call her mother's friends, but maybe not yet, call her uncle Mark. She packed a toothbrush and hand cream and some energy bars and bottled water and the charger for her phone. There was only so much you could keep in your mind at one time.

It wasn't late but it felt late when Grace returned to the hospital and found her way back up to her mother's room. Her mother's head was tilted to one side and her breath made a buzzing sound, like snoring but more mechanical. Her father got up from his chair next to the bed. "She woke up a little while ago. Real groggy. Then she went right back to sleep. But I got to tell her good night."

"So, it's good you were here."

"What do you think of that doctor? There's something about him, I don't know, he seems shady."

"What?" Grace tried to whisper. It was just like her father to dislike someone for no real reason, just because they brought bad news. But was it bad news? Yes. It was bad news until proven otherwise. "Let's not talk in front of her, OK?"

They went out into the hallway, empty and full of glare, and walked to the elevators. There was a nurse's station halfway down, where a nurse, a Filipino man, sat behind the counter working on a computer. Her father said, "I'll be back first thing in the morning. As soon as I can check in with work and get over here. Call me tonight if you need to." He pushed the Down button and it chimed. The elevator door slid open but he didn't get on.

"Dad?"

He shook his head, not speaking. The elevator car stood empty and waiting and then after a moment it closed again. Grace said, "What's the matter?"

"Your mother might be really sick." He stared her down, as if Grace might be inclined to doubt it, or was hearing it for the first time. "We all have to be on our game."

"What's that supposed to mean?"

"We can't let her know how bad things might be. We have to stay strong."

"You can't hide people's conditions from them. Doctors don't do that anymore, it's not ethical."

"I mean, no crying. No hysterics, no scenes."

"Dad, do I look like I'm having hysterics?" Her father was the one who looked worn and unwell. "Are you all right to drive?"

This annoyed him. He didn't like weakness, he was done with it. "Don't worry about me. Worry about your mother." The elevator door opened again, with the magic illogic of machinery. Her father turned and grasped Grace around the shoulders. "Stay strong," he said, then stepped into the elevator and nodded good-bye as the door closed.

Grace stopped at the nurse's station but now there was no one behind the counter. The light over her mother's bed made her mother's skin look dry and even witchlike. Grace turned it off. She lay down on the empty bed by the window. Her mother was now definitely snoring, something that would have embarrassed her. Grace had not been so close to her in sleep since childhood.

She didn't expect to sleep herself, in this strange place with its half-heard noises and buzzing lights. The bed too was strange. She found a scratchy blanket in a closet and used her bag as a pillow. She was too tired to think and too awake to sleep. Instead she dozed and her mind flickered back and forth between dream and dread. Someone was talking loudly. A doctor? He was telling a joke she couldn't follow. She laughed politely anyway, ha ha, so as not to let on she didn't get it. She either woke up or dreamed she woke up. It was very early morning, with gray light at the window. Her mother was awake also, staring at her from across the narrow space between the beds.

"Where's your father?"

"He's at home. He'll be here a little later."

"Did I have a heart attack?"

"No."

"Thank God for that." Her mother closed her eyes and slept again. Grace got up to use the bathroom.

Grace lay back down, but the hospital was waking up around her and after a time she rose and went out into the hallway. She checked her phone for messages. There were none. She said good morning to an aide in scrubs who was pushing a linen cart and asked if the cafeteria was open. It was, and Grace made her way downstairs. She bought two coffees, a banana, orange juice, and a cup of yogurt. Patients would get breakfast, but there was no telling when or what. The coffee tasted murky and she loaded it up with milk and sugar.

Her mother was awake again. "Hi Mom. How are you feeling?"

"What are you doing here?"

"I stayed here, I was here all night."

Her mother closed her eyes again. "I have to go to the bathroom."

"OK, I'll get somebody to help you." Grace went out to the hallway, then walked to the nurse's station, where people were already busy with phone calls and paperwork. They would send an aide, they said. She would have liked to ask them when Dr. Park was coming, but they were all absorbed in their tasks and did not seem eager to have more conversation. It was the way that hospitals always made you feel.

Grace waited at the door of her mother's room for an aide to come, and finally flagged one down. She walked a little ways along the hall to give her mother some privacy. When she came back, her mother was sitting up in bed. The aide had opened the blinds and a square of clear sky showed in the window. "I brought you some coffee," Grace said. She steadied it as her mother took it and drank, wincing.

"Too hot."

Grace set it down on the plastic arm of the bedside table. "How are you feeling?"

Her mother raised both hands to her face. "Do I look terrible? I bet I look just terrible."

"You look fine, Mom." Her mother's hair was lopsided and without her glasses her face seemed unfocused.

"My chest hurts. What did they do to me?"

"I don't know, Mom. I didn't get here until later." She wasn't sure what she was supposed to say or not say. It was better to wait for the doctor.

"I guess I was coming down with something and it just hit me. Oh my goodness, I felt bad."

"Are you hungry? I bet you're hungry. I bet they bring you breakfast pretty soon."

Grace's father arrived just after the breakfast tray. "How's the patient?" He leaned over and kissed Grace's mother, who was struggling with the plastic utensils and scrambled eggs.

"When can I go home? I need a shower and I don't want to take it here."

"We have to wait for the doctor. He has to check you out and make sure you don't end up right back in the hospital."

"I feel fine, just tired," her mother said, giving up on the scrambled eggs. "I feel like somebody beat me up."

"Where's Michael?" Grace asked her father. "Is he coming?"

"I didn't see him this morning, I don't know what he's doing. What else you got here, Laura, a biscuit? How about a biscuit with jelly?"

Michael came in, still smelling of whatever man-scented shampoo or body wash he'd used in the shower. It had been a long time since Grace had shared a bathroom with him and his commercially virile products. "Hey Mom, how you doing?" Michael went around to the far side of the bed so that he could give her a hug. "Wow, you seem a lot better than you were last night."

"Everybody agrees on that," their mother said. "And that's a comfort."

Grace asked him how he got to the hospital, and Michael said he called somebody for a ride. He and his father avoided looking at each other. Couldn't they even manage to get here in the same car? She guessed not.

Grace said she had to call work and tell them she wouldn't be in, and her mother protested that she didn't have to do that, somebody else could stay, and Grace said that no, she wanted to. In fact it was the last thing she wanted to do, be there when two tons of doctor news landed on them all. Her head hurt from her bad night's sleep and her throat had been sandpapered. The coffee had been a mistake. "I'll be right back, OK?" So chickenshit glad to have an excuse to get out of that room. She called from the lounge, not staying on the phone long enough for her coworker to express great amounts of her shock and sympathy. Then she stopped at the nurse's station to ask about Dr. Park, who he or she might be, and when they might be expected to put in an appearance. As soon as he can, she was told.

Most of what you did in a hospital was wait. A nurse came in and took Grace's mother's temperature and blood pressure and listened to her heart. Grace's father tried to find out more about Dr. Park and when he or anybody else in this place might bother to show up. The nurse was a pro and didn't rise to the bait. Michael turned on the television and ran through the channels but their mother said there was nothing she wanted to watch. Michael said he was going to the cafeteria and did anybody want anything. "I don't know why I can't just get up and go," Grace's mother complained, and Grace's father said that wasn't the way they did things.

Dr. Park arrived midmorning, a carefully smiling presence. He was accompanied by a medical student who typed into a laptop. The doctor used the laptop to illustrate the anatomy and function of the lungs: bronchi, plcura, alvioli, bronchioles. He had her mother's X-rays on the computer also and he pointed out the areas of concern. The masses. That was what he called them. He said he was ordering a CT scan and would arrange an appointment with a specialist who would perform a diagnostic bronchoscopy.

Grace's mother asked what that meant, did it mean she had lung cancer? Looking around at the rest of them for support; how ridiculous was that? "I'm not a smoker. Honestly, I'm not."

Dr. Park explained the episode of discomfort she'd had the day before as a symptom, a complication, of what was going on in the lung. A pericardial effusion, it was called. They were fortunate it was discovered and treated promptly. Someone would be here soon to take her for the CT scan. She should consider this a step-by-step process. He wanted to be reassuring. At each step they would get more information, and as they got more information they would better know what to do. How to help her. There would be treatments, monitoring, goals. She and her family would be involved and informed. Active participants. It was made to sound a little like one of those television series where people competed in teams and exhorted each other in the performing of tasks and stunts.

Once the doctor had gone, her mother looked around at the rest of them. "I'm not even fifty-four years old," she said.

Michael said, "Come on, Mom. I didn't hear him say anything all that bad. This is early days, there's all this stuff they don't know yet."

Grace's father said, "We're going to research this. We're going to find out who the top doctors are for this kind of thing. Experimental treatments. We're going to be all over it."

Grace said nothing, and she was the one her mother's gaze sought out. In the look that passed between them they seemed to know what was to come, and what would be required of each of them.

Things started off well. They all learned to think in centimeters, which was how tumors were measured. They became familiar with the names of heavy-duty, cancer-killing drugs like methotrexate and Abraxane. The doctors were encouraging. It was a Stage III diagnosis. Several lymph nodes were involved, and there were several tumor sites. That sounded bad, but it could have been worse. They could work with Stage III, they'd seen it before. Grace's mother had pneumonia as well, it was discovered. She admitted that she'd had a cough for, oh, a while now, but hadn't thought much of it. And wasn't that just like her, to ignore a problem with her own health, while she worried and fussed about everybody else's? It was exasperating, it was enough to make you angry, if you let it, for the backward reason that she had not valued herself enough to spare the rest of them her sudden need.

Then again, lung cancer, whose fault was that? How angry could you be, and what could you blame? Her mother hadn't smoked, or been around smokers, or worked with asbestos, or anything else you could point to as a risk factor. The doctors said that 10 percent of lung cancer cases had no identifiable cause. "Ten percent!" her mother said. "Well, aren't I special!" She was wry and humorous, as always.

Although there were also times she would say things about life going on without her, or what her family ought to do once she was no longer here. But that was when Grace, or her brother, or her father, would tell her not to be negative, it did not help anything to dwell on the negative. They were all of them vigilant against negativity. People died of cancer. It happened every day. Fear was another disease that could kill you from the inside out if you let it. No no no, there was to be no talk of doom and gloom! And Grace's mother would say she supposed they were right.

She spent a few days in the hospital so she could get IV antibiotics to clear up the pneumonia. The family brought her magazines and warm socks and a bathrobe she could wear in bed. People called and sent cards and flowers. Her mother made friends with the doctors and nurses. She said it was all so much easier when you got along with people, wasn't it? Grace supposed that was true, although there was something too eager and placating about it, something childlike, as if jollying up the medical staff might help the course of the disease.

Of course they were all of them busy jollying things up, just to get her mother through it. There was a week of daily radiation treatments, followed by once-a-week chemotherapy for six weeks. She was a trouper, she was doing great. And she was, on balance, although the radiation made her throat so sore she had trouble swallowing, although her chest hurt, although the chemo gave her diarrhea. Her white blood cell counts were worrisome; they had to back off the chemo for a bit. But you had to expect some of that. You had to push on through.

Grace's father talked to the doctors and satisfied himself that they knew what they were doing. He followed the latest cancer news online, the targeted therapies for genetic mutations and all the clinical trials going on. It was hard to say if anything he found was helpful, but then, it was hard to say if anything was helpful, including her actual treatment. The scans of the tumors were sometimes good news and sometimes did not show the kind of improvement the doctors would have liked to see. Surgery was discussed; surgery was ruled out. Nothing was certain except the nerve-jamming uncertainty of it all.

There was even a truce of sorts between Michael and his father. Grace had come to realize, or perhaps she had always known, that their quarrels were a competition between them for her mother's attention and approval. And now they were competing to see who could be the best behaved, the most helpful, the most sympathetic. Michael spent more time at home. He kept his music down, or plunked away on his old acoustic guitar. Their father backed off his automatic complaints. Grace brought chicken broth with garlic and ginger, rice pudding, yogurt with honey, green tea. They were all making an effort at getting along and pulling together and whatever else families were supposed to do at such times. What did they know about cancer? What did they know about how families were meant to be?

By Christmas, Grace's mother was through with the first round of treatment. They set up a tree in the usual spot and brought the boxes of decorations down from the attic. Michael and Grace strung lights across the front porch and hung a wreath on the door. Their mother cried a little because, she said, it all looked so lovely, just lovely. Uncle Mark flew out for a few days before the holiday, and there was an early Christmas dinner, supervised by her mother, assembled by the rest of them. Michael produced some cookies that approximated the ones their mother made, though the Santa heads were lopsided, as if Santa had been squeezed in a vise. But it was good to have something to joke about.

And it was good to have Uncle Mark there, someone who was outside the push and pull of their daily routines and aggravations. He told stories about things that had happened when he and their mother were kids, like the time he'd put the thermometer under the hot-water tap to get out of going to school, and had overshot any normal range and registered a temperature of 125.

"The jig was up. Your grandmother smacked me a good one."

It was a funny story, he made it funny. Grace's mother laughed along. She was so much thinner than she'd been, whittled down. One morning she had woken up to find handfuls of her hair on the pillow. She had muscle weakness and fatigue. Foods developed unpleasant, metallic tastes. Chemo was a bitch. Hang in there, the doctors said. Like you had any choice. She sat at the dinner table wearing a fancy lounge outfit that Grace's father had bought her, a dark blue velvet top and pants. She'd tied a scarf around her head to cover the patchy places in her hair. "I know how I look," she told everyone who tried to compliment her. Waving her hand. "Please."

Uncle Mark said, "Hey Laura, do you remember when we went to a football game and Mom got into a fight with some fat lady who kept squeezing her out of her seat?"

Michael said, "How do you do that, just take over somebody else's seat?"

"They're bleacher seats, there's lines to show which one's yours. What, don't you go to the games?" Michael shrugged; they did not. "Sacrilege! How about it, Laura? You remember?"

"A fight, what, she hit some lady this time?"

"No, but she wanted to. Dad had to switch seats with her and try to calm everybody down." Mark chuckled and shook his head.

"I guess I don't remember that," Grace's mother said.

"Who was playing?" Grace's father asked. "Maybe that would jog your memory."

"I doubt it. We got dragged to all the games, I never paid that much attention."

"That's just like you, Laura," Grace's father said. "Can't take you anywhere." He chuckled. He was drinking but it was the benign part of an evening's drinking.

"It might have been a Wisconsin game," Uncle Mark put in. "I think we beat them."

Grace's mother said, "It was always either too hot or too cold.

That's what I remember about those football games. We always had to go because Mom and Dad were such rah-rah boosters."

"Count me out," Grace's father said. "Football, it just goes better with television and beer."

"Good old Memorial Stadium," Uncle Mark said. "Lest we forget." He smiled and looked around the table, as if some other conversation was going on, something humorous. "We heard a lot about the veterans, about war history, you know, on account of Dad being in France and Germany."

Michael, who had been suffering through a spell of polite sitting, roused himself. "Which war was that? First or Second?"

Grace said, "Honestly, Michael."

"Well I don't know. So I'm asking."

"He fought in World War Two," Uncle Mark said. "But the stadium was built in honor of the World War One soldiers who died. I don't much blame you, Mike. They were both well before your time."

Grace's father said, "See, Michael, the First World War was almost a hundred years ago. Your grandfather would have had to be, what, ah, really old." It was the instructive part of the evening.

Michael shrugged. "Thank you. I have it figured out now."

"A war's nothing to joke about. People go and never come back."

"What makes you think I'm joking?"

"A hundred years," Grace's mother said. "A hundred years is nothing. It's like, you stand on the edge of the Grand Canyon and throw a paper airplane into it."

"Well that's kind of a strange thought, Laura," Grace's father said after a moment.

"Is it? I guess I shouldn't have had that glass of wine. I didn't even drink the whole glass."

"It might not have been the best idea, honey."

Her mother waved this away. "I have a better appreciation these days for the passage of time. A different perspective. I think about Mom and Dad a lot. They're in a memorial too someplace. Well, Dad is, at the law school. There's a plaque right inside the front door. More than I'll ever have."

Grace stood up to clear the table. "We have cheesecake, if anybody wants it. And coffee."

"What are you all afraid of?" her mother said. "Dead people? I'm not nearly as afraid of them as I used to be. There's things I've had to think about. Good for you all, if you haven't."

Michael said, "Come on, Mom."

"Come on what? Stop having cancer? That would be nice. I'm sorry, I didn't mean to spoil things. Dinner was really good, thank you, everybody. I'm going to lie down now."

She went upstairs and soon after, Grace's father followed. Michael said he was going out. No one had eaten the cheesecake. Uncle Mark said he'd share a slice with Grace. Grace cut off a portion and put it on a separate plate. She ate two mouthfuls of it but it was too rich and insinuating and she set it aside. She said, "Mom does pretty good, actually. There are just these times."

"How could there not be. It's OK."

"I'm glad you're here, Uncle Mark. It helps."

"She's my only sister. Just like you have only one brother. You know what that's like."

"Sure."

Her uncle took off his glasses, examined them critically, polished them, examined them again, and put them back on. He was younger than Grace's mother but he looked old now too. "And here I've done the same thing with Dylan and Tracy. We were going to have a third kid. But I guess Brenda and I weren't on the same page about that."

"Well, that's . . ." It was mildly embarrassing to hear about such things. And to imagine skinny Aunt Brenda clamping her knees together and refusing access, or whatever the horrid details were. She got up to empty the dishwasher and start in on the kitchen. "No, that's all right, you don't know where anything goes. I don't mind doing it."

"I'm afraid you're going to get stuck with a lot of things, Grace. It seems like women always do."

"I don't mind," she said again, although she did, she minded fiercely. She wouldn't be like her mother, who lived for everybody but herself. She wouldn't get cancer and make everybody feel bad about it. Or maybe she would, maybe it was some kind of freakish genetic destiny.

"You're one of the tough ones. You always have been. The one who wouldn't put up with anybody's crap. It just makes you angry. You remind me of your grandmother."

"Thanks." She didn't want to be like any of them. She said, "You know what I'm hoping? Once Mom's feeling better, I want to move somewhere else. It's a big world and I don't want to spend my whole life in this stupid town. I mean, it's not stupid, I'm stupid. For sticking around . . ."

She shook her head and bent over the dishwasher. She was stupid for saying anything, for her black, unworthy thoughts. She was stupid for starting to cry.

"Don't I know it," her uncle said, and she was grateful that he kept his distance, kept his tone light and did not try to comfort her. "This town, it's like everybody's known your business from way back before you were born."

"Lung cancer survival rates are not what one would wish." Grace came across this sentence two-thirds of the way through one of the informational pamphlets and handouts. It was after the sections on self-empowerment and the benefits of support groups, good diet, and spirituality. Talk about burying a lede.

They'd gotten through Christmas, January, February. In March it was discovered that the cancer had spread to her mother's spine. Grace was angry, as were they all. It did not help anything to be told that anger was one of the common and expected reactions to setbacks in treatments. The phrase "setbacks in treatment" did not help either.

"Am I going to die?" her mother asked. "Am I dying right now?" No one would say. It was understandable that doctors would rather deal in false hopes than false despair. There were still different drugs, therapies, strategies that could be employed. More radiation, more chemo. Did you really want doctors who gave up? But when Grace looked up the prognosis for lung cancer patients whose cancer had metastasized to the spine the first word was "Sadly."

There was another hospitalization to allow for a new kind of scan, involving radioactive particles and hi-tech imaging. The doctors offered biophosphonates to help prevent fractures, anti-inflammatories and medications for pain. Palliative care. There was no point in getting angry at the doctors. They were magicians who had only so many tricks. Her mother came home and said she wasn't going back to the hospital again, no matter what. She didn't have to, the family assured her, although they kept an open mind when it came to no matter what.

Grace's father moved into the guest room because Grace's mother had so much trouble sleeping. None of them slept, not really. Her father sat up late at night in front of the computer, re-searching lung cancer, lung cancer treatments, lung cancer online communities and forums. He had stopped drinking. He said it didn't work anymore. Michael slipped in and out of the house like a ghost. Sometimes he dragged his pillows and blankets into his parents' bedroom and spent the night on the floor so that if his mother couldn't sleep, there was someone to keep her company. Grace washed dishes, washed sheets and towels, sorted the mail, organized medicines. She still spent nights at her own apartment, for now, still went in to work at the food store for occasional shifts. A substitute taught her yoga classes. It was normal life once you took the normal out of it.

Grace's mother said, "You read in all these obituaries about people who died after a long, courageous fight against whatever killed them. Cancer or something else. But what does that mean, fighting?"

"I don't know, Mom. Maybe, they didn't give up hope."

Grace's mother said, "And then they died anyway."

"I guess so."

"I think it's so people can feel better about themselves. You're a fighter, not some miserable whiny victim."

"Mom."

"All right, I'm sorry. I'll try to do better. My poor girl. None of this is fair. It's not fair to you."

"It's OK, Mom."

"You're the one who's getting stuck with me."

"That's not the way it is," Grace said. Although it was. By the end of the month she was spending the nights in her old bedroom so she could manage her mother's pills and her appointments and help her with hair washing and dressing. There was talk of home health aides, but her mother was fierce about resisting these for as long as possible. In theory, Michael and his father were pitching in more around the house, but in practice it meant sour heaps of laundry left in corners, frozen meals, and dust balls rolling across the floors. Grace cleaned up after them with black-hearted efficiency. It was true, the women always got stuck with such things. And here she had been determined not to be that kind of woman.

There were visitors too, all her mother's friends, people who wanted to help, people who thought they were helping. They meant well, but you could not ask them to pitch in and clean the bathrooms. The visitors brought flowers and casseroles and gift shop stuffed animals, and Grace's mother always said, "Thank you, that is so sweet of you."

Her mother's friend from work came on two different Fridays. Becky? No, Becca. A little woman with a mouth stenciled bright pink, and dangling turquoise earrings. "Happy hour," Becca said, producing a pint bottle from her bag and asking Grace for ice and glasses. When Grace said she wasn't sure, with all the medication, if alcohol was advisable, Becca shook her head so that her earrings clinked. Her short, curly hair was streaked and frosted like some elaborate cake.

"It's not going to hurt anything, I promise. Little bit of liquid comfort. Is your father home? You know, I've never met him. But I expect there's times his ears were burning."

Grace couldn't think of anything to say to this, nor to the drinking, when it came down to it. Becca went upstairs with the ice and Grace could hear them laughing together. When Becca came down again, her lipstick was blotted and pale. "She's sleeping like a baby," she told Grace with satisfaction.

On good days her mother was arranged on the downstairs couch with a blanket and pillows. On bad days people were told not to come. There were a great many people who visited or called. Her mother had lived here all her life, and now her life was circling back around her. There were school friends, work friends, friends who had moved away and those who had stayed. Grace ran interference, taking messages, holding her hand over the phone so that her mother could indicate yes or no, who she wanted to talk to, who she wanted to see. One time Laura plucked a greeting card from the pile of mail, opened it, and tossed it directly into the wastebasket. "Do you know the Bible verse about hypocrites?" she asked Grace. "How they are like whited sepulchers, pretty outside, but filled with dead men's bones and uncleanness."

"What are you talking about?" Grace asked her, but her mother wouldn't say any more, and when Grace thought to look for the card, it was gone.

When people did come over, Grace stayed out of their way. She did not want to hear what she did not want to hear. Sometimes it couldn't be avoided. She was in the den folding laundry. Her mother's friend Susie had come over with cupcakes, red velvet cupcakes with cream cheese frosting, because her mother had always liked these. She didn't have much of an appetite these days. The pain meds put her in some zone where eating was as tiring as climbing a flight of stairs. "They look so pretty," Grace's mother said. "Really, they are too pretty to eat."

"You'd better eat them, that's why I made them."

"Maybe later. I'm just not hungry right now. Isn't it silly, all those times we tried not to eat too much? How about I have a little taste of the frosting. Oh that is so delicious. Thanks, Suse. You're the best."

Susie's voice dropped to a murmur. She was asking Grace's mother how she was, really, how are you?

"Scared. I want to get it over with."

"Don't say that."

"Well you asked. Don't ask if you don't want to know."

They talked a while longer, keeping their voices low. Finally Grace's mother said she was tired and she was going upstairs to rest. Grace came out to see if she needed any help, but her mother said she was all right. Susie hugged her for a long time. "Oh for God's sake, Susie, I'm still right here. You can come back tomorrow if you want."

She climbed the stairs and they heard her go down the hallway and the click of the door shutting behind her. Susie was crying. She said, "I'm sorry, I shouldn't carry on so. After all, she's your *mother*. It must feel so much worse."

"I don't know how it's supposed to feel," Grace said, and that was true. How were you supposed to feel, day by day, hour by hour, when it just kept going on? Susie gave her an odd look and told her to make sure they all had some cupcakes.

The times that her mother's pain broke through the medicine, Grace's father was the one who climbed into bed with her and let her cry against him. He was the one who called the hospital and blistered the ears of the nurses until the doctor agreed to a morphine drip and hospice care. He massaged her feet, read the newspaper headlines out loud to her, coaxed her with food. One night Grace said to him, "You're being really, really great. About Mom." Surprising herself with how much she meant it, suddenly shy about her own feeling.

Her father shrugged. Grace saw in his face how tired he was, how tired they all must be. He said, "It's the last chance I have to make things up to her."

Michael was different. He didn't want to talk. Not to anyone about anything. He came and went at all hours, and Grace was never sure if he was home unless she stood at the closed door of his room and listened and knocked and opened it to confront the emptiness and neglect inside. She hoped he wasn't using again, she saw no signs of it, but Michael was going to have to take care of that himself. No one else had energy or time to worry about it.

One night Grace was in the basement, loading up the washer and dryer, when she heard her brother's voice filtering down from overhead, unexpectedly clear, and knew it was coming through the laundry chute in their parents' room. She stopped moving so she could listen. "I can't. You won't be here and I can't do it."

Her mother's voice, less distinct. Grace could barely make out the words, but the tone was soothing, reasonable. "No," Michael said. "Nobody else. I'll be all alone. I can't do it, I'll crash and burn." He might have been crying. More of her mother's reasonable, chiding tone, he was not to talk that way, feel that way, of course he would not be, not be, of course not. "Not like you," Michael said. "Not ever in my whole whole life."

Grace left the laundry for later and took herself quietly back upstairs. You did not want to hear what you did not want to hear.

By now there were the hospice workers, the professionally compassionate. The family had to get used to the presence of other people in the house just as, before long, they would have to get used to an absence. The schedule of visits was posted on the refrigerator. Someone came for four hours in the morning and someone else for four hours at night. There was one bad incident: a new aide had arrived to work the evening shift. When Grace went in to see if anything was needed, her mother was attempting to get out of bed as the aide, a heavy-set woman with black hair, remonstrated with her. "Now there, Mrs. A., let's just relax," and expertly blocked her efforts with one arm.

"What's going on here, what are you doing? Mom?"

Her mother thrashed and panted and fell back on her pillow. Grace had to bend over to make out what she was saying: "She's the one."

"What?"

"She's the one kills you."

"All right, Mom, don't worry. Listen . . ." Grace straightened up. "I'm sorry, it must be her medicine."

Her mother made swimming motions with her hands. "Go away. Her."

"It's all right, Mom, calm down. I'm sorry, I didn't get your name. . . ."

"Angela. It's all right. I don't take it personal. Some of them get that way." The woman gathered up her coat and handbag. "I still get paid for this shift, right?"

Day after day it was almost spring, sometimes a little closer, sometimes farther away. Day after day her mother wandered off, traveled back, disappeared again. The morphine made her float; an oxygen machine tethered her to earth. One morning she was calmer than usual, more awake. She asked Grace to get her some lilacs.

"Lilacs? We don't have any, Mom. Besides, I think it's too early for them."

"Back at the house." It took Grace a moment to realize she meant the house she'd grown up in.

Against all expectations, the house remained unsold. In spite of its character, historic charm, etc. People wanted new kitchens and bathrooms, they didn't want to move in and have to redo things right away. There had been two or three lowball offers. Another offer went to contract but the buyer backed out once the inspection found mold. Mold! There was no mold! It was just an excuse to renegotiate and drive the price down. The lawyers jumped all over it. The whole deal had fallen apart, in expensive fashion.

Now the house was back on the market. Grace parked in the driveway and nodded in wry greeting at the realtor's sign, the realtor herself pictured with arms crossed in an energetic, can-do pose. The lilacs were in the backyard. Her mother was right. One bush of lilacs, the lightest mauve, had formed flower cones and the tight flowers were pushing open.

Grace had brought clippers along with her, but it was a messy job to cut and tear through the woody stems. The skin of her hands bruised, and when she reached up for the higher branches, they sent a shower of cold water down her neck. Everything about her mother's dying had turned into a messy job of one sort or another, a mix of exhaustion, guilt, resentment, fury. She didn't cry often but she was crying now, with no one to see her, bits of leaf and wet petals caught in her hair. Her hands were cold and scraped, and she was crying because it was so damned easy, at this moment, to feel sorry for herself.

Before she headed back, she used her key to open the kitchen door and walk through the empty rooms. They had a smell to them from being closed up. It was just a house. You wanted it to be important, a place where lives you'd known had left some echo. But nothing remained.

Her mother was awake when Grace got back with the lilacs. The aide was just leaving. She said her mother had had a good morning. Grace put the vase of flowers next to her bed, alongside the wet wipes and lip balm and hand lotion and mints, the Kleenex and prescription eyedrops and flexible drinking straws and all the rest that had accumulated there. "Can you smell them?"

"They're wonderful. They're in Walt Whitman."

"What's in Walt Whitman?"

"Lilacs."

She thought her mother was having a morphine moment. Then she remembered. The poem about Lincoln's assassination, though she couldn't recall much of it. Here coffin that slowly passes, I give you my sprig of lilac. What a thing to think about.

"Jesus, Mom. You couldn't come up with anything a little more upbeat?"

Her mother laughed. She had learned to make laugh noises in her throat, not farther down. Too much laughing hurt. She sipped air as if it was water. The oxygen tubing snaked from her nose. Her face was both familiar and not so, both smaller and looser. She was quiet for a while and Grace thought she might have fallen asleep. Then her mother said, "Nuisance."

Grace knew what she meant. Dying was a nuisance. She said, "Do you want to sleep? Do you want me to leave?"

"Stay and talk to me. Prop me up some. I keep sliding down." There were different layers of padding and pillows, all designed to protect and ease her mother's back. No one position stayed comfortable for very long.

"All right then." Grace rearranged the pillows, then sat on a love seat that used to be at the end of the bed. It had been moved against the wall so you could sit and talk to each other. But where were you supposed to start? There was an empty space they should have been filling up with words while they still had time. The faster the time ticked down, the harder it was to say anything.

Her mother said, "Only in the movies."

"What, Mom?"

"People who look good dying. It's all right. I don't care anymore. You have to help them. Your dad and Michael."

"I am helping them. They're completely useless."

"I don't mean housekeeping. Help them get along."

"Come on. How am I supposed to do that?"

"I don't know. You have to try."

Grace shook her head. "No Mom."

"I worry so much."

"Well don't. They'll work things out between the two of them." Grace was less confident than she sounded. The last thing on her list of last things she wanted was to be in charge of their endless stupid pointless fighting. To fret about it and spend her life trying to calm them down and placate them and make them behave when they clearly didn't want to. Why had her mother wasted so much of her time trying? Why should that be part of some female inheritance?

To change the subject, she said, "Anyway, Dad's been a lot better lately. He's really making an effort to get along with Michael." Though that felt too close to the dangerous truth; that up until her mother got sick, he had made very little effort. Her mother's eyes were closed. She might have been sinking into sleep. Then she roused herself.

"I wish you liked him more."

"Hah. I wish you'd picked me a different father."

"Oh Grace."

"I'm sorry, Mom." She'd intended it as a joke, a mean one. "I upset you, I'm really sorry."

"He does the best he can."

"I know he does." She didn't believe it. There was nothing that had stopped him from doing better, except his own bad temper and bad habits.

Her mother said she would tell Grace a story from back before they were married. It took her an effort to get enough breath into her words, and there were pauses and gaps Grace had to fill in for herself, but the story went like this:

I know how you feel about his drinking, and you're not wrong to hate it. I've spent years hating it myself. I can't say I didn't have some warning. But everything's different when you're young. There's nothing you can't wish away or power through or ignore. Nothing you can't imagine bending to your vision of how life ought to turn out, the rightness of it all.

I met Gabe when I'd just finished college and started working for the city. My dad got me the job. A lot of things came our way because of who he was. A prominent citizen. A man who was in the newspaper a lot. There's a way of trading favors and goodwill in a town like this. Anyway, it wasn't much of a job, I never felt like I'd benefited from some corrupt system or anything.

I had an apartment with one of my old college roommates. She had her own not-great job. We got up in the morning and went to work and came home and complained about our crummy jobs. But honestly, work wasn't that important to us. We weren't especially career-minded. Not like my mother, who was spitting mad all her life because she had to settle for being married. No, our biggest life's work was going to be falling in love.

Does that sound dumb or backward to you? Maybe it was. Maybe girls your age have more practical mind-sets and don't let themselves get derailed by foolishness about men. You'll have to let me know.

On some nights, and always on weekends, we got ourselves dressed up and painted up—those hairstyles! You should see the pictures!—and went out to the bars. Sometimes we'd see a movie, or maybe we'd meet up with other friends and go out to dinner. But the bars were where the boys were. I doubt if that's changed much over time. I know it hasn't. I've been to some of the same places with my friend Becca when she was looking for a new boyfriend.

I saw your dad there a few times before I met him. He'd come in with some other grad students. You could tell they were grad students, they didn't actually smoke pipes but it wouldn't have been out of place on them. I don't think I gave him any particular notice, though he was nice-looking enough. He looked like a very smart little blond boy, all grown up and ready to do serious, important things.

So, a bar. I guess you can meet somebody in a bar and it doesn't have to be a sign of trouble to come. Anyway, we weren't the type to hang out at church, or stay home waiting for excitement to come find us. Me, my roommate, our friends, and all the other girls like us, we all believed there was such a thing as genuine true love. It was out there, but you had to make yourself available to it, you had to be open to possibilities. But once you found it, you'd know. There'd be this certainty. I don't mean the room fades away and colored spotlights go on, like the dance scene in *West Side Story*. Nothing corny. Just that feeling of a punch to your heart.

Of course while you were waiting for true love to show up, there were these other characters you kept company with. The guys who'd failed the test they didn't even know they were taking. They weren't cute enough or smooth enough or something enough. But they bought us drinks and we laughed at their dumb jokes and sometimes we went home with them.

On this night I'm talking about, I was getting impatient with these boys and their horsing around and their too-loud voices. All of them in general, and the one I often paired off with in particular. Technically, he wasn't my boyfriend, so we didn't behave toward each other with any particular sentiment. He liked to complain that I never had anything good in the refrigerator. I knew he expected us to spend the night together, not that he'd done such a thing as call and make plans ahead of time, or even pay that much attention to me once I was there. There was a big football game on, Bears and Packers, and he and his buddies and truth be told, a lot of other people in the place, were staring raptly at the televisions mounted in every corner of the place. But at some point in the evening I'd finish my drink and he'd take his time with the rest of his while I stood there, irritated and waiting, until he finally drained his glass and followed me out the door. It was practically foreordained.

All this, and maybe some mischief or meanness, is why I walked over to where Gabe and his friends were sitting at the other end of the bar, and smiled and said, "How are you guys tonight?"

He always makes a point of teasing me about this: I was the one who came on to him.

Well they didn't know what to make of me, those grad student guys, those computer nerds and research geniuses. The idea of a woman making herself available to them, even this casually, seemed beyond their experience and comprehension. They even left off gaping at the Bears and Packers. Gabe was the one who finally found his voice and moved off his bar stool to offer me a seat. "We're good. How about yourself?"

I was introduced all around. There was a little current of talk of the get-to-know-you variety, before the other geniuses went back to their imported bottled beer—this was another way you could tell they were grad students—and the fine points of the ground game. Gabe asked if I needed another drink, and I said I was fine for now. I was drinking my usual, that headache-in-a-bottle white wine they kept behind the bar. I drank more back in those days, that much is true, and so maybe I was less likely to be alarmed by somebody else's drinking.

Anyway, I liked him. He stood behind me, not crowding me, just close enough to indicate a level of interest, and when he reached around me to get to his drink on the bar, we almost touched. He really was the best-looking of the group, with his fair hair and his smile that had something held back in it, maybe something he'd tell you the next minute or two if you stuck around. He said, "I've seen you here before, I know I have."

"You might have." I liked the idea that he'd noticed me. "I come here sometimes with my friends."

"He one of your friends?" He nodded over his shoulder at my not-boyfriend, who was sending us a nasty look from the other end of the bar, the same way a bartender might send a mug of beer sliding down its length. It was halftime, he must have finally noticed I was gone.

I turned back around so I didn't have to see my soon-to-be ex-not boyfriend. I said, "He's not my friend tonight."

Gabe said he guessed I was a femme fatale, and I laughed at that, because nobody before or since ever called me that, even teasing. It made me feel cool and dangerous and sexy, things I never considered myself to be. I was only middling pretty. Even when I was your age, when everybody has good skin and good hair, oh of course you do, don't be silly.

So it was heady stuff, to have a moment of that kind of attention, the titillating prospect of two men fighting over me, even if there wasn't any actual fighting, even if there turned out to be more bad mood than jealous rage. I sat up straighter and arched my back and took a deep breath. It seemed like I might be on the verge of having an actual exciting time.

"Are you a student?" he asked me. Standard opening question in a college town. I told him I'd graduated the spring before. "Why are you still here?"

"I live here. I'm from here. I'm a townie."

"What's a townie?"

"You're kidding."

"No, really, tell me."

"Somebody who grew up here and never left." So much for feeling glamorous and dramatic. I felt all the femme fatale draining out of me.

"Well I'm glad that you townies stick around," he said, which restored a little of my confidence.

He said he was a grad student, and I said I knew that, and he asked if it was that obvious, and I just laughed and slit my eyes at him. He told me about the work he was doing with computers, and I said I didn't know anything about computers. Like, I couldn't be less interested. Like Scarlett O'Hara saying she didn't want to hear about any old war. I guess I really was flying a different flag that night. Usually I'd be doing the typical girl thing where you widen your eyes and act impressed and ignorant and wait for things to be explained to you.

I had another drink and so did he. And maybe another. We were sliding down a slope of blurry alcoholic conversation, of the kind that makes you feel you must be saying really amazing things to each other. He had a sharp edge to his talk, I could tell he was smart and even a little arrogant about being smart. Confident. Like a grown-up. I was ready for a grown-up.

Meanwhile, that other boy was still making a production out of his displeasure. Whenever I turned my head I saw him glowering in my direction, usually with his lip hanging over the neck of a beer bottle. You want a man's attention? Try ignoring him. My roommate waved at me and went through a pantomime that was familiar to me. She had the car, she was ready to leave, was I coming?

Now I had to decide, stay or go. I signed for my roommate to wait a minute. Femme fatales didn't hang around; they vanished mysteriously and left their admirers in a state of fevered impatience. Maybe I couldn't quite achieve that, but it seemed pretty clear what I ought to do.

I got off the bar stool, a little unsteadily, and held out my hand for him to shake. Which he did, though it confused him. "Listen, I have to go, but it's been great talking to you and maybe we'll see each other . . ."

"Sure." He could have asked for my phone number then, should have done so, but when he didn't I thought, well, that's that. I made a wobbly move to get out the door, avoiding the mad boy and watching my roommate head out through the other door. She'd know to meet up outside. We'd done it a time or two before.

Once you get outside and away from all the commotion of a bar, your eyes and ears are blotted out for a minute until you adjust. It was cold, almost November, and I took a deep breath to clear my head. I was still pretty buzzed. So much for my femme fatale moment. Nobody else was out on the sidewalk just then, only a few cars going by and the light from those old-fashioned globe street lamps that they still have downtown. I set off toward the corner, since my roommate would be waiting just on the other side.

From behind me, somebody said, "Hey, wait up."

I didn't turn around, because it was that boy I didn't care to see or talk to anymore, let alone go to bed with. I wasn't afraid of him, exactly; even mad, even drunk, he was whiny and kind of pitiful. I heard his feet scrambling to catch up to me.

At the same time, behind him, I heard Gabe calling, "Hey, hey, hold on." He'd come out after us both, and now we were all piling up on the sidewalk.

I did stop then and turn around. "Oh hi," I said, to nobody in particular.

Gabe took his time. Strolling, very nonchalant. Once he reached us he stuck his hand out. "How you doing. Gabe Arnold."

That other boy looked at the hand like it might have a joke buzzer in it, like, what was a Gabe Arnold anyway? Then they shook hands, one of those clutch-style shakes. This thing has happened to gentlemen, where they aren't sure which way to go with handshakes, traditional ones or cool, styling ones. He announced his name, which was Randy Something. I've honestly forgotten the rest of it.

"So, Randy, how's it going?"

"Ah, going OK. Yeah. We're just talking," Randy said after a befuddled moment. Not true, technically, because I hadn't said much of anything to him, even earlier when we were inside. There was never what you'd call a lot of dazzling repartee going back and forth between us.

"Sure," Gabe said. "Can't go wrong with talking."

There was this little current of something acrid and testosterone-infused between them, and did I mention some drinking that had been going on? We all sounded drunker than we had even five minutes ago. Just then, from the bar behind us, a muted whooping and whistling erupted. The two of them turned toward it, looking in through the window.

"Bears score?"

"Looks like it. They were so-oo close. Red zone."

"Packers had shit for brains tonight."

"You see their first drive?"

"Totally lame."

My roommate peeked around the corner. She spread her arms palms up, as in, Now what?

Randy said, "Is it fourth quarter now? I think it's the fourth."

"Bears are crushing them."

"A good old-fashioned butt kicking."

"Come on," I said. "Football?"

They both glanced at me. Randy said, "It's Bears-Packers." Like that explained something.

Gabe said, "I came out to see if you wanted to wait until the game was over, and then I could give you a ride home."

"That sounds so fun," I said. I was being sarcastic but nobody noticed.

Randy said, "Or look, when the game's over, I can take you." Like either of them should have been behind a wheel.

"You guys make it so difficult to choose."

Another burst of noise from inside, and they both swiveled their heads toward it. "Why don't you go back in and I'll be there in a minute," I told them. "I'll flip a coin or something."

They went back in and I joined my roommate and we walked to the car. She said, "What happened back there? I thought they were getting ready to fight a duel over you or something."

"I don't think anyone does that anymore."

We drove home. The next night, Gabe called and apologized and asked if we couldn't start over. I was mad that he was too easily distracted and yes, too drunk to carry out my fantasy of two men fighting over me. Like I said, fair warning. But he really did put some effort into it. I made him call a couple more times before I said yes. He told me he got my phone number from Randy, and I never got a straight story about how that happened, though there were many versions told to me, each more outlandish than the last one, about how they had arm wrestled for me, or Randy had insisted on Gabe buying him three more beers, or maybe it was three beers and a couple of basketball tickets. Oh he used to tease me to death, the way he kept coming up with ridiculous stories. And he was sweet to me, and funny and smart and good-looking, and I hadn't known him since I was twelve years old, which I thought was a real advantage.

He said he liked that I was unpredictable. He said it like I was somebody who might jump into a fountain in an evening gown. And maybe I was like that back then, a little, because that was what he saw in me. And he was at his best, for a while at least.

Genuine true love, the tragic kind that comes with its own movie soundtrack? I couldn't say. Of course we went on from there, and we settled into our grown-up selves, and somewhere along there you and your brother came along, and life filled up slow, if you measured day by day, and fast, if you try to account for years. There was good and bad. Some things on both sides that shouldn't have happened. But if you want to know who really loves you, look around and see who's still standing next to you.

IV. GRACE

Once the end came, it came on fast. On a Sunday morning in April her mother said she felt well enough to eat a real meal. She slept most of most days now. It was a little bit of an occasion to have her awake and wanting food.

Grace made pancakes and bacon and sliced up some strawberries and her mother made a good effort at cleaning her plate. It was cold outside but the sun was shining. Morphine was a balancing act between pain control and making her breathing that much more difficult, but on this day it seemed to be working right. She said she felt light-headed. "Like I'm drunk!" Grace asked the hospice aide if they should dial the medication back, but her mother said, "No, I am a cloud in the sky, I am changing my shape."

Grace and the aide looked at each other and the aide nodded, which meant this was to be expected. Grace said, "Well that's good, Mom. You can be a cloud if you want to."

Grace kissed her on the forehead, took the breakfast tray downstairs, and started in on the dishes. Her father and Michael had helped themselves to food and left trails of syrup and coffee grounds on the counters. Grace heard their feet on the stairs, going up and going down, a murmur of conversation. They'd each stopped in to the sickroom to say good morning. It was another in a series of abnormal days made normal.

Grace stepped out to the front porch. Pranayama was used to control the energy that animated the lungs. Conscious breathing originated in the more developed parts of the brain, and helped to elevate the functions of mind and body. It was cold and Grace wrapped her sweater closer around her. She breathed in through her nose and exhaled through her closed mouth. It was Ujjayi Pranayama, Victorious Breath. Her mother's breath was now measured out in the smallest things, in grace notes, in the sidereal motion of stars. When and when and when. Grace shivered and went back into the house.

The hospice aide came downstairs with a white plastic garbage bag, which she carried straight outside to the cans at the side of the house. When she was once again inside, Grace asked her if she wanted pancakes; there were extras. The aide said no thank you, but she'd take a little coffee please. The aide's name was Dorothy. She was their favorite, a soft-spoken black woman who kept everything tidy and calm. She said that Mrs. Arnold was asleep now, and that she would go back up and check on her before she left.

Grace said, "I guess people get confused like that. I guess you see that."

"There's no one way to go about it," Dorothy said, and by it, Grace understood her to mean dying.

Dorothy finished her coffee and went back upstairs. Grace started the dishwasher and wondered if she might be able to lie down for a nap. Sleep at night was hit or miss. If Grace woke, she might walk down the hall to her mother's room to check on her or sit for a while and listen to see if the thin current of her breathing was still there. Or she might wake up and hear footsteps, her father or her brother, going in to do the same. She'd listen until she was sure that no alarms were being raised, and all was as it had been. Sometimes she went back to sleep, sometimes she stayed awake until the sky began to lighten, and then she slept a little while longer.

Dorothy came into the kitchen. She said, "I think . . ."

Did she mean . . . Grace hesitated. So much had been uncertain, a measuring out of each day, gauging if her mother was better or worse than the day before. As if that would keep the inevitable at bay. But was this it? What were you supposed to do?

Grace hurried back upstairs with Dorothy. Her mother's eyes were open and her head beat against the pillow, as if trying to get free from it. Grace said, "Mom, what is it, are you in pain?"

"Tell her Bob Malloy said hello."

"What? Tell who?"

But her mother made a sound that was not words, a long, alarming *huuuuunhh,* like a growl without enough air behind it, and her head strained against the pillow and Dorothy moved to the IV pole that held the morphine drip and said that if Grace wished, they could give her a little more.

Grace said yes, they should do that, and she had to go get her father. She knocked on the guest room door and her father opened it. He looked soft-faced and sleepy. Grace said that he should come talk to Dorothy and he should do it now. He didn't seem to understand her. He stood there blinking and scowling and Grace said, "Dad, please," and then he stepped past her and went quickly down the hall.

Michael was in the basement, where he went sometimes to get away. He was wearing headphones and Grace had to stand in front of him to get his attention. "You need to come see Mom," she said once he took the headphones off. His face turned flat and blank and he got up to follow her.

The sickroom had a smell that trapped you as soon as you walked in. In spite of all the efforts at hygiene and air fresheners, in spite of lilacs and candles and fans. The smell was of something stale, something burdened and heavy. The room was both personal and not so. The personal was being erased from it minute by minute. Death was impersonal. It pulled your loves and hates up by the roots. It rolled right over your likes and dislikes. It took as much as it could of history and memory. This was its moment. All else fell back before it. The husband, son, and daughter stood by, uncertain of what came next. Death said, I will show you what comes next.

The dying woman had been further sedated. She lay on her side and every so often the aide stepped in to suction her mouth so as to avoid the aspiration of fluids, and the noises that came along with the mechanics of a failing body. The aide said this part of things could go on for some time, and she would stay as long as they wanted her to. She would step outside now to give them some privacy.

Did the dying woman know they were there? They spoke as if she did. They held her hand and smoothed her hair. Did they want her to linger, or did they want a quick end? It didn't matter what any of them wanted.

The morning wore on. Grace left the room to call her uncle Mark. He had last visited a couple of weeks before, and now he said he wished he'd known, he could have been there right now, and Grace told him that none of them could have known, it was that sudden. She said she would call him again when everything was over, and her uncle told her to stay strong. Grace said nothing to that, although she didn't feel strong. She felt as if some part of her had been severed. She felt as if she had been holding her breath for months.

Michael was at the top of the stairs, looking down as Grace

came up. He had been crying and he had tried to rub the crying away with his knuckles, like a child. He said, "I don't want to go back in there."

"Don't. You don't have to."

"When I die I want to jump off a fucking bridge and get it over with."

"Great. You do that."

"I'm sorry."

"It's all right."

"It's not anything like I thought it would be."

"It's nothing you can really practice for."

She gave him a sideways hug and they leaned into each other. Grace said, "If you don't want to . . ."

"No, I will. Wait a minute."

He turned and went into his bedroom, came back with his acoustic guitar. "Maybe I could . . ."

"Sure. If it's OK with Dad."

Michael made a wry, despairing face, meant to indicate how unlikely this was.

Had anything changed? Maybe they were imagining that her face had lost some of its flesh, so that the architecture of the bones stood out. The aide had repositioned her so that she was closer to upright. Their father sat on the love seat at the end of the bed. The aide was in the adjoining bathroom, running water in the sink. She came back in with a washcloth she'd wrung out. She was wearing latex gloves and a rubber apron over her work smock. She said, "I thought I could put some lotion on her. If you want. That can be soothing."

They looked at each other, nobody knowing the right answer, and eventually came around to yes. The aide moved to the bedside and began undoing clothing, and they all hurried to leave the room.

Out in the hallway, their father said, "What's this?" Pointing to the guitar.

"I thought I could play a little. Something she'd like."

"All right," their father said after a moment. "Just not any of that hoodlum music."

When the aide called them back in, the lotion smell was still in the air. The aide gathered up the washcloth and towels she'd used and took them downstairs. Grace and Michael and their father arranged themselves around the bed. Michael cleared his throat. "Hi Mom. You always liked this song."

He tried a few chords, then picked out a melody. It took a few bars to recognize it. One of the old Simon and Garfunkel songs. "April Come She Will." Sweet and sad, rising and falling.

If the dying woman heard it, if there was still a living spirit inside the chamber of the body, she gave no sign. Perhaps the music was for those watching and waiting. The song ended and he began playing another with the same sort of lift and ache, and then another. It smoothed over the empty spaces in them. It unclenched the fists that had taken the place of their hearts.

The music ended. The silence held for a moment and grew, like a drop of water about to fall. Then Grace said, "Did she . . ."

The aide, Dorothy, came back inside and removed the oxygen tubing and turned the tank off. She unhooked the IV line but left the needle in place, taped to the blue bruised skin of the arm. She said that she would go downstairs and call the hospice, who would send the man who provided service at such times.

She left them there. Grace and Michael held each other and cried and when they stopped, there was a terrible unquiet place where the crying had been. Grace's father turned away from the bed. He walked out into the hallway and Grace followed him. He said, "Ahh, Jesus." Grace put a hand on his arm. He felt loose and restless, ready to push her away. "Did you hear her say anything? Before she stopped talking?"

"No." She hadn't meant to lie. But she didn't want to tell her father that her mother had said another name, Bob Malloy, who- ever that was, and anyway, who knew if it meant anything at all, when her mother had been deep in a morphine dream. "I hope she heard the music. I bet she did. I should call Uncle Mark now."

Her father nodded, as if he had been listening, though Grace didn't think he had. He said, "I'm going to have a drink. Come have a drink with me."

"I don't want a drink, Dad."

"Come on. This once."

First Grace went back into the bedroom. Michael was sitting in a chair next to the bed. "Did you want me to stay with you?" Grace asked, and her brother shook his head. She waited for him to say something, but he stayed silent. She was avoiding looking at what was now only a body on a bed, and not her mother.

Her father had gone downstairs. Grace came into the living room to see the aide, Dorothy, gathering her coat and purse. Dor- othy said, "They send one of the counselors along too, they should be here any minute. I'm so sorry. She had a good end, it was easy for her."

"Thank you for staying. You were wonderful. I don't know how you can do this job."

"You don't ever quite get used to it," Dorothy said, and she and Grace hugged, and Grace opened the front door for her and watched her walk down the porch steps and out to her car. It was early afternoon, not quite two, and the bright day had turned windy.

Her head felt like a sandbag, heavy and lopsided. There was a buzzing sensation behind her eyes. Her father was in the kitchen, filling two highball glasses with ice. He took the bourbon bottle from its place on the shelf and poured. Grace said, "I really don't want any."

"I'm pouring yours light."

He handed her a glass. The whiskey smell was so strong, it assaulted every part of her. It hollowed out her head and roiled her skin. Whiskey was a spirit, she remembered, a distilled spirit. If she drank it, that's what she'd be doing. Taking a spirit into herself. Her father raised his glass.

"To her. Your mother."

"Shouldn't . . ." she began. She wanted to say, Shouldn't Michael be here too? but Michael didn't drink anymore. She took a small sip and recoiled. "Whew!"

Her father drank, gave the glass a considering look, then drank again. "She'd want us to go on with our lives. She'd want us to keep moving forward."

"Yes." She had a sensation of water rushing over her, roaring through her ears.

"She was the best thing that ever happened to me. Your mother. She deserved better than me. Everybody said so."

"No Dad. That's not true." Was it? She wasn't sure.

"Her parents. Your grandma and grandpa. They always thought she could do better."

He was giving her a challenging look. Was it a question? Did he want an answer? Was there a right answer? "I didn't know that," Grace said.

"Oh yes. Especially her father. He'd call every so often and quiz her. Was I treating her right? Behaving myself?"

Again, the challenging look. Grace tried to sort through what she was hearing, and her own whiskey-addled brain. She was so tired.

Her father said, "Aren't you drinking? We're supposed to be drinking together."

"I don't want anymore, Dad. It's not sitting right with me."

"Oh Gracie girl, don't leave me all alone."

"I'm not, Dad. I'm just really, really tired."

He was weeping suddenly, and holding her around her waist and pulling her close to him so that her face was too near to his, and she tried to turn hers away, and his weeping was awful, awful, as was his poisoned breath and his hands on her, and even as she struggled, the doorbell rang. It was the hospice service, coming to do what had to be done.

Late that same night, Grace woke to sounds of rushing, unquiet wind. Still half-asleep; why was she outside? She opened her eyes. Lightning flickered at the windows. The thunder sounded low and far away, like a chord played on an organ. Closer by, inside, a racket as of something come loose, and the wind knocking and pushing against her door, trying to get in.

Frightened, she jumped up, listened at the door, then went out into the hallway. In the room where her mother had died, the windows had been thrown open and the curtains belled in and out and twisted into ropes. "Michael?"

He sat cross-legged in the center of the bed, which had been stripped down to its mattress. "I'll close them in a minute. I didn't want her to be stuck in here."

The funeral had been foreseen, if not really planned. Uncle Mark and his family flew in, and there was talk of what Laura would have wanted. Pictures, flowers, music. None of the family had actually attended the Presbyterian church for years, although they were nominal members. Had her mother been religious, in any recognizable sense, ever talked about Jesus or sin? No, none of them had. It would have felt false and wrong to have a preacher they didn't even know unwrap some prayers for the occasion. The funeral home had reception rooms that would do, even if the furniture was in an elderly style that no doubt matched up with the age of most of the deceased.

There were things to be done and decided. A different kind of energy took over. Neighbors brought more food: chicken divan, manicotti, angel food cake, Crock-Pot chili. Some of the old photographs were put in frames. Her mother looking young and younger, with straight, dark hair and a serious expression. One of both her parents, taken outside on a summer day, both of them with their hands shading their eyes, grinning into the camera and the future. One of her mother with Grace as a toddler, Michael a baby, their mother's face so absolutely happy, it hurt to see it.

Flowers to order. Tulips and daffodils and lilies. Grace could have cut lilacs for bouquets, they were blooming everywhere now, but she had come to hate the smell of them.

Her father picked out the casket, had arranged for cremation. He made it his business not to flinch from doing so. He was made of sterner stuff. Etc. They would have a closed casket, thank God. Grace got the creeps at funerals where they displayed the honoree. Her mother had not been treated kindly by cancer. She would be allowed this one last vanity, that of remaining unseen.

Uncle Mark and Aunt Brenda and the kids stayed at a hotel with an indoor swimming pool and a piano player in the cocktail lounge. There was the usual hubbub that went along with one of their visits. The kids wanted Mexican food, was there a good Mexican restaurant? Brenda had a case of hives, probably from the detergent they used on the hotel sheets, and she needed Benadryl. Grace was kept busy directing traffic and making phone calls. There was a printed program for the service. A guest book. A slide show that would run on a laptop set up at a back table.

What should she wear? Not black, she decided. One of her spring dresses that didn't look too hippieish. Something her mother might have approved of. Why was that important now? Maybe it was stupid, but it did.

What kind of service would it be, would anyone speak? No one seemed anxious to do so. Perhaps just some music. Did Michael wish to play? He said he did not. He said he wasn't even sure he wanted to go. Grace told him he didn't have to want to. Maybe none of them wanted to, but they would.

"I'm worried about him," Grace told her uncle Mark. "About Dad too, sure, but . . ."

"How about yourself," her uncle said. "Who gets to worry about you?"

"I'm OK." They were sitting in the hotel's cocktail lounge. Mercifully, it was too early for the piano player, who went in for medleys of show tunes. Grace was drinking cranberry juice and her uncle a beer. "I mean I will be OK, I'll get through it." She didn't want to try and explain the complicated territory between mothers and daughters, how she and her mother had veered toward and away from each other through the years, how Grace had measured herself against her mother and always took off running in the other direction. "But the two of them, my dad and Michael, and Michael especially, she did so much for them. Propped them up, calmed them down. Made them feel better about themselves."

She stopped talking, aware that she might be saying too much of the truth. She began again. "I was thinking. Maybe we could have a memorial later. Something more like a celebration. A big potluck? She'd like that. Or a tree planting in one of the parks . . ."

"That's a nice idea. Let a little time pass, give everybody a chance to catch their breaths and gather their thoughts."

"A tree planting or even a garden. A place people could visit. You can give money to the park district and they set it up, a dedication. You remember her talking? She didn't think she'd have anything like that. Like, she wasn't important enough."

It wasn't missing her mother that made her cry, not always, but the sadness of her mother's life. Her mother who had always seemed to be apologizing for herself, worrying about everything and everyone else. And now, how would they manage without her?

Her uncle handed her a cocktail napkin. "Here you go."

"Sorry."

"Don't be."

"Crying's stupid. It doesn't help anything."

"You don't have to be so tough, Grace."

She blew her nose. "Good, because I'm not."

"I like the idea of the garden. Let's work on that one. See what your dad and Michael think."

"All right." As if the two of them would agree on anything.

The bartender came by to ask if they wanted another drink. Both Grace and her uncle said no, roused themselves, and smiled wanly at each other. Mark looked at his phone. "Uh-oh. I am summoned."

Grace said that she had better get back also. The service was tomorrow and there was still a lot to be done. They stood, and Grace led the way out to the lobby. "Uncle Mark? Do you know anybody named Bob Malloy?"

"Bob . . . oh yeah, from high school. I used to run track with Bob. Haven't seen him for a hundred years. How come?"

"Nothing. Just a name that came up. So many people talking . . ." Weren't your last words supposed to mean something? Wasn't your life supposed to mean something?

"Yeah. So, tomorrow. It'll be good. We'll make sure it is."

Everything came together as it was supposed to, the pictures, the flowers, the mix of music Michael had put together. Old songs, ones their mother liked to sing along to. Hippie anthems, power ballads, pop songs that weren't inappropriately upbeat. "You did a good job," Grace told her brother. "We need real music, not some stupid hymns played on an organ."

"I wish nobody else was coming."

She knew what he meant. The funeral was for other people. Their mother had been all theirs.

They had arrived early to set things up. Their father had dropped them off, saying he would go get Mark and Brenda and the kids. And probably down a couple of quick drinks in the bar, though Grace didn't care about that, as long as he didn't fall to pieces in some awful way, and even if he did, she guessed people would make allowances. The funeral director greeted them. He was all sad smiles. The room had thick carpet that turned their footsteps soft. The handsome coffin was a rental, as was customary for cremations. There were some things Grace would have been all right not knowing. It sat at the front of the room on a small stage. A spray of lilies and roses was arranged on its polished lid. It was shockingly large. It made you think of pianos and armoires. A row of polished handles glinted along its side.

Grace and Michael contemplated it from a distance. "It's not really her," Michael said.

"No," Grace agreed. She touched his shoulder. "You look nice." He'd shaved and made some effort with combing his hair. He wore a tan sports jacket he must have hauled out from the back of his closet and had cleaned. A deep blue shirt and a soft knit tie and dress pants. Sometimes Grace forgot how handsome he could make himself.

He shrugged. "Mom would have wanted me to dress up."

They arranged chairs and found places for the pictures. People had sent bushels of flowers. There was hardly enough time to read all the cards. Too late, they realized they might have asked for donations, money for cancer research, say, in place of so much floral art. They pushed the fusty drapes aside and opened the blinds and let the spring sunlight warm the place. There was one especially ugly lamp with a base that looked like a soup tureen. They hid it underneath a table.

The service began at noon. At five after, the first visitors arrived. Their father and Uncle Mark's family were still missing. Grace put a lid on her anger and anxiety, and went to the front of the room to greet people. There wasn't any point in having any kind of receiving line if it was just the two of them.

"Thank you," she said, and kept saying. "Thank you for coming." Michael stood behind her, not saying much, unless someone singled him out. Some people she recognized from her mother's book club. Her mother's coworkers from the alumni association. Neighbors. They asked after her father, they wanted to make sure they offered condolences. Grace said he was here just a minute ago, he must have stepped out. Where the hell was he anyway? A bald man with an ostentatious-looking beard wandered in and stopped to look at the video playing on the table in the back. Grace recognized him as someone who worked with her father, though she couldn't remember if he was a boss or not. It was going to be hard to keep making excuses for him. People asked if there was anything they could do, anything, and Grace said she couldn't think of a thing, but they were so kind to offer. She didn't think she could send anyone over to the hotel to do a sweep of the bar.

Aunt Brenda waved to them from the foyer, and Grace went to join her. "Where's my father, is everything all right?"

"Mark's talking to him. He's having a hard time."

Her cousins, Tracy and Dylan, came in behind Brenda and made a beeline for the last row of chairs. They sat down and both of them took out their phones and bent over them. Grace saw that

Michael had taken a seat also, slumping on a sofa against the wall. So much for the family presence. "Is he coming in?" Grace asked.

"Yes, Mark's getting him cleaned up."

Grace gaped at her. "He spilled a drink," Brenda said. "It was an accident, really, not a big deal." She took out her compact and lifted her chin to assess herself. She was wearing a dark blue spring suit and high-heeled tan pumps. Her legs, in panty hose, shimmered. She looked almost painfully appropriate. Grace, in her droopy cotton dress and sweater, wondered if someone should clean her up as well. Never mind that now.

Grace said, "If you think he should go home instead . . ."

"I think he should pull himself together and show up at his wife's funeral." Brenda snapped her compact shut and put it away. "I'm sorry, I don't mean to sound harsh. Everybody reacts differently, sometimes things hit you when you don't expect it." She stopped and gave Grace a measuring look. Assessing her fitness for duty.

"I'm all right," Grace said.

"You only ever have one mother," Brenda said, patting Grace on the shoulder and moving into the reception room.

Grace decided not to tell Michael. Whatever might be going on, he could see it for himself. Anyway, it was a bad idea to stir up trouble between the two of them, when so much trouble already existed there.

It was getting crowded. Some of the same women who had come to visit her mother when she was ill were here now, and they had brought with them their husbands, or best friends, or teenage children. They hugged Grace, they stopped to talk to Michael, who always pulled himself together and was polite when required to be. They signed the guest book and peered at the photos. They stood respectfully before the coffin in attitudes of prayer.

Her father and her uncle Mark came in and paused together

in the entrance, Mark with his arm around her father's shoulders, saying something that looked earnest, even from a distance. When Grace crossed the room to reach them, Mark spotted her and shook his head ever so slightly: caution.

"Hi Dad." Her father's face looked rubbery, blank. Not good. At least there was no evidence of a spilled drink, although it was possible, now that she regarded him, that the shirt he wore was not his own. "Come on and sit down, there's people who want to talk to you."

She and Mark deposited him in an easy chair that was part of a conversational grouping of other chairs. "Here you go. Want some water? How about we get you some ice water."

Her father looked up at her, his expression darkening. "I'm not some damned baby."

"Right."

"Your mother's gone." He lifted his gaze to the coffin at the front of the room. "My God, we put people in boxes and then we bury them."

Grace and her uncle traded looks. "Just sit here a minute, can you do that?" Grace told her father. She and Mark retreated to a corner. "At least he's here," she said. "It would be worse if he wasn't."

"People understand these things," Mark said, although he did not seem convinced.

Grace was distracted by the arrival of people she knew, some of her old school friends and a couple of people from the food co-op. She was so grateful to see them, people who were there for her, people who were on her side, that she turned teary. It was such a relief not to feel entirely alone. Alone! Wasn't this her family, or all she had left of it? Nevertheless, alone.

She hugged her friends and they said all the right things about how sorry they were, how it sucked, how she should hang in there.

They'd call her tomorrow, see if she wanted to go out, get food, talk. They went off to sign the guest book, and when Grace looked back at her father, a woman had seated herself next to him.

The woman was holding his hand and leaning over to speak to him, and if it looked odd and overcozy, at least her father was paying attention and nodding along and not doing anything belligerent. Grace remembered her as one of her mother's visitors, but couldn't come up with her name. Betty? Beth? Her hair was different now, colored a resolute blonde. Other people were edging in, waiting for their turn to speak to him. As Grace approached, she heard the woman say, "She was the best. She was dynamite. Nobody like her."

"Damned straight," Grace's father said.

"And I know she'd want us to be happy. Even without her. She'd want us to tend to that little green shoot of happiness and make sure it got enough water and sunlight. You know what I mean, Gabe?"

"Water the plants."

"Oh, aren't you silly. A big silly Billy."

"Ha ha."

Grace realized that neither the blonde woman nor her father was entirely sober. She stepped forward, into the circle of chairs. "Dad? The Klingermans are here."

The woman stood and people moved in to shake her father's hand. He got out of his chair to greet them. Maybe he would be all right. Maybe he would at least be all right for the next hour and a half.

The blonde woman's hand was on her arm. "How are you, honey, I mean, really?"

"I'm sorry, I can't remember . . ."

"Becca."

"Yes, of course. Sorry, I couldn't place . . ."

"I worked with Laura at the alumni association. AA, we used to call it. For fun. Hah."

Becca's hand lay on her arm like a small animal you were supposed to pet. Grace said, "We're all doing our best."

"You meant the world to her. You and your brother." A whiff of alcohol breath.

"Thank you." There was something blurred or out of focus about Becca's makeup, as if she'd used a stencil that had slipped. The blue lines around her eyes wavered and her lipstick was bleeding through. And, because it seemed she ought to keep talking, Grace said, "My dad won't know what to do with himself."

"I only just now met him," Becca said. "And he's exactly the way your mom said."

Grace had no idea what that meant, and no time to wonder, because now the ladies from her yoga classes, Peggy, Helen, Rita, and Flo, had arrived and were yoo-hooing at her from the back of the room. "You'll have to excuse me," she told Becca. "Thanks for talking to my dad."

Becca sighed. "Men. They never know what they feel until it's too late."

Grace was glad to see that some of Michael's friends were here as well, some not very dressed-up kids who gave the impression of having smoked pot out in the parking lot. They gathered around Michael and draped themselves over the furniture. It was hard to tell if their presence cheered Michael up, since none of them were talking to each other, only glumly slouching. But at least he was not alone either.

Grace went to meet Peggy Helen Rita Flo, her hands outstretched. "It was so very nice of you all to come."

The event was scheduled to go on until three o'clock, but three came and went, and people still lingered, or rather, had made themselves comfortable and were visiting back and forth. The funeral director kept checking on them, popping in and out like the cuckoo in a clock. Uncle Mark had taken her father home in a cab. Mark said he'd sit with him until Grace and her brother got back. Aunt Brenda and Dylan and Tracy had gone shopping. Grace supposed she would have to go back to the house, although she was looking forward to sleeping in her own apartment that night. Michael had left with some of his friends, saying it was only for a little while. That had been a little while ago.

Grace was weary, and tired of people being dead, and while it was a tribute to her mother that so many people had come, and later she would appreciate this, right now she only wanted everyone to leave so that she could go home. Home home. It had been close to three weeks since she'd slept in her own bed, lived her own life. It was time to move on to whatever came next after your mother died.

The people still here seemed to all know one another, the long-ago friends from her mother's early days. Some of these Grace had met before, or had pointed out to her, some of them she had not. Maybe they only got together for funerals these days. She sat in one of the upholstered chairs placed midway in the room, and watched the group of sociable mourners milling and chatting around her, and wondered why she was the only one left to maintain any family presence, the only one who was not allowed to abandon her post.

"Now, you must be Grace."

The woman stood in front of her, and Grace got to her feet. She allowed that yes, she must be.

"I knew your mom and dad before you were born. Back in prehistoric times."

Grace had nothing to say to this. Her brain was too flaccid to respond to funnies. The woman went on. "Not that we'd kept up over the years. Still, such a shock. Terrible. So sad for you."

"Thank you." The woman was perched on a pair of high heels that seemed to be a bad fit. She had red hair and green eyes and her face gave the impression of being dusted with flour. Good Lord, what happened to women at this age, that so many of them got themselves up to look so scary? "I'm sorry, I don't know your name."

"Jeanine Franks. Back in the old days, I was Jeanine Darlington. Maybe your mother spoke of me?"

"No, I don't recall . . ."

"I sent her a prayer card."

"That was nice of you," Grace said, although the woman looked as if she expected to hear more.

"Is your father here?" Jeanine swiveled her neck to take in the room. The face powder she used was a bad idea. It settled unkindly into wrinkles. Still, you could see where she might once have been pretty. "I can't remember the last time we saw Gabe. My husband and I. Oh, I want you to meet him too." She made a windshield wiper–like wave at a stout man in a polo shirt across the room, who either did not see her or was pretending not to.

"My father wasn't feeling well, he went on home."

"What a shame. You make sure you tell him hello from us, and how sorry we are."

Grace promised, although she had already forgotten the woman's name. Jeanine Somebody. She was waiting for the woman to leave so she could go find the funeral director and start closing things down.

But she didn't leave. Instead she scrutinized the program that Grace and her father had put together. "Is there a burial service? I don't see . . ."

"Mom wanted to be cremated."

"Won't you miss having a headstone? Never mind. Just a thought."

"Mom wanted to be cremated," Grace repeated, and the two of them stood, trapped on this conversational ledge. How many more awkward encounters was she going to have to have?

"Could I ask you, dear, does your family have a regular church home?"

"Church home? Oh. Well, the Presbyterians, but I guess none of us is very . . . Presbyterian."

"Then I'd like to invite you to worship with us at Christ the Victim."

"The what?"

"It's a Lutheran congregation. Very welcoming."

"Why is it called Christ the Victim?"

"Victor, dear. I said Victor."

"I'm sorry, I misheard you. I'm just so tired . . ."

"Of course you are. What a terrible time for you."

"I guess it gets easier," Grace said, although she was only saying it to say something.

"Come on, sit down." Jeanine sat and patted the chair next to her. Grace sat too. "And here you don't even know me, and I come sailing in and talking your ear off."

"It's all right," Grace said, liking Jeanine a little better. "Mom would have wanted people to come together. Share memories and all."

"I have plenty of those. We went to high school together, Laura and I. She was such a dear. One of those shy girls."

"I guess she outgrew that," Grace said.

"It seems like a whole different lifetime. You're still young, you haven't felt the, what do they call it, the march of time yet. One day you're turning heads, then it's like, you look in the mirror and . . ."

Jeanine spread her hands, as if to encompass the whole of her. The shoes that made her ankles overflow them like bread dough, her top-heavy figure, the powdery face and lurid red-green of her hair and eyes. Grace made some mild noise meant to disagree, mildly, with Jeanine's self-criticism. "Oh it's all right," Jeanine said. "That's life. When I think back on those days, all the parties and the bars and the carrying on, I have to shake my head. I don't think your mother ever enjoyed that scene much, you know? She tended to hang back from things."

Jeanine waited for Grace to remark on this, but Grace was unsure what she should say. Agree or disagree? How could she possibly know? And there was something Grace didn't care for in this fond recounting, something disagreeable, although maybe she was imagining it. . . .

When Grace didn't speak, Jeanine went on. "Anyway, Ian and I are much happier now. We settled down, raised our kids. We found our church home and a whole new, Christ-centered life. Which is why I want to share it with people. So they can find a higher purpose also."

Grace's attention had slipped once Jeanine's talk had turned churchy. She came out of her blankness to see Jeanine looking at her expectantly. What? Grace said, "I wonder if you know, that is, if you could help me figure out something my mother said toward the end of things. Since you went back a ways with her."

"Well I'll try, dear. That sounds very mysterious."

"I don't know. She was on a lot of morphine. It was about someone, maybe you knew this person? It was, 'Tell her Bob Malloy said hello.'"

Jeanine stared at her. Two red dots appeared in her white cheeks. She pulled herself out of her chair and wobbled away in her badly fitting shoes. She crossed the room to where her husband was talking to two other men. They appeared to be discussing golf swings. Jeanine said something to her husband and headed for the door, the husband walking backward after her, still trying to demonstrate grips.

Well that was . . . Grace looked around her. There was no one there she could have told how peculiar everything had been and was still being.

Grace gathered the photos, and the laptop, and the iPod that Michael had hooked up to the speakers. She made trips back and forth to load all the flowers. The funeral director said that if a family had extras, the county nursing home was always glad to have them dropped off. Finally the room was restored to its generic, impersonal self, like the display in a furniture store. Nothing intruded except for the coffin, which would soon be returned to its place in the showroom.

She stood at the entrance looking back at it and trying to formulate some kind of farewell. There would be the cremated remains later, but she didn't want to think about that right now. "Bye, Mom," she said, the best she could come up with, and then she went out to the parking lot.

Grace had placed the bouquets and their vases into cardboard boxes to keep them upright. When she got behind the wheel, they crowded in on her from behind. Roses and stalky carnations, bunches of daisy mums, baby's breath, wax flowers, tulips, love in a mist, something she didn't know, birds-of-paradise, more roses. She rolled down the windows to air out the smell of them, which was close and overwhelming, with a faint undertone of staleness. She was too tired to stop at the nursing home. Everything could sit until tomorrow. She would have plenty of room for her bags, which were already packed.

Her father and her uncle were in the den, watching the golf channel. What was it about men and golf? Was it just something they did to get away from women? They looked up at her when she came in. Her uncle got to his feet. "Hey kiddo, would you mind running me back to the hotel? I have to get the crew to the airport."

"Sure. Dad, I'm going to take your car. Mine's full of stuff. OK?"

Her father waved a hand: Whatever. There was a coffee cup on the table next to him, and a plate with a half-eaten sandwich. He'd changed out of the shirt he'd worn at the funeral home and into a sweatshirt. Mark bent over him. "Gabe, you know I'll be talking to you. Hang in there."

"Don't go, man. Stay another day."

"Got to get back to work. You know how it is."

They shook hands, though her father did not get out of his chair. His face was red and he gave an impression, somehow, of having been beaten up. Grace hoped he'd fall asleep before she came back. She took his car keys from their hook in the kitchen and she and Mark went out to the driveway. "Have you seen Michael?" she asked him.

"No, you'll have to tell him good-bye for us."

"Sure." Goddamn him. "Half a sec." Mark got in the passenger side and Grace got out her phone to send her brother a text:

ARE YOU COMING HOME?

What was wrong with him? With her father? Couldn't either of them keep it together for one day?

It wasn't a long drive to the hotel; nothing in town was a long drive. Grace said, "Thanks for babysitting Dad. I'm worried about him."

"Yes, well . . ." Her uncle seemed to want to come up with something reassuring to say, but gave up. "I'll call. I'll call whenever I can. Besides, there's your mother's estate to sort out. I'm the executor."

"I hadn't thought about any of that." And she hadn't. Money, the machinery and enterprise of money, that took up so much of people's time and imagination, didn't have much claim over her. It wasn't that she was so much purer than other people; she just lost interest in it. "I guess you or somebody else will tell me if I need to do anything."

"They will. We will." They'd reached the hotel. Grace pulled into the drive and Mark got out. "Thanks for the ride. Hey did you get a chance to meet Bob Malloy? Since you were asking about him. He was there today."

"He was? No, I didn't."

"I guess he was only around for a little while. Tall guy. Skinny. Gray hair. No? It was early on. I had my hands full with your dad. We said hello, but when I looked around for him again, he was gone."

Not that she would have known what to say to him. It would have been too weird. Oh well. "Tell Aunt Brenda and the kids good-bye for me." She was too tired to pretend she wanted to see them again.

"Sure." He leaned in through the car window and kissed her on the cheek. "Take care of yourself, Gracie girl. Make it job one. Call me if you need anything."

Grace said that she would, and when she drove off, she saw him in the rearview mirror, waving, and she had a passing wish that he could have been her father, although that wasn't a logical thought when you considered that he was her mom's brother.

She drove back to the house and parked her father's car in the drive and before she went inside she texted Michael again.

ARE YOU HOME?

No answer. He wasn't here, she knew it. She went in through the kitchen and put her father's car key on its hook. Next to it was the key to her mother's car. What would they do with the car now? And her mother's clothes, her books, her framed flower prints, her box of old Christmas cards, her magazine subscriptions, cookbooks, jewelry, flower seed catalogs, demitasse set, and more? She'd hardly let herself think about everything that remained to be done, probably because she would have to be the one to do it all.

"Dad?" He wasn't in the den. The television had been turned off. He might have gone upstairs to sleep. There was no sign of her brother.

She went back into the kitchen and wrote a note that she propped up on the kitchen table. She wrote that there was a casserole of lasagna in the freezer and he could have it for dinner, just put it in the microwave on defrost setting for ten minutes, then in a 350-degree oven for forty minutes. She said that she would call him tomorrow.

She climbed the stairs and listened at the landing. The door to the guest room was closed and everything was quiet. She set her bags out in the hall and went through the bathroom for her toothbrush and shampoo and anything else she'd brought with her. She packed these up in a plastic grocery bag and unzipped her duffel to put the bag inside. Then she took the bags downstairs one at a time.

"What are you doing?"

Her father stood on the landing, looking down at her. He still wore his sweatshirt but he had removed his pants. He had on shrunken-looking white briefs.

They were not a family who walked around the house in their underwear. Grace's heart bumped and skidded. She looked away from the lumpy pouch and the pale territory of his bare legs. "I'm going back to my place."

"Why are you in such a hurry?"

"I'm going in to work tomorrow, early, and I want to get settled."

"Honey, nobody expects you to go to work. Your mother just died."

"No, I want to. I want to get back to my normal routine." Did he even know he didn't have pants on? Was he still drunk? She kept talking to tamp down her rising panic. "I left you a note, there's some frozen lasagna you can defrost and heat up for supper."

"Lasagna. Great."

"Or you could—"

"I don't want to be alone."

"Dad, I'll come back and help clear out Mom's stuff, and we can talk about, maybe there are things we need to talk—"

"You can't leave me like this. My little girl."

He started down the stairs. Grace picked up one of her bags and pushed the other ahead of her to the front door. She scrambled with the latch, then swung it open and got herself and the bags outside. Her car was parked on the street. She managed to get everything down the porch stairs, then out to the sidewalk. She thought he might come after her, underpants and all, in full view of God and the neighbors. But the front door stayed closed.

She found space for the bags among the flower vases and started the car. One of the bouquets toppled forward and lay against the back of her neck, the stalks feeling damp and unclean. She yelped and shook it off and hit the accelerator and she didn't care about anyone's death as long as it was not hers.

V. GRACE

There were weeks when she did not see or speak to either her father or her brother. They had not been in the same room together, all three of them, since the funeral.

Grace went back to the house while her father was at work and cleared out her mother's clothing, putting most of it aside in plastic bags for Goodwill, though she couldn't yet bring herself to drop them off. It depressed her that there was so little—next to nothing, really—of her mother's that she wanted for her own. A couple of pairs of earrings that she might or might not end up wearing. Her mother's wardrobe had been sturdy and serviceable. Oxford button-down shirts, cardigans, elastic-waist pants. Her dress-up clothes on their hangers had a disappointed look; they had never lived up to their promise. Grace chose two pullover sweaters in Nordic patterns to take with her. They were heavy, expensive sweaters. They had most likely been Christmas presents. Perhaps her father had bought them? She couldn't remember. Anyway, they were too good to give away, although it was hard for Grace to imagine herself skiing or drinking cocoa by a fireplace or any other such winter wonderland fantasy.

Tubes of lipstick worn down to waxy nubs. A dresser drawer filled with tangled panty hose. The contents of her purse, a collection of Kleenex scraps, receipts, breath mints, and many cheap ballpoint pens from the credit union. Tube of hand cream, small nonworking flashlight. Matchbook. A loose Band-Aid in a soiled wrapper. Anyone's life could be reduced to this impersonal compost.

Some things stayed as they were. In the kitchen, the small blue teapot on its shelf. Her striped apron hung on the pantry door. Mail addressed to her still arrived, advertisements, catalogs, appeals from charities. Over time, such things would be moved or changed, disappear by increments, like chalk on a sidewalk. Less and less of her presence.

She took her mother's house plants home with her, and waited for her father to notice, but if he did, he said nothing.

Michael had moved out to stay with friends who had couch space. He didn't earn enough from any of his jobs to get his own apartment. Grace knew he was broke, or mostly broke. She was pretty sure their mother had given him money when he needed it, and now that was at an end. Was he still going to his classes at the community college? Grace asked, and the answer was vague. She guessed that meant he wasn't.

"Are you drinking and drugging? Don't bullshit me."

They were talking on the phone, and Grace listened to the humming, clicking space of silence. Finally Michael said, "How about you stop asking me that."

"Crap."

"Step Five: rigorous honesty. Ha ha."

"Are you at least still going to your counselor? Come on, do you think Mom would want you to trash yourself to prove how unhappy you are that she died? Huh?"

Another space of silence. "No and no," Michael said.

"Well . . ." What came next? What was she meant to say? Channel her mother's anxious fussing concern, keep nagging him? She didn't want to and what good would it do anyway. She said, "I'm worried about you. Try not to be stupid."

"I'm not drinking."

What came next? A conversation about Don't. She heard him exhale, waiting. "I love you," Grace said.

"I love you too," he said after an uncertain beat.

"All right, talk to you later." Grace hung up quickly. There wasn't anywhere else to go from there.

Her father often called in the evenings, once he was home from work and settled into his chair in front of the television. "I should get a dog," he told her.

"How about an aquarium instead. You're not home enough to take care of a dog."

"No. 'Sitting home with just me and the fish' doesn't have the same resonance as 'Sitting home with just me and the dog.'"

"Don't get a dog." Grace had the phone pressed to her ear and was trying to fold laundry. It was easier to talk to him if she was engaged in doing something else. "A cat, maybe."

"I don't like cats."

"Fine, don't get one." She could just about gauge his alcohol consumption by: the time of night, the normal (or dragging) pace of his words, and whatever degree of belligerence or plaintiveness came through the receiver. It was a totally awful skill and she was sorry she'd ever developed it.

"Your mother," he began, and Grace considered putting the phone down while she tried to get the edges of the sheets straight. The Your Mother portions of the conversations were the hardest to deal with. Your Mother would have wanted you, Grace, to do one or another thing, nearly all of them burdensome or unpleasant. Your Mother would have wanted you to call the HVAC guy and have the air-conditioning serviced, tell your brother to move his crap out of the bathroom if he wasn't going to live here, come over and keep your old dad company once in a while, why didn't she ever do that?

This last request was the one that went along with his worst and sloppiest drinking, and it made her skin start a slow, creeped-out dance. So she met him for dinner at a casual barbecue restaurant. She visited the house when her mother's friend Susie and her husband were expected. She called his office and offered to meet him for coffee, though that never came to pass. And then she stopped making such efforts.

She could feel sorry for him. She did feel sorry for him, but she also felt sorry for herself, and for her brother, and she had no idea of how any of them might be helped. Her mother's death had sent each of them into some private space of hurt. None of the rituals of mourning eased them. Her mother's cremated remains were deposited in a grave site, or so she understood. She refused to accompany her father when he went to the cemetery. She had a healthy understanding of all things bodily, including the body's end and the spirit's release. You understood such things, but that did not mean that you wished to bear witness to what was left of a body, packaged in a metal cylinder and lowered into a cement-lined space.

Her father moped and drank, her brother did whatever he did with his drugs of choice. Grace slept badly and had a series of dreams in which she was lost, trapped, smothered, struggling, all of them variations on a theme. How much of it was missing her mother, how much was the profound shock of death itself? Some friend of her mother's had sent a condolence card, a Catholic one with saints and sacred bleeding hearts and a verse Grace did not recognize: *Be praised, my Lord, through our Sister Bodily Death, from whose embrace no living person can escape.* Was that meant to be comforting? *Our Sister Bodily Death.* Grace could imagine Sister Bodily Death, the family member you didn't want showing up, a black-gummed vampire with oily, stinking skin.

She guessed that things got better over time. Time dragged its feet and now it was summer, and if Grace was no longer preoccupied, every waking and sleeping minute, with death and loss, there were still days when her head was filled with static, like a bad television channel, moments her familiar routines slid sideways and turned strange.

The summer heat descended, humid and glassy. You got used to squinting, to the painful look and feel of car hoods, concrete, windows. Grace let her hair grow long and pulled it up into a waterfall on top of her head. She wore halter dresses that left her thin, tan arms and collarbones bare. She was used to men trying to flirt with her or attract her attention as they went through the checkout at the health food store, though most of these were earnest, awkward guys who gave the impression they wanted to engage her in a serious conversation about their recent reading material. It was easy to smile at them and move them along harmlessly while they fumbled their dairy-free frozen dessert and fair trade coffee into cloth bags. Men were so dumb. She was glad to be through with them.

Grace was taking her lunch break in the community room, as it was called, which was off to one side of the store and was furnished with wooden tables, mismatched chairs, and a bulletin board with advertisements for chicken coops, art therapy, and handmade soaps. She finished her salad and gathered up her plate and silverware and tray to stow them in the right bins for recycling or trash or the dishwasher. The only other person in the room was a man in a far corner, sitting by himself with a cup of coffee. As Grace watched, he took out a pack of cigarettes, extracted one, and tapped it against the table's surface.

"Excuse me, sir? Sir? There's no smoking in the store."

He looked up at her. He might have been one of the homeless men who found their way inside and were tolerated for long
enough to buy food or use the bathroom before they were eased
out again. Or no; he was only odd-looking, in a rough sort of way,
like a biker, maybe. Not much taller than she was, she guessed,
and skinny, with a narrow chest and a long face. A graying mus-
tache. The top of his head was balding and the long blond-gray
hair around the crown was pulled back into a ponytail. He wore
jeans and a black T-shirt with a yin-yang symbol in the center.

"Right," he said, putting the cigarette carefully back into its
pack. "Forgot where I was." He tilted his head back to smile up at
her. He seemed to find her amusing.

"I don't know why anybody smokes," Grace said. She was annoyed by him.

"What else don't you know. Grace." He leaned forward to read
her name tag.

She didn't answer, and took her tray to the row of recycling
bins. She thought he was a creep.

She saw him again a few days later. He was sitting outside the
store this time, at one of the picnic tables set on the concrete ter-
race at the entrance. He sat on the edge of the farthest table and
he had a cigarette going, which might be technically permitted but
was still bad form. "Uh-oh," he said. "The smoking police."

"Why do you want to hang around a health food store smoking? Why don't you go somewhere that makes more sense, like, a
pool hall?"

"Pool hall. Funny. I wanted to show you something."

"I have to start work now." How old was he? Not old old. Forty?
His face was younger than the gray ponytail, but you wouldn't
have called him good-looking, not at any age. One of those small
guys who was all mouth.

"Won't take but a minute. See?" He was wearing the same black T-shirt with the yin-yang symbol. The symbol was made up of some intricate design she couldn't make out. "This side here is heaven. The other's hell."

Grace looked and saw that one side, the white part of the design, had pictures of sunbeams, hummingbirds, twining vines. The black portion had a skull, a lightning bolt, some sort of unwholesome-looking flower. "All right," she said. "Now I've seen it."

"But you don't get it. It's the yin and the yang. Opposites. They balance each other out. No hell, no heaven."

"That's deep."

He inhaled and sent the smoke out the side of his mouth. "All right, Miss College. I guess nobody can teach you anything."

"I'm not in school anymore."

"My mistake."

"Anyway, I don't expect to learn a lot from a T-shirt." Somehow she'd gotten herself trapped in this false, sneering voice that was not really hers. "And everybody's heard about yin and yang, it's one of those popularized concepts."

He raised his eyebrows at this. "Well shit. Never mind, then. The meaning of the universe has already been all scoped out."

"I meant, if you can put it on a T-shirt, it's common knowledge. I have to go in now, my shift's starting."

"Hey." He threw the cigarette down and put it out beneath his foot. "You're pretty."

Grace started to say something like, Oh really, gee, thanks, when he said, "I'm not." And laughed. "See? Yin and yang."

He grabbed her hand in both of his, too quick for her to stop him. "You feel that? That's the energy balance between us."

Grace snatched her hand away and walked off. She heard him say, "Now don't be mad," and then the automatic doors whooshed open and shut and she was inside.

Although she kept an eye out for him, he didn't come into the store, and later when she looked out at the picnic tables, he had gone.

She wished she could sort things out in her mind the same way you could the recycling: trash, cans only, and so on. Here was a space for work, here was one for yoga, one for money, one for the worries about her father, another for the worries about her brother. And there would be a different kind of space, with soft edges like a mouth, where she could put everything else that was bitter and wrong, everything broken or unquiet. She no longer pretended to be a wild woman.

The man with the gray ponytail came through her line three days later. "Oh great," Grace said. "Crap."

"Look, I wanted to say I'm sorry about the other day. I was, what do you call it, inappropriate."

He raised his eyebrows at her expression. "What, you think I don't know any good vocabulary words?"

Grace muttered "All right, fine," not looking at him. She really was a snob sometimes. He had a basket of different kinds of produce—peaches, tomatoes, onions—that he had not sorted into bags, so that Grace had to do that and weigh them out. The store wasn't busy and no one was lining up behind him.

"I bought us lunch too." He put two tuna sandwiches and two bottles of juice on the conveyor belt. "You get a break? Come on outside and eat with me."

"No, that's OK. Thanks."

"I won't smoke. Promise." He smiled, hamming it up. "What big teeth you have, Grandma." He had such an odd face. Long and oversized, like a cartoon.

Another customer came up behind him. Grace said, "I don't think I—"

"I'll be outside." He paid and scooped up his change. It took him a while to get out the door. He kept stopping and shifting the weight of the groceries, and hitching up his jeans, which seemed about to fall off his skinny hips.

When the crew leader told her to take her break, she looked through the front windows and saw him sitting at one of the tables in the shade. His back was to her and if he was doing anything at all, Grace couldn't tell. She hadn't decided about him, or rather, if she ought to bother about him at all, but now she took off her crew apron, hung it on the hook by the office, and stepped outside.

"I only have twenty minutes," she announced, and he looked up at her and put his lips together and exhaled, a soft whistle.

"She don't know how good she looks," he said, as if to an invisible someone next to him.

"Please stop saying things like that."

"Oh, I said it out loud? Sorry. Thought I was alone with my thoughts. You going to sit down?"

She sat. He'd unwrapped the sandwiches and set them out on paper plates, along with plastic forks and napkins. He asked if she was all right with tuna and Grace said that she was. He took a short-bladed knife from his pocket and used it to slice into one of the peaches and lay it out in segments on a separate plate. Then he did the same with a tomato, taking care to make the slices even and to fan them out. "Dig in," he said, wiping the knife blade down and folding it shut. His hands weren't large, but the fingers were long and swollen, either from arthritis or hard use. He wore two cheap-looking rings, one solid turquoise, the other alternating bands of turquoise and some red stone, and this one was worn around the base of his forefinger.

She was a little freaked out by the knife. Men she knew didn't carry knives. "Are you a biker or something?"

"Define 'biker.'"

She didn't answer. Even in the shade it was hot. Currents of ticklish heat traveled across her bare legs. She ate some of the sandwich and used a fork to spear a piece of peach. She was too cautious around him to be very hungry. He was wearing a different T-shirt today, dark blue, with a faded white silhouette of two palm trees. He said, "My name's Les, by the way."

He held out his hand. He was one of those men who didn't know that it was up to the lady to decide if she wanted to shake hands, though so many people were ignorant of this point that she couldn't hold it against him. They shook, and Grace was glad that there wasn't any funny business to it. "Les Moore," he added.

"You're kidding."

"My dad thought it was funny."

It was at least a little funny, though she wasn't sure she believed him either. "See," he said, "with a name like that, I'm a walking yin and yang. Like, happy and sad. Hot and cold. That's how I come by my interest in it. Understand?"

"I guess so." They each ate without speaking for a time. A co-worker of Grace's walked past their table, giving Grace a sidelong look. *None of your damned business.* She picked out a slice of tomato and put it in her mouth. It tasted watery.

"I'm not any hard-core biker. I was just having fun with you. I'm more of a philosopher type. I read a lot. I'm a self-educated person. You can look down on that if you want. I work at Plastipak, I'm a forklift operator. I guess you can look down on that too."

"Why do you keep saying that, you don't know me and you don't know what I think about things."

"I guess it's another energy vibe I get from you."

Grace rolled her eyes at this. Energy vibe was one more thing you might read on a T-shirt.

"I just meant, you're particular. A pretty woman like yourself,

I hope I can say that without you getting steamed, anyway, you have to be particular, you got good bait and you have to keep the scrub fish away."

"That's kind of gross."

"It's something my dad used to say. He was a character, my old dad was. Anyway, you have to be careful who you let get in close to you. Because every man who sees you wants to."

"Everybody has boundaries," Grace said after a moment. She couldn't tell if he was trying to run some kind of scam, talk her into something. She wasn't used to thinking of herself as all that pretty. Certainly not as irresistible. "Thank you for taking such an interest in my welfare."

"You are welcome. You going to finish that sandwich before you run away again?"

"It's a twenty-minute break. I told you." She wrapped the rest of the sandwich in a napkin. "I'll save it for later. Thank you for lunch."

Les picked up her fork and put a peach slice on it. "One more bite. Open up."

She opened her mouth and he put the peach up to her lips. It felt weird and unwholesome to be fed in this way, and she swallowed it down quickly. Then she stood. "All right, back to work. Thanks again."

"Maybe next time I see you, we can talk a little more. Now you know I don't bite."

"OK," Grace said, just to get away. *Oddball,* she thought.

Her brother called, all upset and aggrieved at their father, who had done and said more awful things. "Why do you even go over there?" Grace asked him. "Or don't go over when you know he's going to be home or don't go over when you know he's going to be drinking. Have some sense about it." In the background she heard music playing, some churning, dark track she recognized from the show she'd gone to. His band had booked some other shows since, and Michael was happy about that.

"All my stuff is still there. I can't always wait for him to clear out if I need something. Have you talked to him lately? He's all worked up about Grandma's house not being sold yet, he wants to change realtors again."

"It has taken a while." The sign out front now said New Price. Meaning it had been lowered once more. It was said to be a difficult market.

"So I was thinking, what if I moved in there?"

"At Grandma's? No, come on."

"Seriously. They show houses all the time with people living in them. I'd keep the place clean, it's not like I'd be having big parties or anything. It's not like we'd have band practice there."

As soon as he said this, Grace had the inevitable image of parties, big parties, going on at the old house, cars parked up and down the brick streets, a bra draped over the realtor's sign, the band playing in the living room, colored lights, pissed-off neighbors. Cops at the door. "I don't think that's a great idea."

"Why not? It's just sitting there empty. It's not like I need the whole house, just one of the bedrooms."

"What's the matter with Jonesy's?" Jonesy was the friend he'd been staying with.

"Ah, his girlfriend's over there a lot now."

It wasn't hard for Grace to imagine all the ways that might cause problems. She said, "Have you asked Dad about the house?"

"I was hoping you could."

"He's not going to listen to me."

"Like he ever listens to me? Just give it a shot, please?" He had to raise his voice over the music, an erupting volcano of noise. "Tell him it's either that, or I might have to move back in with him. Ha."

"All right, I'll talk to him, but don't get your hopes up. Try to come up with some other idea." They said good-bye and Grace let her shell-shocked ears adjust back to a normal decibel range. She was just as glad her own apartment was too small for Michael to move in with her. She wondered if he was doing anything stupid with drugs, but there was no way to bring it up without going into nagging mode.

As soon as she agreed to talk to their father, she was sorry she'd done so. He was never going to give Michael permission to camp out at the empty house. It would only annoy him to be asked, and would probably make him associate Michael, irrationally, with the unsold real estate, and add another layer of grudge. So when she called her father, she said, "Michael needs money so he can get his own apartment."

"He put you up to this, didn't he."

"No," Grace said truthfully. "But I was thinking about what would be best for him."

"What would be best for your brother is if he quit hiding behind women and fought his own fights."

"Dad."

"First your mother and now you."

"Come on," Grace said, but even as she denied it, the idea found a home in her. Was that what Michael did? Was she expected to be someone's mommy now, God forbid? "Well, the two of you never listen to each other, you just start in hollering, so that's why I'm the one talking to you, and I wish you'd help him get his own place. He can't stay where he is and he's afraid you don't want him back home."

"Huh." If she was hoping her father was going to deny this, he didn't.

"Dad? Why is it so hard for you and him to get along? Help me understand."

A silence while her father did something away from the phone. Put something down, picked something up. Not a drink, at least she hoped not, since it was nine thirty on a Saturday morning. Or say it was a drink, say that things had unraveled that much for him since her mother died. Say she was a bad, neglectful daughter, who turned her back on her needy, messed-up, difficult father. She waited until he came back to the phone.

"Your mother said I didn't like to see him having fun, screwing around, when I was always working."

"Oh." Grace considered this. She doubted if her mother had used the words "screwing around." "He works hard at his music. You don't give him enough credit."

"And then his little druggie trip," her father went on, either not hearing her feeble defense or dismissing it. "Yeah, he had his fun. It cost everybody else big-time, but who cares?"

"It was a mistake. It's a disease. Addiction. It happens to people." Like alcoholism, she could have said, but she knew her father, like most drunks, did not consider himself to be an alcoholic. A magical sifting of fairy dust descended and addled their vision.

"Drugs happen to people who play around and don't take anything seriously."

She didn't say anything. She was tired of the clucking and fussing and ritual denials that were her part of the conversation.

"I'm sorry, Gracie, I know how I sound. Killjoy Dad. But I work hard, I always have, and it's not just the work, it's the stress and worry that go along with it. And then here's your brother, who wants to live like a, what do they call it, a flower that doesn't want to get a job. Like in the Bible."

"A lily of the field that toils not, and neither does it spin." Maybe he was drinking. A small, unwelcome alarm went off in her head. "OK, but the point of that verse is not to worry so much about material things. The Lord will provide, it's saying."

"Yeah, well, I have some utility bills that could use a little providing for."

"Oh you're hopeless." She didn't want to explore the depressing idea that her own lack of a high-paying, hard-charging career was of no real consequence because she was female. Only a son was invested with the full burden of her father's expectations. "Would you please think about helping him? And maybe not looking down on him for playing music?" She considered bringing up Bruce Springsteen. Her father was a fan of Springsteen. She decided this would be unhelpful.

"Better he should think about getting a real job so he can pay his own freight." There was a category of jobs that her father thought of as "real." It excluded all jobs of the sort that Michael was able to acquire.

"All right," Grace said. "Maybe you're right, maybe he needs to up his game." It was weak of her, she knew, to give in, agree with him, and what did she mean anyway, up his game? What sort of high-paying job was her druggie musician brother likely to stumble into? "But is it all right if he moves back home? Can you make an effort to get along, or at least leave each other alone?"

"As long as he shows some respect and stays out of my way."

"I wish you could—"

"What?"

"Nothing. Just, I wish you could see him for who he is, not what he does."

"You're a good girl. Yes you are."

"I don't think so, Dad. I'm not very . . . warmhearted."

"Warmhearted gives me a pain."

And didn't that all sound like a wholesome emotional climate. But it seemed like the best any of them could do, at least for now. Michael moved back into the house and he and their father seemed to come to some grumpy agreement about sharing space, or at least ignoring each other. Life seemed to be settling down, settling into place. The yoga institute brought in a visiting yogi who taught master classes and got Grace excited about her practice in a way that energized her. She made plans to go to a conference in Chicago later in the fall. She went out with a few friends in the evenings. She priced plane fares for a trip out west, to places she'd never been: Portland, Seattle, San Francisco, though checking fares was as far as she was going to get for now.

She talked with her uncle Mark about how they might set up a memorial for her mother, a garden, she had decided. She approached the park district about it. Michael thought the idea was "OK," though he had no special enthusiasm for gardens. She was still waiting for the right time to talk about it with her father. He did not speak of Grace's mother except in passing, or perhaps in drinking. That was when Grace might get a late-evening phone call. Her mother had been one hell of a woman. He wanted Grace to know that. He wanted everyone to know that. He dared anyone to say a word against her. Not that anyone was, to Grace's knowledge. Her father and her brother kept their griefs separate and took no comfort from each other. That was sad. That was her family.

Les Moore came around the store often enough that her co-workers teased Grace about having a new boyfriend. Now that she was more used to him he didn't seem so strange, only entertaining, in a goofy way. He was different from anyone she knew, but she had to remind herself there were more people like Les in the world than people like herself. People who didn't have much of an education and who didn't worry about it, people who worked for a paycheck instead of some windy, aspirational sense of personal fulfillment. Les worked second shift, three to eleven. No one else she knew worked that late into the night. She felt sheltered and naive and more than a little spoiled.

There were people who didn't know or care what yoga was.

Grace tried to explain it to Les, that it was a set of spiritual and physical practices that emphasized harmony and consciousness. Balance, in every sense of the word. Les said it sounded a lot like yin and yang, and Grace said it might. She was a little tired of hearing about yin and yang.

"I do push-ups," Les offered. "I do curls with ten-pound weights. See?" He pushed his shirt sleeve up and flexed his biceps. She never knew what you were supposed to say when men did this. His arm was thin and hard, and the muscles looked as if pieces of broken crockery had been piled up and shoved beneath his skin.

"Yoga is good for flexibility," said Grace, a little primly.

"Flexibility, I like that in a woman." He grinned, showing his big teeth. He often said things like that, flirtatious and sexual, which Grace tolerated because he was so outrageous, so unattractive, that it was comical. What was it with gray ponytails, why did anyone think that was a good look? He talked as if he'd had a lot of women, and maybe he had. Or maybe it was just bullshit. She was never sure with him.

He'd grown up here in town, but in a part she'd never had much to do with, the middle-aged subdivisions of small houses and duplexes built on slabs, the kind of places that must have looked rundown almost as soon as they were built. The streets were named Ivanhoe or Carriage Way or Essex Lane, like bad jokes meant to distract you from the shabbiness. His father had been a truck driver, an owner operator, who had up and died from meanness almost twenty years ago. That's what it was, though the death certificate said heart attack. His mom was gone as well, she'd had female cancer. He guessed he wasn't going to live all that long himself. It was just the breaks. Grace told him about her mother dying. Les said he knew how that one felt, he'd been down that road already and it was a tough one.

They didn't know any of the same people. He'd gone to a different high school than Grace, and anyway he was almost fifteen years older than she was and they hardly ran in the same crowd. He and his friends spent their free time in driveways or garages, drinking beer and working, or not working, on projects like re-painting boats or building cabinetry. Their cars had bumper stickers about guns (for) and taxes (against). Their kids rode ATVs and did unsafe stunts on backyard trampolines. Yes, she looked down on such things and yes, she was a hideous snob. Les didn't have any kids, well, he did and he didn't. He'd been married once. Or twice, but only one of them was legal. Both times to crazy women. He had one kid, a boy, but Les hadn't seen him since he was a baby, his mother had made sure of that. Her whole family was crazy. Her old man got a sheriff's star from a pawnshop and drove around the county pulling people over and pretending he was the law. Her brother liked to race as fast as he could on the old slab roads, and then one day him and his girlfriend slid two hundred feet trying not to hit a train but they went underneath it and got their heads cut off.

"Stop," Grace ordered, waving her hands. "Why do you think I want to hear things like that?"

"Begging your pardon. I keep forgetting, you're kind of a sissy."

She had heard this before from him. She made a particular kind of face, meant to express forbearance.

"How about, you come home with me sometime?"

"No. What brought that on?"

"What, you think you're too good for me?"

"That's not it." That was exactly it.

"You need a real man."

"Thanks, I'll go find one."

"I will make you howl like a dog. Promise."

"Stop it." She tried to be angry but she was laughing, he was so ridiculous. Skinny and undersized and totally full of himself.

"Why not? You got something better to do?"

"Yes. Yoga."

"Well you can teach me some of the, what do you call them, poses. Then I can teach you some I know."

She shouldn't let him talk to her that way. It wasn't always funny, and he didn't always seem to be kidding. Grace didn't know why she went along with it. It was such a strange time in her life. She had lost a parent, but that happened to people all the time, and people moved forward with their lives, as she was doing. And if there was now a piece of her missing, how could you hope to see the shape of something that was not there? And how was this empty place filled by allowing a goofy-looking guy, a goofy-look-ing *old* guy, to talk dirty to her? "Life is strange," she took to telling people, and they agreed with her, though they had to be thinking about their own kinds of strangeness.

She told Les about her father and her brother not getting along. She had already told everyone else she knew. They'd said, Oh man, that really sucks. Les said he'd been on one side of that fight, the son side, and it was just something guys did, a power struggle thing. "It's completely stupid," Grace said. "My dad won't cut him any slack, and my brother eggs him on by acting like a punk."

"It's biology. The young buck and the old buck smash into each other with their antlers to see who's boss. The winner gets the fe-males."

"That's stupid too."

"It's the way nature intended. See, men—"

"And gross," Grace said, before he could start talking about yin and yang again. "Women don't want to be fought over."

"If you say so."

"Not fought over so they get carried off to be part of some harem, come on."

"The man always makes the moves. That's what I'm saying."

"Oh give me a break." He had a lot of such notions on human affairs that she disagreed with, although she didn't always do a good job of arguing against them. The weather was colder now and they were back in the community room. Grace wore a heavy sweater and jeans, but Les still wore T-shirts, or today, an open-necked knit shirt that showed a patch of chest hair and some kind of gold charm on a chain.

He saw her looking at it. "Go ahead, here." He leaned forward and she took the charm between her fingertips, feeling self-conscious. The charm was a small twist of gold, like a teardrop bent around itself. "You like it? I got it off a guy at the plant in a pinochle game. He threw in a couple of squaws to go along with it."

"Don't say squaws, it's racially insensitive." She let the charm fall back.

"Lighten up. I said it to bug you. I wouldn't have, if there was any squaws around."

Grace ignored that one. There were times he tried to be funny and missed by a mile.

"Hey, don't be mad. Why're you always getting mad at me? You know something I regret about not growing up with my boy? Well there's lots of things. I could have been the exception to the rule. The kind of dad who doesn't beat the crap out of his son. Like I got beat."

Grace murmured that she was sorry, and she was. There were times she needed to be taken out of her own boo-hoo problems and realize that other people had it rough too.

After that she had a dream that she touched his chest right where the gold charm hung and put her hand on the springy, gray-dark hair beneath it. Cool it, she told herself soberly when she woke. Down, girl. She must have been lonelier than she thought. She needed to get out more, make herself take up the misery that was dating again.

Ten days before Thanksgiving, Grace's father called the police and said that his son was assaulting him. Two squad cars came and spent some time in the driveway, their red-blue lights whirling, then left without taking anyone into custody. Grace did not witness this; she first heard about it from a neighbor who called her, pretending solicitousness, but who was avid for details. "Everything's fine," Grace said, trying to get off the phone. "Just a misunderstanding. Thanks for your concern." Nosy old bitch hag. But were either her father or brother going to tell her?

She called her brother, who said, unconvincingly, that he'd been about to call her himself. "It was one of those idiotic Dad things, where he gets in your face and starts screaming and spitting."

"About what?"

"The usual. How I'm doing everything wrong."

"Did you hit him?"

"Excuse me, you mean, did I assault him? Hell yes. He was shoving me and I shoved back. He lost his balance because he was shit-faced, and wound up on the floor, that's all. Am I sorry? No."

"What else happened, did either of you get hurt?"

"No, I only—"

"What did you do to him?"

"Jesus, nothing. He kept trying to get up and I had to—"

"What?"

"I had to kick him back down so he wouldn't come at me again."

Grace let this settle for a minute. Then she said, "What did the police tell you?"

"They said we should give each other some time to cool off and they gave me a ride to Jonesy's, I'm staying over there again for a while."

"All right. But how did the whole thing start?"

"He said Mom would be ashamed of me."

"Shit. I'm sorry."

"It's a fucked-up situation."

Her father didn't want to talk about it when she called. Grace thought that meant he'd probably gotten the worst of the fight. Neither of them were the fighting type, she would have said, at least they hadn't been. They weren't the kind of guys who went around flexing their biceps. Now here they were, going at it like two small, vicious animals, was it minks or voles who were supposed to be so bloodthirsty? It was a fucked-up situation.

Her father said, "If I have to get a restraining order, I will."

"Come on, Dad."

"He's a drug user. That's documented. And now the police have been involved."

"All right, you're mad, I get it. But don't turn it into a war. How is this supposed to end up, are you going to fight with each other forever? You're both acting like ten-year-olds. Are you going to put a sign on the front door, Secret Clubhouse?"

Her father was not in the mood to be coaxed or teased. "I have applied for a firearms permit. I think you ought to know that things have gotten to that point."

"You can't be serious." Exasperated. He carried everything too far.

Her father said nothing, meaning that he was being serious. She felt her own helplessness and failure. He carried things too far and she couldn't drag him back from the brink. Only her mother had been able to do that. She said, "You're scaring me. Is that what you want? Scare me and Michael so you don't ever see us again?"

"I only said I got a permit," her father said, sounding sulky now. "Don't make it some big deal. I have some safety concerns. Your brother tried to extort money from me."

"Extort."

"He wanted money."

This hardly came as a surprise, although Michael had not mentioned it. "Is that what started everything?"

"He's a legal adult. I'm not obligated to provide for him. I'm certainly not obligated to pay for his drugs."

Grace gave up on him. The two of them could carry on all they wanted and leave her out of it. Easy enough to say. You could announce yourself emancipated from your family and its wars and scars, but you weren't, not really. She was right in the stupid middle of everything. The gun talk was stupid. Her father disapproved of guns. He'd said so often enough. He was being a jerk. They both were. She wasn't going to take up her mother's anxious work of trying to smooth things over. If she had to live with the guilt of that, so be it.

Then a week later their father announced that he wanted them both, Grace and Michael, to come over for Thanksgiving dinner. This was unexpected. He said that he had been thinking about it and it was what their mother would have wanted. How could they say no? Although they considered it.

"I don't trust him," Michael told Grace. "He's got some notion in his head about getting back at me."

"Like what, poisoning the mashed potatoes? Come on, maybe he's sorry and this is the only way he can bring himself to say so. Were you planning on doing anything else? Maybe he doesn't want to try and get through the holidays alone."

"Alone doesn't sound so bad to me."

But they agreed to go. Their father said he would cook the turkey and dressing and gravy and all that. He would prepare a vegetarian stuffed-squash dish for Grace. He would supply the apple and pumpkin pies they always had, though he would not promise to bake them himself. They could bring things if they wanted. Appetizers. Beverages. "No alcohol," their father announced, which was every bit as surprising as the invitation itself. "Nobody needs it, right?"

Grace imagined he meant Michael. She had the uncharitable suspicion that her father would engage in what the literature of alcoholism called predrinking, that is, getting himself liquored up before the guests arrived for the sober feast.

Nevertheless, she went shopping for nonalcoholic beer and wine and some fancy bottled soft drinks, Green River and Sarsaparilla and cream soda, things that nobody would really want to drink, but that could be the subject of harmless conversation. NuGrape, strawberry soda. One of the other groceries in town stocked such things. She filled a cardboard holder with them. One more, Orange Crush.

"You really drink that stuff?"

It was Les Moore, grinning at her. He had his own six-pack under his arm, Budweiser Light. Grace was unaccustomed to seeing him anywhere other than the health food store, and for a moment she gawked at him. "Oh, hey. They're for Thanksgiving dinner. But I'm not going to drink them. I don't think anybody is. Never mind. It was just this idea I had."

"Sure," Les said, nodding with elaborate encouragement. "Great idea. Awesome. What's the main course, hot dogs and chips?"

She was so used to regarding him from her position of enlightened understanding, tolerating his amusing peculiarities. And here she was, dithering over peculiar soda products while he looked on with raised eyebrows. A solid citizen, a respectable working man who knew what people drank and what they did not. Or perhaps she had just grown so used to him that she experienced one of those shifts of perception, where the idea of him became more plausible. She set the carton of sodas in her shopping cart. She said, "What are you doing for Thanksgiving?"

When Grace told her father and brother she would be bringing a guest for dinner, of course they thought, boyfriend. She found ways to tell them that this was not the case. He was just a friend who didn't have anywhere else to eat the holiday meal. She knew him from the store. That made it sound as if they worked together, which was good enough for now.

She explained things to Les this way: "We'll all behave better if somebody else is there, somebody who isn't family. And it'll be more festive, you know, having a guest."

"I don't think anybody's ever before told me I was festive." Les was getting a kick out of the whole thing. He wanted to know if he should dress up.

"No," Grace said. "Nobody else will. But I'd love to see your dress-up wardrobe."

"I'd rather show you my undressed wardrobe."

Grace ignored this. She told him about the nonalcohol pact and Les said he was cool with that, he could drink anytime.

What was he going to wear, anyway? And what were they all going to talk about, what kind of intersection was there between forklifts, computers, and indie music? She asked him if he wasn't turning down some other invitation, one he'd enjoy. She was beginning to have second thoughts.

"Who says I'm not going to enjoy this? A real old-fashioned family Thanksgiving."

Grace felt a headache coming on, pushing its way behind her eyes. "We're not exactly a real old-fashioned type of family."

"You want to know something, cutie? Nobody's really is. Not nobody's."

Grace said she would pick him up at noon on Thanksgiving, then they would swing over to give Michael a ride. Les lived in an apartment building not that far from the health food store, an ordinary brick cube with narrow, utilitarian windows. She pulled up to the front door and waited, and a few minutes later, Les emerged, a skinny figure walking with his usual jauntiness, and came around to the passenger side.

"Don't you want to come up?" he asked, leaning in the open window.

"I don't think so."

"You're no fun."

"Why thank you."

He was carrying one of those cellophane-wrapped fruit baskets the groceries sold. This one had a whole pineapple, some oranges, an apple, and a stiff red bow on the handle. "Hostess gift," he said, hoisting it. "Well, host." He was wearing a clean pair of blue jeans and a shirt with a collar. Also a coat she hadn't seen before, a black wool peacoat with an elderly look. His hair in the ponytail still showed damp comb tracks. There was a whiff of aftershave.

He saw her examining him. "What, I don't look good enough for you?"

"You look very nice." The effort he'd made seemed both endearing and misplaced to her, like the generic fruit basket. "Thanks for coming."

"I don't guess I can smoke there, huh. I'll just go outside."

Michael shook hands with Les once he was settled in the backseat, then occupied himself with staring out the window. At least he didn't seem to find Les especially odd or remarkable, but maybe he was preoccupied with his own problems, and the coming trial by holiday with their father. The two of them had not seen each other since the police call. Grace eyed Michael in the rearview mirror. Nothing visibly worrisome, certainly not the weight loss or twitchiness she remembered from the worst of his worst days. Instead he was glum and quiet. He was there under protest.

"I brought some stuff to drink," Grace said, attempting small talk. "I got some Sierra Mist, you like that, don't you?"

"Sure."

"I mean, what kind of carbonated beverage goes with turkey? There must be guidelines. You like white meat, right? We're definitely talking lemon-lime."

Silence. Grace looked over at Les: *What did I tell you about them?* Les shrugged and turned on the radio. He punched the buttons and fiddled with the dial until he found the classic rock station. The Allman Brothers were playing "Sweet Melissa." Les sat back and sang along under his breath in a wheezy voice.

Michael stirred. "Could we maybe—"

Grace gave him a savage look in the mirror. Les half turned toward the backseat, waiting. "Nothing," Michael said. Les turned around again. Grace sent another meaning glance behind her, willing her brother to behave. She knew that among the many things he was particular about in music were his dislike of southern rock bands and of people who sang along to the radio. Here she'd thought it was only her father who was going to be a problem.

They reached the house. Her father's house, although Grace still thought of it as her parents'. She watched Les take it in and decide to remain visibly unimpressed. And really, it wasn't any grand or extravagant piece of real estate. She'd grown up there but it had not been built to inspire sentimental attachments. It was enough like all the other houses in the neighborhood to seem entirely unimaginative, a house that had always been at war with the imagination and determined to impose its functionality on those who lived there, to impress them with its hierarchies of closets and bathrooms. Nevertheless, she saw Les appraise it and she could see, as clearly as if it were written on a screen, his thought: *And these people think they have problems?*

Grace opened the trunk and took out the tray of stuffed mushrooms she'd fixed that morning. Les carried his fruit basket and one of the bags of drinks, and after she called it to his attention, Michael took the other one. They walked up the driveway to the side door. "Hello," Grace called, stepping inside. The kitchen had a good smell, a good Thanksgiving smell, of onion and sage and celery. The oven was on and throwing waves of heat. "Dad?"

They crowded into the kitchen and put down the things they carried. "Dad?" Grace went further into the house, calling him. The dining room table was set with the harvest-themed plates that her mother had used for Thanksgiving, along with some fancy cut glass serving dishes that had also been part of the holiday. But the place where her mother had sat was left empty. This sight stopped her cold. She could not have said what she was feeling, except that it sent her stomach into a slow, slow revolving orbit, like certain restaurants on top of skyscrapers. She went into the den and then called him at the foot of the stairs and finally went up to look for him.

He wasn't anywhere. It looked as if he was still sleeping in the guest room. The bed was made up and one of his shirts lay across it. His plaid bathrobe was on a hook behind the door.

Grace went back downstairs. Her brother and Les had come out of the kitchen and were standing in the living room, still wearing their coats. "I don't know where he is," Grace said. She wondered if they should check unlikely places, like the basement.

"His car's gone," Michael pointed out. "Maybe he had to go out for something."

"Yeah, maybe." Grace looked at Michael, a question, and he stared back. Who cared where their father had gone? his look said. Les seemed as if he was trying to stay within sight of the front door, in case he had to make a quick exit. Grace went back into the kitchen. She opened the oven. It was filled by a roasting pan and a still-pale turkey, doing its best to cook.

Investigating further, she saw other evidence of meal planning. A gravy boat, next to a jar of premade gravy. A foil pan of dinner rolls. In the refrigerator, some quivering cranberry sauce in a dish. She missed all the other things they were accustomed to eat at Thanksgiving. Deviled eggs, celery sticks. Different kinds of potatoes. Last year, her mother had been well enough to do the cooking. This year's meal was already threatening to go off track.

"I'm going to call him," Grace said to the others, getting out her phone. Les and Michael were in the den by now, watching a football game. Making the best of things. They kept their eyes on the television as she dialed.

She was surprised when he answered. Her father didn't much like cell phones and often enough turned his off or left it at home "Hello, Dad? Where are you, we're all here at the house."

"Ah, I forgot the ice cream. For the pie. I forgot the pies too."

"All right, no problem. Where are you now?"

"Some store that has a bakery. I just wound up here. I should've planned ahead more."

"Looks like. How about you get those pies and come on home. How about I get started on the rest of the food."

"That would be great," her father said expansively. "You know what to do. It's Thanksgiving. We need all kinds of goodies."

"Good-bye," Grace said, ending the call before he could say any more. "He went to the grocery," she told her brother and Les. "Dinner's going to be a while. If you're hungry, there's things like chips."

Neither of them made any response to this, as if watching football was a task requiring skill and concentration. Grace returned to the kitchen and rummaged around. There were potatoes. An entire acorn squash, perhaps meant for her own dinner. A head of lettuce. She put half a dozen eggs in a pot, ran water, and set them to boil.

Les came in, holding up his pack of Marlboros. "Smoke break."

Grace watched him through the kitchen window, exhaling

smoke. She'd told him that her mother had died of lung cancer and he'd said that he was hoping the heart attack got him first. When he came back inside he said, "So where's your dad?"

"If I had to guess? Drinking in the parking lot of the Safeway."

"This is a weird-ass type of situation."

"You think? Here." She handed him a potato peeler and pointed at the bin she'd set on the counter. "I figured this would be messed up or bad. I just didn't know exactly how."

He came up behind her, put a hand beneath her elbow, and tried to turn her toward him. "Don't," Grace said.

"Just trying to offer, you know, aid and comfort."

"Then peel some potatoes." She moved away from his hand. It was setting off unwelcome sensations in her skin, which felt, absurdly, like popcorn popping.

"Want the fruit basket? Would that cheer you up at all?"

Her father arrived an hour later, in too good a mood and with an apple pie in a foil pie pan. "Would you believe, I went all over town, and this is the best I could do." He held out the pie, as if willing it to testify for him. The pie was undersized, with a crumb topping. It looked slightly shopworn, as if it had been passed over for a day or two, or perhaps someone had briefly sat on it.

"It's OK, Dad. We got it under control. This is my friend Les."

Her father and Les shook hands. She saw her father register Les's cheap rings and ponytail. Her father must have forgotten that she was bringing a guest, although the table was set with four places. Her father nodded and his face assumed an all-purpose, serious expression. Les said, "Hey, thanks for having me," and her father said sure, sure. He looked suspiciously at Grace.

"Dad? When did you put the turkey in the oven? Do you remember?"

"You don't even eat turkey." A chemical smell wafted from him. Scotch, Grace figured. Why couldn't he just drink at home?

"Is it the kind where the thermometer pops out? Never mind. Do you want to go watch the football game? I don't know who's playing."

"Kentucky and Louisville," Les said. "That's the one we've got going."

"Yeah, OK. Give me a minute." Her father planted himself in the center of the room, waiting. Les tilted his head at Grace and raised his eyebrows, as in, What the hell. He stayed in the doorway until Grace nodded: *It's all right, I can handle him.* Then he walked out. Grace heard the television in the distance, the bright noise of a commercial.

"Where did you get that character?"

"He's a friend. I told you."

"He's too . . ." Her father appeared to be struggling with exactly what was objectionable about Les. ". . . old for you," he managed.

"He's a friend and anyway it's none of your business."

"Baby girl," her father said, opening his arms as if to embrace her. He was both earnest and ridiculous, red-faced, his mouth hanging open. Grace dodged him. "Baby girl, there's so much in life that you don't understand. A guy like that—"

"Like what?"

"Did he even go to college?"

Grace moved to put the kitchen table between them. "Go on," she said. "Leave me alone, you're drunk. No, he did not go to college and since when do you care what I do or who I do it with? Since when did you even notice?" She was furious with him for insisting on this fiasco of a dinner and then screwing it up. She opened a cupboard, took out a bag of potato chips, and shook them into a bowl. "Here, take these out to the den. Les is a guest and I expect you to have some manners. Go on, get out."

"If your mother was here, she'd be very concerned."

"Leave."

"I bet she'd have dinner on the table by now."

"Get," Grace said, pointing. To her surprise, he left the room without saying anything more, though he gave her a bitter look.

She put on her mother's striped apron, hoping it might convey some of her mother's domestic expertise. In a funny way it did, or else it was just her mother's kitchen, the long habit of being in her mother's kitchen. It would always be her mother's, with its pretty dishes and the stoneware canisters that had been there as long as Grace could remember.

The room calmed her and allowed her to move from task to task. She quartered the acorn squash and set it to bake. She found the dish in which her mother had served pickles and olives, she even found pickles and olives. She peeled the eggs, riced the yolks, and dressed them with mayonnaise, mustard, and paprika. She washed the lettuce and made salad dressing. The turkey was doing its thing. She'd forgotten, all you had to do was let it roast long enough. The hard part was the physics of it, hoisting it up and getting it to come apart into serving portions.

She put the stuffed mushrooms under the broiler and took them out to the den, where the three men were watching the football game in silence. She couldn't tell if that was because they were comfortably engrossed in the game, or because they were sunk in silent loathing. At least her father and brother weren't slugging each other. "Who's winning?" Grace asked.

After a moment, her brother said, "Kentucky."

"Go team," Grace said, hoping to sound ironic, or sprightly, or something, and when no one said anything else, she went back to the kitchen.

Her brother followed her a minute later. "How about I help?"

"Maybe later, thanks. What, you're not having fun in there?"

"I keep waiting for Dad to light into me."

"He's ignoring you. Be thankful. You know what would really

help? Go back in there and keep him from picking a fight with Les. Or Les from spouting off."

"He's kind of weird, that guy."

"Then he'll fit right in. Go."

Grace didn't believe in ghosts or spirits, at least she didn't think she did. But it was hard not to think of her mother as she moved from the sink to the oven and back again, tasting and chopping and doing her best impersonation of her mother. She felt, not a presence, exactly. Something more earthbound, a better understanding, perhaps, of her mother and the life she had lived. The endless small chores, the worries, never enough time, and always the barely movable obstacles of her husband and children.

Grace knew how difficult she herself had been, how impatient and judgmental, how often she had turned tail and run the other way when she might have stayed. Her father and her brother had been worse only because they were louder, as well as more insistent and destructive.

Although perhaps as her mother's daughter, she had been the bigger disappointment.

Her mother's illness and death had brought them together, if only for a time. Had made the three of them better. Her mother's last, ultimate sacrifice.

"Stop," Grace said out loud. It made her unhappy to be thinking such things.

The little red nipple of the turkey thermometer popped out, and Grace called into the den for someone to help. After a minute, Michael appeared. "Yeah?"

"Can you lift the roaster out of the oven and onto the counter?"

He did so, awkwardly. The roaster spit grease and it was hard to maneuver the pan without getting burned. The bird had browned and with the built-in thermometer, Grace was pretty sure it was cooked through as it was supposed to be. She was a little nervous.

She'd never been in charge of a Thanksgiving turkey before, plus she was squeamish about all things carnivorous. "Can you lift the turkey onto the cutting board? Here, use these string things."

"Now what," Michael said, straightening up.

"It has to cool off for a while before we carve it." She remembered that much. She poked at the thing. It looked distressingly dead, or rather, too much like it was recently walking around on these fat, glistening drumsticks. It appeared to be full of stuffing, which she'd have to extract somehow. "How's it going in the den?"

"I guess Dad doesn't like your friend much."

"Why, what is he doing?"

"Just kind of making faces."

"Fine, he can do that. Help me with the food, let's get this over with."

The potatoes needed to be brought to a boil, the dinner rolls heated through. She dressed the salad and put it onto plates, which Michael carried out. Grace scooped the stuffing out of the turkey, put it in a casserole dish, and set it in the oven to keep warm. She didn't trust the supermarket gravy but used some of the pan drippings to give it a boost. Michael said he didn't know how to carve. Grace imagined going into the den and asking either her father or Les to do it. She was pretty sure it was a chore right up Les's alley, but her father would probably insist on doing it, and waving the knife around and doing some sort of damage.

In the end Grace overcame her distaste and carved the bird herself. The white meat wasn't that hard, but she struggled to joint the thighs and drumsticks, as if performing some hideous surgery. Finally she sent Michael into the den to tell the others that dinner was ready.

Les ducked out the kitchen door for another smoke break. He was being uncharacteristically quiet, which didn't seem like a good sign, but she couldn't worry about him right now. She'd filled glasses with ice water, and brought out the peculiar soda pop, but her father went to the pantry and came out with two bottles of red wine, which he uncorked. Grace said, "I thought we weren't going to . . . Never mind."

Les came back inside. They took their seats. Her mother's empty place and empty chair gave the table an unbalanced look and crowded the rest of them in together. Her father and Les were drinking the wine. Grace settled for water, and she was glad to see that Michael was also. Her brother's expression was closed off and grim, the silent version of I told you so. She didn't want to think what her own face looked like. Her father hitched his chair closer. "This all looks great, Gracie." He raised his glass. "Here's to the cook."

The others did the same, in an embarrassed, halfhearted way. Grace acknowledged them, attempting a proper irony. "And," her father went on, "to your mother, who . . ." He waved his free hand at the expanse of empty table that had been her mother's place. "Ah, God. There's some things, they're tough."

"Let's just eat, Dad," Grace said.

"Yes," her father said, recovering himself, speaking briskly. "Let's everybody dig in. Because life goes idiotically on."

No one said anything. Grace knew that her father was unhappy, that was genuine enough, but why did he have to be so histrionic and messy about it? Why did he act like he was the only one who missed her mother? Les, sitting next to her, was careful not to meet Grace's eye. She had the sense he was practicing the kind of manners that meant not saying anything. Then her father roused himself once more. "Everything looks great," he said again. "Let's eat."

They filled their plates. It always took a long time to do this at Thanksgiving, and even today, with the food being pulled together at the last minute, there was a lot of it to pass around and load up. Then there would be an interval of eating, always disappointingly brief, given the preparation time. Then plates passed around for second helpings. Then Grace supposed she'd have to at least get the cleanup under way. Then they could go home.

Her father put his fork down, taking a rest. "Did you guys like the stuffing? You didn't say."

Grace said, "It's good, Dad." Michael also said it was good. Les kept on eating. He gauged, correctly, that his opinion was not required.

"I was trying to remember how your mother fixed it. I thought she put apple in it, so that's what I did."

"Yeah, you got it. It's a lot like hers."

"She wasn't the fanciest cook, but everything she made always tasted just right."

No one answered, or rather, no one carried the thought forward. Her father drank some of his wine. If he'd begun on the bright, hectic edge of drunkenness, and then had passed into melancholy, now he had slowed down and considered everything with weighty attention. He noticed Les, who was doing his best not to be noticed, working away at his plate with his head down. "You getting enough to eat?"

"Yes, sir. My compliments to the chef." Les turned and gave Grace a smile that he managed to make look suggestive, as if the two of them spent their time feeding each other pomegranate seeds in bed.

This too had the effect of halting conversation. Grace felt her insides coiling and tightening. She said, "Les comes into the store for lunch sometimes."

"Huh," Grace's father said. "You a health food guy?"

"Absolutely. Can't get enough of it."

"Huh," her father said again. He turned to Grace with another of his dark, suspicious glances. "You're not all of a sudden selling burgers and fries over there, are you? Some kind of fried healthy stuff?"

She let that pass and bent her head over her food again. They would eat all the food, and then the meal, and the day, would come to an end. "Michael," her father said. *Leave him alone,* Grace prayed, but it was no use. "Tell me something about your music. What you're doing nowadays."

"I don't talk about it, I play it."

"What, you took some vow of silence? I want to know. Help me understand what it is you play. It's not jazz. It's not classical. Not that old-time rock and roll." Her father held up a hand and counted off on his fingers. "Not the blues. Not rap."

"It has influences of rap and blues," Michael said. He gave Grace a glance that indicated how patient and tolerant he was being in the face of their father's bullheaded questions. "It's like the product of everything you've heard and take in, then you try to make it into something new and original."

That seemed to Grace to be a sound and appropriate answer, under the circumstances, Art for the Simple-Minded, maybe, but their father started over, wiggling his fingers. "It's not country and western. Not folk music. Not, what else is there."

Les said, "You know who was a really great band? Black Sabbath."

"I guess I don't know them very well," Grace said.

Her father said, "I like a song you can sing along to. One with real words."

"I saw one of their concerts out in Denver. It kicked ass." Les was getting over his unnatural silence. Maybe it was the wine.

Michael said, "How about I write a song about you, Dad? With real words and everything."

"No. I don't think I'd like that."

"I'm all kinds of inspired."

"I said, Don't."

"It could be this great song. We'd play it everywhere and you couldn't stop us."

"The hell you will."

"Like Neil Young, 'old man take a look at my life.' I just have to find something that rhymes with 'bullshit.'" Michael grinned and mugged, playing air guitar.

"You do that and I will beat your punk ass."

"Neil Young is a righteous dude," Les said reflectively.

"Oh, big talker. Who was the one who ended up on the floor?"

"Stop it," Grace said. "Just stop it. Both of you, what are you fighting about? A song nobody wrote yet?"

"You heard him. He's going to beat my punk ass."

"I'll do more than that, sport. Don't push your luck."

"Big talker," Michael said again. "But I'm the one who can sing."

"Are you both crazy?" Grace demanded. "Am I related to crazy people?"

They subsided then. Her father mumbled something. "Didn't quite catch that. Was that an apology?" Grace asked. Her father said that he guess he got carried away sometimes. Michael was even more reluctant, but he managed to come up with a sorry. "Thank you," Grace said. They exhausted her. There was something wrong with them. Something wrong with her whole family that could not be fixed, like original sin.

They finished the meal. No one wanted any apple pie. Grace let the others clear the table and set the dishes to soak. She was done with them and with trying to make them behave. Her father offered to give them some of the leftovers. No one wanted them either. It was early dark by now and Grace went out to the car and started it and turned the lights on, waiting for the others.

Michael and Les came out together and got in without speaking. They seemed to recognize the extent of her mood. Les turned the radio on, then off again. She drove to Michael's, or rather, to the house of the friend he was now staying with, having had to move on from the previous friend's. This friend's house was in the seedier part of campus, a district of houses allowed to run down until only students of the most careless sort would live in them, moving in and out every few months. A string of blue Christmas lights sagged across the front porch. One of the downstairs rooms showed lights behind the curtain, or rather, the piece of fabric stretched across the window. Grace wasn't sure who lived there. Somebody in the band, she thought. The place had the look of a musical crash pad. Michael opened the car door but didn't get out. "So, anyway . . ."

"I don't want to talk about it," Grace said, and Michael told Les it was good to meet him and Les said the same. Michael got out and they watched him go down the walk and up the front steps. The door opened and admitted him and then closed again.

"Are you mad at me too?" Les asked. They were circling back from the residential neighborhoods through campus itself, its streets quiet for the holiday and its enormous redbrick buildings vacant under the glare of anticrime lights. It looked like a civilization that had suffered some plague or other catastrophe, everything intact but abandoned.

"No, I'm not mad at you. I'm not related to you."

They left campus behind. Les's street was one of those the city had tried and failed to call Old Town. It had never caught on. It was a district of workingmen's cottages and newer, but still elderly, single-family homes, interrupted by the occasional apartment building, like Les's, where a developer had fought the zoning code and won. Grace parked the car at the curb, stopped the engine, and got out.

"You're coming in," Les observed, shutting the car door behind him.

She was. She followed him up to the front door and into a small lobby with a number of metal mailboxes on the wall. He worked the lock to an inner door and stood aside to let her enter. He said he lived on the second floor. They climbed a short flight of concrete stairs. Like all such buildings it had an industrial look to it, although that had to do with budget, not design. Les unlocked the apartment door, saying something about things being sort of a mess, he wasn't exactly an AI housekeeper.

"I don't care," Grace said, and she didn't. She waited for him to switch on the lights in the living room with its oversized television and shapeless upholstered couch. There was a small kitchen behind it. A weight bench was set up in one corner. The heavy denim jacket he usually wore was draped over a chair.

"Bathroom," Les said, walking down a small passage. He switched on another wall light. "Bedroom."

A queen bed took up most of the space. It was made up with a plaid cotton spread of the sort that people bought for young boys' rooms, that is, with nothing about it that could be accused of being too decorative or girly. Grace took off her coat and hung it on the doorknob. She sat down on the bed and bent to remove her boots and socks. She pulled her sweater overhead, unhooked her bra, and tossed them aside. Les said, "Whoa." She stood up enough to unzip her pants and pull them and her panties over her hips and kick her ankles free of them. You were supposed to ask about condoms at this point but she had reached the limits of her nerve, getting this far, and she didn't trust herself to speak.

Les was already out of his shirt and working at his belt buckle. His chest was narrow and unmuscular but deeply furred. "You want a drink or anything?" She shook her head. "Then move your ass over."

When he was out of his clothes he said, "So now you know what I look like and I know what you look like." Naked, he was even skinnier, all collarbones and knees and elbows. His penis looked small but it wasn't yet hard. Now he lowered himself onto her and rubbed himself against her.

When he tried to kiss her, she turned her head away. "No? How about here?"

He lowered his mouth to one breast and sucked at the nipple. When he drew away he said, approvingly, "Getting hard," and turned his attention to her other breast. With his head below hers she saw how thin the gray hair was, pulled tight over the bare scalp, and the very ugliness of the sight was part of what aroused her, along with the shock of what she was doing, the very last thing she would have expected of herself, which was probably why she wanted it.

His hand was between her legs and his fingers entered her, pushing hard, and she wanted that too, she wanted nothing gentle or skilled, just insistence and shame. When he lowered his head to use his mouth and tongue on her, she tried to push him away. It was too much, she was too self-conscious and it never worked, but he had her pinned down so there was no escaping, and then it did begin to work. Always before when she came it was a matter of focus and effort and a sense of pushing through a barrier. Now it was like something pulled out of her against her will.

"You make a lot of noise," he told her. "Who would have thought you're that kind. You need a rest? Then it's my turn."

How brief it was, this respite, and how quickly the rest of her life rushed back in to fill the blessed empty space she'd made with her body. She closed her eyes and felt him shifting his weight, changing position, and she readied herself for what would be required of her. Who would have thought she was this kind. But she had hardly escaped any part of her life at all, even for a moment. Because she would never manage to break free from her family or cast off its legacy of unhappy women.

VI. GRACE

The week before Christmas, Grace met her father for lunch at a franchise Italian restaurant, the kind of place that was one big commercial for itself. Lunch had been her idea, this particular restaurant her father's. There were placards on easels, full-color, oversized representations of food that wanted nothing more than to be devoured. The servers wore signs below their name tags, ASK ME ABOUT OUR SHRIMP SPECIALS! The menu was composed of so many choices, so many combos and platters, so many adjectives and yummy options, it either inflamed appetite or bewildered it, as it did for Grace. It would feel like sitting down to eat paper pictures of food.

Her father was late. Grace waited by the entrance, occupying her attention with the restaurant's holiday decorations. There were evergreen garlands set with twinkle lights. A Della Robbia–style wreath of fruit, groupings of red candles, silver bells. She'd always loved Christmas decorations, even the impersonal commercial variety like these. She'd driven past her parents' house one night last week. Her father had not put up any sort of Christmas lights or items. She hadn't really expected him to but she'd wanted to see it for herself, so as to get over anything sentimental or wounded.

Here was her father, coming in with the cold day at his back, looking around for her. The entrance was crowded and he didn't see her until she stood up and waved at him. "Gracie, sorry, they dragged me into a conference room just when I was trying to get away."

"No problem, they're just now getting to us on the list." The place was mystifyingly popular, or maybe there was no mystery, just advertising. Once they were seated in a booth in one of the noisy side rooms, once they'd gotten out of their winter coats and had the oversized menus under control, they sat back and smiled at each other, as if willing away their miserable awkwardness. Before her mother died, Grace couldn't remember the last time she and her father had gone out on their own together, for lunch or for anything else.

"You look good," her father pronounced, and Grace said thanks, and that he did too. Although he didn't, especially. He seemed distracted, skittish, as if he expected to be interrupted or called away. He might have had a cold or something else that had inflamed his nose and turned his skin blotchy. They had not seen each other since Thanksgiving. Unless one of them made some effort, today's lunch might be their Christmas.

They studied the menus. When the waitress came, Grace ordered minestrone and a salad. Her father said he'd try the sausage rigatoni. Grace dug into the shopping bag she'd brought. "This is for you," she said, handing over a wrapped package. "And here, cookies. I made some of them and some came from the store's bakery."

"Thanks, honey. Should I open it now? No, I want to save it."

"Sure, you can open it later." It was a watch, the kind with annoying features that registered your heart rate and allowed other people to track you down. It was something he didn't yet have. It was the sort of gift her mother would have bought for him.

He looked embarrassed. "I was going to write checks for you and your brother. I'm not feeling the holiday vibe, you know?"

"That's fine, Dad." It wasn't fine.

"It's been a hell of a year."

"It absolutely has."

"You keep thinking you're back on track and then, pow, right in the kisser."

The waitress brought bread sticks, hot, puffy fingers of dough, and some dipping sauces. Grace put one on her plate but didn't eat it. Her father said, "How's your friend, you know, the one I met?"

"Les? He's fine too." He wasn't fine. Pow, right in the kisser.

"You're not encouraging him, I hope." Grace gave him a withering look and her father raised his hands in protest. "Never mind, just asking. It's hard not to have an opinion."

"Yeah, but it's not that hard to keep it to yourself."

"Forget I said anything. I guess I'll help myself to some of these fine bread sticks."

Two days ago Les had called while Grace was still at work, trying to get her to come over. "I can't, you know I'm working."

"Tell them your boyfriend needs a blow job."

"You're not my boyfriend."

"Well, he probably needs a blow job too."

She'd made some excuse and gone to his apartment. She thought that something was wrong with her, perhaps it had always been wrong and it was just now surfacing.

Her father asked her how work was, and Grace said it had been busy, and her father complained that his work was impossible, really, they wanted the impossible from him. He had been complaining about work for as long as Grace could remember. But then, the only thing she ever said about her own work was, busy.

"How's Michael?" her father asked, as if it was a casual question, and Grace said that she didn't know. "Well, if you see him, tell him to give me a call, OK?"

"You can't call him yourself?"

"You know how things are," her father said vaguely. And she did.

Whose fault was it? Each blamed the other. The two of them were warring states, bound up in their historic grievances. How long had it been going on? Probably ever since her father looked at Michael and saw him as a reproach. They were too much alike, as Grace's mother said, and it was both their similarities and their differences that irritated them and set them against each other, each reflecting back at the other an imperfect version of himself.

"Just tell him to call. No big deal."

"I don't like being put in the middle of things."

"It's better if it comes from you," he said, and Grace knew this was true.

She said, carefully, "Maybe if you weren't drinking when you talked to him."

"Excuse me, what's this in my glass? Iced tea."

"All right."

"You make it sound like I'm the one who wrecked the car and got arrested and had to be hauled off to the rehab ranch."

"All right, never mind."

"You want to worry about somebody, worry about him. I'm just hoping he's OK." Her father looked around the room, taking note of the other tables. "You'd think we'd have our food by now. Everybody else does."

At least there were times that one or both of them, her father or brother, had these tentative impulses, hoping to blunder into some kind of reconciliation. At least they had the peculiar and intimate connection of their long hostility.

Because Grace had no such bond and never had. Not with any of them. Something was wrong with her, and perhaps it had always been wrong.

Their food arrived. Her father's pasta was an enormous piggy portion, immobilized by melted cheese. He offered her a bite. "Oh, sorry, forgot. Vegetarian." Grace's soup had been revived by a microwave and was too hot to eat. She tried one spoonful and scalded her tongue.

She started in on her salad. It was hard to taste anything. She felt pointlessly sad, the way she had been sad as an adolescent, without any one particular reason and with no cure for it, unless the reason was the falsity of everything around her: the facsimile of family, the approximation of holiday cheer, the impersonation of Italian food.

One thing you could say about Les Moore and their often brutal sexual usage of each other: it didn't pretend to be anything other than what it was. He knew what she looked like and she knew what he looked like. Yin and yang. "I guess you're not so much better than me after all," he said, and she guessed that was true. She did not deserve anything better.

How was Michael? Grace had not really wanted to know, even as she tried to find out. The times she'd attempted to reach him by phone, her messages and texts weren't returned. Screw him, but that didn't get her off the hook. She wasn't sure where Michael was living, or rather, sleeping. There wasn't any news of the band that she could track. Either they weren't getting any bookings, or else they had broken up and reformed under a different name, as happened often enough. Every so often one of Michael's friends would show up at the food store, or she'd run into them around town and she'd ask about him.

The friends were always noncommittal. Yeah, he was OK. He was keeping busy with the music. He was staying in this place or maybe that one. They weren't sure. Grace couldn't tell if they were covering for him, protecting him, or they just weren't paying attention. Grace tried his Facebook page but he hadn't touched it in months. How worried should she be? Maybe he just needed a break from family. That wasn't so hard to imagine.

She and her father finished their meal. Her father said that his pasta had been pretty good. A place like this, you always knew what you were going to get. There were some nights he called in a dinner order and picked it up on the way home from work. He said it was a nice break from his own cooking. "Well, it's not cooking, not really. Lots of microwave action."

"Yeah, I can believe that."

"There's that whole big kitchen that hardly gets any use."

"Uh-huh." She was thinking about Thanksgiving.

"You could move back in. Put it to good use."

"You don't like my food, remember?" It occurred to her that he was serious. "No," Grace said, shaking her head. "Honestly, no."

"Why not? I've been thinking about it. It would save you money. There's plenty of space. Come and go as you please."

"No Dad." It seemed incredible that he should ask. "I like where I am now. I like my privacy." Privacy being the excuse of last resort.

"Just consider it. That's all I'm asking."

"You know what's a better idea? Michael."

"Michael is never a better idea."

"All right, but don't pester me about this. I don't want to move."

"Look, you're not married, you don't seem like you're on track to get married anytime soon—"

"What does that have to do with anything?"

"Take it easy, I only meant, you haven't settled down. It's been all right up until now to live in some crummy apartment—"

"It's not crummy."

"—so maybe, now don't get me wrong, you could still get married and have children of your own, nothing would make me happier, and you're a very attractive girl. But time marches on, you know? And men don't always go for the headstrong types."

"You think I'm an old maid?"

"Did I say that? Maybe you're just one of those modern women who goes her own way. So you might want a little more comfort. Stability. You might want to consider that."

"God."

"We could help each other out."

"No," Grace said, and they stared at each other across the table. She saw how needy, sad, and infuriating he was. How he would always go about everything wrong. And what did he see when he looked at her?

That was the end of their talking, although it would take more words for them to get themselves up from the table and walk out of the restaurant and away from each other.

"What's the matter?" Les asked her the next time they were together. He'd gotten out of bed to find a cigarette, and turned to look at her. "Don't say 'nothing.'"

"I don't know. Everything."

"Not much of a clue."

"Do men not like independent women? Smart women?"

"What brought that on?"

Grace shook her head. Nothing. Everything.

"Well I'll tell you the awful truth, you can get away with more when you have stupid whore girlfriends like I mostly had. Of course you have to tell them what to do every minute, and that gets old."

It served her right for asking. Stupid whore girlfriends; who talked like that?

"But hey, you're not like them. You've got brains, I respect that."

"Maybe I'm not as smart as I thought I was." She was about to complain that her job was not anything that required much intelligence, but stopped herself. It was complicated, complaining to a man who worked in a factory, which you might look down on, except that he earned much more money than she did. Of course, working at the health food store wasn't meant to be a way of life for her. She was supposed to advance to something more high-powered. Except that she gave no indication of doing so anytime soon.

She wasn't on track to get married. She didn't have to get married, you didn't these days. Even if you wanted a baby, you could have one on your own, it was no big deal. If you didn't want some annoying baby daddy hanging around, you could go to a fertility clinic and choose a desirable donor. You could marry another woman. You could marry another woman and go to the fertility clinic, you could adopt an African orphan, or both. Or forget the kids, you could devote your life to art, or a cause, you could travel the world or start a religion, whatever you wanted, except it seemed that what you wanted at present was knock-down, drag-out sex with someone who profoundly embarrassed you. She was twenty-six going on twenty-seven. One of those modern women who was completely screwed up.

Les lit his cigarette and took some efficient drags from it. She always smelled like smoke when she'd been here and had to wash her clothes. When she complained, he suggested she strip down at the front door and save them both some time.

"Women worry about all the wrong shit. Their hair, their fingernails. But am I too smart, that's a new one on me." He put the cigarette out and sat down on the edge of the bed. His gray hair had come loose from its holder and the thin strands hung loose around his face. He was the ugliest man she'd ever seen naked. His hand strayed between her legs. "You want to go again?"

"No."

"Your mouth's saying no, but your pussy's saying yes."

In January the weather turned viciously cold. No surprise. Always there were two or three weeks when the temperature crept a few degrees above or below zero, when new snow fell on top of old snow, and a constant wind set in from the northwest. The cold followed you inside and made you curl into yourself, made you lose heart.

The health food store served up thick, hippie soups made of lentils, beans, and rice, yellow curries, pepper pot. Grace wore fingerless gloves when she worked at the cash register, and a mohair scarf wrapped twice around her neck. She never felt warm, either at work or at home.

What would it be like to live in a place where the weather didn't fight you, where you didn't have to give yourself a pep talk just to walk outside? She wished she could get in her car and drive south or west, out of winter, to somewhere you could see the sun and the whole sky. She told herself she didn't have the money, which was true, but she didn't have the nerve either. There might not be much that she felt good about in her present life, but she was afraid to walk away from it. Who were you when nobody knew you?

One frigid night her phone rang late, after ten, a bad-news time for calls, and when she saw it was her father, she thought, *Michael.* Her father started off shouting. She couldn't make out what he was saying. "What, slow down." Yes, it was Michael, something about Michael. "What did he do? Is he there now?"

No, he wasn't. Grace could make out that much. Her father said he was going to change the locks, he might even do it tonight, they had twenty-four-hour locksmiths. They had them for just such situations.

"What situations," Grace said uselessly. He wanted to kick and scream a while longer, he wanted, she understood, to complain to her and only her about the bad character and worse behavior of her brother. Drinking involved.

"I'll tell you what. The police are looking for him. They'll settle his hash."

"Why police, did you call them? What do they want him for?"

"For being a damn druggie."

"Tell me—"

"He can run but he can't hide."

From what Grace could tell, her brother had showed up at her father's house earlier, saying he wanted to talk. But that was just an excuse to get in the door. He wanted money for drugs. He was stoned to the eyeballs. How did her father deduce that? Oh well, maybe you had to be there all those other times, when he swore up and down he didn't touch the stuff, or sometimes he did but not tonight, or he did, but he was never going to do so again. How can you tell if a druggie is lying? Their lips are moving.

"What happened?" Grace repeated. She needed to know the police part.

"He wanted to talk. So we're talking. He says he's sorry we don't get along better."

Here her father went silent. Grace had to prompt him. "And?"

"You think I'm not sorry too? You think I don't want things to be different?"

"Of course you do." Maybe he did. That would be the sad part.

"Jesus Christ."

"Dad? Where's Michael now, do you know?"

"But it's a scam," her father said, sounding suddenly drunker. "Get old Dad right where you want him, all fat, dumb, and happy, and then you go for the kneecaps. Ask the guy if he can afford a lawyer. You tell him, he's going to learn some lessons."

"No, wait, why is it a scam? I don't understand."

Her father put the phone down but kept talking from somewhere else in the room. She heard him, far away, furious, his words just beyond the edge of her hearing, then footsteps coming closer to the receiver again. There was a shocking loud noise in her ear, something he was doing to the receiver, hanging it up, or trying to.

Then the null space of dead air.

The phone rang again. "Do you think I was a bad father?" he asked. "Honest Injun."

"I think you and Mom both did your very best."

"Ha," her father said as if he'd caught her in a falsehood.

"Why? Were you and Michael arguing about it? Did he say you weren't?"

"Just tell him, I'm not kidding around." The phone went dead again.

Grace waited, but he didn't call back. She raised the blinds in the living room and looked out on the parking lot, lit by a single mercury vapor street lamp that gave the humps of frozen snow a blue cast, like winter on a different planet. She texted her brother:

WHAT HAPPENED?

She hardly expected an answer, but it wasn't more than a couple of minutes before her phone screen lit up:

HE IS TOTALLY SICK.

WHERE ARE YOU?

Grace texted, and waited, but the phone stayed black and silent. She tried calling and got the blast of music noise that was his voice mail and hung up without leaving a message. Goddamn them both, goddamn whatever failed and guilty part of her made her put on her boots and coat and hat and gloves and find her keys and start the car that didn't want to start.

First she drove to her parents' house. Her father's house. She no longer had parents. The house was dark except for one light on upstairs, in the room where her mother had died. There was no police presence, nothing to see. The street was dark and quiet, stupefied by cold. The snow underfoot had hung on like a curse. A small white moon sat high up in the sky, emitting no light. Grace pulled up to the curb and stayed there with her motor running for as long as she dared, risking the attention of a vigilant neighbor. The upstairs light remained on.

Finally she drove off. Where was Michael, would he call her if he'd been arrested? Maybe that had only been part of her father's angry carrying on. What if Michael was using again. And of course he was. She knew it as an ugly certainty.

It was now almost eleven, but that wasn't late for the people Michael kept company with, even in this kind of near-hibernation weather. They'd still be up having grubby fun. She drove with care on the imperfectly plowed side streets, where the tire tracks had been frozen in place and sometimes the steering wheel left her hands as the car grabbed and slipped on the rutted surface. Grace knew where some of them lived, his friends, and the friends of friends, the bad influences and lost causes. She was going to find him one way or another, she had the sudden notion that she would take custody of him. He needed to be sent away or taken away, kept safe.

She let herself imagine it. She would call her uncle Mark. He could break off a chunk of their grandmother's estate, surely there was enough money for whatever Michael needed, rehab, a new start. A new start for both of them, somewhere that was not here. Desert, mountain, ocean: they'd pick a place they could look at every day and marvel. They'd find a house together, one with plenty of space, with good light and a garden. She imagined floors made of gleaming blond wood, oversized windows, a shady porch. Imagined her brother shaking off his sickness and sadness. She'd cook him healthy food that he'd make fun of, but he'd eat it and be better for it. There would be things they wouldn't talk about, not for a while, not until they were a long way away from this night.

But tonight, right now, was here, and she made herself pay attention to traffic signals and the other occasional cars on the road, sitting at intersections in clouds of exhaust or cruising up alongside her. Her car's defroster didn't work very well and she kept having to wipe her windows free of ice, so that even if a car pulled up next to her, she couldn't see who was inside, a friend, a stranger, a threat. Why would anyone be out on such a night, why was she out in it? *Because my mother is dead, my father is drunk, my brother is sick.* What she'd say in case somebody stopped her, stuck a gun or a flashlight in her face. Any or all of those reasons.

The first place she went was Jonesy's, the friend Michael had stayed with for a while before moving on. Jonesy lived on campus in one of the new high-rises, vertical playpens that promised students the good life. Cable, Wi-Fi, exercise studio, bike storage, grilling in the courtyard, parties in the hall. Grace wouldn't have lived in such a place, and neither would her friends. They would have scorned the whole consumerist, hedonistic vibe, so devoid of authenticity, individuality, etc. Well, she and her friends had graduated and were blazing trails at the health food stores and coffee shops, while the pampered children would go on to business school and earn their six-figure salaries and never worry about it for a minute.

She found Jonesey's apartment number on the list in the lobby and rode the elevator up. When she walked down the corridor, the different closed doors throbbed with barely contained amplified noise.

She knocked, and after a time the door cracked open. It was one of the roommates she didn't know, a baby-faced kid with a fuzzy chin beard that didn't help anything, and Grace had to explain herself. Oh yeah, Mike, no, he wasn't here. They hadn't seen him. There was something going on in the room behind the boy, something he wasn't going to let her see. Someone was talking loudly, saying fuck a lot, either angry or drunk or both. No, Jonesy wasn't here either. She could try calling him. The kid actually yawned in her face then. Sleepy or just rude. It was so not his problem.

Grace had to stick her foot in the door to keep him from closing it on her. Well where might her brother be, did he know anywhere else could she try? He didn't know. Well ask somebody. It was important.

Grace waited. The boy came back and said there was a girl, maybe her brother was with this girl named Georgia. She lived downtown someplace. There was another consultation away from the door. Yeah, over the shoe repair place. "Did old Mike get into something?" the boy asked.

"What?"

"Did he get into some kind of shit? You know." The boy had an avid look she didn't like. Energized, finally, by the possibility of bad news. She hoped he wasn't in school. His tuition would be a waste of somebody's money. "Trouble."

"What are you talking about?" Grace asked sharply. "What kind of trouble?"

But he wasn't going to say anything more. He drew his head back inside the door, smirking, and closed it and left her standing there.

Now she had to imagine trouble, the great flapping bat shape of it, the different varieties of dangerous and stupid. Dealing? Stealing? And which substance or substances in the witch's brew of possibilities was he taking? She didn't know, but most likely crack. It was the cheapest and dirtiest and the one you heard the most about, and now she was probably going to have to find out for sure, find out every ugly truth.

The girl Georgia wasn't home, or at least no one answered the buzzer at the street door next to the shoe repair. She texted Michael again, nothing. Miserable with cold, Grace trudged from one downtown bar to another, but Michael was not in any of them. She saw a group of his friends, who maintained their record of perfect ignorance as to his whereabouts. She saw a couple of people she knew too but she didn't want to stay; the crowded bars felt exactly like one of those movies where people were photographed from grotesque angles, meant to show how depraved the whole thing was.

It was past midnight. She got back in the car, ready to give up. She thought about Les Moore, who would be off work now. She could call him or just show up there. But more and more, he was feeling like her own kind of drug, something unwholesome and illicit you kept hidden. She texted Michael one more time,

ARE YOU ALL RIGHT?

Stupid question. No wonder he didn't answer.

Last stop. She drove to the house he'd been staying at over Thanksgiving. She'd wanted to avoid it; it was a run-down crash pad for outlaw band members and the rest of the damn druggies. Or so she gathered. She'd never been inside. But here she was, trying to be brave, though she was reaching the end of her nerve, and thinking there was no point in trying to help someone who would not help themselves, and working herself into some pointless melodramatic state.

Nevertheless. The blue Christmas lights sagged over the porch. Grace walked with care up the unshoveled pathway to the door.

Other lights inside, television noise. The doorbell was taped over, broken. She knocked, waited, knocked again. As she was turning away to leave, the door opened.

"Oh, hey . . ."

She recognized a boy from Michael's band, or one of his bands. A tall kid who moved as if his arms and legs were fastened with paper clips. She couldn't remember his name, but Grace could tell he didn't remember hers either.

"I'm looking for my brother, is he here?" The boy shook his head. "Has anybody here seen him recently?"

"I wouldn't say recent."

She put on her polite, questioning face: Then what would he say? "Come on in," the boy said. "I'll ask around."

He held the door open for her. "Cold out there," he said, by way of indifferent conversation, and Grace agreed, although it didn't seem that much warmer inside.

It was a big bare room with a staircase leading to a second floor. The boy headed upstairs and Grace stayed by the door. Along one wall, a flat-screen television was turned to some true crime drama. On a couch in front of the television, giving it their entire attention, a boy and a girl. They looked young, high school age, like they should be home studying for an algebra test.

The couple on the couch paid her no mind, and that was fine with Grace. They were huddled under a blanket and the boy had his arm around the girl's shoulders and was nuzzling at her neck. The television was on too loud, blaring its hyped-up and breathless account of gruesome crime scenes, autopsies, murder weapons.

Grace examined the room. It wasn't messy, exactly; there wasn't enough in it for that. More like unkempt and inhospitable. People had drawn and painted on the walls, inexpertly, in most cases scrawls and drips and spray-painted smiley faces. But on the back wall, a door had been surrounded by a pair of giant, bleeding crimson lips, rendered with unpleasant accuracy.

The boy came down the stairs again, swinging his arms in that strange, stiff-jointed way. "Nobody's seen him for a few days." To the boy and girl on the couch, he said, "Kenny's on his way."

"So . . ." Grace tried to sort this out. "So he does stay here?"

"I don't know about stay," the boy said, again sounding judicious, as if word choice was important to him.

"He's not answering his phone."

"Huh. Well, phones."

Meaning maybe he doesn't want to talk to you. Something Grace had considered herself. He spoke to the couple: "I'm telling you, five or ten minutes."

"Is Michael . . ." Grace wanted to dump out her worries and demand answers, but either nobody knew anything or nobody was going to tell her. Her brother might as well have been a runaway slave being hidden in the underground railroad. "How's the band?" she asked instead.

"Oh, we kind of quit." He stepped closer to the couch. "Hey. Seriously."

"I didn't know that," Grace said. Except she did, or she sort of knew. "I guess it's hard to keep everybody motivated."

"Yeah. If you talk to your brother, tell him we're all real motivated to see him around here."

"Why's that?" Grace asked.

"Just tell him."

"But I don't know where he is."

"Hopeless," the boy said. It was unclear who he meant, Grace, Michael, or the couple on the couch, who were still going at each other and ignoring them. He turned and walked through the door shaped like a bloody mouth, which was designed to make it look as if he was being swallowed, an evil visual joke.

She let herself out the front door and into the cold, which felt almost welcoming after the strangeness of indoors. Before she reached her car, the door opened again. "Hey, wait up."

It was the boy who had been on the couch. "You think you could give me a ride?"

"A ride?" Grace repeated, then, "A ride to where?" Because she needed to know but also because she had to process the realization that he was not a boy but a girl, the kind of girl who attempted not to be a girl.

"Not real far. The other side of downtown. Fuck, it's cold."

"Hop in," Grace said, because she was tired and it was easier than saying no, and anyway she was thrown off her stride, having to recalibrate what she'd seen. "I'm Grace," she told her passenger once they were settled. The girl slouched on her tailbone with her legs crossed, her feet in heavy ugly boots grazing the dashboard.

"Tig. Head back down to University and keep going east. Thanks. I so did not want to walk."

"No problem." OK, she got it now. It had just taken her a moment. Tig, short for Tigger? Or perhaps signifying nothing at all.

A light, sleety snow was falling. "Oh, excellent," Tig said, drawling with sarcasm. "More snow." She wore a green army jacket and a gray hoodie sweatshirt underneath. Camo pants and those ugly boots. She was slim and small, with dark hair cut short across her forehead, and buzzed on the sides. A girl's voice, a little on the husky side. At least Grace had figured the age right. Sixteen or seventeen. Really, too young to be hanging out at the neighborhood bad-vibes place. Probably a not-good story in there somewhere.

"You're Mike's sister?"

"That's right." Grace waited a beat. "You know where he is?"

"No."

Of course not. He had dematerialized. Then Tig said, "OK, look, since you're helping me out. His name's like a swear word around there. I think he owes some of those dudes a lot of money."

He probably did. Oh goddamn. It was so stupid and predictable. Money for drugs, her father said. He wasn't always wrong. Tig said, "Sorry. I didn't mean to upset you."

"That's all right."

"It's not like I know for sure. It's something Heather was talking about."

"Heather," Grace repeated, trying to concentrate on her driving. The snow was freezing as it fell, and the road surface was treacherous.

"My girlfriend."

Grace was careful to look straight ahead. "So who's Kenny?"

"Ah, she doesn't know what she wants." Tig's foot took a swing and connected with the dashboard. She took her feet down and sat up straighter.

They were both quiet then. The wind had picked up and was sending a fine, icy layer of snow skittering across the road. Grace slowed the car so that they only crept along. Tig said, "Turn left at the next light."

"Where is it we're going, exactly?"

"My place. Well, my parents' place. As they like to remind me."

"They worry about you being out this late?"

"No."

"Nice neighborhood," Grace said, because it was, one of the brick street blocks, with the old-fashioned globe streetlights that shone dim and misty in the snow. The houses were solid dark sleeping shapes.

"I guess it's fine," Tig said. "If you're like, into total seclusion. It's only a couple more blocks, you can let me off."

"No, I'll take you all the way." The windshield wipers were

dragging, piling up ice. Grace made herself focus on the steering and braking. She thought she knew now where Michael was.

"I liked him. Mike," Tig said unexpectedly. "The times I talked to him. So maybe he's a little screwed up. . . ."

"Why do you say that?" Grace immediately regretted asking. There were things she might not want to hear.

"Sorry. He's your brother."

"No, really, tell me."

"All that bad-boy rock-and-roll stuff, you know, the devil teaches you how to play the guitar? And all the drugs? You better respect them or they peel your brain like a banana. Anyway. It doesn't seem like that's really him, you know? It's like, he puts on a Halloween costume and scares himself."

"Maybe that's right." It seemed entirely right.

"He's another one who doesn't know what he wants."

"Not like you," Grace said, liking the girl in spite of herself.

"That's right. That's why I'm going to be just fine. No matter what anybody else says."

Tig got out at a house on the corner, a tidy redbrick with a colonnade of white pillars. At the front door she raised a hand in a jaunty salute. Grace watched her until she got inside. If she accomplished nothing else tonight, at least she'd gotten Tig home safely.

The snow had stopped and the streets had a shell-shocked look. Her grandmother's house wasn't far away. Grace drove past it once, circled the block, and came back to it. There were no lights and there was nothing to see. A good place for total seclusion. By now the realtor's sign looked like a bad joke, as if they were attempting to sell a haunted house. Grace slowed at the drive, turned in, and promptly slid into the curb. She killed the engine and left the car where it was.

The snow cover reflected frozen light. The house itself was entirely dark. The realtor's bulky key box was hooked over the doorknob. She rang the doorbell and heard the faraway, underground sound of the chimes. She rang again, waited, then used her key to wrestle the locks and push the door open.

She hung back on the porch and called into the dark hallway. "Is anybody here?"

Nothing. Her voice echoed back to her.

"Michael?"

The hallway was a pool of darkness. She could make out the white banisters of the stairs. She listened. Nothing.

Or maybe something. A distant, skittery sound. She found her phone in her purse. As if anyone on the other end of a phone could help her. She didn't feel brave, only stupid, slow-brained from cold and fatigue. "If you're here, come out. I'm not going in there."

She waited. More of the skittery noise. Footsteps. A light went on in the hallway overhead. She heard Michael at the top of the stairs, calling down. "You alone?"

"Yes."

He descended halfway, slowly, one step at a time. He was barefoot, wearing sweatpants and a black T-shirt. "What are you doing here?" His voice was hoarse.

"No, what are you doing here?"

He sat down on the stairs. "What time is it?"

"Late. Almost two. Hey."

He was having trouble holding his head up. It sagged between his knees. "Are you going to be sick?"

He shook his head. Grace advanced into the hallway and shut the door behind her. "What are you doing here, this is dumb. Are you listening to me? Are you high? Huh?"

"Leave me alone." He coughed and spit something to one side.

"No. Get your shoes. You have shoes, right? And a coat?" He didn't move or look up. "Michael, you can't stay here. What?" He was talking, but to himself. "I can't hear you."

"I can't stay anywhere."

"Come home with me and we'll sort it all out in the morning."

"This is it for me."

"What? What are you talking about? Do you need to go to the ER? Did you take something?" His head wobbled. He was shaking it no. "Then let's go."

"Are you going to call the police?"

"I'm not going to call the police." She wondered if she'd have to. "What's the matter?"

"You think you can fix it but you can't."

"Fix what?"

"Me."

Grace sighed, as if he was only being obstinate, and it was only a matter of using more patience and persuasion to budge him. She was trying to think things through. She shivered inside her coat. "Is the heat on?"

"The realtor keeps it pretty low."

"Yeah, I guess they would." That was a mistake. They should blast the heat in the old place, turn on all the lights. Make it look as if all the life hadn't long gone out of it. "I guess you took Dad's key."

"He won't miss it."

"How long have you been here?"

"I don't know. A few days. They should probably change realtors. Nobody's even come around."

"Well. Bad weather." At least he seemed more awake now, less out of it. She wanted to keep talking, saying normal things. "They should move some furniture back in, what do they call it, stage the rooms."

Michael looked around him as if there was something to see besides darkness. "Mom grew up here."

"Yes."

"It was Grandma and Grandpa's house. You remember coming here when we were little kids? Mom used to make jam from the grapes in the arbor. Grandma scared me. I don't think she ever smiled."

"I don't think she had that much to smile about."

"It's an important place. It's part of our memories. And now they want to sell it."

"Well, nobody needs it, Michael. Nobody has the money to keep it up. Pay the taxes."

"Yeah, I know. Nothing lasts, everything dies. Get over it."

Oh God, now he was going to go down that track: loss, death, self-pity. How to get him off it?

Michael said, "I think about Mom a lot."

"So do I," Grace said, rather too quickly. "Little things, usually. How she kept a jar of Jergen's hand cream by the sink. If I see it or smell it someplace, it brings her right back."

"After a while, everybody stops remembering. I mean, the people who knew you, they're dead too."

"Come on."

"Sorry. That's how I feel."

"You're being maudlin. It's a useless, silly way to think."

"Well that's me. Useless and silly. It's all I got."

It was the kind of talk that made her impatient. She wanted to tell him that it was all a bad mood, a bad spell, a bad habit, it would pass. But it had already gone on too long, and she didn't know how to argue against the implacable force of his self-hatred. The house seemed to be getting colder by the minute. Yes, she could see her breath.

Grace said, "How much money do you owe people?"

He scowled. "Who says I owe anybody money?"

"Because it's just money. It's not the most complicated thing in the world. The cure for money problems is money, right?"

"How about you leave and forget you saw me. Seriously."

"And who says we have to stay here? Live here? We can get out of this town, go someplace else. Anywhere in the world. Yes we can." He was shaking his head. "You can get away from Dad for a while. You guys are toxic together."

"Yeah, but he's right about me, I'm a fuckup."

"No, you just . . . don't know what you want."

"Yeah, whatever. Where is it we're supposed to go, anyway?"

"Wherever you want. Anywhere."

"Anywhere's the same as nowhere."

"Then pick a place."

"You're only talking about this to make me feel all shiny and hopeful."

"I want to get out of here too. Yes I do." She was thinking about Les Moore, and the person she was with him, and the person she was everywhere else, and how none of this made her happy. "Let me take care of you."

"No."

"You're the only family I have left. Not Dad." As soon as she said it, she knew it was the sad truth.

He was quiet and for a moment it seemed she might win out, that he might give himself over to her, allow himself to be taken in, comforted, understood. Then he said, "I guess there's some happy-talk stuff I can't believe in anymore."

"Well anyway." She had reached the end of what she had to say and she had lost. She kept on, not yet knowing how to stop. "You can at least come home with me. You can sleep on the couch, it has to be more comfortable than here."

"I've got a bedroll."

"Oh, a bedroll. Great."

"Not tonight. It's late, it's cold, I have guitars and all kinds of shit here."

"Tomorrow, then. I'll come get you."

"Not too early," he said, and Grace said afternoon, around one. At least he was agreeing to this much. He came down the rest of the stairs to see her out, and she hugged him. He had a faintly grubby smell of unwashed hair, unwashed clothes.

"You'll be all right here?"

"Sure. Careful driving."

"When you're the only fool on the road, it makes it easy."

She stepped out onto the porch and motioned to him to shut the door, it was too cold to stand there barefoot, and he drew back inside.

She had failed him. She knew that, but she didn't yet know how badly.

Grace went home and slept until almost noon. The local television news was all about the weather, the disruptions of travel, the closing of schools. Her brother wasn't answering his phone. By now she hardly expected him to. She showered and dressed and set out again. The sun was out, trying to burn a hole in the cold. When she reached her grandparents' house, it glittered with frost and the windows shone with reflected light.

As before, she let herself in with her key and called her brother's name. When he didn't answer, she climbed the stairs and looked through all the rooms. Her footsteps echoed. The house was empty. She knew it without looking further.

He'd gone and taken everything with him. The floors were bare and swept, and she couldn't tell where he might have lain down to sleep.

Two nights later. Grace was asleep, or rather, since she had not been aware of being asleep, she was awake in the dark. Someone trying to get in. Or no, knocking, loud and insistent. "What?" Grace said in her sleep, and then again, speaking it. "What?"

She pulled a sweatshirt over her pajamas. Turned on a light in the kitchen but hung back from the door. "Michael?"

"Police," someone said, a woman's voice, and that was a strange enough thing that she opened it.

Two blue uniforms crowded the alcove that was her entryway. Grace stared at the woman officer. "Becky?"

"Hi Grace."

"You're a cop? Wow."

They'd been in high school together. Grace hadn't seen her since. Becky had the same small, round blue eyes and a face that looked like someone had used their thumbs to put it together. Except that now she was encrusted with cop gear: badge, belt, shoulder mic, something that was probably Mace, and a holster with a real-looking gun sticking out of it. It was like seeing somebody you knew on television.

"This town," Grace said. "People keep turning up. Wow." She was awake, but her brain hadn't yet caught up with her body. Becky had been one of those quiet, phlegmatic girls who took up space in classes and lunch hours and study halls. She and Grace had not been friends, especially, but once, in a restroom, Becky had provided Grace with a tampon when she needed one. Becky had a musclehead older brother who lifted weights and got his girlfriend pregnant. Useless bits of memory, surfacing.

The other cop was a man, older, bigger, more obviously cop-like, who managed to stare at Grace without ever actually looking in her direction. She was wearing particularly embarrassing pajamas, pink flannel with a pattern of kittens chasing butterflies.

"Could we come in?" Becky Who Was Now A Cop asked, and an alert, an alarm, went off in Grace's brain, something she needed to pay attention to, but what? "Sure," Grace said.

She stepped aside and they trooped in, crowding around the door, though there wasn't enough room for the three of them.

Grace turned on the overhead light. They didn't seem to want to sit, and she wasn't sure if you were meant to invite them. "So how long have you been a cop?" she asked Becky. She couldn't think what else to say.

"Couple of years. I went into the army after school, I was an MP."

"You must like it, huh?"

"I do. It makes you feel like you're giving back."

"Sure." Grace wondered what she'd done, if they would get around to telling her. She had a little pot in the nightstand. Did anybody care about that these days? The worrying part of her brain was awake now.

She and Becky spoke at the same time.

"There was a—"

"What—"

"An incident."

"What's an incident?"

"At your father's residence. Involving firearms."

She must have blanked out then, or fallen asleep on her feet, because Becky had a hold of her arm. "Steady there."

They steered her to the couch in the living room and sat her down. "I'm so sorry," Becky said. The other cop took up a lot of space. His big stomach was level with Grace's eyes. She shook her head to try and clear it. "What?"

"Your father gave us a statement."

"So he's all right."

"He's in custody."

She'd reached the end of her understanding and only stared.

"There was a confrontation. An argument. Between your father and your brother, Michael. Your father produced a weapon and shot him. I'm so sorry, Grace. He didn't survive. He was gone by the time we got there."

*   *   *

She was asked when was the last time she'd seen her brother. She said that she hadn't known it was going to be the last time.

The only place she would see her father ever again would be in a courtroom.

People wanted to help. And they did. Her friends sat with her and cried with her and said the right things, which sometimes was to say nothing at all. They kept track of her and fed her as she moved through the following days and weeks as if she were made of glass. But no one thought to prevent her, the morning after her brother's death, from walking behind the house to the place where he had fallen and seeing the bright shock of his blood in the snow.

The father admitted that he had been drinking. He didn't know how much. He didn't know what that meant, "impaired." Was that really the most important thing here? After everything that had happened? My God. He had been drinking, let it go at that. He was doing his best to explain. His account was composed of things he remembered and things he thought he remembered, how one thing might have led to another. He had been afraid for his safety. He had only meant to scare his son. He had meant to teach him a lesson. All of these.

    He and his son had a difficult relationship. This was no secret. His son had a history of substance abuse. This too was well-known. Things between them had only grown worse since the death of his wife. She was the boy's mother, so of course she had stuck up for him. Smoothed things over. Let him get away with things. Allowances were made for him because he was talented. And he was, a talented musician. When he was a kid they'd paid for lessons, encouraged him. He was a natural. Keyboards and guitar, mostly, though he could play his way around a banjo and a mandolin too. Times he'd be practicing and everybody in the house would stop what they were doing to listen.

The trouble came when he got older and the music got angrier, louder. His music turned into this whole mangy way of life, drugs included.

Growing up, they were always buddies. He'd taught his son how to throw a ball, how to hammer a nail. People used to say they looked exactly alike. What the hell happened to kids? How did they go from the babies you held next to your heart to . . . Jesus Christ.

On a previous occasion, his son had attacked him physically. It was on record; the police had been involved. It was after this that he had purchased a firearm. It was entirely for the purpose of protection. He wasn't some gun nut.

His son had not been living at the house. He lived here and there, one place or another. He led an irregular life, as you would expect of someone who abused drugs. The same with work. Nothing seemed to last very long for him or provided him with much of a living. Music sure wasn't making him rich. It was a source of many of their disagreements. Money, and why his son was so careless and indifferent about it. Not to mention drugs, the money that went to buy drugs and was worse than wasted, worse than sending it down a sewer. Money they had spent on rehab and counseling, another waste.

His son had come to the house late, a little after ten. He was not expected there. They had argued. He could not remember exactly what was said. By time time all their arguments were connected, so that it was like trying to unsnarl a knot, pulling and tugging until you found a loose place. So that a complaint by one of them would lead to an accusation by the other, and so on.

His son had been agitated and upset. He had talked about his mother. That much he remembered, because it had been so infuriating. He had said intolerable things about his father's lack of care and consideration. Did he think he was the only one who grieved for her? That was what their argument had become. Who missed her most, loved her the most.

He kept the gun upstairs. He must have gone up and found it and brought it back down. There were actions, and sequences of actions, which were unclear to him. He must have felt threatened. It was reasonable to feel that way. He did not know how they had ended up outside. Perhaps one of them had chased the other. He had no memory of being outside. He was inside, in the kitchen, drinking orange juice from the container in the refrigerator.

His son had been shot once in the chest. He must have been the one to shoot him. There was no other explanation. It must have been cold outside, so he had come back in. He was in the kitchen, drinking orange juice from the container in the refrigerator. The police had come to the door, beating and pounding and shouting. They had found the gun on the middle shelf of the refrigerator, where he'd set it down.

He did not think he was a bad person. He was a person who had made a bad mistake.

He had done it, there was no question. He had not meant to do it. This was his only son, his boy. He was so very sorry. He couldn't account for it. He really wished he could remember more, explain it right.

part three

THE GIRL OF MY DREAMS

The blue of her eyes and
the gold of her hair
are a blend of the western sky

And the moonlight beams
On the girl of my dreams
She's the sweetheart of Sigma Chi

"The Sweetheart of Sigma Chi"
Byron D. Stokes and F. Dudleigh Vernor, 1911

I. GRACE

Her grandfather's archive was brought to Grace in sealed, dust proofed, and cataloged boxes. She was given white cotton gloves to wear and cautioned that if she wished to take notes, only pencils were allowed. The room was kept chilly, since heat was one of the enemies of preservation. A state-of-the-art HVAC system monitored humidity and kept out pollutants. Nothing had been exposed to light since it had been deposited. "How long is everything supposed to last?" Grace marveled, and the archivist said they were aiming for the half-life of plutonium, which was twenty-four thousand years. She added, quickly, that this was an archivist joke.

Everything was ordered and recorded and there was a digitized guide to the contents. Grace went through the guide and located what she was looking for, but she asked the archivist if she might browse a bit. "Of course," the woman said. "You should take as long as you need." Grace thought the archivist was probably trying to be nice to her, because of everything that had happened. It was unavoidable and it wasn't all bad, but she would be glad to get away from it.

She was leaving town, in a little more than a month. It had all come together fast. She had an old college friend who lived in Oregon, in Eugene, and she would go there first, and then to California, to another friend who lived in Santa Rosa, and see if either place suited her enough to settle there. She didn't expect to be coming back, not to live, at least.

There was even some money. Her uncle Mark had explained it to her, how her mother's portion of her grandparents' estate was settled on her children. Her surviving child, that is, herself. The old house had finally sold. The sensational events involving her family had generated a certain interest. Buyers saw opportunities. It was a complicated and awful sort of good luck and Grace had given up trying to decide just how bad she ought to feel about it.

Her grandfather's materials were stored in glassine folders and wrapped in acid-free paper. Here were his diplomas and credentials, letters of appointment, his legal correspondence. His honors and promotions. Speeches he had given, newspaper articles that someone had clipped and saved, most probably her grandmother. Pictures of him that Grace remembered seeing before, as a child, images that she had forgotten she'd forgotten, until she held them in her gloved hands. Her grandfather in a long overcoat and a fedora, leaning on the hood of what was probably his first car, a dark, beetle-shaped Chevy. Part of a group portrait of his law school class. Her grandmother, neither young nor old, unsmiling, standing next to him and wearing a gardenia corsage. In this picture her grandfather was looking down on her with an expression that suggested wariness.

And here was the letter she'd been looking for typed on university letterhead, the printing small and gray. Dated 1952, addressed to Dear Andrew, and signed with a squiggle, Bob. Thanking him for taking over the care and management of the "living memorial to that earlier generation who have made the supreme sacrifice."

The solemn importance of which her grandfather was uniquely suited to appreciate.

Attached to this letter, an even older paper, written in careful script in brown ink—or ink that had faded to brown—a map showing the placement of the trees. One hundred and seventy-three of them, each of them honoring a university student or staff member who had died in the Great War.

The trees had been planted in 1920. By the time her grandfather took over their care, they would have been fully grown. They wouldn't have needed the kind of nursing along that you did with new trees. Most likely her grandfather's duty was an honorary one, and workers had done whatever inspection or pruning was required. Still, he had undertaken it. Perhaps he had sought it out, seen it as important. He'd been a soldier himself. A new war always took the place of the old one.

Each tree was labeled with a name. Privates first class and sergeants, mostly. A few captains. One major. She read through each name. Charles, Robert, Vaughn, Frances. Later, when the stadium was built, the names would be carved in the stone columns. But the trees had come first.

The trees had been laid out in lines along several blocks, surrounding a field identified as the parade ground. Grace didn't think there was a parade ground anymore. But the street names were the same, and the day after she visited the archives, she went in search of it.

It took her a while to orient herself. Buildings had gone up on the east and west sides, and to the south was a parking lot. There was still a green field in the center, currently in use as a soccer field. Indian or Pakistani boys from the residence halls across the street were playing a match.

The trees had not fared well. Either they had died away on their own, or else they'd been taken down for the new construction.

There was only one line of trees, shading the sidewalk along one block, but none of them looked to be close to a hundred years old. Grace parked her car and got out to examine them. She walked along the tree line, each tree in its tidy circle of mulch. It was May and they were beginning to leaf out. What kind were they anyway? Honey locusts, she thought. She knew that honey locusts had been planted to replace all the elms that had died from Dutch elm disease. Maybe the original trees had been elms. The papers in the archive hadn't said.

It was disappointing, but what did you expect? Grace reached the end of the tree line and turned to head back to her car. Then she saw it, just to the side of the redbrick gymnasium, which was itself now nearly as old as the Great War. A large, spreading tree, slightly offset from the line of other trees, growing in its own island of grass, surrounded by post and chain fencing.

She felt sure it was one of the memorial trees. She stepped carefully over the chain fence and put her hand on the tree's trunk. She only knew the easiest trees, oaks and maples. This was something else. There was probably someone in charge of trees who could tell her, if she made an effort. She wondered which of the names on the list it had been intended to honor. She could go back and find that out also. But for right now it was enough to stand next to it and touch its cool, rough bark, and send her thoughts back to that distant war, and the young man who had died, or perhaps all the young men who had died, and her grandfather, who might have stood where Grace did now, resting his hand on the tree's living skin.

Les Moore said, "I guess you went a little crazy. Everything with your family was pretty crazy. I'm sorry about them. So now you're done with me, well OK. I hope you'll miss me a little. Hey, it wasn't love, but it wasn't bad."

*   *   *

Before her grandparents' house sold, Grace went through the last stray items that had been left behind in the garage and the basement, things her mother had sorted through but hadn't been able to either throw out or find space for at home. Among these were the framed mirrors and pictures. Grace found her grandmother's print of *Guernica* and took it out of its frame, thinking that the frame, at least, was worth saving. A small envelope fell out of the backing. Inside it was a single sheet of lined notebook paper, covered with spiky, earnest handwriting.

Dear Professor,

I know, you are not a real professor, but maybe you are one by now, ha!

I hope the history people know how to find you if you are not there. How are you? It's me, your old pal. It sure has been a long time, so I apologize for not writing until now. Anyway you know that writing is not my best subject. I hope things are good with you. I am pretty good. I am married and have three boys. My wife and I still farm but I am mostly busy with the equipment sales and service which I have had for twelve years now. It is a pistol and it keeps me running. My dad passed away but my mother is still with us Thank God. I am busy and happy in my life but I still think about you sometimes. I am sorry that after the time we spent together I just up and left and I hope I did not leave you in a bad spot. I was so young and dumb. Now I am old and dumb, ha! Because my life right now is very good but maybe it all could have turned out different and you and me might have had a good life too. Even if I was not your best student! So I want you to know I think of you and I hope you think of me if you have the time. God bless.

Very truly yours,

Russell Hatch
January 10, 1961

The garden would be dedicated before it was entirely finished, since there were still plantings to go in, and some of the brickwork needed completion. But enough was done so that you could see the shape and plan of it, and how it would grow. At the last possible minute before the official opening, the plaque that had been commissioned arrived and was installed on a brick column at the entrance:

IN LOVING MEMORY OF
LAURA WISE ARNOLD
AND
MICHAEL ARNOLD

A lot of people had made donations through the GoFundMe page. Grace was kept busy tracking them and writing thank-yous and talking every day to the park district about one or another thing that needed to be done or redone. It was fortunate that she had been thinking about the garden ever since her mother died, about what her mother would have wanted and how it might be arranged. It was fortunate that she had talked to the park district last summer and knew what was needed for a proposal, for pricing and budgeting. Once she had the money in hand, they were able to make things happen quickly.

They had broken ground in March. Dry weather that month helped the construction along, just as the rain in April was good for the plants. May was all about pushing to get things done. Grace surprised herself with a previously unsuspected efficiency. She made phone calls and called again when people didn't respond. She visited the site and made sure the workers were actually at work. Sometimes after they'd left for the day she went back with a spade and did some of the digging herself. It felt good to dig until her muscles were ropy and sore and her head was free of thought.

A doctor had prescribed sleeping pills, and it was made clear that if she felt the need, other soothing pharmaceuticals were available to her. The pills made her head feel as if it was stuffed with cotton and she gave up on them after two nights. It was easier to stay awake and commune with her ghosts.

Now it was early June. There had been some days of chilly rain, but the weather had cleared and was holding. The night before the opening, Grace walked through the garden, liking what she saw. A low brick wall enclosed the space. Existing shade trees had been left in place beyond this border, so that the effect was that of coming into a sunlit glade. Trimmed boxwood hedges set off the different beds, a formal element, but within the beds themselves there were casual plantings, flowers and shrubs that were meant to mingle and grow dense. Roses and Shasta daisies, daylilies and Orientals, bee balm. Vining honeysuckle trained over a trellis, hydrangeas in different forms. Blazing star. Iris, phlox, black-eyed Susan, peonies. Chrysanthemums for fall color and spaces left for the spring bulbs that would go in later, daffodils and tulips and hyacinths. White and magenta coneflowers, purple salvia, painted daisies, ornamental grasses with seed heads that looked like fine sprays of water. Witch hazel, dogwood, dwarf forsythia. Some of it wouldn't bloom until the following year, so annuals filled in the bare spots for now, red and white and pink petunias, verbena, blue Angelonia, Dragon Wing begonias. A grape arbor to one side, the new vines pruned back and ready to climb. And although lilacs made for painful memories, Grace had made sure that some of her grandmother's old-fashioned favorites were included.

The white oak tree on the north side was for Michael.

The hackberry tree on the south was for her grandfather.

It was possible that someday her father would walk free and come here. It was possible that someday she would feel differently about this.

The head gardener was still here, working into the evening, setting up sprinklers and spreading a few last wheelbarrows of mulch. Grace spoke with him and was glad that he seemed pleased with everything. He said that in a year or two, the plantings would start to fill in. By year three, you could expect everything to take off. He'd be taking good care of it, not to worry. Grace said that she planned to be back from time to time and would look forward to seeing how things grew. He said that she'd gotten a good deal for her money and Grace said it was actually a lot of other people's money and he said then it was an especially good deal. They said good night and Grace drove home through the summer twilight. Fireflies were sparking in the tall grass by the side of the road.

The garden would outlast the memory of those to whom it was dedicated. When the garden itself was gone, you could hope that someone would plant a new garden.

The next day Grace met her uncle Mark and aunt Brenda and Dylan and Tracy for an early lunch. Now that they were, in effect, her only family, Grace was trying to like her aunt and cousins a little better. At least the kids were growing out of their carefully maintained boredom and occasionally expressing interest in their surroundings. Dylan asked her if she was really going to California. When Grace said she was, he said "Cool," in the hopeless tone of a boy who was certain he was never going to get laid, since he had been denied access to surfer girls, free and easy hippie girls. Brenda said that she hoped Grace would not experience any earthquakes, the west coast being the place for so many frequent and destructive earthquakes, and Grace said she would be certain to enter only those buildings that had been retrofitted.

She excused herself and went home to change into a pale green summer dress that she liked because it reminded her of a picture in a book she'd had when she was a little girl, a green-gowned fairy with gauze wings. She didn't know what had happened to that book. She wished that her mother was here so that she could ask, Do you remember that storybook with the red cover? Do you remember which story it was, the one with the fairy lady? She wished that there was someone left for her, someone who might bear witness to her past.

The official opening of the garden was at one o'clock, although that was a little silly, opening, since nothing was blockaded off and people had already been checking the place out and wandering around in it for some time now. Grace picked up two sheet cakes she'd ordered at the grocery, along with a case of water bottles, and some fizzy pink nonalcoholic wine. The park district was supplying a long table and tubs of ice. There weren't going to be any speeches, Grace had insisted on that, but she was determined that there be something in the way of occasion and celebration.

It was perfect June weather. The air was warm and full of blossom scent, the sky a profound blue, the clouds white and drifting. There had been no way of knowing how many people might show up, or how long they might stay. There had been an article in the newspaper, and a short mention on one of the local television news shows. The parking lot filled up. Grace put Tracy and Dylan in charge of cutting cake slices and pouring drinks. The park district people needed to talk with her about the last-minute maintenance.

Other people wanted to tell her how very sorry they were, to inquire after her health and well-being, and others, she suspected, wanted to set eyes on her as the survivor of a tragedy. Her friends ran interference, claiming her whenever the crowd became overwhelming. She was kept busy, distracted, marveling at the number and variety of people, the dense connected web of her family's history. Here were her mother's friends, and a younger group of Michael's, who sat on the grass to one side. Some majestic old couples who navigated the garden paths with canes and had opinions about the plantings. High school teachers of Grace's and of Michael's, former bosses, neighbors, schoolmates, people from the near and distant pasts.

There was nowhere else in the world where, for good or bad, she would be such a known quantity. She was beginning to sense how hard it would be to leave it behind. She was beginning to wonder if she ever really would, no matter where else she settled.

Her uncle Mark took her aside during a lull. "I went to see your dad yesterday."

Grace felt her face harden. She hoped he would not start talking about forgiveness. She was tired of hearing about forgiveness.

"I said I'd tell you hello from him. He wanted to know how you were."

"Tell him whatever you want."

"He's not doing so good in there, Grace. It's tough on him."

"He'd better get used to it." There was going to be some delay before any trial. The lawyers were keeping busy with motions. It was confounding to Grace that there could be so many qualifications attached to outright guilt, so many side issues and efforts at argument and mitigation. At least he was not going to be out on bond. The judge had been unimpressed by the rationale that since he had no son left to murder, her father was unlikely to commit any new crime.

Her uncle began explaining some point of order in the legal process, then stopped himself. "Hold on a minute."

He walked away and returned with another man at his side. "Grace, I want you to meet Bob Malloy."

"Oh, sure, how do you do," Grace said, shaking hands with him, and Bob Malloy said he was pleased to meet her, and her uncle began to speak and then stopped himself, and a strange, humming sort of silence descended on the three of them. Grace felt her face reddening, at the same time she was watching the color rise in Bob Malloy's.

"Well," Mark said after a moment. "How about I let you two get acquainted."

Left alone, they fumbled through one or two attempts at speech. Bob Malloy said, "I'm an old friend of Mark's. From way back in the day."

"Way back in the day," Grace repeated. "My mom . . ."

Dead stop. He looked away. "Would you excuse me for a moment?" Grace said. She cut a path through the crowd, waving off people who wanted to speak to her, pretending some urgent errand. She had never before in her life fainted, but she thought she might now. She and Bob Malloy looked way too much alike, uncannily alike.

He found her sitting beneath one of the shade trees, her knees drawn up and her green dress tented over them. "Is it OK if I talk to you?" he asked, and Grace motioned for him to sit beside her. He did so, letting himself down carefully. "Bad knees," he explained, and Grace nodded. He had her same big forehead and wide-set eyes, or rather, she had his. Same high-bridged nose and curving mouth, same tall and rangy frame. Lines around his eyes and mouth. Not old yet. Just older, some of his sharp edges worn down. What she might look like, in time.

She said, "My mom said your name. At the very end."

He pulled up a handful of grass and scattered it. "I hadn't seen her in—"

"I'm twenty-six."

"In about that long."

"She never said."

"I guess she wouldn't." He looked at her straight on now, appraising. "Look, I'm sorry about—"

"Sure."

"It's kind of a lot to think about," Bob Malloy said, and Grace agreed that it was. She was trying to decide how it changed things, and how it didn't. She was trying to sneak looks at him. He was wearing a pair of jeans with the creases still in them, as if they had been bought new for the occasion, and a long-sleeve button-down shirt in a small blue check. The dress-up clothes of somebody who didn't dress up often. He said, "How are you holding up these days?"

"I don't know yet," Grace said, which was the truth. "Sometimes I'm pretty normal. Then something sets me off and I get reminded all over again what happened. Like I'm hearing the news for the first time. I think it's like, this sounds stupid, but, PTSD."

"That's not one bit stupid."

Grace shrugged. She felt stupid because she was stupid, although it was nice of him to try and talk her out of it. She said, "Anyway, it helps to keep busy. This whole garden project, it's been . . . enormous."

"Your mom would love it."

"I hope so." She looked away. Her eyes were filling with tears, which she guessed was all right, but she didn't want to make a big deal out of it.

"She was a wonderful lady."

Grace nodded and kept quiet. A little breeze sifted through the tree leaves. Overhead, the clouds formed and reformed themselves. They watched the milling crowd, the people eating cake, the people bending down to read the tags on the plantings. He said, "Maybe we could grab a bite to eat one of these days. Get to know each other a little. If that's all right with you."

"Oh, that would be great, but I'm going to be moving pretty soon. Leaving town." She saw him drop his eyes, ready to give up. "But not right away," she qualified. "Not so soon that we couldn't have dinner. Anyway, I'll have to come back to town. For a while, at least. I'll have business here."

She had meant the trial, but he nodded at the garden. "Sure. You'll want to see how it's doing." He squinted at something. "Whoa, what's this?"

A procession was making its way from the parking lot, a group of young men armed with guitar cases, a drum kit, amplifiers, extension cords. One of them wore a blue satin tuxedo coat over cut-offs. Another, a kind of Tyrolean hat with a feather, like Pinocchio. Well, it wasn't like there was a dress code. "The entertainment," Grace explained. "Some of my brother's friends. You know he was a musician, right?"

"Oh, right. Do you need to go help them?"

Grace shook her head. "They know what to do. But listen, I'll have to go talk to people in a minute. I should give you my phone number."

"Sure. But sit here a little while longer. If you can."

Grace said that she could. And after all, things would go on without her once she left, things were going on with and without her, and always had and always would. Her heart hurt. It would always hurt. Sometimes more than others, the way bad weather might make an old injury throb and come to life again.

They watched the band members set up their instruments on the level concrete in front of the garden, watched them string their extension cords across the grass and plug in the guitars. The band members took up their instruments. The boy in the blue satin coat counted down and they launched into a song that was immediately cut short by alarming, amplified squawks.

They stopped playing. Onc of them bent over an amp, adjusting something, while another boy ran off toward the parking lot for whatever it was they'd forgotten and now required. Then he ran back and he too examined the amp.

People waited. You never knew how these things would go. Amateur hours, open stages. You hoped they would either play well or give up entirely, before everyone, both playing and listening, was embarrassed. Grace closed her eyes, willing them to get it together. Just this once, for her brother's sake, let it fly.

A guitar tried a single note and found it good. Again the countdown and the first chord, then the rhythm kicked in, then the sweet and urgent melody. The boys knew their business. The music was a scroll of sound unrolling, rolling, rising, swinging for the fences, connecting. Everyone hearing it felt themselves to be lucky. And Grace felt blessed, because for just this little while, on this particular day, there was no better place to be.

ABOUT THE AUTHOR

Jean Thompson is a novelist and short story writer. Her works include the novels *She Poured Out Her Heart, The Humanity Project, The Year We Left Home, City Boy, Wide Blue Yonder, The Woman Driver,* and *My Wisdom* and the short story collections *The Witch and Other Tales Re-Told, Do Not Deny Me, Throw Like a Girl, Who Do You Love* (a National Book Award finalist), *Little Face and Other Stories,* and *The Gasoline Wars.* Thompson's short fiction has been published in many magazines and journals, including *The New Yorker,* and anthologized in *The Best American Short Stories* and *The Pushcart Prize.* Thompson has been the recipient of Guggenheim and National Endowment for the Arts fellowships, among other accolades, and has taught creative writing at the University of Illinois at Urbana-Champaign, Reed College, Northwestern University, and other colleges and universities. She lives in Urbana, Illinois.